New York Times bestselling author **Sherrilyn Kenyon** lives a life of extraordinary danger . . . as does any woman with three sons, a husband, a menagerie of pets and a collection of swords that all of the above have a major fixation with.

Writing as Sherrilyn Kenyon and Kinley MacGregor, she is an international phenomenon with more than twelve million copies of her books in print, in twenty-eight countries. She's the author of several series including: The Dark-Hunters, The League and Lords of Avalon. Her books always appear at the top of the *New York Times*, *Publishers Weekly* and *USA Today* lists.

Visit Sherrilyn Kenyon's new UK website www.sherrilyn kenyon.co.uk or follow her on Twitter at www.twitter.com/kenyonsherrilyn

D1395727

Kiss of the Night

Sherrilyn Kenyon

piatkus

PIATKUS

First published in the US in 2004 by St. Martin's Press, New York
First published in Great Britain in 2005 by Piatkus Books
This paperback edition published in 2011 by Piatkus

A CIP catalogue record for this book
is available from the British Library.

ISBN 978-0-7499-5525-0

Typeset by Palimpsest Book Production Limited, Falkirk, Stirlingshire
Printed and bound by CPI Mackays, Chatham ME5 8TD

Papers used by Piatkus are from well-managed forests
and other responsible sources.

MIX
Paper from
responsible sources
FSC
www.fsc.org   FSC® C104740

Piatkus
An imprint of
Little, Brown Book Group
100 Victoria Embankment
London EC4Y 0DY

An Hachette UK Company
www.hachette.co.uk

www.piatkus.co.uk

Kiss of the Night

Thrylos

Atlantis:

Fabled. Mystical. Golden. Mysterious. Glorious and magical.

There are those who claim that it never was.

But then there are also those who think they are safe in this modern world of technology and weapons. Safe from all the ancient evils. They even believe that wizards, warriors, and dragons are long dead.

They are fools clinging to their science and logic while thinking it will save them. They can never be free or safe, not so long as they refuse to see what is right before their very eyes.

Because all ancient myths and legends are rooted in truth, and sometimes truth doesn't make us free. Sometimes it enslaves us more.

But come, fair ones, and listen to me tell a tale about the history of the most perfect paradise that ever existed. Beyond the mythical Pillars of Heracles, out in the great Aegean, was a once proud land that nourished a race of people far more advanced than any who came before or since.

Founded in the ancient mists of time by the primordial

god Archon, Atlantis took her name from Archon's eldest sister, Atlantia, whose name meant "graceful beauty." Archon conjured the isle with the help of his uncle, the ocean god Ydor, and his sister Eda (earth) to give the land to his wife Apollymi so that they could populate the continent with their divine children, who would have all the room they needed to romp and grow.

Apollymi wept with such joy at her gift that her tears flooded the land and made Atlantis a city within a city. Twin islands ringed by five channels of water.

Here she would birth her immortal children.

But it was soon discovered that the great Destroyer, Apollymi, was barren. At the request of Archon, Ydor spoke to Eda and together they created a race of Atlanteans to populate the islands and to bring joy again to Apollymi's heart.

It worked.

Golden and fair in honor of the god-queen, the Atlanteans were far superior to any other race of man. They alone gave Apollymi pleasure and made the great Destroyer smile.

Peace-loving and just, like their ancient gods, the Atlantean people knew no war. No poverty. They used their psychic minds and their magicks to live harmoniously within the balance of nature. They welcomed all foreigners who came to their shores and shared with them their gifts of healing and prosperity.

But as time passed and other pantheons and peoples arose to challenge them, the Atlanteans were forced to fight for their homeland.

To protect their people, the Atlantean gods came into constant conflict with the upstart Greek pantheon. To them, the Greeks were children fighting for possession of things they could never understand. The Atlanteans tried to deal with them as any parent would an angry toddler. Fairly. Patiently.

But the Greeks wouldn't listen to their ancient wisdom. Zeus and Poseidon, among others, were jealous of the Atlantean riches and serenity.

Yet it was Apollo who coveted their island the most.

A ruthless, cunning god, Apollo set into motion a means to take over Atlantis from the older gods. Unlike his father and uncle, he knew the Greeks could never defeat the Atlanteans in open warfare. It was only from within that one could conquer the ancient advanced civilization.

So when Zeus banned Apollo's warring race, the Apollites, from their native Greece, Apollo gathered his children together and led them across the sea to the shores of Atlantis.

The Atlanteans sympathized with the psychic, godlike Apollite race that had been persecuted by the Greeks. They looked to the Apollites as cousins and welcomed them so long as they abided by Atlantean law and caused no strife.

Publicly the Apollites did as they were told. They made sacrifices to the Atlantean gods while never breaking their covenant with their father, Apollo. Every year they picked the most beautiful virgin among them and sent her to Delphi as an offering to Apollo for his kindness in giving them a new home where they would one day reign as gods.

In the year 10,500 B.C. the beautiful aristocrat Clieto was sent to Delphi. Apollo fell instantly in love and sired five sets of twins on her.

It was through his lover and her children that he foresaw his destiny. At long last, they would lead him to the throne of Atlantis.

He sent his mistress and children back to Atlantis where they married into the Atlantean royal family. As Apollo's older children had intermarried with the native Atlanteans and blended the two races together, making his children even stronger, so would they. Only he would keep the royal bloodline pure to ensure the strength and loyalty of the Atlantean crown to him.

He had plans for Atlantis and his children. Through them, Apollo would rule the entire earth and cast down his father as his father had cast down the old god Cronus before him.

It was said that Apollo himself would visit the queen of every generation and father the male Atlantean heir on her.

As every eldest son was born, Apollo would then go to his oracles to find out if this son would be the one to overthrow the Atlantean gods.

Every year he was told no.

Until 9548 B.C.

As was his custom, Apollo visited the Atlantean queen whose king had died more than a year before. He came to her as a phantom and fathered his son on her while she slept dreaming of her dead husband.

It was also that year that the Atlantean gods became aware of their own destinies. For the queen of the Atlantean gods, Apollymi, found herself pregnant with Archon's child.

After all the centuries of aching for a child of her own, the Destroyer at long last had her desires granted. It was said the island of Atlantis flourished that day and knew more prosperity than ever before. The god-queen celebrated joyously as she told all the other gods of her news.

As soon as the Fates heard her announcement, they looked at Apollymi and Archon and proclaimed that

Apollymi's unborn son would bring about the death of them all.

One by one, the three Fates each spoke a single line of prophecy.

"The world as we know it will end."

"All our fates will rest in his hands."

"As a god, his every whim will reign supreme."

Terrified of their prediction, Archon ordered his wife to slay the unborn infant.

Apollymi refused. She had waited too long to have her child to see him needlessly dead over the words of the jealous Fates. With the help of her sister, she birthed her son prematurely and hid him away in the mortal world. To Archon, she delivered a stone baby.

"I've had enough of your infidelities and lies, Archon. From this day forward you have hardened my heart toward you. A stone baby is all you will ever have from me."

Enraged, Archon trapped her in Kalosis, a nether realm between this world and theirs. "There you will stay until your son is dead."

And so the Atlantean gods turned on Apollymi's sister until they forced a confession from her.

"He will be born when the moon swallows the sun and Atlantis is bathed in total darkness. His queenly mother will weep in fear of his birth."

The gods went to the Atlantean queen whose son's birth was imminent. As predicted, the moon eclipsed the sun as she struggled to give birth, and when her son was born, Archon demanded the baby be slain.

The queen wept and begged for Apollo to aid her. Surely her lover wouldn't see his own son killed by the older gods.

But Apollo ignored her and she watched helplessly as her newborn son was slain before her eyes.

What the queen didn't know was that Apollo had already been told what was going to happen and it wasn't his son she bore, but another child he had switched in her womb to save his own.

With the help of his sister, Artemis, Apollo had taken his son home to Delphi where the boy was raised among Apollo's priestesses.

As the years passed and Apollo failed to return to the Atlantean queen to father another heir, her hatred of him grew. She despised the Greek god who couldn't be bothered to give her a child to replace the one she had lost.

Twenty-one years after she had witnessed the sacrifice of her only child, the queen learned of another child fathered by the Greek god Apollo.

This one was born to a Greek princess who had been given to the god as an offering in hopes of swaying the god's benediction toward the Greeks, who were at war with the Atlanteans.

As soon as the news reached the queen, her bitterness swelled deep inside until the tide of it overwhelmed her.

She summoned her own priestess to ask where the heir to her empire would be found.

"The heir to Atlantis resides in the house of Aricles."

The same house where Apollo's new infant son had been born.

The queen screamed in outrage at the proclamation, knowing Apollo had betrayed his own children. They were forgotten while he forged a new race to replace them.

Calling out her personal guards, the queen sent them off to Greece, to make sure that Apollo's mistress and child were killed. She would never allow either of them to sit on her beloved throne.

"Make sure to rip them apart so that the Greeks will

believe it was done by a wild animal. I want nothing to make them look to our shores for this."

But as with all acts of vengeance, this one, too, was uncovered.

Heartbroken, Apollo, without thought, cursed all of his once chosen race. "A plague to all who are Apollite born. May you reap all you have sown this day. None of you shall ever live past the age of my precious Ryssa. You shall all perish painfully on the day of your twenty-seventh birthday. Because you acted as animals, you shall become them. Let you find your nourishment solely in the blood of your own kind. And never again will you be able to walk in my realm where I will see you and be forced to remember what it is that you did to betray me."

It wasn't until the curse was spoken that Apollo remembered his own son back in Delphi. A son he had foolishly damned along with the others.

For once spoken, such things can never be undone.

But more than that, he had sown the seeds for his own destruction. On his son's wedding day to Apollo's most treasured high-priestess, Apollo had entrusted his son with everything in life he valued.

"In your hands, you hold my future. Your blood is mine and it is through you and your future children that I live."

With those binding words, and in one fit of anger, Apollo had damned himself to extinction. For once his son's bloodline died, so then would Apollo and with him the sun itself.

You see, Apollo isn't just a god. He is the essence of the sun and holds in his hands the balance of the universe.

On the day Apollo dies, so dies the earth and all who dwell here.

Now the year is A.D. 2003 and there is only one Apollite child left who bears the blood of the ancient god . . .

Chapter 1

"Oh, honey, *major* stud alert. Three o'clock."

Cassandra Peters laughed at Michelle Avery's lust-filled tone as she turned in the crowded bar to see an average-looking, dark-haired man facing the stage where their favorite local band, Twisted Hearts, played.

Swaying to the music's beat as she sipped her Long Island Iced Tea, Cassandra studied him for a minute. "He's a *Milk* Man," she decided after a thorough scan of his "attributes" that comprised his looks, his carriage, and his lumberjack attire.

Michelle shook her head. "No, ma'am, he's a *Cracker* for sure."

Cassandra smiled at their rating system, which hinged on what they wouldn't toss a man out of bed for. Milk Man meant he was attractive in an unusual way and could bring a glass of milk to bed anytime. Crackers were one step up, and Cookies were gods.

But the ultimate in masculine desirability rated a Powdered Donut. Not only was a powdered donut messy, it violated their perpetual diet mentality and begged a woman to bite into it.

To date, none of them had ever met a Powdered Donut in the flesh. Still, they were ever hopeful.

Michelle tapped Brenda and Kat on their shoulders and inconspicuously pointed to the man she was eye-balling. "Cookie?"

Kat shook her head. "Cracker."

"Definitely Cracker," Brenda confirmed.

"Oh, what do you know? You have a steady boyfriend," Michelle said to Brenda as the band finished their song and took a break. "Jeez, you guys are tough critics."

Cassandra looked back at the guy, who was talking to his buddy and drinking a longneck beer. He didn't make her heart pound, but then very few men did. Even so, he had an easy, open manner and a nice, friendly smile. She could see why Michelle liked him.

"Why would you care what we think anyway?" she asked Michelle. "If you like him, then go up and introduce yourself."

Michelle was horrified. "I can't do that."

"Why not?" Cassandra asked.

"What if he thinks I'm fat or ugly?"

Cassandra rolled her eyes. Michelle was a very thin brunette who was a far cry from ugly. "Life is short, Michelle. Too short. For all you know, he might be the man of your dreams, but if you stay back here, drooling and not acting, you'll never know."

"God," Michelle breathed, "how I envy you that live-for-today attitude. But I can't."

Cassandra grabbed her by the hand and hauled her through the crowd, over to the man.

She tapped him on the shoulder.

Startled, he turned around.

His eyes widened as he looked up at Cassandra. At six feet one, she was used to being a freak of nature. To his credit, the guy didn't appear offended by the fact that she was a good two inches taller than him.

He looked down at Michelle, who was a normal five feet four.

"Hi," Cassandra said, drawing his gaze back to her. "I'm taking a quick survey. Are you married?"

He frowned. "No."

"Seeing someone?"

He passed a puzzled look to his friend. "No."

"Gay?"

His jaw dropped. "Excuse me?"

"Cassandra!" Michelle snapped.

She ignored both of them and held tight to Michelle's hand as her friend tried to run away. "You like women, yes?"

"Yes," he said, sounding offended.

"Good, because my friend Michelle here thinks you're exceptionally cute and she'd like to meet you." She pulled Michelle between them. "Michelle, this is . . ."

He smiled as he met Michelle's stunned gaze. "Tom Cody."

"Tom Cody," Cassandra repeated. "Tom, this is Michelle."

"Hi," he said, extending his hand to her.

From Michelle's expression, Cassandra could tell her friend wasn't sure if she should strangle her or thank her.

"Hi," Michelle said, shaking his hand.

Assured that they were semicompatible and that he didn't bite on the first date, Cassandra left them and headed back to Brenda and Kat, both of whom had their mouths hanging wide open as they stared at her in disbelief.

"I can't believe you just did that to her," Kat said as soon as Cassandra rejoined them. "She's going to kill you later."

Brenda cringed. "If you ever do that to me, I *will* kill you."

Kat draped an arm over Brenda's shoulders and gave her an affectionate hug. "You can yell at her all you want to, hon, but I can't let *you* kill her."

Brenda laughed at Kat's comment, not knowing that Kat spoke from her heart. She was Cassandra's covert bodyguard and had been with her for five years now. A record. Most of Cassandra's bodyguards had a job expectancy of about eight months.

They either ended up dead or quitting the minute they caught a look at exactly who and what was after her. To their way of thinking, not even the exorbitant amount of money her father paid them to keep her alive was worth the risk.

But not Kat. She had more tenacity and chutzpah than anyone Cassandra had ever met. Not to mention the fact that Kat was the only woman Cassandra had ever known who was actually taller than her. At six feet four, and stunningly beautiful, Kat made quite an entrance everywhere she went. Her blond hair hung just past her shoulders and she had eyes so green they didn't look real.

"You know," Brenda said to Cassandra as she watched Tom and Michelle talking and laughing. "I would give anything to have your confidence. Do you ever doubt yourself?"

Cassandra answered truthfully. "All the time."

"You never show it."

That's because, unlike her companions, there was more than just a slim chance Cassandra might only have another eight months left to live. She couldn't afford to be scared or timid of life. Her motto was to grab everything by both hands, and run with it.

Then again, she'd been running all her life. Running from those who would kill her if they had a chance.

But most of all, she'd been running from her destiny, hoping that somehow, some way, she could avert the inevitable.

Even though she'd traveled the world since she was six years old, she was no closer to discovering the truth about her heritage than her mother had been before her.

Still, with every day that dawned, she was hopeful. Hopeful that someone would tell her that her life didn't have to end on her twenty-seventh birthday. Hopeful that she would be able to stay someplace for more than a few months or even days.

"Hub-ba!" Brenda said, her eyes wide as she looked toward the entrance. "I think I just found our cookies! And ladies, there are *three* of them."

Laughing at her awed tone, Cassandra turned around to see three incredibly sexy men entering the club. They were all well over six feet in height, golden in skin and hair, and drop-dead gorgeous.

Her laughter died instantly as she felt a horrible, stinging tingle run through her. It was a sensation she was all too familiar with.

And it was one that branded terror into her heart.

Dressed in expensive sweaters, jeans, and ski jackets, the three men scanned the bar's occupants like the deadly predators they were. Cassandra trembled. The people in the bar had no idea how much danger they were in.

None of them.

Oh, dear God . . .

"Hey, Cass," Brenda said. "Go introduce me to *them*."

Cassandra shook her head as she made eye contact with Kat to warn her. She tried to herd Brenda away from the men and out of their dark, hungry sight. "They're bad news, Bren. *Really* bad news."

The one virtue of being half Apollite was her ability to spot others of her mother's kind. And something in her gut told her the men walking through the crowd, scanning women with seductive smiles, were no longer simple Apollites.

They were Daimons—a vicious breed of Apollite who chose to prolong their short lives by killing humans and stealing their souls.

Their unique, powerful Daimon charisma and their hunger for souls bled from every pore of their bodies.

They were here for victims.

Cassandra swallowed her panic. She had to find some way to get out of here before they got too close to her and discovered who she really was.

She reached for the small handgun in her purse, and looked for an escape.

"Out the back," Kat said, pulling her toward the rear of the club.

"What's going on?" Brenda asked.

Suddenly, the tallest of the Daimons stopped dead in his tracks.

He turned to face them.

His steely eyes narrowed on Cassandra with intense interest and she could feel him trying to penetrate her mind. She blocked his intrusion, but it was too late.

He grabbed his friends' arms and inclined his head toward them.

Damn. This sucked.

Literally.

With the bar's crowd, she couldn't open fire on them and neither could Kat. The hand grenades were in the car and she had opted to leave her daggers under the seat.

"Now would be a good time to tell me you have your sais with you, Kat."

"Nada. You got your kamas on you?"

"Yeah," she said sarcastically, thinking of her weapons that looked like small handheld scythes. "I tucked them into my bra before I left home."

She felt Kat force something cold into her hand. Looking down, she saw the closed uchiwa fighting fan. Made of steel, the fan was sharpened on one side so that it was as dangerous as a Ginsu knife. Folded up and only eleven inches long, it looked like an innocuous Japanese folding fan, but in the hands of either Kat or Cassandra, it was lethal.

Cassandra tightened her grip on the fan as Kat pulled her toward the stage where there was a fire exit. She drifted back into the crowd near the exit, away from the Daimons, and away from Brenda before she endangered her by being close to her when the Daimons struck.

She cursed both their heights as she realized there was no way to hide. No way to keep the Daimons from seeing them even in this heavy crowd when she and Kat stood so tall against everyone else.

Kat stopped dead in her tracks as another tall, blond man cut off their escape.

Two seconds later, all hell broke loose on their side of the club as they both became aware that there were more than just three Daimons in the bar.

There were at least a dozen of them.

Kat shoved Cassandra toward the exit, then kicked the

Daimon back, into a group of people who shouted and shrieked at the disturbance.

Cassandra opened her fan as another Daimon came for her with a hunting knife. She caught the blade between the slats and twisted it from his hands, then used the knife to stab the Daimon in the chest.

He disintegrated instantly.

"You'll pay for that, bitch," one of the Daimons growled as he charged her.

Several men in the bar moved to help her, but the Daimons made quick work of them while other patrons headed for the exits.

Four Daimons surrounded Kat.

Cassandra tried to get to her to help fight them off, but couldn't. One of the Daimons caught her bodyguard with a vicious blow that sent Kat flying into a nearby wall.

Kat hit it with a thud, then landed on the floor in a heap. Cassandra wanted to help her, but the best way to do that would be to get the Daimons out of the bar and away from her friend.

She turned to run, only to find two more Daimons standing directly behind her.

The collision of their bodies distracted her enough so that one of the Daimons could wrench the fan and knife from her hand.

He put his arms around her to keep her from falling.

Tall, blond, and handsome, the Daimon held a rare sexual aura that pulled anything female toward him. It was that essence that enabled them to prey effectively on humans.

"Going some place, princess?" he asked, taking her wrists in his hands and blocking her ability to fight for her weapon.

Cassandra tried to speak, but his deep, dark eyes held her completely captive. She felt his powers reaching into her mind, numbing her ability to flee.

The others joined him.

Still, the one before her kept his hands on her wrists, his mesmerizing gaze on hers.

"Well, well," the tallest said as he dragged a cold finger down her cheek. "When I came out to feed tonight, the last thing I expected to find was our missing heiress."

She snapped her head away from his touch. "Killing me won't free you," she said. "It's only a myth."

The one holding her turned her around to face his leader.

The Daimon leader laughed. "Aren't we all? Ask any human in this bar if vampires exist and what will they say?" He ran his tongue over his long canine teeth as he eyed her evilly. "Now, come outside and die alone, or we'll feast off your friends."

He slid his predator's gaze over to Michelle, who was far enough away and so captivated by Tom that she wasn't even aware of the fight that had gone on over on Cassandra's side of the large, crowded bar. "The brunette is strong. Her soul alone should sustain us for at least six months. As for the blonde . . ."

His gaze drifted over to where Kat lay surrounded by humans who didn't appear aware of how she'd gotten hurt. No doubt the Daimons were using their powers to fog the minds of the humans around them to keep them from interfering.

"Well," he continued ominously, "a little snack never hurt anyone."

He grabbed her arm at the same time the Daimon holding her let go.

Unwilling to go quietly to her slaughter, Cassandra reverted to her strict and intensive training. She stepped back into the arms of the Daimon behind her and brought her heel down on his instep.

He cursed.

She buried her fist into the stomach of the Daimon before her, then darted between the other two and headed for the door.

With his inhuman speed, the tallest Daimon cut her off halfway there. A cruel smile curved his lips as he pulled her viciously to a stop.

She kicked out, but he prevented her from hurting him.

"Don't." His deep voice was mesmerizing and filled with the promise of lethal harm should she disobey him.

Several people in the bar turned to look at them, but one vicious glare from the Daimon and they headed off.

No one would help her.

None dared.

But it wasn't over yet . . . She would never surrender to them.

Before she could attack again, the front door of the club swung open with an arctic blast.

As if he sensed something even more evil than himself, the Daimon turned his head toward the door.

His eyes widened in panic.

Cassandra turned to see what held him transfixed and then she, too, couldn't tear her gaze away.

The wind and snow swirled into the entranceway around a man who stood at least six feet six.

Unlike most people who walked around in ten-degree weather, the newcomer wore only a long, thin black leather coat that rippled with the wind. He had on a solid black sweater, biker boots, and a pair of tight black leather pants that hugged a lean, hard body that beckoned with wild, sexual promise.

He had the confident, deadly swagger of a man who knew he had no equal. Of a man who dared the world to try and take him on.

It was the gait of a predator.

And it made her blood run cold.

Had his hair been blond, she would have presumed him another Daimon. But this man was something else entirely.

His shoulder-length jet-black hair was blown back from a perfectly sculpted face that caused her heart to pound. His black eyes were cold. Steely. His face was set and impassive.

Neither pretty, nor feminine, the man was such a Powdered Donut, he wouldn't even have to share it in her bed!

Drawn like a homing beacon, and oblivious to the crowd in the bar, the newcomer swept his dark, deadly gaze from one Daimon to the next, until it settled on the one by her side.

A slow, evil smile spread over his handsome face, displaying the tiniest hint of fangs.

He headed straight for them.

The Daimon cursed, then pulled her in front of him.

Cassandra fought his hold, until he took a gun out of his pocket and held it to her temple.

Screams and shouts erupted in the bar as people ran for cover.

The other Daimons moved to stand by his side into what appeared to be a battle formation.

The newcomer gave a low, sinister laugh as he sized them up. The light in his jet eyes told her how much he looked forward to the fight.

His gaze actually goaded them.

"Bad form to take a hostage," he said in a deep,

smoothly accented voice that rumbled like thunder. "Especially when you know I'm going to kill you anyway."

In that instant, Cassandra knew who and what the newcomer was.

He was a Dark-Hunter—an immortal warrior who spent eternity hunting down and executing the Daimons who fed off human souls. They were the defenders of mankind and the personification of Satan for her people.

She'd heard of them all her life, but much like the bogeyman, she'd attributed them to urban legends.

But the man before her wasn't a figment of her imagination. He was real, and he looked every bit as deadly as the stories she'd heard.

"Out of my way, Dark-Hunter," the Daimon holding her said, "or I'll kill her."

Appearing amused by the threat, the Dark-Hunter shook his head like a parent scolding an angry child. "You know, you should have stayed in your bolt-hole one more day. Tonight's Buffy night, and it's a whole new episode, too."

The Dark-Hunter paused to sigh irritably. "Have you *any* idea how angry it makes me that I have to come out here in the freezing cold to slay you when I could be at home all toasty warm, watching Sarah Michelle Gellar kick ass in a halter top?"

The Daimon's arms shook as he tightened his grip on Cassandra. "Get him!"

The Daimons attacked at once. The Dark-Hunter caught the first one by the throat. In one fluid motion, he picked the Daimon up and slammed him against the wall where he held him in a tight fist.

The Daimon whimpered.

"What are you, a baby?" the Dark-Hunter asked.

"Jeez, if you're going to kill humans, the least you could do is learn to die with some dignity."

A second Daimon dove for his back. As the Dark-Hunter twisted his lower body, a long, evil-looking knife shot out of the toe of his boot. He buried the blade in the center of the Daimon's chest.

Instantly, the Daimon exploded into powder.

The Daimon in the Dark-Hunter's grip flashed his long canine teeth as he tried to bite and kick him. The Dark-Hunter tossed him into the arms of the third Daimon.

They stumbled back and landed in a heap on the floor.

The Dark-Hunter shook his head at the two Daimons as they stumbled over each other, trying to regain their feet.

More attacked and he cut through them with an ease that was as scary as it was morbidly beautiful.

"Come on, where did you learn to fight?" he asked as he killed two more. "Miss Manners' School for Girls?" He sneered contemptuously at the Daimons. "My baby sister could hit harder than you when she was three years old. Damn, if you're going to turn Daimon, the least you could do is take a few fighting lessons so you can make my boring job more interesting." He sighed wearily and looked up at the ceiling. "Where are the Spathi Daimons when you need them?"

While the Dark-Hunter was distracted, the Daimon holding her moved the gun from her temple and fired four shots into him.

The Dark-Hunter turned very slowly toward them.

Fury descending over his face, he glared at the Daimon who had shot him. "Have you no honor? No decency? No damn brains? You don't kill me with bullets. You just piss me off."

He looked down at the bleeding wounds in his side, then pulled his coat out so that light shone through the holes in the leather. He cursed again. "And you just ruined my friggin' favorite coat."

The Dark-Hunter growled at the Daimon. "For that, you die."

Before Cassandra could move, the Dark-Hunter whipped his hand toward them. A thin black cord shot out and wrapped itself around the Daimon's wrist.

Faster than she could blink, the Dark-Hunter closed the distance between them, jerked the Daimon's wrist, and wrung his forearm.

She stumbled away from the Daimon and pressed herself against the broken jukebox, out of their way.

With one hand still on the Daimon's arm, the Dark-Hunter grabbed him by the throat and lifted him off his feet. In a graceful arc, he slung the Daimon onto a table. Glasses shattered under the weight of the Daimon's back. The gun hit the wooden floor with a cold, metallic thud.

"Didn't your mother ever tell you the only way to kill us is to cut us into pieces?" the Dark-Hunter asked. "You should have brought a wood chipper instead of a gun."

He glared at the Daimon, who fought desperately against his hold. "Now, let's see about freeing the human souls you've stolen." The Dark-Hunter pulled a butterfly knife from his boot, twirled it open, and plunged it into the Daimon's chest.

The Daimon decayed instantly, leaving nothing behind.

The last two ran for the door.

They didn't get far before the Dark-Hunter pulled a set of throwing knives out from under his coat and sent them flying with deadly precision into the backs of the fleeing killers. The Daimons exploded, and his knives hit the floor ominously.

With an unbelievably deliberate calmness, the Dark-Hunter headed for the exit. He paused only long enough to retrieve his knives from the floor.

Then he left as quickly and silently as he'd come.

Cassandra struggled to breathe as the people in the bar came out of hiding and went berserk. Thankfully, even Kat pushed herself up and stumbled toward her.

Her friends came running up to her.

"Are you okay?"

"Did you see what he did?"

"I thought you were dead!"

"Thank God, you're still alive!"

"What did they want with you?"

"Who were those guys?"

"What happened to them?"

She barely heard the voices that hit her ears so fast and blended that she couldn't tell who asked what question. Cassandra's mind was still on the Dark-Hunter who'd come to her rescue. Why had he bothered to save her?

She had to know more about him . . .

Before she could think better of it, Cassandra ran after him, looking for a man who shouldn't be real.

Outside, blaring sirens filled the air and were getting progressively louder. Someone in the bar must have called the police.

The Dark-Hunter was halfway down the block before she caught up to him and pulled him to a stop.

His face impassive, he looked down at her with those deep, dark eyes. Eyes so black that she couldn't detect the pupils. The wind whipped his hair around his chiseled features and the cloud from his breath mingled with hers.

It was freezing out, but his presence warmed her so much that she didn't even feel it.

"What are you going to do about the police?" she asked. "They'll be looking for you."

A bitter smile tugged at the edges of his lips. "In five minutes no human in that bar will ever remember they saw me."

His words surprised her. Was that true of all Dark-Hunters? "Will I forget too?"

He nodded.

"In that case, thank you for saving my life."

Wulf paused. It was the first time anyone had ever thanked him for being a Dark-Hunter.

He stared at the wealth of tight, strawberry-blond curls that cascaded without order around her oval face. She wore her long hair plaited down her back. And her hazel-green eyes were filled with a brilliant vitality and warmth.

Though she wasn't a great beauty, her features had a quiet charm that was inviting, tempting.

Against his will, he reached his hand up to touch her jaw, just below her ear. Softer than velvet, her delicate skin warmed his cold fingers.

It had been so long since he last touched a woman.

So long since he had last tasted one.

Before he could stop himself, he leaned down and captured those parted lips with his own.

Wulf growled at the taste of her as his body roared to life. He'd never sampled anything sweeter than the honey of her mouth. Never smelled anything more intoxicating than her clean, rose-scented flesh.

Her tongue danced with his as her hands clutched at

his shoulders, pressing him closer to her. He became hard and stiff with the thought of how soft her body would be in other places.

And in that moment, he wanted her with an urgency that stunned him. It was a desperate need he hadn't felt in a long, long time.

Cassandra's senses swirled at the unexpected contact of his lips on hers. She'd never known anything like the power and hunger of his kiss.

The faint smell of sandalwood clung to his flesh and he tasted of beer and wild, untamed masculinity.

Barbarian.

It was the only word to describe him.

His arms flexed around her as he plundered her mouth masterfully.

He wasn't just deadly to Daimons. He was deadly to a woman's senses. Her heart hammered as her entire body burned, wanting a mad taste of his strength inside her.

She kissed him desperately.

He cupped her face in his hands while he nibbled her lips with his teeth. His fangs. Suddenly, he deepened his kiss as he ran his hands over her back, pressing her closer to those lean, masculine hips so that she could feel just how hard and ready he was for her.

She felt him all the way down her entire being. Every hormone in her body sizzled.

She wanted him with a ferocity that terrified her. Not once in her life had she known such hot, wrenching desire, especially not for a stranger.

She should be pushing him away.

Instead, she wrapped her arms around his broad, rock-hard shoulders and held him tight. It was all she could do not to reach down, unzip those pants, and guide him straight into the part of her that throbbed with demanding need.

Part of her didn't even care that they were on the street. It wanted him right here. Right now. No matter who or what saw them. It was an alien part of herself that scared her.

Wulf fought the urgency inside him that demanded he pin her to the brick wall beside them and have her wrap those long, shapely legs of hers around his waist. To push her sinfully short skirt up over her hips and bury himself deep inside her body until she screamed out his name in sweet release.

Dear gods, how he ached to possess her.

If only he could . . .

Reluctantly, he pulled back from her embrace. He ran his thumb over her swollen lips and wondered what she would feel like writhing beneath him.

Worse, he knew he could have her. He had tasted her desire fully. But once he was finished with her, she would have no memory of him.

No memory of his touch. His kiss.

His name . . .

Her body would only soothe his for a few minutes.

It would do nothing to ease the loneliness in his heart that yearned for someone to remember him.

"Good-bye, my sweet," he whispered, touching her lightly on the cheek before he turned around.

He would remember their kiss forever.

She wouldn't recall him at all . . .

Cassandra couldn't move as the Dark-Hunter walked away from her.

By the time he had vanished into the night, she had completely forgotten he'd ever existed.

"How did I get out here?" she asked as she wrapped her arms around her to banish the biting cold.

Her teeth chattering, she ran back into the bar.

Chapter 2

Wulf was still thinking of the unknown woman when he pulled his dark green Expedition into his five-car garage. He frowned at the sight of the red Hummer parked against the far wall, and turned his car off.

What the hell was Chris doing home? He was supposed to be spending the night at his girlfriend's house.

Wulf went inside to find out.

He found Chris in the living room, putting together a huge . . . something. It had metallic arms and things that reminded him of a poorly designed robot.

Chris's wavy black hair was sticking out in front as if he'd been tugging at it in frustration. There were parts and papers strewn all over the room, along with various tools.

Wulf watched in wry amusement as Chris battled the long, metallic post he was trying to fit into the base.

As Chris worked, one of the arms fell and smacked him on the head.

Cursing, he dropped the post.

Wulf laughed. "Been watching QVC again?"

Chris rubbed the back of his head as he kicked at the base. "Don't start with me, Wulf."

"Boy," Wulf said sternly, "you better check that tone."

"Yeah, yeah, ya scare me," Chris said irritably. "I'm even wetting my pants while in your terrifying, gut-wrenching presence. See me shiver and quiver? Ooo, ahhh, ooo."

Wulf shook his head at his Squire. The boy had no sense whatsoever to taunt him. "I knew I should have taken you out in the woods as an infant and left you there to die."

Chris snorted. "Ooo, nasty Viking humor. I'm actually surprised my father didn't have to present me to you for inspection at birth. Good thing you couldn't afford the *barnaútburðr,* huh?"

Wulf glared at him—not that he thought for one second it would do any good. It was only force of habit. "Just because you're the last of my bloodline doesn't mean I have to put up with you."

"Yeah, I love you, too, Big Guy." Chris went back to his project.

Wulf shrugged his coat off, then draped it over the back of his couch. "I swear, I'm going to cancel our cable subscription if you keep this up. Last week it was the weight bench and rowing machine. Yesterday that facial thing, and now this. Have you seen the crap in the attic? It looks like a rummage sale."

"This is different."

Wulf rolled his eyes. He'd heard that one before. "What the hell is it, anyway?"

Chris didn't pause as he set the arm back up. "It's a sun lamp. I thought you might be tired of your pasty-pale complexion."

He looked at him drolly. Thanks to his mother's dark Gaulish genes, Wulf wasn't really pale, especially given the fact that he hadn't been in daylight in over a thousand years. "Christopher, I happen to be a Viking in the middle of winter in Minnesota. Lack of a deep tan goes with the whole Nordic territory. Why do you think we raided Europe anyway?"

"Because it was there?"

"No, we wanted to thaw out."

Chris flipped him off. "Just wait, you'll thank me for this once I get it hooked up."

Wulf stepped over the pieces. "Why are you here, screwing with this? I thought you had a date tonight."

"I did, but twenty minutes after I got to her place, Pam broke up with me."

"Why?"

Chris paused to give him a hateful, sullen stare. "She thinks I'm a drug dealer."

Wulf was completely stunned by that unexpected declaration. Chris was barely six feet tall, with a gangly frame, and an honest, open face.

The most "illegal" thing the boy had ever done was to walk past a Salvation Army Santa Claus, once, without dropping money into the kettle.

"What made her think that?" Wulf asked.

"Well, let's see. I'm twenty-one, and I drive a custom-built, armor-plated Hummer worth about a quarter million dollars, with bulletproof tires and windows. I live on a remote, massive estate outside of Minnetonka all alone as far as anyone knows, except for the two bodyguards who trail me whenever I leave the property. I keep weird hours. You usually page me three or four times while I'm on a date to tell me to get down to business and give you an heir. And she accidentally saw some of your oh-so-wonderful toys I picked up from your weapons dealer in the cargo storage."

"Those weren't sharpened, were they?" Wulf interrupted. Chris was never allowed to handle sharpened weapons. The fool might cut off a vital body part or something.

Chris sighed and ignored the question as he continued his tirade. "I tried to tell her I was independently wealthy, and liked to collect swords and knives, but she didn't go for it." He pinned Wulf with another glacial stare. "You know, there are times when this job really bites. And the pun *was* intended."

Wulf took his bad temper in stride. Chris was perpetually irritated at him, but since Wulf had raised the boy from the instant he was born and Chris was the last surviving member of his bloodline, Wulf was extremely tolerant of him. "So sell the Hummer, buy a Dodge, and move into a trailer."

"Oh, yeah, *right*. Remember when I traded the Hummer for an Alpha Romeo last year? You burned the car and bought me a new Hummer and threatened to lock me in my room with a hooker if I ever did it again. And as for the perks . . . Have you bothered to look around this place? We have a heated indoor pool, a theater with surround sound, two cooks, three maids, and a pool guy I get to boss around, not to mention all kinds of other fun toys. I'm not about to leave Disneyland. It's the only good part in this arrangement. I mean, hell, if my life has to suck there's no way I'm going to live in the Mini-Winni. Which knowing you, you'd make me park out front anyway with armed guards standing watch in case I get a hangnail."

"Then you're fired."

"Bite me."

"You're not my type."

Chris tossed a wrench at his head.

Wulf caught it, and dropped it to the floor. "I'm never going to get you married off, am I?"

"Damn, Wulf. I'm barely legal. I have plenty of time left to have kids who can remember you, okay? Sheez, you're worse than my father was. Duty, duty, duty."

"You know, your father was only—"

"Eighteen when he married my mother. Yes, Wulf, I know. You only tell me that three or four times an hour."

Wulf ignored him as he continued thinking out loud. "I swear, you are the only man I've ever known who missed the whole teenage hormonal surge. Something's not right with you, boy."

"I am not taking another friggin' physical," Chris snapped. "There's nothing wrong with me or my abilities other than the fact that I'm not a horn-dog. I would rather get to know a woman first before I take my clothes off in front of her."

Wulf shook his head. "There is something *seriously* wrong with you."

Chris cursed him in Old Norse.

Wulf ignored his profanity. "Maybe we should look into hiring a surrogate. Maybe buy a sperm bank."

Chris growled low in his throat, then changed the subject. "What happened tonight? You look even more pissed now than when you left. Did one of the panthers say something nasty to you at their club?"

Wulf grunted as he thought about the Katagaria panther pack who owned the club he'd gone to tonight. They had called him first thing this evening to let him know one of their scouts had spotted a group of unknown Daimons in the city, out on the prowl. It was the same group who had caused some problems for the panthers a few months back.

The Inferno was one of many sanctuaries set up throughout the world where Dark-Hunters, Were-Hunters, and Apollites could gather without fear of an enemy coming at them while they were inside the building. Hell, the were-beasts even tolerated Daimons so long as they didn't feed on the premises or bring unwanted attention to them.

Even though the Were-Hunters were more than capable of killing the Daimons themselves, as a rule they usually abstained from doing so. After all, they were cousins to the Apollites and Daimons, and as such took a very hands-off approach to dealing with them. Likewise, the Weres weren't overly tolerant of the Dark-Hunters who killed their cousins. They worked with them when they had to or when it benefitted them, but otherwise kept their distance.

As soon as Dante had been notified the Daimons were heading for his club, he had paged Wulf with an alert.

But as Chris had insinuated, the panthers had a way of being less than friendly to any Dark-Hunter who stayed too long at their place.

Flipping his weapons out of his clothes, Wulf returned them to the armoire against the far wall. "No," he said, answering Chris's question. "The panthers were fine. I just thought the Daimons would put up more of a fight."

"Sorry," Chris said sympathetically.

"Yeah, me too."

Chris paused, and by his expression, Wulf could tell the boy had laid aside his ribbing and was trying to cheer him up. "You feel up to training?"

Wulf locked up his weapons. "Why bother? I haven't had a decent fight in almost a hundred years." Disgusted with the thought, he rubbed a hand over his eyes, which were sensitive to the bright lights Chris had on. "I think I'll go insult Talon for a while."

"Oh, hey!"

Wulf paused to look back at Chris.

"Before you go, say 'barbecue.' "

Wulf groaned at Chris's usual last resort to attempt to cheer him up. That was a standing joke that Chris had used to irritate him with since Chris was a small child. It stemmed from the fact that Wulf still held on to his ancient Norse accent which made him lilt when he spoke, especially when he said certain words, such as "barbecue."

"You're not funny, rugrat. And I am not a Swede."

"Yeah, yeah. C'mon, make the Swedish Chef noises."

Wulf growled. "I should never have allowed you to watch *The Muppets*." More to the point, he shouldn't have pretended to be the Swedish Chef when Chris was a child. All it did was give the boy one more thing to aggravate him with.

But still, they were family, and at least Chris was attempting to make him feel better. Not that it was working.

Chris let out a rude noise. "Fine, you decrepit old Viking grump. By the way, my mother wants to meet you. Again."

Wulf groaned. "Can you put her off another couple of days?"

"I can try, but you know how she is."

Yes, he did. He'd known Chris's mother for more than thirty years.

Unfortunately, she didn't know him at all. Just like everyone else not born of his blood, she forgot him five minutes after he left her presence.

"All right," Wulf relented. "Bring her over tomorrow evening."

Wulf headed to the stairs that led to his rooms underneath the house. Like most Dark-Hunters, he preferred to sleep where there was no possibility of accidental sun exposure. It was one of the very few things that could destroy their immortal bodies.

He opened the door, but didn't bother with the overhead light since Chris had lit the small candle by his desk. The eyes of a Dark-Hunter were designed to need almost no light. He could see better in the darkness than humans could see in broad daylight.

Taking his sweater off, he gently prodded the four bullet wounds in his side. The bullets had passed cleanly through his flesh and the skin had already started to heal.

The injury stung, but it wouldn't kill him, and in a couple of days, there would be nothing left except four tiny scars.

He used his black T-shirt to wipe the blood from his side, and went to the bathroom to wash and bandage it.

As soon as he was clean and dressed in a pair of blue jeans and a white T-shirt, Wulf switched on his stereo. The preprogrammed songs started off with Slade's *My Oh My* while he grabbed his cordless phone and brought up his computer screen to log on to the Dark-Hunter.com Web site to update the others on his latest kills.

Callabrax liked to keep up with how many Daimons were slain each month. The Spartan warrior had some weird notion that Daimon crossovers and attacks were related to moon cycles.

Personally, Wulf thought the Spartan had way too much time on his hands. But then, being immortals, they all did.

Sitting in the darkness, Wulf listened to the words of the song as it played.

I believe in woman, my oh my. We all need someone to talk to, my oh my . . .

Against his will, the lyrics conjured up images of his

ancient home, and of a woman with hair as white as the snowfall, and eyes as blue as the sea.

Arnhild.

He didn't know why he still thought of her after all these centuries, but he did.

He took a deep breath as he wondered what would have happened had he stayed on at his father's farm and married her. Everyone had expected it.

Arnhild had expected it.

But Wulf had refused. At seventeen, he'd wanted a different life than that of a simple farmer paying taxes to his jarl. He'd wanted adventure, and battles.

Glory.

Danger.

Maybe if he'd loved Arnhild, it might have been enough to keep him home.

And if he'd done that . . .

He'd have been bored out of his friggin' mind.

Which was his problem tonight. He needed something exciting. Something to stir his blood.

Something like the hot, tempting strawberry-blonde he'd left behind on the street . . .

Unlike Chris, getting naked with a strange woman wasn't something he shirked from.

Or at least something he used to not shirk from. Of course his willingness to be naked with unknown women was what had led him to his current fate, so maybe Chris had some sense after all.

Seeking a distraction from that irritating thought, Wulf dialed Talon's number and clicked the remote to change his song over to Led Zeppelin's "Immigrant Song."

Talon answered his cell phone at the same time Wulf logged on to the Dark-Hunters' private message boards.

"Hey, little girl," Wulf said tauntingly, switching to his

headset so that he could type and talk at the same time. "I got your 'Dirty Deeds Done Dirt Cheap' T-shirt today. You're not funny and I don't work cheap. I expect a lot of money for what I do."

Talon scoffed. "Little girl? You better lay off or I'll come up there and kick your Viking ass."

"That threat might carry some weight if I didn't know how much you hate the cold."

Talon laughed deep in his throat.

"So what are you up to tonight?" Wulf asked.

"About six feet five."

Wulf groaned. "You know, that crappy joke doesn't get funnier every time I hear it."

"Yeah, I know. But I live only to harass you."

"And you succeed so well. You been taking lessons from Chris?"

He heard Talon cover the phone with his hand and order black coffee and beignets.

"So you're already out and about tonight?" he asked Talon after the waitress had walked away.

"You know it. It's Mardi Gras time and Daimons abound."

"Bullshit. I heard you order coffee. You ran out again, didn't you?"

"Shut up, Viking."

Wulf shook his head. "You really need to get yourself a Squire."

"Yeah, right. I'll remind you of that the next time you're bitching about Chris and his mouth."

Wulf leaned back in his chair as he read through the postings of his fellow Dark-Hunters. It was comforting to know he wasn't the only one who was bored out of his mind in between assignments.

Since Dark-Hunters couldn't gather together physically without draining each others' powers, the Internet and phones were the only way they could share information and stay in touch.

Technology was a godsend to them.

"Man," Wulf said, "is it just me or do the nights seem to be getting longer?"

"Some are longer than others." Talon's chair squeaked over the phone. No doubt the Celt was leaning back in it to scope out some woman walking past his table. "So, what has you down?"

"I'm restless."

"Go get laid."

He snorted at Talon's stock answer for everything. Worse, he knew the Celt really believed sex was a cure-all for any ailment.

But then as his thoughts turned back to the woman at the club, Wulf wasn't so sure it wouldn't work.

At least for tonight.

However, in the end, a night with another woman who wouldn't remember him didn't appeal to him.

It hadn't in a long time.

"That's not the problem," Wulf said as he scanned the messages. "I'm aching for a good fight. I mean, damn, when was the last time you really had a Daimon fight back? The ones I took out tonight just laid down on me. One of them even whimpered when I hit him."

"Hey, you should be glad you got them before they got you."

Perhaps . . .

But then Wulf was a Viking and they didn't look at things the same way the Celts did.

"You know, Talon, killing a soul-sucking Daimon without a good fight is like sex without foreplay. A total waste of time and completely un . . . satisfying."

"Spoken like a true Norseman. What you need, my brother, is a mead hall filled with serving wenches and Vikings ready to fight their way into Valhalla."

It was true. Wulf missed the Spathi Daimons. Now, they were a warrior class that put the fun in war.

Well, from his way of thinking anyway.

"The ones I found tonight knew nothing about fighting," Wulf said, curling his lip. "And I'm sick of the whole 'my gun will solve all' mentality."

"You get shot again?" Talon asked.

"Four times. I swear . . . I wish I could get a Daimon up here like Desiderius. I'd love a good down-and-dirty fight for once."

"Careful what you wish for, you just might get it."

"Yeah, I know." In a way Talon couldn't even begin to imagine. "But damn. Just once can't they stop running from us and learn to fight like their ancestors did? I miss the way things used to be."

There was a pause on the other end as Talon let out a slow appreciative breath.

Wulf shook his head. There was definitely a woman nearby.

"I tell you what I miss most are the Talpinas."

Wulf frowned. That was a term he'd never heard before. "What are those?"

"That's right, they were before your time. Back in the better part of the Dark Ages, we used to have a clan of Squires whose sole purpose was to take care of our carnal needs."

It was nice to know his best friend had a one-track mind, and Wulf would pay money to meet the one woman who could derail the Celt from his earthy ways.

"Man, they were great," Talon continued. "They knew what we were and they were more than happy to bed us.

Hell, the Squires even trained them on how to pleasure you."

"What happened to them?"

"About a hundred or so years before you were born, a Dark-Hunter made the mistake of falling in love with his Talpina. Unfortunately for the rest of us, she didn't pass Artemis's test. Artemis was so angry over it, she stepped in and banished the Talpinas from us, and implemented the oh-so-wonderful "you're only supposed to sleep with them once" rule. As further backlash over it, Acheron came up with the "never touch your Squire" law. I tell you, you haven't lived until you've tried to find a decent one-night stand in seventh-century Britain."

Wulf snorted. "That's *never* been my problem."

"Yeah, I know. I envy you that. While the rest of us have to pull ourselves back from our lovers lest we betray our existence, you get to cut loose without fear."

"Believe me, Talon, it's not all it's cracked up to be. You live alone by choice. Do you have any idea how frustrating it is to have no one remember you five minutes after you leave them?"

It was the only thing that bothered Wulf about his existence. He had immortality. Wealth.

You name it.

Except that if Christopher died without having children, there would be no human left alive who could remember him.

It was a sobering thought.

Wulf sighed. "Christopher's mother has come over here three times in the last week alone just so she can meet the person he works for. I've known her for what? Thirty years? And let's not forget that time sixteen years ago when I came home and she called the cops on me because she thought I had broken into my own house."

"I'm sorry, little brother," Talon said sincerely. "At least you have us and your Squire who can remember you."

"Yeah, I know. Thank the gods for modern technology. Otherwise I'd go insane." He fell silent for a bit.

"Not to change the subject, but did you see who Artemis relocated to New Orleans to take Kyrian's place?"

"I heard it was Valerius," Wulf said in disbelief. "What was Artemis thinking?"

"I have no idea."

"Does Kyrian know?" Wulf asked.

"For an obvious reason, Acheron and I decided not to tell him that the grandson and spitting image of the man who crucified him and destroyed his family was being moved into the city just down the street from his house. Unfortunately, though, I'm sure he'll find out sooner or later."

Wulf shook his head. He supposed things could be worse for him. At least he didn't have Kyrian's or Valerius's problems.

"Man, human or not, Kyrian will kill him if they ever cross paths—not something you need to cope with this time of year."

"Tell me about it," Talon concurred.

"So, who got Mardi Gras duty this year?" Wulf asked.

"They're importing Zarek."

Wulf cursed at the mention of the Dark-Hunter from Fairbanks, Alaska. Rumors abounded about the ex-slave who had once destroyed the very village and humans he'd been charged with protecting. "I didn't think Acheron would ever let him leave Alaska."

"Yeah, I know, but word came from Artemis herself

that she wanted him here. Looks like we're having a psycho reunion this week . . . Oh wait, it's Mardi Gras. Duh."

Wulf laughed again.

He heard Talon let out a happy sigh.

"Coffee arrived?" Wulf asked.

"Oh yeah."

Wulf smiled, wishing he could find pleasure in something as simple as a cup of coffee.

But no sooner had that thought crossed his mind than he heard Talon snarl, "Ah, man."

"What?"

"Friggin' Fabio alert." Talon spat the words out contemptuously.

Wulf arched a brow as he thought about Talon's own blond hair. "Hey, you're not too far from the mark either, *blondie.*"

"Bite me, Viking. You know if I were a negative person, I would be seriously annoyed right now."

"You sound annoyed to me."

"No, this isn't annoyed. This is mild perturbance. Besides, you should see these guys." Talon dropped his Celtic accent as he invented a conversation for the Daimons. He raised his voice to an unnaturally high level. "Hey, Gorgeous George, I think I smell a Dark-Hunter."

"Oh no, Dick," he said, dropping his voice two octaves, "don't be a dick. There's no Dark-Hunter here."

Talon returned to his falsetto. "I dunno . . ."

"Wait," Talon said, again in the deep voice, "I smell tourist. Tourist with big . . . strong soul."

"Would you stop?" Wulf said, laughing.

"Talk about inkblots," Talon said, using the derogatory term Dark-Hunters had for Daimons. It stemmed from the strange black mark that all Daimons developed on their chests when they crossed over from being simple Apollites to human slayers. "Damn, all I wanted was a drink of coffee and one little beignet."

He heard Talon tsk-tsking. Then his friend started debating out loud. "Coffee . . . Daimons . . . Coffee . . . Daimons . . ."

"I think in this case the Daimons better win."

"Yeah, but it's *chicory* coffee."

Wulf clicked his tongue. "Talon wanting to be toasted by Acheron for failure to protect humans."

"I know," he said with a disgusted sigh. "Let me go expire them. Talk to you later."

"Later." Wulf hung up the phone and switched off the computer. He looked at the clock. It wasn't even midnight yet.

Damn.

It was just after midnight when Cassandra, Kat, and Brenda returned to their college apartment complex. They let Brenda out in front of her unit, then drove around back to where they shared an apartment. They got out of the car and made their way inside their two-bedroom flat.

Ever since she'd left the Inferno, Cassandra had had a terrible niggling in the back of her mind, like something wasn't right.

She went through the entire evening again in her mind as she got ready for bed. She'd driven down to the club with her friends after Michelle's class, and they had spent the night listening to Twisted Hearts and then the Barleys play.

Nothing unusual had happened other than Michelle meeting Tom.

So, why did she feel so . . . so . . . strange.

Uneasy.

It didn't make sense.

Rubbing her brow, she picked up her Medieval Lit book and did her best to struggle through the Old English version of *Beowulf*.

Dr. Mitchell loved embarrassing graduate students who hadn't prepared for his class, so Cassandra wasn't about to show up tomorrow without having read the assignment.

No matter how boring it might prove.

> *Grendrel, chomp, chomp,*
> *Grendrel, chomp, chomp,*
> *See the Vikings in their boats,*
> *Someone hand me the Cliff's Notes . . .*

Not even her little singsong ditty could revive her interest.

Yet as she read the Old English words, she kept imagining a tall, dark-haired warrior with black eyes and full, warm lips.

A man of incredible speed and agility.

Closing her eyes, she saw him standing out in the cold, wearing a long black leather coat and a look on his face that said . . .

Decadence.

She tried to make the image clearer, but it evaporated and left her aching for want of him.

"What in the world is wrong with me?"

She widened her eyes and forced herself to read.

Wulf locked his bedroom door and went to bed early—just after four. Chris had been asleep for hours. There was nothing on TV, and he was bored with playing online computer games against the other Dark-Hunters.

He'd already taken out the "pressing" Daimon menace tonight. He sighed at the thought. During the winter months, they tended to take a hiatus south, since Daimons weren't real big on the whole cold thing. They hated to have to "unwrap" their food and found it extremely cumbersome to attack humans wrapped in layers of coats and sweaters. Things would pick up in the spring, after the thaw, but in the meantime, the nights were long and the battles few and far between.

Maybe if he got a good day's sleep, he might feel better tomorrow evening.

It was worth a try.

But as soon as Wulf fell asleep, his dreams started drifting. He saw the club again and felt the lips of the unknown woman against his.

Felt her hands on him as she clutched him . . .

What would it be like to be remembered by a lover again?

Just once?

A strange, swirling mist engulfed him and the next thing he knew, he was in an unfamiliar bed.

Wulf grimaced at the size of it—It was only a full-sized bed so he had to bend his legs to keep his feet from dangling over the edge of it.

Frowning, he looked around the dark room. The white walls were stark and covered with art posters. Something about it had an institutional quality to it.

There was a desk built into the wall by the window, a boxlike dresser with a TV and stereo, and a lava lamp burning in the corner, casting strange shadows over the walls.

It was then he realized he wasn't alone in the bed.

Someone was lying next to him.

Wulf studied the woman who was dressed in a prudish pink flannel gown that obscured her body as she lay with her back to him. Leaning over her, he saw the curly, strawberry-blond hair that she wore plaited.

He smiled the moment he recognized the woman from the club. He liked this dream . . .

But not as much as he liked the look of her serene face.

And unlike the Daimons, he didn't mind "unwrapping" his food.

His body instantly stirring, he rolled her over onto her back and started unbuttoning her gown.

Chapter 3

Cassandra's eyes fluttered open as she felt strong, hot hands unbuttoning her flannel gown. Startled, she stared up at the Dark-Hunter who had saved her life at the club.

His midnight eyes were hungry with desire as he looked down at her.

"It's you," she breathed, her head fuzzy from her dreams.

He smiled at that and appeared delighted by her words. "You remember me?"

"Of course. How could I ever forget the way you kiss?"

His smile widened wickedly as he parted her gown and ran his hand over her bared skin. She moaned at the warmth of his palm on her flesh. Against her will, a stab of desire tore through her as her breasts tingled from his fiery touch. The calluses of his rough fingers lightly, gently scraped her swollen nipples. It made her stomach contract even more. Made her throb as moisture pooled itself between her legs, making her want even more to take his entire strength into her body.

She realized her Viking savior was completely naked in her bed. Well, maybe not completely. He did wear a silver necklace of Thor's hammer and a small crucifix.

Okay, that was pushing it. But he wore the necklace well against his tawny skin.

The dim light caressed every contour of his magnificent body. His shoulders were wide and well muscled, his chest a perfect sculpting of male proportions.

And his rear . . .

It was the stuff of legends!

His chest and legs were lightly covered by dark hair. His strong, lightly whiskered chin begged for a woman to lick her way down it until she could tilt his head back and continue on to his luscious neck.

But what fascinated her was the intricate Norse tattoo that covered his entire right shoulder and ended in a highly stylized band that encircled his biceps. It was beautiful.

And yet it didn't hold a candle to the man in her arms.

He was gorgeous. Mouthwateringly so.

"What are you doing?" she asked as he traced circles around her breasts with his hot tongue.

"I'm making love to you."

Had she not been asleep, those words would have terrified her. But all thoughts of fear and everything else scattered as he cupped her breast in his hand.

She hissed in pleasure and expectation.

Gently, he massaged her, rubbing his callused palm against her taut nipple until it was so tight that she wanted to beg him to kiss her. Beg him to suckle her.

"So soft," he whispered against her lips before he claimed them as well.

Cassandra sighed. Her body burned with an astounding intensity as she ran her hands over his bare, broad shoulders. She'd never felt the likes of them. Well formed and perfect, they rippled with his power and strength.

And she wanted to feel more of him.

He moved his hand away from her and reached for her braid. She watched him study her hair as he loosened it. "Why do you wear your hair like this?" he asked in that intoxicatingly deep, accented voice.

"The curls tangle if I don't."

His eyes snapped fire as if he thought her braid were some kind of abomination. "I don't like it. Your hair is too beautiful to be bound."

He ran his hands through her freed curls and his gaze instantly turned tender. Soft. He brushed her hair with his fingers until it covered her bared breasts. His breath fell against her skin while he teased her nipples with her curls and his touch.

"There now," he said, his Norse accent smooth and lilting. "A more beautiful woman, I've never seen."

Her body molten, Cassandra could do nothing but watch him watch her.

He was stunningly handsome. Masculine in a barbaric way that made the woman in her thrum with primal need.

It was obvious this was a dangerous man. Basic. Hard. Unyielding.

"What is your name?" she asked as he dipped his head to nibble her neck. His whiskered cheeks prickled her flesh, raising chills all over her as he tasted her.

"Wulf."

She shivered as she realized the source of this midnight fantasy. "Like Beowulf?"

He smiled hungrily, flashing her a brief glimpse of his long, canine teeth. "Actually, I'm more like Grendel. I come out only at night to devour you."

She shivered again as he gave one long, deliciously wicked lick to the underside of her breast.

Now this was a man who knew well how to pleasure a

woman. And better yet, he didn't seem to be in a hurry to finish, but rather took his time with her.

If there was any doubt before, that alone told her this was a dream!

Wulf ran his tongue over her soft skin and delighted in her murmurs of pleasure as he tasted her salty-sweet flesh. He loved the warm, soothing feel and smell of this woman.

She was delectable.

He hadn't had a dream like this in centuries. It was so real, and yet he knew it wasn't.

She was only a figment of his starving imagination.

Even so, she touched him in a way he'd never before known. And she smelled so good . . . like fresh roses and powder.

Womanly. Soft.

A tender morsel just waiting for him to sample her. Or better still, devour.

Pulling back, he returned to her hair that reminded him of the color of sunshine. The fiery gold strands captivated him as the curls wrapped themselves around his fingers and tugged at the edges of his stone heart. "You have such beautiful hair."

"So do you," she said as she brushed his hair back from his face.

She scraped his whiskers with her fingernail as she traced the curve of his jaw. Gods, how long had it been since he'd last had a woman?

Three, four months?

Three, four decades?

It was hard to keep track of time when it stretched out interminably. All he knew was that he had long ago given up the dream of having a woman like this under him.

Since no woman could remember him, he refused to take decent women into his bed.

All too well, he knew what it was like to wake up after sex and have no idea what had been done to him. To lie there wondering how much of it had been real and how much had been a dream.

So, he had relegated his encounters to women he could pay for their services, and then only when he absolutely could stand his celibacy no more.

But this one had remembered his kiss.

She had remembered *him*.

The thought made his heart soar. He liked this dream, and if he could, he'd stay in it forever.

"Tell me your name, *villkat*."

"Cassandra."

He felt the word rumble under his lips as he kissed the column of her throat. She trembled in response to his tongue stroking her flesh.

And he loved it. Loved the sounds she made as she returned his caresses. She ran her hot, eager hands over his naked back and paused her right hand over the brand on his left shoulder.

"What is this?" she asked curiously.

He glanced down at the sign of a bow and arrow. "It's the mark of Artemis, the goddess of the hunt and of the moon."

"Do all Dark-Hunters have it?"

"Yes."

"How strange . . ."

Wulf couldn't stand the flannel barrier anymore. He wanted to see more of her.

Wulf lifted the hem of her gown. "This should be burned."

She frowned. "Why?"

"Because it keeps me from you."

With one tug, he pulled it over her head.

Her eyes widened for an instant, then turned dark with her own passion.

"Now, that's better," he whispered, feasting on the sight of her taut breasts, her narrow waist, and best of all, the strawberry-blond curls at the juncture of her thighs.

He skimmed his hand between her breasts, down over her stomach, and around her hip.

Cassandra reached out and ran her hand over the glorious skin of his chest, delighting in the rocky terrain of his muscles. He felt so wonderful. His body rippled with every move he made.

The deadly power of him was undeniable, and yet he was as gentle as a tamed lion in her bed. She couldn't believe the tenderness in his hot, masterful touch.

His dark, moody features stirred her deeply, and his eyes held such a vital intelligence as they took in the world around him.

She wanted to tame this wild beast.

To feed him from her hand.

With that thought, Cassandra reached down between their bodies and took his hard cock into her palm.

He growled low in his throat, then kissed her senseless.

Like some sleek, muscled predator, he moved over her mouth, burning her with his kisses.

"Yes," he gasped as she sheathed him with her hands. His breathing ragged, he stared at her with a hunger so raw that it made her shiver with anticipation.

"Touch me, Cassandra," he whispered, covering her hand with his.

She watched as he closed his eyes and showed her how

to stroke him. Cassandra bit her lip at the feel of him between her hands. He was a large man. Large and thick and powerful.

His jaw steely, he opened his eyes and singed her with a hot stare. She knew playtime was over.

Like an unleashed predator, he rolled her onto her back and separated her thighs with his knees. He lowered his long, lean body over hers and, like he had promised, devoured her.

Cassandra gasped as his hands and lips sought out every inch of her body with a furious intensity. And when he buried his hand between her legs, she shook all over. His long fingers stroked and delved deep inside her, teasing her until she was weak from it.

"You're so wet," he growled in her ear as he pulled back from her.

Cassandra trembled as he spread her legs wider.

"Look at me," he commanded. "I want to see your pleasure when I take you."

She looked up at him.

The moment their gazes locked, he buried himself deep inside her.

She moaned in pleasure. He was so hard and thick, and he felt wonderful as he thrust against her hips.

Wulf pulled back so that he could watch her face while he took his time making love to her and savoring the feel of her warm, wet body beneath his. He bit his lip as she ran her hand down his spine, then scored his back with her nails.

He growled in response, wanting her wildness.

Her passion.

She placed her hands against his lower back, urging him faster. He obliged her more than willingly. She lifted her hips to him and he laughed.

If she wanted to be in control, he was certainly in the mood to let her. Rolling over, he pulled her on top of him without leaving her body.

She gasped as she looked down at him.

"Ride me, *elskling*," he breathed.

Her eyes dark and untamed, she leaned forward, spilling her hair across his chest as she slid herself down the length of him until he was barely still sheathed by her body, then fell back, pulling him into her all the way to his hilt.

He shook from the force of it.

He cupped her breasts and squeezed gently as she took control of their pleasure.

Cassandra couldn't believe the way he felt underneath her. It had been a long time since she'd made love to a man and she had never had one like this.

One who was so innately masculine. So virile and wild.

One she knew nothing about except that he made her mother's people tremble in terror.

And he had saved her life.

It must be her repressed sexuality that had summoned him into her dreams. Her need to make contact with someone before she died.

That was her biggest regret. Due to the curse of her mother's family, she had been fearful of approaching other Apollites. Like her mother before her, she had been forced to live in the human world as one of them.

But she had never been one of them. Not really.

All she had ever wanted was to be accepted. To find someone who could understand her past and not think her mental when she told tales of a cursed lineage.

And monsters who stalked the night.

Now she had a Dark-Hunter for her own.

At least for tonight.

Grateful for that, she laid herself over him and let the heat of his body soothe hers.

Wulf cupped her face and watched as she experienced the height of pleasure. He rolled over with her then, and took control. He thrust deep inside her as her body convulsed around him. Her gasp punctuated his motions in a way that sounded like she was singing.

He laughed.

Until he felt his own body explode.

Cassandra wrapped her entire body around him as she felt his release. He collapsed on top of her.

His weight felt so good there. So wonderful.

"That was incredible," he said, lifting his head up to smile at her while they were still joined intimately. "Thank you."

She returned his smile.

Just as she reached up to cup his face, she heard her alarm clock go off.

Cassandra jerked awake.

Her heart was still pounding as she reached to turn the clock off. And it was only then she realized her hair was no longer braided and her gown was lying on the floor in a crumpled heap . . .

Wulf came awake with a start. His heart pounding, he looked over at his clock. It was just after six and by the activity upstairs he could tell it was morning.

Frowning, he glanced around in the darkness. There was nothing unusual.

But the dream . . .

It had seemed so incredibly real.

He rolled over, onto his side, and clutched his pillow in

his fist. "Damn psychic powers," he growled. They never left him any peace. And now they tortured him with things he knew he couldn't have.

As he drifted back to sleep, he could almost swear he smelled the faint scent of roses and powder on his skin.

"Hey, Cass," Kat greeted as Cassandra took a seat at the breakfast table.

Cassandra didn't respond. Over and over she kept seeing Wulf. Kept feeling his hands on her body.

If she didn't know better, she would swear he was still with her.

But she didn't know who her dream lover was. Why he haunted her.

It was so weird.

"Are you okay?" Kat asked.

"Yeah, I guess. I just didn't sleep well last night."

Kat placed her hand against Cassandra's forehead. "You look feverish, but you're not."

She was feverish all right, but not from illness. There was a part of her that wanted nothing more than to go back to sleep, find her mysterious man, and continue making love with him for the rest of the day.

Kat handed her the cornflakes.

"By the way, Michelle called and told me to thank you for introducing her to Tom last night. He wants her to meet him back at the Inferno tonight and she wanted to know if we could go with her."

Cassandra flinched as Kat's words jogged something loose in her memory.

All of a sudden, she saw the Inferno the night before. Saw the Daimons.

She remembered the terror she'd felt.

But most of all, she remembered *Wulf*.

Not the tender lover of her dreams, but the dark, terrifying man who had killed the Daimons in front of her.

"Oh, my God," she breathed as every detail became crystal clear.

"In five minutes no one in that bar will ever remember they saw me." His words tore through her mind.

But she did remember him.

Well.

Had he come home with her?

No. Cassandra calmed a degree as she clearly remembered him leaving her. Of her going back inside and rejoining her friends in the club.

She had gone to bed alone.

But she had awakened naked. Her body damp and sated . . .

"Cass, I'm starting to get worried."

Cassandra took a deep breath and shook everything off. It was a dream. It had to have been. Nothing else made sense. But then when dealing with such supernatural things as Daimons and Dark-Hunters things seldom made sense.

"I'm fine, but I'm not going to my morning class. I think we need to do some research and run an errand."

Kat looked even more worried than before. "You sure? It's not like you to miss class for anything."

"Yeah," she said, offering her a smile. "Just go grab the laptop and let's see what we can find out about Dark-Hunters."

Kat arched a brow at that. "Why?"

In all the years Cassandra had been chased by her mother's people, she had only confided the truth of her world to two bodyguards.

One who had died when Cassandra was only thirteen, in a fight that had almost killed her.

The other had been Kat, who had taken the truth a lot easier than the first bodyguard. Kat had merely looked at her, blinked, and said, "Cool. Can I kill them and not go to prison?"

Since then, Cassandra had never kept anything secret from Kat. Her friend and bodyguard knew as much about the Apollites and their customs as Cassandra did.

Which wasn't much. Apollites had a nasty habit of not letting anyone know they existed.

Still, it had been such a relief to find someone who didn't think she was insane or delusional. But then in the course of the last five years, Kat had seen enough Daimons and Apollites come after them to know the truth of it.

Over the last few months as Cassandra neared the end of her life, the Daimon attacks had backed off enough so that she had a small semblance of normality. But Cassandra wasn't foolish enough to think that she was safe. She would never be safe.

Not until the day she died.

"I think we met a Dark-Hunter last night."

Kat frowned. "When?"

"At the club."

"When?" she repeated.

Cassandra hesitated to tell her. Several details were still sketchy even to her, and until she remembered more of them, she didn't want to worry Kat.

"I saw him in the crowd."

"Then how do you know he was a Dark-Hunter? I thought you told me they were fables."

"I don't really know. He could have just been some weird guy with dark hair and fangs, but if I'm right and he's here in town, I want to know because he might be able to tell me whether or not I'm about to drop dead in eight months."

"Okay, points well taken. But you know, he could have also been one of the fake Goth vamps who hang at the Inferno." Kat went to her bedroom to retrieve the laptop and set it up on the kitchen table while Cassandra finished eating.

As soon as it was ready, Cassandra signed online and headed to Katoteros.com. It was an online community that she had found a little over a year ago where Apollites could talk to each other. On the public side, it looked like a Greek-history site, but there were password-protected areas.

There was nothing on the site about Dark-Hunters. So she and Kat spent some time trying to hack into the private areas, which proved to be even more impossible than breaking into the government's servers.

What was it about preternatural beings that they didn't want others to discover their whereabouts?

Okay, so she understood the need for secrecy. Still, it was a major pain in the ass for a woman who needed some answers.

The closest thing she could find for help was an "Ask the Oracle" link. Clicking it, Cassandra typed in a simple e-mail. "Are Dark-Hunters real?"

After that, she did a search for Dark-Hunters and came up with bubkes. It was as if they didn't exist anywhere.

Before she signed off, her e-mail came back from the Oracle with only two words for a response.

Are you?

"Maybe they are just legends," Kat said again.

"Maybe." But legends didn't kiss women the way Wulf

had kissed her, nor did they find their way into her dreams.

Two hours later, Cassandra decided to utilize her last resort . . . her father.

Kat drove her to her father's high-rise office in downtown St. Paul. All things considered, the late-morning traffic was light and Kat only managed to give her one small heart attack with her dodge-car style of driving.

No matter the time of day or how bad the traffic congestion, Kat always drove as if the Daimons were after them.

Kat whisked the car into the parking garage, clipping the automatic gate on her way in before she whipped around a slow-moving Toyota and beat it into a good spot.

The driver flipped them off, then kept going.

"I swear, Kat, you drive like you're playing a video game."

"Yeah, yeah. Wanna see the ray gun I have under the hood to zap them if they don't get out of my way?"

Cassandra laughed, even though part of her wondered if maybe Kat really had something hidden there. Knowing her friend, it was possible.

As soon as they left the car in the parking lot and entered the building, they attracted a lot of attention. But they always did. It wasn't every day people saw two women who were both over six feet tall. Not to mention that Kat was so strikingly beautiful, Cassandra would have to cut the woman's head off to make her blend in anywhere not Hollywood.

Since a headless bodyguard was rather useless, Cassandra was forced to tolerate a woman who should be working for LA Models.

The company guards greeted them at the door with a nod and waved them inside.

Cassandra's father was the infamous Jefferson T. Peters of Peters, Briggs, and Smith Pharmaceuticals, one of the world's largest drug research and development companies.

Many of the people she passed as she walked through the building cast a jealous eye toward her. They knew she was her father's sole heir, and they all thought she had it made.

If they only knew . . .

"Good day, Miss Peters," his administrative assistant greeted her when she finally made it to the twenty-second floor. "Should I buzz your father?"

Cassandra smiled at the extremely attractive, skinny woman who was very sweet, but always made her feel like she should lose ten pounds and brush her hand self-consciously through her hair to straighten it. Tina was one of those scrupulously well dressed people who never had a molecule out of place.

Dressed in an impeccable Ralph Lauren suit, Tina was the total antithesis to Cassandra, who was dressed in her college sweatshirt and jeans.

"Is he alone?"

Tina nodded.

"I'll just go in and surprise him."

"You'll definitely do that. I know he'll be glad to see you."

Leaving Tina to her work and Kat waiting in a chair near Tina's desk, Cassandra entered her father's sacred workaholic domain.

Contemporary in design, his office had a "cool" feel to

it, but her father was anything but a cold man. He'd loved her mother passionately and since the hour of Cassandra's birth, he had doted on her with everything he had.

Her father was an exceptionally handsome man with dark auburn hair that was laced with distinguished gray. At fifty-nine, he was fit and trim and looked closer to his early forties.

Even though she'd been forced to grow up away from him, for fear of the Apollites or Daimons finding her if she stayed anywhere too long, he had never been far away from her even when she'd been halfway around the world. Only a phone call or even a plane ride away.

Over the years, he'd turned up unexpectedly on her doorstep with gifts and hugs—sometimes in the middle of the night. Sometimes in the middle of the day.

As children, she and her sisters used to make bets on when he'd turn up again to see them. He had never let any of them down, nor had he ever missed a single birthday.

Cassandra loved this man more than anything else in the world and it terrified her what would happen to him if she were to die in eight months like other Apollites. Too many times, she had witnessed his grief and sorrow as he buried her mother and four older sisters.

Every death had torn apart his heart, especially the car bomb that had killed her mother and her last two sisters.

Would he even be able to stand another blow such as that?

Pushing that terrifying thought aside, she approached his steel-and-glass desk.

He was on the phone, but he hung up the minute he looked up from his stack of papers and saw her.

His face lighting instantly, he got up and hugged her, then pulled back with a worried frown. "What are you doing here, baby? Shouldn't you be in class?"

She patted his arm and urged him back to his side of the desk as she flopped into one of the comfy chairs in front. "Probably."

"Then why are you here? It's not like you to cut class to come see me."

She laughed as he echoed Kat's earlier sentiments. Maybe she needed to alter her habits a bit. In her position, predictable behavior was a dangerous liability. "I wanted to talk to you."

"About?"

"The Dark-Hunters."

He paled, making her wonder just how much he knew and how much he was going to share. He had a nasty tendency to overprotect her, hence her long legacy of bodyguards.

"Why do you want to know about them?" he asked cautiously.

"Because I was attacked by Daimons last night and a Dark-Hunter saved my life."

He shot to his feet and rushed over to her side of the desk. "Were you hurt?"

"No, Daddy," she hastened to assure him as he tried to inspect her body for damage. "Just scared."

He pulled back with a stern frown, but kept his hands on her arm. "All right, listen. You need to withdraw from school, we'll—"

"Daddy," she said firmly, "I'm not going to withdraw less than a year from graduation. I'm through running."

Even though she might not live past eight months, there was a possibility that she would. Until she knew for certain, she had vowed to live her life as normally as possible.

She saw the horror on his face. "This is not something debatable, Cassandra. I swore to your mother that I would keep you safe from the Apollites and I will. I'll not let them kill you too."

She clenched her teeth at the reminder of an oath he took as sacred as he did this office and company. She knew the legacy she had inherited from her mother's family all too well.

Centuries past, it had been her ancestor who had caused the Apollites to be cursed.

Out of jealousy, her great-great-whatever had sent out soldiers to murder the son and mistress of the god Apollo. In retaliation, the Greek sun god had banished all Apollites from his favor.

Since the Apollite queen had ordered her men to make it appear as if a beast had destroyed the mother and child, Apollo gave all the Apollites the features of beasts—long canine teeth, speed, strength, and predator's eyes. They were forced to feed off each other's blood in order to survive.

He had banished them from the daylight so that the angry god would never again have to see them.

But the cruelest blow of all, he had cursed them to a life span of only twenty-seven years—the same age his mistress had been when she'd been slain by the Apollites.

On his or her twenty-seventh birthday, an Apollite spent the entire day slowly, painfully decaying. It was so awful a death that most of them committed ritual suicide the day before their birthday to escape it.

The only hope an Apollite had was to slay a human and take the human soul into their own body. There was no other way to prolong their short lives. But the minute they turned Daimon, they crossed over and invoked the wrath of the gods.

It was then the Dark-Hunters were called in to kill

them and free the stolen human souls before the souls that were trapped withered and died.

In eight short months, Cassandra would turn twenty-seven.

It was something that terrified her.

She was part human and because of that she could walk in daylight, but she had to stay covered up and couldn't be out too long without burning severely.

Her long canine teeth had been filed down by a dentist when she was ten, and though she was anemic, her need for blood was satisfied by bimonthly transfusions.

She was lucky. The handful of other half-Apollite, half-humans she had met over the years had leaned mostly toward their Apollite heritage.

All of them had died at twenty-seven.

All of them.

But Cassandra had always held on to the hope that she had enough human in her to make it past her birthday.

Ultimately, though, she didn't know, and she'd never been able to find anyone who knew more about her "condition" than she did.

Cassandra didn't want to die. Not now when there was so much living she had left. She wanted what most everyone else did. A husband. A family.

Most of all, a future.

"Maybe this Dark-Hunter knows something about my mixed blood. Maybe he—"

"Your mother would fly into a panic if their name ever came up," he said as he stroked her cheek. "I know very little about the Apollites, but I know they all hate the Dark-Hunters. Your mother called them evil, soulless killers that no one could reason with."

"They're not the Terminator, Daddy."

"The way your mother spoke of them, they are."

Well, that was true. Her mother had spent hours warning her and her sisters to stay away from three things: Dark-Hunters, Daimons, and Apollites—in that order.

"Mom never even met one. All she knew was what her parents had told her and I'll wager they never met one either. Besides, what if this Dark-Hunter is the key to helping me find a way to live longer?"

His grip tightened on her hand. "What if he was sent to kill you just like the Daimons and Apollites who killed your mother? You know what the myth says. Kill you, and the curse is lifted from them."

She thought about that for a second. "What if they're right? What if my death would allow all the other Apollites to live normally? Maybe I should die."

His face flushed with rage. His gaze burned into hers as he tightened his grip on her hand. "Cassandra Elaine Peters, I better never hear you say that again. Do you understand me?"

Cassandra nodded, contrite for having raised his blood pressure when that was the last thing she wanted to do. "I know, Daddy. I'm just upset."

He kissed her forehead. "I know, baby. I know."

She saw the torment on his face as he got up and returned to his chair.

He didn't say what they both thought. Long ago he'd entrusted a small group of researchers with the duty of finding a "cure" for her rare disease only to learn modern science was helpless before the wrath of an ancient god.

Maybe he was right, maybe Wulf was as dangerous to her as everyone else. She knew the Dark-Hunters were sworn to kill Daimons, but she didn't know how they would deal with Apollites.

Her mother had said to trust no one, most especially not the ones who made their living by killing their people.

Still, her gut told her that a race that had spent eternity hunting hers would know everything about them.

Then again, why would a Dark-Hunter ever help an Apollite when they were sworn enemies?

"It was a stupid idea, wasn't it?"

"No, Cassie," her father said gently. "It wasn't stupid at all. I just don't want to see you hurt."

She got up and went to hug and kiss him. "I'll go on to class and forget about it."

"I still wish you'd think about leaving for a while. If those Daimons saw you, they might have told someone else you were here."

"Trust me, Daddy, they didn't have time. No one knows I'm here and I don't want to leave."

Ever.

The word hung unspoken between them. She saw her father's lips quiver as they both thought about the fact that the clock was ticking for her.

"Why don't you come over for dinner tonight?" her father asked. "I'll leave work early and—"

"I promised Michelle we could do something. Catch you tomorrow?"

He nodded and gave her a squeeze so strong that she winced from the pressure of his arms around her waist. "You be careful."

"I will."

By the look on his face, she could tell he didn't want her to go any more than she wanted to leave. "I love you, Cassandra."

"I know. I love you too, Daddy." She offered him a smile and left him to his work.

Cassandra made her way from his office and out of the building, while her thoughts drifted back toward her dreams of Wulf and the way he'd felt in her arms.

Kat fell in behind her and remained completely silent, giving her the space she needed. It was what she loved most about her bodyguard.

Sometimes it seemed as if Kat were psychically linked to her.

"I need some Starbucks," Cassandra said to Kat over her shoulder. "What about you?"

"Always game for java. Give me ground-up beans or give me death."

As she walked down the street toward the coffee shop, Cassandra started thinking more and more about the Dark-Hunters.

Since she had discounted them before as myths her mother had used to frighten her, she'd never really researched them while she'd studied ancient Greece. Ever since she was a child, she'd spent her spare time looking into her mother's history, and ancient legends.

She couldn't recall ever finding a mention in her readings about the Dark-Hunters, which only confirmed in her mind that her mother was relaying stories of bogeymen and not real people.

But maybe she'd overlooked—

"Hey, Cassandra!"

She looked up from her musings to see one of the guys from school waving at her as she drew near Starbucks. He was a couple of inches shorter than her and was cute in a very Boy Scout kind of way. His short black hair was curly and he had friendly blue eyes.

Something about him reminded her of Opie Taylor from *The Andy Griffith Show* and she half-expected him to call her "ma'am."

"Chris Eriksson," Kat whispered under her breath as he came over.

"Thanks," Cassandra said in an equally low tone,

grateful Kat's name recall was much better than her own. She could always remember faces, but names often eluded her.

He stopped before them.

"Hi, Chris," she said, smiling at him. He was really nice and always tried to help anyone who needed it. "What brings you here?"

He looked instantly uncomfortable. "I . . . uh . . . I was picking up something for someone."

Kat exchanged an interested look with her. "Sounds kind of dubious. I hope it's not illegal."

He blushed profusely. "No, not illegal. Just kind of personal."

For some reason, Cassandra liked the sound of it being illegal better. She waited a minute or two while he looked rather awkward.

Chris was an undergraduate student in her Old English class. They hadn't really spoken to each other much except to compare notes whenever she'd had trouble translating something. Chris was the professor's pet and maintained a perfect score on all the tests.

Everyone in the class wanted to hang him for blowing the curve.

"Did you do the assignment for class this afternoon?" he asked finally.

She nodded.

"It was great, wasn't it? Really exciting stuff." By his face, she could tell he truly meant that.

"Like having my teeth drilled without Novocain," she said, intending it to be funny and playful.

He didn't take it that way.

His features fell. "I'm sorry. I'm being a geek again." He pulled nervously at his ear and dropped his gaze to the ground. "I better go. I have some other things I need to do."

As he started away from her, she called out to him, "Hey, Chris?"

He stopped and looked back at her.

"Overprotected Child Syndrome?"

"Excuse me?"

"You're an overprotected child too, aren't you?"

He scratched the back of his neck. "How'd you know?"

"Trust me, you have the classic symptoms. I used to have them too, but after years of intensive therapy, I learned to hide them and can almost function normally now."

He laughed at that. "Got the name of that therapist handy?"

She smiled. "Sure." Cassandra inclined her head toward the coffee shop. "You got time to join us for a cup of coffee?"

He looked as if she had just handed him the keys to Fort Knox. "Yeah, thanks."

She and Kat led the way into Starbucks with Chris right behind them like a happy puppy whose owner had just come home.

After they had their drinks, they sat down in the back, away from the windows where the light couldn't burn her.

"So why are you taking Old English?" Chris asked after Kat had excused herself to go to the restroom. "You don't seem like the type who volunteers for that kind of punishment."

"I'm always trying to research old . . . things," she said for lack of a better term. It was hard to explain to a stranger that she researched ancient curses and spells in hopes of elongating her life. "What about you? You seem like you'd be more at home in a computer class."

He shrugged. "I was after the easy As this semester. I wanted something I could coast through."

"Yeah, but Old English? What kind of home do you have?"

"One where they actually speak it."

"Get out!" she said in disbelief. "Who in the world actually speaks that?"

"We do. Really." Then he said something to her that she couldn't understand.

"Did you just insult me?"

"No," he said earnestly. "I would never do anything like that."

She smiled as she glanced down to his backpack where she did a double take. There was a distressed brown day planner exposed by an unzipped pouch. The planner held a burgundy ribbon hanging out with an interesting badge attached to it. The badge had the picture of a round shield with two swords crossed and over the swords were the initials D.H.

How strange to see that today when she had her mind on a whole other kind of D.H.

Maybe it was an omen . . .

"D.H.?" she asked, touching the emblem. She turned it over and her heart stopped as she saw the words "Dark-Hunter.com" engraved into it.

"Huh?" Chris looked to her hand. "Oh . . . Oh!" he said, getting instantly nervous again. He took it from her and tucked it back into his backpack, then zipped it closed. "That's just something I play with sometimes."

Why did it make him so tense? So obviously uncomfortable? "You sure you're not doing anything illegal, Chris?"

"Yeah, trust me. If I even had an illegal thought, I'd get busted and get my tail kicked."

Cassandra wasn't so sure about that as Kat rejoined them.

Dark-Hunter.com . . .

She hadn't tried to search them out with a hyphen between the words. And now she had a Web address to try.

They chatted a few more minutes about class and school, then parted ways so Chris could finish his errands before their late-afternoon Old English class and she could get back to campus before her next one.

She might blow off one class a day, but two classes . . .

Nah. Cassandra was nothing if not dedicated.

Before long, she was safely ensconced at her desk and waiting for her Classics professor to show while other students talked around her. Kat was just down the hall in a small waiting area where she was reading a Kinley Mac-Gregor novel.

While Cassandra waited for the professor, she opened up her Palm Pilot and decided to do a little Web surfing. She typed in Dark-Hunter.com.

She waited as the page loaded.

The minute it did, she gasped.

Oh, this was getting good . . .

Chapter 4

Chris sighed as he neared his Old English classroom. It was a typical day of suckage and blowage. His life should be great. He had all the money in the world. Every luxury known. There was nothing on the planet he could dream of that couldn't be his for the asking.

For that matter, Wulf had even flown Britney Spears in to sing at Chris's twenty-first-birthday party last spring. The only problem was that the attendees had consisted of him, his bodyguards, and Wulf, who ran around the whole time trying to make sure Chris didn't get a head wound or racked.

Not to mention the three million times Wulf had urged him to make a pass at Britney. Or at the very least propose to her—which she had rejected with a great deal of laughter that still rang in his ears.

All Chris really wanted was a normal life. More than that, he wanted his freedom.

Those were the only two things he couldn't have.

Wulf wouldn't let him leave the house unless he was tagged and tailed. The only time Chris could fly anywhere was if Acheron himself, the leader of the Dark-Hunters, came and picked him up and kept him within his eyesight the entire time. Every member of the Squires'

Council understood that Chris was Wulf's last blood link to his brother. As such, he was guarded more zealously than a national treasure.

He felt like such an alien species, he wished he could find someplace where he wouldn't be a complete freak.

But it was impossible. There was no escaping his destiny.

No escaping what he was . . .

The last heir.

Without Chris and his children, Wulf would be alone for eternity because only a human born of Wulf's blood could ever remember him.

The only problem with that was finding a mother for those kids, and no one wanted to volunteer.

His ears still rang with Belinda's rejection from ten minutes ago.

"Go out with you? Pah-lease. Call me when you grow up and learn to dress right."

Grinding his teeth, he tried not to think about her harsh words. He'd put on his best khaki pants and navy sweater just to ask her out. But he knew he wasn't suave or cool.

He had the social graces of an idiot. The average face of the boy next door and the confidence of a snail.

God, he *was* pathetic.

Chris paused at the door of his classroom to see the two male Theti Squires trailing him at a "discreet" distance. In their mid-thirties, both of them were over six feet tall, with dark hair and stern faces. Assigned to him by the Squires' Council, their sole duty was to watch over him and make sure nothing happened to him until he spawned enough kids to make Wulf happy.

Not that there was any big threat during the daylight. On rare occasions a Doulos—human servants for the

Apollites—might attack a Squire, but those were so rare these days as to be worthy of national news coverage.

At night, Chris was forbidden to leave the property unless he was on a date. Which seemed impossible after his one-and-only girlfriend had dumped him.

He sighed at the prospect of trying to find someone else to go out with him. Why would they when they would have to be subjected to blood tests and physicals?

He groaned under his breath.

While he was in class, the Thetis would take up stations outside the door, thus guaranteeing Chris's freak status even more than his solitary nature.

And who could blame him for being solitary? Jeez, he'd grown up in a house where he wasn't allowed to run in case he hurt himself. If he ever got a cold of any sort, the Squires' Council called in specialists from the Mayo Clinic to treat him. What few children his father had imported to play with him from other Squire families had been given strict orders that they were never to touch him, or make him angry, or do anything to make Wulf angry at them.

So his "friends" would come over, sit and watch television with him. They seldom spoke for fear of getting into trouble and no one dared to even bring a present or share so much as a potato chip. Everything had to be thoroughly searched and detoxed before Chris was allowed to play with it. After all, one little germ and he might become sterile or, God forbid, die.

The burden of civilization was upon him, or more to the point, the burden of Wulf's lineage was upon him.

The only real friend Chris had in his life was Nick Gautier, a Squire recruit he'd met online a couple of years ago. Too new to their world to understand Chris's gilded status, Nick had treated him like a human being and the

Cajun agreed that Chris's life seriously sucked in spite of the benefits that came along with it.

Hell, the only reason he'd been able to convince Wulf to let him go to college, instead of hiring professors to come to the house and teach him, was the fact that here he might actually meet an eligible ovary donor. Wulf had been giddy at the prospect and interrogated him every night on whether or not he met a new woman.

More to the point, had he scored with her?

Sighing again, Chris entered the room and kept his gaze lowered so that he wouldn't see the glares or sneers most of the students directed at him. If they didn't hate him for being Dr. Mitchell's pet, they hated him for being an overprivileged geek. He was used to it.

He flopped down in a vacant chair in the back corner and dug out his notebook and text.

"Hi, Chris."

He started at the friendly feminine voice.

Looking up, he saw Cassandra's beaming smile.

Totally dumbstruck, it was a full minute before he could respond to her. "Hi," he answered back lamely.

He hated himself for being so damned stupid. Nick could probably have had her eating out of his hand.

She sat down next to him.

He broke out into a sweat. Clearing his throat, he did his best to ignore her and the light scent of roses that drifted from her over to him. She always smelled incredible.

Cassandra opened her book to the assignment and watched Chris. He seemed even more nervous now than he had at the coffee shop.

She glanced down at his backpack, hoping to see another glimpse of the shield, but he'd concealed it completely.

Damn.

"So, Chris," she said softly, leaning a little closer to him. "I was wondering if I might be able to study with you later."

He blanched and looked like he was almost ready to bolt. "Study? With me?"

"Yeah. You said you knew this stuff really well and I'd like to make an A on the test. What do you think?"

He rubbed the back of his neck nervously—clearly a habit since he seemed to do it so frequently. "You sure you want *me* to study with *you*?"

"Yes."

He smiled sheepishly, but refused to meet her gaze. "Sure, I guess that would be okay."

Cassandra sat back with a satisfied smile as Dr. Mitchell came in and commanded everyone to silence.

She'd spent hours on the Dark-Hunter.com Web site after her last class, going through every part of it. On the surface, it appeared to be some kind of role-playing group or book site.

But there were entire sections of it that were password protected. Secret loops and areas that she couldn't access no matter how hard she tried. There were many things about it that reminded her of the Apollite site.

No, this wasn't a gaming group. She had stumbled upon the real Dark-Hunters. She knew it.

They were the last great mystery of the modern world. Living myths that no one knew about.

But she knew they were there. And she was going to find a way into their society and find some answers even if it killed her.

Sitting through that class while the professor droned on about Hrothgar and Shield was the hardest thing she'd ever done in her life. As soon as it ended, she packed up and waited for Chris.

As they neared the door, she saw the two men dressed in black who immediately flanked them while eyeballing her.

Chris let out a disgusted sound.

Cassandra laughed in spite of herself. "Are they with you?"

"I really wish I could say no."

She patted his arm in sympathy. She jerked her chin to indicate down the hall where Kat was standing up and tucking away her book. "I got one myself."

Chris smiled at that. "Thank God, I'm not the only one."

"Nah, don't worry about it. I told you I understand completely."

The relief on his face was tangible. "So when would you like to study?"

"How about now?"

"Okay, where?"

There was only one place Cassandra was dying to get into. She hoped it would hold more clues about the man she'd met last night. "Your place?"

His nervousness was back instantly, confirming her suspicions. "I don't know if that's a good idea."

"Why?"

"I just . . . it's just . . . I, um, I just don't think it's a good idea, okay?"

Stymied already. Cassandra forced herself to hide her irritation. She'd have to tread carefully if she was to get past his defenses. But then she understood that. She had her own secrets to hide.

"Okay, you pick the place."

"The library?"

She bristled. "I can't ever get comfy there. I'm always afraid of being told to hush. Want to come back to my apartment?"

He looked totally stunned by her offer. "Really?"

"Sure. I mean, I don't usually bite or anything."

He laughed. "Yeah, me either." He took two steps off with her, then turned to the men trailing them. "We are just going to her place, okay? Why don't you guys go get a doughnut or something?"

They didn't acknowledge him in the least.

Kat laughed.

Cassandra led the way to the students' parking lot and then gave Chris directions to her apartment. "See you there?"

He nodded and made his way toward a red Hummer.

Cassandra dashed to her gray Mercedes, where Kat was waiting in the driver's seat. They headed home, while Cassandra hoped Chris didn't wait too long or, worse, change his mind.

Not until she had a chance to search his backpack, anyway.

It took her two hours of boring *Beowulf* study and a pot of coffee before Chris left her alone with his backpack while he went to the bathroom. Kat had long since retired to her bedroom, claiming the dead language and Chris's enthusiasm for it was giving her a migraine.

As soon as Chris vanished, Cassandra went searching.

Luckily, it didn't take long to find what she was looking for . . .

She found the day planner in his backpack where she had seen it earlier. The binder of it was hand-tooled leather with a strange emblem on the front: a double bow and arrow that was tilted up with the arrow pointing to the right.

Just like the one she had seen on Wulf's shoulder in her dream . . .

She ran her hand over the brown leather, then opened it to find that everything was written in Runic. The language was similar to Old English, but she couldn't read it.

Old Norse, perhaps?

"What are you doing?"

She jumped at Chris's sharp question. It took a few seconds for her to think of anything to say that wouldn't make him even more suspicious. "You're one of those gamers, aren't you?"

His blue gaze narrowed on her and turned sharp. "What are you talking about?"

"I . . . um, I went to this site called Dark-Hunter and found all these teasers about a book series and game. Since I had seen your book earlier, I was wondering if you were one of the members who plays there."

She could tell he was searching his mind and her face to see what, if anything, he should say.

"Yeah, my friend Nick runs the site," he said after a long pause. "We have a lot of interesting people who play there."

"I saw that. Do you have one of those names like Hellion or Rogue that you play under?"

He came forward and took the day planner from her. "No, I just use 'Chris.' "

"Ah. So what goes on in the private areas?"

"Nothing," he said a little too fast. "Just a bunch of us BSing each other."

"Then why is it private?"

"It just is." He grabbed the book from her hand and

shoved it back into his backpack. "Look, I have to go now. Good luck on the test."

Cassandra wanted to stop him and ask more questions, but it was painfully obvious he had no intention of letting her know anything else about them or him.

"Thanks, Chris. I appreciate the help."

He nodded and made a hasty exit.

Alone in her kitchen, Cassandra sat in the chair, chewing her thumbnail as she debated how to proceed. She thought about tailing Chris to his house, but that wouldn't do much good. No doubt his bodyguards would catch her, even with Kat's cockamamie driving.

Getting up, she went to the laptop in her room and booted it up.

Okay, the Dark-Hunter site was designed as if the Dark-Hunters were characters in a book. Most people would accept that, but what if she reviewed it again from the angle that nothing on the site was false?

She'd spent her life in hiding and one thing she had learned . . . the best place to hide was out in the open. People had a tendency to not see what was right before them.

And even if they saw it, they came up with ways to explain it away. They would say it was a figment of their imagination or youthful pranks.

No doubt the Dark-Hunters thought the same thing. After all, in this modern world where everyone knew about vampires and demons and thought them a Hollywood myth, they wouldn't even necessarily have to hide. Most people would write them off as eccentrics.

She watched the intro to the site, then switched to the profile pages of the individual Hunters who were listed.

There was one there for a character named Wulf Tryggvason whose Squire was named Chris Eriksson. Supposedly, Wulf was a Viking warrior who had been cursed . . .

Cassandra copied Wulf's name and then searched the Nillstrom—an Old Norse legend-and-history search engine.

"Bingo," she whispered as several entries popped up.

Born of a Christian mother from Gaul and a Norse father, Wulf Tryggvason had been a renowned adventurer and raider of the mid-eighth century whose death was unrecorded. In fact, it only said that he had vanished one day after he had won a battle against a Mercian warlord who had been trying to kill him. Popular belief had it that one of the warlord's sons had vengefully slain him that night.

Cassandra heard her bedroom door open. Looking up, she saw Kat standing in the doorway.

"You busy?" Kat asked.

"I was just doing some more research."

"Ah." Kat moved forward to read over her shoulder. " 'Wulf Tryggvason. Pirate, risk-taker, and warrior, he fought his way across Europe, hiring himself out to both Christian and pagan alike. It was once written that his only loyalty was to his sword and to his brother Erik who traveled with him . . . ' Interesting. You think this might be the guy you saw at the Inferno?"

"Maybe. You ever heard of him?"

"Not at all. You want me to ask Jimmy? He's all into Viking history."

Cassandra considered it for a second. Kat's friend was in the Society of Creative Anachronism and lived to study Viking culture.

But it wasn't Wulf's past that interested her at the moment. It was his present, and what she wanted most was a modern-day address for him.

"It's okay."

"You sure?"

"Yeah."

Kat nodded. "Fine then, I'll just head back to my room and finish my book. You want me to bring you something to munch on or drink?"

Cassandra smiled at the offer. "A soda would be great."

Kat vanished only to return a few minutes later with a Sprite. Cassandra thanked her, then went back to work while Kat left her alone.

Cassandra sipped her drink leisurely as she surfed. About an hour later, she was so tired, she couldn't keep her eyes open any longer.

Yawning, she checked the time. It was barely five-thirty. Even so, her eyelids were so heavy that she couldn't stay awake no matter how hard she tried.

She shut down her computer, then headed for bed to take a short nap.

She fell asleep the instant her head touched the pillow. Normally, Cassandra didn't dream much whenever she took an afternoon nap.

Today was completely different.

Today her dreams started almost as soon as she closed her eyes.

How strange . . .

But the oddest part of all was that her fantasy realm bore no resemblance to anything she'd ever dreamt before. Instead of her normal dreams of glamour or horror, this one was peaceful. Gentle. And it filled her with warm security.

She was dressed in a soft dark green gown like some medieval lady. Frowning, she ran her hand over the material, which was softer than chamois.

Alone inside a stone cottage where a warm fire blazed

in a large hearth, she stood off to the side of an old wooden table. The winds howled outside a window that was covered by a wooden shutter that clattered noisily as it tried to keep the winter winds out.

She heard someone at the door behind her.

Cassandra turned around just in time to see Wulf shoulder it open. Her heart stopped as she caught sight of him dressed in a chain-mail vest of sorts. His massive arms were bare with his torso and mail covered by a leather vest that had Nordic designs burned into it. The designs matched the tattoo on his right shoulder and biceps.

His conical helm covered his head and had more mail attached to it that covered his face, virtually obscuring it. But for those intense, heated eyes, she would never have known it was Wulf under there. He held a small battle-axe in one hand, resting it over his shoulder. He looked primitive and wild. The kind of man who had once owned the world. One who was afraid of nothing.

His dark gaze swept the room, then stopped on her. She watched a slow, seductive smile break across the lower half of his face, showing off his fangs.

"Cassandra, my love," he greeted, his voice warm and enchanting. "What are you doing here?"

"I have no idea," she answered honestly. "I'm not even sure where *here* is."

He laughed at that, a deep, rumbling sound, then shut the door and bolted it. "You're in my home, *villkat*. At least what was once my home long ago."

She looked about the spartan place, which was furnished with a table, chairs, and one very large fur-covered bed. "Strange, I would have thought Wulf Tryggvason had a better place than this to call his own."

He set the axe down on the table, then removed his helm and placed it over the axe.

Cassandra was floored by the masculine beauty of the man before her. He oozed a raw, sexual appeal that no one could ever rival.

"Compared to the small farm where I grew up, this is a mansion, my lady."

"Really?"

He nodded as he pulled her up against him. His eyes scorched her and filled her with a deep, aching need. She knew exactly what he wanted, and though she barely knew him at all, she was more than willing to give it to him.

"My father was once a warring raider who took a vow of poverty years before I was born," Wulf said huskily.

His confession surprised her. "What made him do that?"

His grip on her tightened. "The downfall of all men, I'm afraid . . . Love. My mother was a captured Christian slave who had been given to him by his father after one of their raids. She beguiled him, and in the end she tamed him and turned a once-proud warrior into a docile farmer who refused to lift his sword lest he offend his newfound God."

She could hear the raw emotions in his voice. The contempt he felt for anyone who would choose peace over war. "You disagreed with his choice?"

"Aye, what good is a man who cannot protect himself and those he loves?" His eyes turned dark, deadly. The rage inside them made her shiver. "When the Jutes came to our village to loot and take slaves, I am told he held his hands out and let them run him through. Everyone who survived mocked him for his cowardice. He who had once made his enemies quake in terror at the mention of his name died at the slaughter like a defenseless calf. I have never understood how he could just stand there and take a killing blow without trying to defend himself."

She reached up to smooth his brow with her fingers as his pain reached out to her. But it wasn't hatred or condescension she heard in his voice. It was guilt. "I'm so sorry."

"As was I," he whispered, his eyes turning even stormier. "It wasn't bad enough that I left him there to die, but I took my brother as well. There was no one there to protect him in our absence."

"Where were you?"

He dropped his gaze to the floor, but still she could see his self-recrimination. He wanted to go back and change that moment, just as she wished she could take back the night the Spathi Daimons had killed her mother and sisters.

"I had left the summer before in search of war and riches." He released her and looked about his modest home. "After word of his death reached me, riches no longer seemed important to me. Disagreements aside, I should have been there with him."

She touched his bare arm. "You must have loved your father greatly."

He let out a tired breath. "At times. At others I hated him. Hated him for not being the man he should have been. His father was a respected jarl and yet we lived like starving beggars. Mocked and spat upon by our own kin. My mother took pride in the insults, saying it was God's will that we suffer. It was somehow making us better people, but I never believed her. My father's blind devotion to her beliefs only angered me more. We fought, he and I, constantly. He wanted me to follow in his footsteps and to take their abuse and say nothing."

The torment in his eyes touched her even more than the gentleness of his hand on hers. "He wanted me to be something I wasn't. But I couldn't turn the other cheek.

'Twas never in my nature to not answer insult with insult. Blow with blow."

He turned and looked at her with a scowl. "Why am I telling you this?"

Cassandra thought about it for a second. "The dream, I'm sure. It's probably on your mind." Though why it would be in *her* dream, she couldn't imagine.

In fact, this dream was getting odder by the minute and she couldn't figure out why her subconscious would come here.

Why was she conjuring up this fantasy about her mysterious Dark-Hunter . . . ?

He nodded. "Aye, no doubt. I fear I am doing to Christopher what was once done to me. I should let him live his life as his own and not interfere with his choices so often."

"Why can't you?"

"Honestly?"

She smiled. "I certainly prefer honesty to lies."

He gave a light laugh, then his face turned brooding again. "I don't want to lose him too." His voice was so deep and aching that it made her heart clench. "And yet I know I have no choice except to lose him."

"Why?"

"Everyone dies, my lady. At least in the mortal realm. Yet I go on as everyone around me perishes over and over again." He lifted his gaze to hers. The agony on his face reached deep inside her. "Have you any idea what it is like to hold a loved one in your arms while they die?"

Cassandra's chest drew tight as she thought of her mother's and sisters' deaths. She had wanted to go to them after the explosion, but her bodyguard had pulled her away while she howled in grief for their loss.

"It's too late to help them, Cassie. We have to run."

Her soul had screamed that day.

Sometimes it screamed even now at the injustice of her life.

"Yes, I do," she whispered. "I, too, have seen everyone I love die. My father is all I have left."

His gaze sharpened. "Then imagine doing it thousands of times, century after century. Imagine watching them be born, live, and then die while you carry on and start over with each new generation. Every time I see a member of my family die, it is like watching my brother Erik die all over again. And Chris . . ." He winced as if the very mention of Chris's name caused him pain. "He is my brother made over in face and form." One corner of his mouth lifted in wry amusement. "And mouth as well as temperament. Of all the family I have lost, his death will be the hardest to bear, I think."

She saw the vulnerability in his eyes and it affected her deeply that this fierce man would have so human a fault. "He's still young. His whole life is ahead of him."

"Perhaps . . . but my brother was only twenty-four when he was slain by our enemies. I will never forget the look on his son Bironulf's young face when he saw his father fall in battle. All I could think of was saving the boy."

"Obviously you did."

"Aye. I swore I would never let Bironulf die as his father had. All his life, I kept him safe and he died an old man, in his sleep. Peacefully." He paused for a moment. "I guess in the end I do follow my mother's beliefs more than those of my father. The Norse believed in dying young in battle so that we could enter the halls of Valhalla, but like my mother, I wanted a different fate for those I loved. 'Tis a pity I came to understand her feelings far too late."

Wulf shook his head as if to banish those thoughts. He

frowned at her. "I can't believe I'm thinking of this while I have such a beautiful maid with me. I am truly growing old when I would rather talk than take action," he said with a deep laugh. "Enough of my morbid thoughts."

He pulled her forcefully against him. "Now why are we wasting our time when we could be spending it much more productively?"

"Productively how?"

His smile was wicked, warm, and it devoured her. "I am thinking my tongue could be put to much better use. What say you?"

He ran said member up the column of her throat until he could nibble her ear. His warm breath scorched her neck, causing her to shiver.

"Oh yeah," she breathed. "I'm thinking that is a much better use of your tongue."

He laughed while he unlaced the back of her gown. Slowly, seductively, he pulled it from her shoulders and let it fall straight to the floor. The fabric slid sensuously against her flesh as it left her body and cold air caressed her.

Naked before him, she couldn't suppress a deep tremble. It was so odd to be exposed while he stood before her wearing his armor. The firelight played in his dark eyes.

Wulf stared at the unadorned beauty of the woman before him. She was even more luscious than she had been the last time he'd dreamed of her. He ran his hand tenderly over her breast, letting the nipple tease his palm.

She reminded him of Saga, the Norse goddess of poetry. Elegant, refined. Gentle. Things he had spurned as a mortal man.

Now he was captivated by her.

He still didn't know why he had confided in her. It

wasn't like him to speak so freely, and yet she had lured him.

But he didn't want to make love to her here. Not in the past where his memories and guilt over those he had failed slashed at him.

She deserved better than this.

Closing his eyes, he conjured them into a facsimile of his modern bedroom. Only he made a few modifications . . .

Cassandra gasped as she pulled back slightly and looked around. The walls surrounding them were reflective black with white trim, except the wall to her right, which was made up of floor-to-ceiling windows. The open windows were framed by gauzy white curtains that fluttered in the wind, reaching out toward them and making the candlelight from dozens of candles in the room dance.

But the candles didn't go out. They twinkled all around them like stars.

There was a large bed in the center of the room, up high on a raised platform. It had black silk sheets and a thick black silk duvet over a down comforter. The bed was made of ornate ironwork that formed an intricate square canopy between the four posts. More of the white gauzy material was wrapped around it and was left to twist in the wind.

Wulf was naked now. He scooped her up in his arms and carried her toward the huge, welcoming bed.

Cassandra sighed as she felt the soft mattress under her while Wulf's weight pressed down on her from above. It was like being pressed into a cloud.

Looking up, she laughed as she realized there was a mirror on the ceiling, and she saw that Wulf was holding a long-stemmed rose behind his back.

The walls flashed, then they too became mirrors.

"Whose fantasy is this?" she asked as Wulf brought the rose forward and brushed its soft petals over the swollen nipple of her right breast.

"Ours, *blomster,*" Wulf said as he parted her thighs and laid his large body between her legs.

She moaned at the rich sensation of having all his lush power lying over her. The masculine hairs of his body teased hers into an overload of sensual ecstasy.

He moved over her sinuously, like some dark, forbidden beast who was out to consume her.

Cassandra watched him move in the mirror above her. How odd that she had created him in her dreams. She'd always been so cautious in her life. So careful of whom she let touch her. So she had conjured a glorious lover in her subconscious whereas she dared not allow one in real life.

Because of her death sentence, she didn't want anyone to fall in love with her or care for her. She didn't want to bear a child who would mourn her. A child who would be left alone, frightened.

Hunted.

The last thing she wanted was to leave someone like Wulf behind to grieve her death. Someone who would have to watch his child die in the full bloom of youth because of a curse that had nothing to do with any of his actions.

But in her dreams, she was free to love him with her body. There was no fear here. No promises. No hearts to be broken.

Just them and this one perfect moment.

Wulf groaned deep in his throat as he nibbled her hip. She hissed and cupped his head. He let the softness of her hands in his hair soothe him.

For so long he had wandered through the past in his dreams. Always searching for the one who had tricked him into trading places. He was never destined to be a Dark-Hunter. He had never sworn his soul to Artemis or received an Act of Vengeance in exchange for his service.

Wulf had been seeking someone to soothe the pain he felt at his brother's death. A tender body he could sink himself into and forget for just a moment that he had led Erik into battle far away from their homeland.

Morginne had seemed the perfect answer. She'd been as eager for him as he had been for her.

But the morning after his one night with the Dark-Huntress, everything had changed. Somehow either during their sexual encounter or right after it, she had traded souls with him. Mortal no longer, he had found himself born into a new life.

And viciously cursed by Morginne so that no mortal could remember him. Meanwhile she had escaped Artemis's service so that she could spend eternity with the Norse god Loki.

Her parting curse had been the cruelest blow of all and it was one he didn't understand to this day.

Not even his nephew Bironulf had known him afterward.

Wulf would be completely lost now had Acheron Parthenopaeus not taken pity on his situation. Acheron, the leader of the Dark-Hunters, had told him that no one could undo Morginne's trickery, but that Acheron could modify it. Taking a drop of Bironulf's blood, Acheron had made it so that all who carried his blood would remember Wulf. Furthermore, the Atlantean had given Wulf psychic powers and explained to Wulf how he had become immortal and what his limitations were, such as his sensitivity to sunlight.

So long as Artemis held Wulf's "new" soul, he had no choice except to serve her.

Artemis had no intention of ever letting him go. Not that he really minded. Immortality had its benefits.

The woman under him was definitely one of them. He ran his hand down her thigh and listened to her breathing. She tasted of salt and woman. Smelled of powder and roses.

Her scent and taste stirred him to a level he'd never known before. For the first time in centuries, he felt possessive toward a woman.

He wanted to keep this one. The Viking in him roared to life. In his human time, he would have carried her off and slain any who dared try to keep him from her.

Even after all these centuries, he was no closer to being civilized. He took what he wanted. Always.

Cassandra yelped the moment Wulf took her into his mouth. Her body sizzled with desire for him. She arched her back and watched him in the mirror above the bed.

She'd never seen anything more erotic than the sight of Wulf teasing her while the muscles of his back flexed. She could see every inch of his tawny, naked body while he pleased her. And he had an incredible body.

One she wanted to touch.

Moving her legs under his body, she used her feet to gently caress the hard length of his cock.

He growled in response. "You have very talented feet, *villkat.*"

"All the better to stroke you with," she said, her voice light as she thought about the fact that she felt like Little Red Riding Hood being eaten by the Big Bad Wulf.

His laughter joined hers. She buried her hands in the soft waves of his hair and let him have his way with her. His tongue was the most incredible thing she'd ever known as he swirled it around her. Licking, teasing, tasting.

Just when she didn't think she could feel any better, he slid two fingers deep inside her.

Cassandra came immediately.

Still he continued caressing her until she was on fire and weak from the bliss.

"Mmm," he breathed, pulling away from her. "I think my kitten is hungry."

"Famished," she said, pulling him up her body so that she could feast on his skin the way he had feasted on hers.

She buried her lips against his neck and nibbled with every part of her that was desperately hungry for him. What was it about this man that drove her wild with desire? He was magnificent. Hot. Sexy. She'd never wanted anyone like this.

Wulf couldn't stand the way she grabbed at him. It made him insane for her. It heightened his need until he was practically dizzy.

Unable to tolerate any more, he rolled her onto her side and entered her.

Cassandra cried out at the unexpected pleasure that filled her. Lying completely on her side, she'd never had a man inside her in this position. Wulf was so deep that she swore she could feel him all the way to her womb.

She watched him in the mirrored wall as he thrust into her over and over, deeper and deeper, until she wanted to scream with pleasure.

The power and strength of him was unlike anything she'd ever known. Every forceful stroke made her weak, breathless.

She came again an instant before he did.

Wulf pulled back from her and lay down beside her.

His heart was pounding from the fury of their passion. But still he wasn't sated. Reaching for her, he pulled her across his chest so that he could feel her with every inch of his body.

"You are spectacular, *villkat*."

She nuzzled his chest with her face. "You're not too bad either, *villwulf*."

He laughed at her made-up endearment. He really liked this woman and her wit.

Cassandra lay in the peace of Wulf's arms. For the first time in her life, she felt completely safe. As if nothing or no one could touch her. She'd never felt this way. Not even as a child. She'd grown up always afraid whenever someone unknown had knocked on the door.

Every stranger was under suspicion. At night, it could easily be a Daimon or Apollite out to see her dead. During the day, it could be a Doulos after her.

But something told her that Wulf wouldn't let them threaten her at all.

"Cassandra?"

She frowned at the sound of a woman's voice intruding into her dream.

"Cassandra?"

Against her will, she was pulled out of her dream only to find herself asleep in her own bed.

The knocking continued.

"Cass? Are you all right?"

She recognized Michelle's voice. It was a struggle to awaken enough so that she could sit up in bed.

She was naked once more.

Frowning, Cassandra saw her clothes in a crumpled heap. What the hell was this? Had she been sleepwalking or something?

"I'm here, Chel," she said as she got up and pulled on

her red bathrobe. She opened the door to find her friend and Kat on the other side.

"Are you okay?" Michelle asked.

Yawning, Cassandra rubbed her eyes. "I'm fine. Just taking a nap."

But she didn't really feel fine. She felt much more like some sort of narcoleptic.

"What time is it?"

"It's eight-thirty, hon," Kat supplied.

Michelle looked back and forth between them. "You said you guys would go back to the Inferno with me, but if you don't feel like it . . ."

Cassandra caught the disappointment in Michelle's voice. "No, no, it's okay. Let me get dressed and we'll go."

Michelle beamed.

Kat looked at her suspiciously. "Are you sure you feel up to it?"

"I'm fine, really. I didn't sleep well last night and I just needed a nap."

Kat made a rude noise. "It's all that *Beowulf* you and Chris were reading. It sucked all the energy right out of you. Beowulf . . . incubus . . . same thing."

Now that was just a little too close to home for Cassandra's comfort.

She laughed nervously. "Yeah. I'll be out in a few minutes."

Cassandra shut the door and turned back toward her crumpled clothes.

What was going on here?

Was Beowulf really an incubus?

Maybe . . .

Brushing the ridiculous thought aside, she picked up her clothes and added them to the laundry hamper, then dressed herself in a pair of jeans and a dark blue sweater.

As she prepared to leave, a strange tingle ran through her. Something was going to happen tonight. She knew it. She didn't have her mother's psychic powers, but she did get strong feelings whenever something good or bad was going to happen.

Unfortunately, she just couldn't tell which one it would be until it was too late.

But something was definitely up tonight.

Chapter 5

"Welcome to *kolasi*," Stryker said under his breath, speaking the Atlantean word for hell as he surveyed the leaders of his Daimon army that was ever ready to attack at his command.

For eleven thousand years, he, as the son of the Atlantean Destroyer, had led them.

Handpicked by the Destroyer herself and trained by Stryker, these Daimons were all elite killers. Their own brethren referred to them as Spathi Daimons. A term that had been bastardized by both the Apollites and Dark-Hunters who didn't understand what a true Spathi was.

Instead they applied the term to any Daimon who fought them. But that wasn't right. The true Spathi were something else entirely.

They weren't the children of Apollo. They were Apollo's enemies, just as they were the enemies of the Dark-Hunters and humans. The Spathis had long ago forsaken whatever Greek or Apollite heritage they might have had.

They were the last of the Atlanteans and were proud of it.

Unbeknownst to the Dark-Hunters and humans, there

were thousands of them. Thousands. All far older than any pathetic human, Apollite, or Dark-Hunter dared dream. While the weaker Daimons lived in hiding on earth, the Spathis used *laminas* or bolt-holes to travel from this realm to the human one.

Their homes existed in another dimension. In Kalosis, where the Destroyer herself resided under imprisonment and where the lethal light of Apollo never shone. They were her soldiers.

Her sons and daughters.

Only a very select few of them could summon the *laminas* on their own—it was a gift the Destroyer didn't bequeath often. As her son, Stryker could come and go at will, but he chose to stay near his mother's side.

As he had for the last eleven thousand years . . .

All this time, they had planned well for this night. After his father Apollo had cursed them and left Stryker and his children to die horribly, Stryker had embraced his mother willingly.

It was Apollymi who had shown him the way. She who had taught them to take the souls of humans into their bodies so that they could survive even though his father had damned them all to die at twenty-seven.

"You are my chosen ones," she had told him. *"Fight with me and the world shall belong to the Atlantean gods once more."*

Since that day, they had recruited their army with care. The three dozen generals who lounged around him in the "banquet" hall were the best fighters among them. They all waited for word from their spy as to when the missing heiress would reappear.

She'd been out of their reach all day. But now that the sun had set, she was within reach once more.

Any moment now and they would be free to run the night and rip her heart out of her.

It was a precious thought Stryker cherished.

The doors to the hall opened and from the darkness outside came Stryker's last surviving son, Urian. Dressed all in black like his father, Urian had long blond hair that he wore in a queue secured by a black leather cord.

His son was more handsome than any other, but then all of their race were beautiful.

Urian's deep blue eyes flashed as he walked with the pride and grace of a lethal predator. When Stryker had first brought his eldest son over, it had been strange to play father to a man who was physically the same age as him, but that aside, they were father and son.

More than that, they were allies.

And Stryker would kill anyone who threatened his child.

"Any word?" he asked his son.

"Not yet. The Were-Hunter said he has lost her scent, but that he will pick her up again."

Stryker nodded. It had been their Were-Hunter spy who had brought the news to them last night of the fight where a group of Daimons had died in the bar.

Normally such a fight would be meaningless to them, but the Were-Hunter had told them that the Daimons had called their victim "the heiress."

Stryker had been searching the earth for her. Five years ago, in Belgium, they had almost killed her, but her bodyguard had sacrificed himself to them and allowed her to escape.

Since then, there had been no sightings of her. No tell-tale encounters with any of their people. The heiress had proved herself to be every bit as crafty as her mother.

So they had played the game.

Tonight, that game would end. Between the patrols Stryker had out in St. Paul and the Were-Hunter who served him, he was sure she would be found tonight.

He clapped his son on the back. "I want at least twenty of us standing by. There's no way she'll escape us all."

"I'll summon the Illuminati."

Stryker inclined his head in approval. The Illuminati comprised him and his son, as well as thirty others who were the bodyguards of the Destroyer. Each of them had taken a blood oath to his mother to see to it that she would be free of her netherworld so that she could rule the earth once again.

When that day came, they would be the princes of the world. Answerable only to her.

That day was finally upon them.

Wulf didn't know why he was headed for the Inferno tonight, other than he felt a compulsion inside him that wouldn't listen to reason.

He suspected it was from his insane need to feel closer to the woman who haunted his dreams. Even now he could see the beauty of her smile, feel her body welcoming his.

Or better yet, taste her.

Thoughts of her tormented him. They opened up feelings and needs that he had cast aside centuries ago without ever looking back.

Who needed it? Yet there wasn't anything he wanted more than to see her again.

It didn't make sense.

The chances of her being in the same place tonight were next to impossible.

Still, he went. He couldn't help it. It was as if he had no control over himself, but was being driven by some unseen force.

After parking his car, he walked down the quiet street like a silent phantom in the cold frigid night. The winter winds whipped around him, biting his exposed skin.

It had been a night much like this one that had brought him into service for Artemis. He'd been on a quest then too. Only then the nature of the quest had been different.

Or had it?

You're a wandering soul, looking for a peace that doesn't exist. Lost you will be until you find the one inner truth. We can never hide from what we are. The only hope is to embrace it.

To this day, he didn't really understand what it was the old seer had tried to tell him the night he'd sought her out, wanting her to explain to him how Morginne and Loki had swapped their souls.

Perhaps there was no real explanation. After all, it was a freaky world he lived in and it seemed to get stranger by the minute.

Wulf entered the Inferno. Painted black inside and out, it had iridescent flames painted inside and out, as well, that sparkled eerily under the muted, dancing lights of the club.

The club's owner, Dante Pontis, met him at the door where he and two other "men" were taking cover charges and checking IDs. In human form, the Katagari panther was ironically dressed like a "vampire." But then Dante thought such things were funny—hence the name of the club.

Dante wore black leather pants, biker boots that sported red and orange flames, and a black poet's shirt. The panther had left his shirt unlaced and the ruffled collar curled around his neck while the silk laces fell down his chest. His long black leather coat had a nineteenth-century look to it as well, but Wulf knew it to be a copy— one of the advantages to having been alive then was that he well remembered the fashions of that time period.

Dante's long black hair fell freely about his shoulders. "Wulf," he said, flashing a set of fangs Wulf knew weren't real.

The panther only had teeth like that in his true animal form.

Wulf cocked his head at the sight. "What the hell are those?"

Dante smiled wider, displaying his teeth. "Women love them. I'd tell you to get a set, but you already come well equipped."

Wulf laughed at that. "I'm not going there."

"Please don't."

Still, bad double entendres aside, it always felt good to come to the Inferno, even if the Were-Hunters didn't really want him there. It was one of the few places where someone remembered his name. Yeah, okay, so he felt like Sam Malone on *Cheers,* but there was no Norm or Cliff sitting at the bar here. More like Spike and Switchblade.

The "man" beside Dante leaned over. "Is he a DH?"

Dante's eyes narrowed. He grabbed the man beside him and shoved him toward the other bouncer. "Take the friggin' Arcadian spy out back and deal with him."

The man's face went pale. "What? I'm not Arcadian."

"Bullshit," Dante snarled. "You met Wulf two weeks ago and if you were really Katagaria, you'd remember him. Only a fucking were-panther can't."

Wulf arched a brow at the insult that none of the Katagaria used lightly. The root of the term "were" meant human. To place that term before their animal name was a gross insult to the Katagaria, who prided themselves on the fact that they were animals who could take human form, not the other way around.

The only reason they were tolerant of being called Were-Hunters was the fact that they did in fact hunt and kill the Arcadians, who were humans capable of taking animal form. Not to mention the fact that the male of their species often hunted human females for sexual purposes. Apparently, sex was much more enjoyable to them in human form, and the males had voracious appetites in that department.

Unfortunately for Wulf, the female Were-Hunters who could remember him never looked outside their species for partners. Unlike the men, the females had sex in hopes of finding mates. The men were simply after the pleasure of it.

"What are you going to do to him?" Wulf asked as Dante's bouncer dragged the Arcadian away.

"What's it to you, Dark-Hunter? I don't screw with your business, you don't screw with mine."

Wulf debated what to do, but then if the other man really was an Arcadian spy, most likely he could handle the situation on his own and wouldn't relish the thought of help, especially from a Dark-Hunter. The Weres were extremely independent and hated for anyone or anything to interfere with them.

So Wulf changed the subject. "Any Daimons in the club?" he asked Dante.

Dante shook his head. "But Corbin's inside. She came in about an hour ago. Said it was slow tonight. Too cold for the Daimons on the street."

Wulf nodded at the mention of the Dark-Huntress who was also assigned to the area. He wouldn't be able to stay long then, not unless Corbin was ready to leave.

Going inside, he went to say hi to her.

There was no band on stage tonight. Instead a DJ played loud, operatic music he vaguely remembered Chris calling Goth Metal.

The club was dark with bright strobe lights flashing. It played havoc with his Dark-Hunter sight, an attempt on Dante's part to keep Dark-Hunter interference at a minimum while they were in the club. Wulf pulled out his sunglasses and put them on to help alleviate some of the pain it caused him.

People danced on the floor, oblivious to everything around them.

"Greetings."

He jumped at the sound of Corbin's voice in his ear. The woman had the power of bending time and teleportation. She lived to surprise people by sneaking up on them.

He turned to see the extremely attractive redhead behind him. Tall, lithe, and deadly, Corbin had been a Greek queen in her human lifetime. She still had that regal bearing and a look of such haughty supremacy that it could make anyone feel like they should wash their hands before they touched her.

She'd died trying to save her country from invasion by some barbarian tribe who were no doubt the forerunners to his own people.

"Hi, Binny," he said, calling her by a nickname she only allowed a chosen few to use.

She placed a hand on his shoulder. "You okay? You look tired."

"I'm fine."

"I don't know. Maybe I ought to send Sara over to replace Chris for a few days and take care of you."

He covered her hand with his, warmed by her concern.

Sara Addams was her Squire. "That's all I need. A Squire who can't remember she's supposed to serve me."

"Oh, yeah," Corbin said, wrinkling her nose. "I forgot that one drawback."

"Don't worry. It's not Chris. I just haven't been able to sleep well."

"Sorry to hear that."

Wulf noticed several of the Weres were staring at them. "I think we're making them nervous."

She laughed as she looked around the club. "Maybe. But my money says that they sense what I do."

"Which is?"

"Something is going to happen here tonight. It's why I came in. Don't you feel it too?"

"I don't have that power."

"Be grateful then, it's a bitch." Corbin stepped away from him. "But since you're here, I'll step out for a breath of fresh air and leave the club to you. I don't want my powers drained."

"Later, then."

She nodded and in a flash vanished. He only hoped no human had seen her do that.

Wulf walked through the club feeling odd, detached. He didn't know why he was here. It was so stupid.

He might as well leave too.

Turning around, he froze . . .

Cassandra had felt so weird being in the Inferno tonight. Her mind kept flashing back to the night before. Even Kat was sensing her discomfort.

There were two warring voices in her head. One telling her to leave immediately and one telling her to stay.

She was beginning to fear that she might be schizophrenic or something.

Michelle and Tom came up to them. "Hey, guys, I hate to bang out on you, but Tom and I are going someplace quiet to talk, okay?"

Cassandra smiled at them. "Sure. You two have fun."

As soon as they left, she looked at Kat. "No need in us staying, huh?"

"Are you sure you want to leave?"

"Yeah, I think so."

Cassandra got up from her chair and grabbed her purse. Shrugging on her coat, she wasn't paying attention to anything until she walked into someone who was standing as still as a wall.

"Oh, I'm sor—" Her words broke off as she looked up a good four inches into the face that had haunted her dreams.

It was him!

She biblically knew every inch of that solid, gorgeous male body.

"Wulf?"

Wulf was stunned beyond comprehension as he heard his name on her lips. "You know me?"

A becoming blush stained her face and it was then he knew . . .

Those hadn't been dreams.

She started away from him.

"Cassandra, wait."

Cassandra froze as she heard her name on his lips.

He knew her name . . .

Run! It sounded like her mother's voice in her head, but the order was drowned out by the part of her that didn't want to run away from him.

He reached his hand out toward her.

Cassandra couldn't breathe as she stared at it, wanting his touch. His *real* touch.

Before she could stop herself, she reached out to him.

Just as she was about to touch him, a shimmer over his shoulder caught her eye.

She looked past him to see a strange mirrorlike image appear on the dance floor. Out of its midst stepped a man who was evil incarnate.

Standing at least six feet eight, he was dressed all in black with short ebony hair that framed the face of perfection. He was every bit as handsome as Wulf. And like Wulf, he wore a pair of dark sunglasses. The only color on him was a bright yellow sun with a black dragon in its center that was painted on the front of his motorcycle jacket.

In spite of his black hair, he was a Daimon. She knew it with every Apollite instinct she possessed. What's more, he was followed through the opening by more Daimons. All of whom were blond and dressed in black.

They oozed an unnatural attraction and virility. Most of all, they oozed deadly precision.

They weren't here to feed. They were here to kill.

She stepped back with a gasp.

Wulf turned to look at what had startled Cassandra. He felt his jaw go slack as he watched the Daimons coming through a bolt-hole in the center of the club.

Dante came running from the front in human form that shifted to panther as he ran. Before he could get near them, the Daimon with black hair shot a god-bolt straight at him.

The Katagari hit the ground with a yelp as the electrically charged bolt shifted him from panther to human and back again.

The bar went wild.

"Mind-shield the humans!" the DJ shouted over the intercom, alerting the Katagaria who were present that the humans needed to be gathered and their memories of the night reorganized and/or purged, just as they routinely did anytime something "strange" happened in their club.

Most of all, the humans needed to be protected.

The Daimons fanned out, circling the club and attacking any Katagari who came near them.

Wulf rushed through the crowd to attack.

He caught the Daimon with a blond ponytail and swung him around. The Daimon jumped back out of his reach. "This isn't your fight, Dark-Hunter."

Wulf pulled two of his long daggers out from his boots. "I think it is."

He attacked, but to his amazement, the Daimon moved like lightning. Every move Wulf made to attack was countered and returned.

Holy shit. He'd never in his life seen Daimons move like this.

"What are you?" Wulf asked.

The blond Daimon laughed. "We're Spathis, Dark-Hunter. We are the only thing that is truly deadly in the dark of night. While you . . ." He raked a repugnant look over Wulf's body. "You're just a pretender."

The Daimon caught him by the neck and threw him to the ground. Wulf hit the deck hard. His breath left his body with a vicious *woof* as his knives flew out of his grasp.

The Daimon jumped on top of him, slugging him as if he were a helpless babe.

Wulf knocked him off, but it was hard. There were fights all over the room as the Were-Hunters engaged the Daimons.

Worried about Cassandra, he looked to see her hiding with a blond woman in a far corner.

He had to get her out of here.

The Daimon he was fighting looked to where Wulf had glanced. "Father," he called out. "The heiress." He pointed straight at Cassandra.

Wulf took advantage of the distraction to kick the Daimon back.

As one cohesive unit, the Spathis disengaged their opponents and jumped from their locations to where Cassandra and the blond woman were hiding.

They literally dropped out of the sky and landed in formation.

Wulf ran for them, but before he could reach the women, the blonde with Cassandra came out of her crouch.

The Daimon leader froze instantly.

The blonde held her arms straight out as if to bar the Daimons from Cassandra. Suddenly, a wind of unknown origin whipped through the club.

The Daimons froze.

Another shimmery doorway opened on the dance floor.

"It's the *laminas*," the Daimon who had been fighting Wulf said, sneering. He turned toward the blond woman and glared.

Their faces angry, the Spathis disengaged the formation and walked one by one back through it.

Except for the leader.

His gaze unwavering, he glared at the blond woman. "This isn't over," he snarled.

She didn't move or flinch. It was as if the woman were made of stone. Or comatose.

The Daimon leader turned around, and walked slowly through the portal. It vanished the instant he was through it.

"Kat?" Cassandra asked as she rose to her feet.

The blond woman staggered back. "Oh, God, I thought I was dead," Kat breathed, her body trembling. "Did you see them?"

Cassandra nodded as Wulf joined them.

"What were they?" Kat asked.

"Spathi Daimons," Cassandra breathed. She stared in disbelief at her companion. "What did you do to them?"

"Nothing," Kat said, her face innocent. "I just stood here. You saw me. Why did they leave?"

Wulf looked at Kat suspiciously. There was no reason for them to leave. They had been winning the fight.

For the first time in his life, he had actually felt a momentary doubt in his ability to defeat them.

Corbin came up to them. "Did you get any of them?"

Wulf shook his head, wondering when Corbin had returned. He hadn't even noticed the drain on his powers but then, given the way the Spathis were kicking his ass, it was no wonder.

Corbin rubbed her shoulder as if she'd been injured in the fighting. "Neither did I."

The impact of that statement wasn't lost on either of them.

The two of them turned to Cassandra.

"They were after you?" Wulf asked.

Cassandra looked extremely uncomfortable.

"You see to Dante and his crew," Wulf told Corbin. "I'll handle this one."

Corbin headed off while Wulf turned back to the women. "How can you remember me?"

But then the answer was so obvious that he already knew. "You're Apollite, aren't you?" She damn sure wasn't a Were-Hunter. They had an unmistakable aura to them.

Cassandra dropped her gaze to the floor as she whispered, "Half."

He cursed. It figured. "So you're the Apollite heiress they have to kill to lift their curse?"

"Yes."

"Is that why you've been fucking with my dreams? You thought I'd protect you?"

Offended, she raked him with a furious glare. "I haven't been doing anything to you, bud. You're the one who's been coming to me."

Oh, that was a good one. "Yeah, right. Well, it didn't work. My job is to kill your kind, not protect you. You're on your own, princess."

He turned and stalked away.

Cassandra was torn between the desire to slap him and to cry.

Instead, she went after him and pulled him to a stop. "Just for the record, I don't need *you* or anyone else to protect me, and the last thing I would do is ask the Satan of my people to help me. You're nothing but a killer and not a bit better than the Daimons you hunt. At least they still have their souls."

His face hardening, Wulf jerked his arm free of her grasp and left.

Cassandra wanted to scream at the way this had turned out. And it was then she realized some part of herself had actually started to like him. He'd been so tender in her dreams.

Kind.

So much for her thoughts of asking him about her people. He wasn't the same man she'd dreamed about. He was horrible in the flesh. Horrible!

She looked about the club where tables were overturned and the Katagaria were trying to clean up the mess.

What a nightmare all of this had turned into.

"C'mon," Kat said. "Let's get you home before those Daimons come back."

Yes, she wanted to go home. She wanted to forget this night had ever occurred and if Wulf came to her tonight . . .

Well, if he thought the Spathis were tough on him, he hadn't seen tough.

Stryker left his men in the hall and went to see Apollymi. He alone of the Spathis was allowed in her presence.

Her temple was the grandest building in all of Kalosis. The black marble glistened even in the dim light of their netherworld. Inside, the temple was guarded by a pair of vicious ceredons—creatures with the head of a dog, the body of a dragon, and the tail of a scorpion. The two of them snarled at him, but stayed back. They had learned long ago that Stryker was one of four beings the Destroyer allowed to come near her.

He found his mother in her sitting room with two of her Charonte demons flanking her couch. Xedrix, her own personal guard, was to her right. His skin was navy blue in color, his eyes vibrant yellow. Black horns stood out from his equally blue hair and his wings were a deep blood red. He stood unmoving with one hand near the Destroyer's shoulder.

The other demon was of a lesser order, but for some

reason his mother favored Sabina. She had long, green hair that complemented her yellow skin. Her eyes were the same color as her hair and her horns and wings an odd deep shade of orange.

The demons watched him closely, but neither moved nor spoke while his mother sat as if lost in thought.

Her windows were open, looking out onto a garden where only black flowers grew, in memory of his dead brother. The Destroyer's other son had perished untold centuries ago and to this day she mourned his death.

Just as she rejoiced in Stryker's continued life.

Her long white-blond hair fell around her in waves of perfection. Even though she was older than time, Apollymi had the face of a beautiful young woman in her mid-twenties. Her black gauzy gown blended into the black of her couch, making it hard to see where one ended and the other began.

She was motionless as she stared outside, holding a black satin pillow in her lap. "They are trying to liberate me."

He paused at her words. "Who?"

"Those stupid Greeks. They think I will side with them in gratitude." She laughed bitterly.

Stryker smiled wryly at the very thought. His mother hated the Greek pantheon zealously. "Will they succeed?"

"No. The Elekti will stop them. As he always does." She turned her head to look at him. Her pale, pale eyes had no color. Ice glittered on her eyelashes and her translucent skin was iridescent, giving her a delicate, fragile appearance. But there was nothing fragile about the Destroyer.

She was as her name declared, destruction. She had consigned every member of her family to the death realm from where they would never return.

Her power was absolute and it was only through betrayal that she had ended up imprisoned here in Kalosis, where she could see the human world, but not participate in it. Stryker and his fellow Daimons could use the boltholes to come and go out of this realm, but she could not.

Not until the seal of Atlantis was broken, and Stryker had no idea how to do it. Apollymi had never disclosed that to him.

"Why did you not kill the heiress?" she asked.

"The Abadonna opened the portal."

Again his mother was so still as to not appear real. After several seconds, she laughed. The sound was soft and gentle, ringing through the air like music.

"Good one, Artemis," she said out loud. "You're learning. But it won't save you or that scabby brother you protect." She pushed herself up from her couch, put the pillow down, and walked over to Stryker. "Were you hurt, *m'gios*?"

He always felt a rush of warmth whenever she referred to him as her son. "No."

Xedrix moved to whisper into the Destroyer's ear.

"No," she said out loud. "The Abadonna is not to be touched. She has torn loyalties and I will not take advantage of her kind nature, unlike some goddesses I can name. She is innocent in this and I will not have her punished for it."

The Destroyer drummed two fingers on her chin. "The question is, what is that bitch Artemis planning?"

She closed her eyes. "Katra," she breathed, calling out to the Abadonna.

After a few seconds, Apollymi let out a disgusted noise. "She refuses to answer . . . Fine," she said in a voice Stryker knew could transcend this realm and be heard by Katra. "Protect Artemis and Apollo's heiress if you must. But know you can't stop me. No one can."

She turned back to Stryker. "We will have to separate Katra from the heiress."

"How? If the Abadonna continues to open the portal, we are powerless. You know we must step through it whenever it opens."

The Destroyer laughed again. "Life is a chess game, Strykerius, haven't you learned that yet? Whenever you move to protect the pawns, you leave your queen open to attack."

"Meaning?"

"The Abadonna can't be everywhere at once. If you can't get to the heiress, then attack something else the Abadonna cares for."

He smiled at that. "I was so hoping you would say that."

Chapter 6

Cassandra was so angry that she didn't know what to do. Actually, she did. But that involved having Wulf tied up in a room and her having a very large broom in her hands to beat him with.

Or better yet, a stick with thorns!

Unfortunately, it would take more than her and Kat to tie up the obnoxious oaf.

As Kat drove her back to her apartment, she fought against screaming and railing at the imbecile who had all the compassion of a leek pea.

She hadn't realized just how much she had opened herself up to the Wulf of her dreams. How much of herself she had given to him. She had never been the kind of woman to trust anyone, least of all a man. Yet she had welcomed him into her heart and body.

How much more—

She paused her silent tirade as her thoughts shifted.

Wait . . .

He remembered their dreams too.

He had accused her of trying to—

"Why didn't I think of that while we were at the club?" Cassandra asked out loud.

"Think of what?"

She looked over at Kat, whose face was illuminated by the light of the dashboard. "Do you remember what Wulf said in the bar? He remembered me from his dreams and I remember him from mine. Do you think our dreams could be real?"

"Wulf was at the bar?" Kat asked as she frowned at Cassandra. "The Dark-Hunter you've been dreaming about was there tonight? When?"

"Didn't you see him?" Cassandra countered. "He came right up to us after the fight and yelled at me for being an Apollite."

"The only person who came right up to us was the Daimon."

Cassandra opened her mouth to correct her, then remembered what Wulf had said about people forgetting him. Good grief, whatever it was had made her bodyguard completely forget him too.

"Okay," she said, trying again. "Forget about Wulf being there and let's go back to the other question. Do you think the dreams I've been having could be real? Maybe some kind of alternate consciousness or something?"

Kat snorted. "Five years ago I didn't think vampires were real. You've shown me differently. Honey, given your freaky life, I would say most anything is possible."

True. "Yeah, but I've never heard of anyone who could do this."

"I don't know. Remember that thing we saw online about the Dream-Hunters earlier today? They can infiltrate dreams. You think they could have had something to do with this?"

"I don't know. Maybe. But the Dream-Hunter.com site said that they infiltrated dreams themselves. It didn't have anything on there about them putting two people together in a dream."

"Yeah, but if they are sleep gods, it only stands to reason they could put two people together in their own domain."

"What are you saying, Kat?"

"I'm just saying maybe you know Wulf better than you think you do. Maybe every dream you've had with him *has* been real."

Wulf had no real destination in mind as he drove through St. Paul. All he could focus on was Cassandra and the betrayal he felt.

"It figures," he snarled. All this time and he had finally found an eligible woman to remember him only to have her turn out to be an Apollite—the only kind of woman who was completely taboo for him to interact with.

"I'm such an idiot."

His phone rang. Wulf picked it up and answered it.

"What happened?"

He flinched as he heard Acheron Parthenopaeus's thickly accented voice on the other end. Anytime Ash became really angry, he reverted to his Atlantean accent.

Wulf decided to play ignorant. "What?"

"I just got a call from Dante about the attack tonight in his club. What exactly went down?"

Wulf let out a tired breath. "I don't know. A bolt-hole opened and a group of Daimons came out. The leader of them had black hair, by the way. I didn't think that was possible."

"It's not his natural hair color. Trust me. Stryker discovered L'Oréal a while back."

Wulf pulled off the road as that tidbit went through him like a hot-bladed knife. "You know this guy?"

Acheron didn't respond. "I need you and Corbin to pull back from Stryker and his men."

There was something in Acheron's tone that made Wulf's blood run cold. If he didn't know better, he'd swear he heard real warning there. "He's just a Daimon, Ash."

"No he's not and he doesn't come out to feed like the others."

"What do you mean?"

"It's a long story. Look, I can't leave New Orleans right now. I've got enough shit to deal with down here, which is probably why Stryker is pulling his crap now. He knows I'm distracted."

"Yeah, well, don't worry about it. I've never met a Daimon yet I couldn't take."

Acheron made a noise of disagreement. "Guess again, little brother. You just met one, and trust me, he's not like any you've ever met before. He makes Desiderius look like a pet hamster."

Wulf sat back in his seat as traffic raced by him. There was definitely something more to this than Acheron was spilling. Of course, the man was good at that. Acheron kept secrets from all the Dark-Hunters and never revealed any personal information about himself.

Enigmatic, cocky, and powerful, Acheron was the oldest of the Dark-Hunters and the one they all turned to for information and advice. For two thousand years, Acheron had fought the Daimons all alone without any other Dark-Hunters. Hell, the man had been around since before the Daimons had even been created.

Ash knew things they could only guess at. And right now, Wulf needed some answers.

"How come you know so much about this one when you didn't know much about Desiderius?" Wulf asked.

As expected, Ash didn't answer. "The panthers said you were with a woman tonight. Cassandra Peters."

"You know her too?"

Again Ash ignored the question. "I need you to protect her."

"Bullshit," Wulf snapped, angered over the fact that he already felt used by her. The last thing he wanted was to give her another shot at messing with his head. He'd never liked anyone toying with him, and after the way Morginne had used and betrayed him, the last thing he needed was another woman out to screw him to get what she wanted. "She's an Apollite."

"I know what she is and she has to be protected at all costs."

"Why?"

To his amazement, Acheron actually answered. "Because she holds the fate of the world in her hands, Wulf. If they kill her, Daimons are going to be the very least of our problems."

This was not what he wanted to hear tonight.

Wulf growled at Ash. "I really hate it when you say things like that." He paused as another thought occurred to him. "If she's so important, why aren't *you* here guarding her?"

"Mostly because this ain't *Buffy* and there's not one single Hellmouth to guard. I'm up to my armpits in Armageddon down here in New Orleans and not even I can physically be in two places at once. She's your responsibility, Wulf. Don't let me down."

Against his better judgment, Wulf listened to Ash give him Cassandra's address.

"And Wulf?"

"Yeah?"

"Have you ever noticed that salvation, much like your car keys, is usually found where and when you least expect it?"

He frowned at Ash's esoteric words. The man was really, really strange. "What the hell does that mean?"

"You'll see." Ash hung up.

"I really hate it when he plays Oracle," he said between clenched teeth as he turned his SUV around and headed toward Cassandra's.

This sucked. The last thing he wanted was to be near a woman who had seduced him so completely.

A woman he knew he could never touch in the real flesh. That would be an even bigger mistake than the one he'd already made. She was an Apollite. And for the last twelve hundred years, he had spent his life pursuing her kind and killing them.

And yet the woman called out to him in a way that tore through him.

What was he going to do? How could he uphold his code as a Dark-Hunter and keep away from her when all he really wanted to do was take her into his arms and see if she tasted as good in real life as she had in his dreams . . .

Kat thoroughly searched the apartment before she allowed Cassandra to lock the door.

"Why are you so nervous?" Cassandra asked. "We defeated the Daimons."

"Maybe," Kat said. "I just keep hearing that guy's voice in my head telling me that it's not over. I think our friends are going to be back. Real soon."

Cassandra's nervousness came back with a vengeance. It had been way too close tonight. The mere fact that Kat had refused to let them fight the Daimons and had opted instead to hide in a corner of the bar told her just how dangerous these men were.

She still wasn't sure why Kat had pulled her away from them.

Neither one of them cowered from anyone or anything.

Not until now.

"So what should we do?" Cassandra asked.

Kat triple-locked the door and pulled the gun from her purse. "Put our heads between our knees and kiss our butts good-bye."

Cassandra was stunned by the unexpected words. "Excuse me?"

"Nothing." Kat offered her an encouraging smile that didn't quite reach her eyes. "I'm going to go make a call, okay?"

"Sure."

Cassandra went to her room, and did her best not to relive the night her mother had died. There had been a bad feeling in the pit of her stomach all day long. Just like she had now.

She wasn't safe. No Daimon had ever attacked the way they did tonight.

The Daimons at the club hadn't come out to feed or to play. They had been specially trained and had come out as if they had known exactly where she was.

Who she was.

But how?

Could they find her even now?

Terror filled her. She went to her dresser and pulled open the top drawer. In it was a small arsenal of weapons, including the dagger of her mother's people that had been handed down to her.

She didn't know how many people had a dagger for a

security blanket, but then there weren't many people who grew up the way she had either.

She secured the sheath to her waist and hid it at the base of her spine. Her death might be imminent in a few months, but she had no intention of dying one day sooner than she had to.

A knock sounded on her front door.

Cautiously, she left her room and walked into the living room, expecting to see Kat in there curious about their unannounced visitor too.

Kat wasn't there.

"Kat?" she called, taking a step toward Kat's room.

No one answered.

"Kat?"

The knocking continued, more demanding than it had been before.

Scared now, she went to Kat's room and pushed open the door. The room was empty. Completely. There was no sign that Kat had ever been in there.

Her heart hammered. Maybe Kat had gone out to the car for something and gotten locked out?

She went back to the door. "Kat, is that you?"

"Yeah, let me in."

Cassandra laughed nervously at her stupid behavior and swung open the door.

It wasn't Kat outside.

The dark-haired Daimon smiled at her. "Did you miss me, princess?" he said in a voice identical to Kat's.

She couldn't believe this. It couldn't be real. This kind of stuff happened in movies, not in real life.

"What are you, the friggin' Terminator?"

"No," he said calmly in his own voice. "I'm the Harbinger who is merely preparing the way for the Destroyer."

He reached for her.

Cassandra stepped back. He couldn't enter the house without an invitation. Reaching behind her, she pulled out her dagger and sliced his arm.

He drew back with a hiss.

She spun as she saw someone behind her.

It was another Daimon. She caught him in the chest with her dagger.

He evaporated into a golden-black cloud.

Another shadow passed over her.

Spinning around, she kicked Stryker back, but he didn't go completely out the door. Instead, he only blocked it more.

"You're quick," he said as his arm healed instantly before her eyes. "I'll give you that."

"You don't know the half of it."

Daimons came at her from all directions. How the hell had they gotten into her home? But she didn't have time to contemplate that. Right now, all she could focus on was survival.

She kneed the next Daimon who reached her and fought a second one. Stryker stayed back as if the fight amused him.

Another Daimon, this one with a long blond ponytail, attacked. Cassandra flipped him over. As she went to stab him, Stryker came out of nowhere to grab her arm.

"No one attacks Urian."

She shrieked as he wrenched the dagger from her hand. Cassandra moved to strike him, but the instant her gaze met his, all thoughts scattered.

His eyes turned to a strange, swirling silver. They moved in a hypnotic dance that held her spellbound and turned her thoughts to oatmeal.

All the fight inside her instantly vanished. A sly, seductive smile curved Stryker's lips. "See how easy it is when you don't fight?" She felt his breath against her throat.

Some unseen force tilted her head to the side to give him access to her neck and to the throbbing carotid artery she could feel pounding in terror.

Inside, Cassandra was screaming at herself to fight.

Her body refused to obey.

Stryker's laughter rumbled a moment before he sank his long teeth into her neck. She hissed as pain sliced her.

"Am I interrupting?"

Cassandra could only vaguely recognize Wulf's voice through the numbed haze of her mind.

Something jerked Stryker away from her. It was a few seconds before she realized it was Wulf knocking the Daimon back.

Wulf whisked her up into his arms and ran with her. Cassandra could barely keep her head from lolling back as he headed for a large dark green Expedition and tossed her inside it.

The instant Wulf was in the car, something struck it hard. Out of the darkness, a large, black dragon appeared on the hood.

"Let her out and you can live," the dragon said in Stryker's voice.

Wulf answered by putting his SUV in reverse and gunning it. He turned the wheel and sent the beast flying.

The dragon shrieked and blew a blast of fire at them. Wulf kept going. The dragon took flight and dove at them, then arced up, high into the sky, before it vanished into a shimmery cloud of gold.

"What the hell was that?" Wulf asked.

"He's Apostolos," Cassandra murmured as she struggled to snap herself out of her daze. "He's the son of the

Atlantean Destroyer and a god in his own right. We're so screwed."

Wulf let out a disgusted sound. "Yeah, well, I don't let anyone screw me until they kiss me, and since there's not even a snowball's chance in hell of me kissing that bastard, we're not screwed."

But as his Expedition was suddenly surrounded by eight Daimons on motorcycles, he reconsidered that.

For three seconds at least.

Wulf laughed as he surveyed the Daimons. "You know the beauty of driving one of these?"

"No."

He swerved his Expedition into three of the bikes and knocked them from the road. "You can swat a Daimon like a mosquito."

"Well, since they're both bloodsucking insects, I say go for it."

Wulf glanced sideways at her. A woman who could keep her humor even in the midst of death. He liked that.

The remaining Daimons must have rethought acting out Mad Max with him and dropped back from his SUV. He watched as they faded out of sight in his rearview mirror.

Cassandra let out a relieved breath as she pushed herself up more in the seat. She turned her head and tried to see where the Daimons had vanished. There was no sight of them.

"What a night," she said quietly as her thoughts cleared and she remembered everything that had happened in the apartment. Once more, panic consumed her as she remembered Kat hadn't shown up. "Wait! We have to go back."

"Why?"

"My bodyguard," she said, gripping his arm. "I don't know what happened to her."

He kept his gaze on the road ahead of them. "Was she in the apartment?"

"Yes . . . maybe." Cassandra paused while she thought it over. "I'm not exactly sure. She went to make a phone call in her room and then she wasn't in there when I went to see if she'd go with me to the door." She released his arm. Fear and grief warred inside her heart. What if something had happened to Kat after all these years they'd been together? "Do you think they killed her?"

He glanced at her, then changed lanes. "I don't know. Was she the blond woman in the bar?"

"Yes."

He pulled his cell phone off his belt and made a call.

Cassandra chewed her nails as she waited.

She heard someone's faint voice on the phone.

"Hey, Binny," Wulf said. "I need a favor. I just left the Sherwood student apartments over by the University of Minnesota and we may or may not have a casualty there . . ." He glanced at Cassandra, but his eyes betrayed no clue as to what he was thinking or feeling. "Yeah, I know tonight's been a real freakfest. You don't even know the half of it." He switched hands with the phone.

"What's your friend's name?" he asked Cassandra.

"Kat Agrotera."

He frowned. "Why do I know that name?" He relayed it to whomever he was speaking to.

"Shit," he said after a brief pause. "Do you think they might be related to her?"

Once again, he glanced in Cassandra's direction. Only this time, his scowl was most sinister. "I don't know. Ash told me to guard her and now her bodyguard holds a last name that ties her to Artemis. Could it be a weird coincidence?"

Cassandra cocked her head at that. She'd never before thought about the fact that Kat's last name was also one of the many epithets the ancient Greeks had used for Artemis.

She'd met Kat in Greece after she had fled from Belgium with a load of Daimons hot on her heels. After helping her out in a fight one night, Kat had told her she was an American come to touch base with her Greek heritage that summer.

It had been a bonus that Kat had said she was a martial arts expert with a knack for using explosives. Cassandra had explained to her that she was looking for a new bodyguard to replace her old one and Kat had signed on with her immediately.

"I just love to put a hurt on evil things," Kat had confessed.

Wulf sighed. "I don't know either. Okay. You go look for Kat and I'll take Cassandra home with me. Let me know what you find. Thanks." He hung up, then returned his phone to his belt.

"What did she say?"

He didn't answer her question. Not exactly anyway. "She said Agrotera is one of the Greek names for Artemis. It means 'strength' or 'wild hunter.' Did you know that?"

"Sort of." A drop of hope welled inside her. If that were true, maybe the gods hadn't abandoned her family after all. Maybe there was some hope for her and for her future. "Do you two think Artemis sent Kat to protect me?"

His grip tightened on the steering wheel. "I don't know what to think at this point. I was told by Artemis's mouthpiece that you are the key to the end of the world and that I had to protect you and—"

"What do you mean, 'key to the end of the world'?" she asked, interrupting him.

He looked as surprised as she felt. "You mean you don't know that?"

Okay, so it was obvious Dark-Hunters could get high and delusional.

"No. In fact, I'm thinking right now that one, if not both of us, needs to put down the crack pipe and start this night over."

Wulf gave a light laugh at her comment. "If it wasn't for the fact I can't get high, I might agree with that."

Cassandra's mind raced. Was there any truth to what he had just said? "Well, if you're right and I'm key to the world's destruction, then if I were you I'd be making out a will."

"Why?"

"Because in less than eight months, I turn twenty-seven."

Wulf heard the catch in her voice as she spoke those words and he more than understood the doom she was facing. "You said you were only half-Apollite."

"Yeah, but I've never known a half-Apollite to survive the curse, have you?"

He shook his head. "Only the Were-Hunters seem immune to the Apollite curse."

Cassandra sat silently, watching the traffic out the window while she contemplated what had happened tonight.

"Wait," she said as she remembered the Daimons coming into her apartment. "How did that guy get into my house? I thought Daimons were forbidden to enter your home without an invitation."

Wulf's answer was far from comforting. "Loophole."

"Excuse me?" she asked, arching both brows. "What do you mean, 'loophole'?"

He turned off the expressway onto an exit ramp. "Got to love those gods. The same loophole that allows Daimons to enter malls and public areas allows them to enter condos and apartments."

"How so?"

"Malls, apartments, and such are owned by one entity. When that person or company allows their building to openly serve for multiple groups of people, they essentially put out a cosmic welcome mat to everything, including Daimons."

Oh, this was un-friggin-believable! She blinked in shock. "*Now* you tell me this? Why didn't someone tell me this before? I thought I was safe all this time."

"Your bodyguard should have known better. If she really is tied to Artemis."

"Then maybe she's not. You know, she could just be a normal person."

"Yeah, one who holds her arms out and scares off Spathi Daimons?"

He had a point there. Sort of. "She said she didn't know why they ran."

"And later she left you there alone to face them . . ."

Cassandra rubbed her hand over her eyes as she caught his implication. Could Kat be working with the Daimons? Did Artemis want her dead or alive?

"Oh, God, I can't trust anyone, can I?" Cassandra breathed tiredly.

"Welcome to the real world, duchess. The only person any of us can trust is ourselves."

She didn't want to believe that, but after tonight, it seemed to be the only real truth she had.

Could Kat really be a traitor after all they had been through together?

"Lovely, just lovely," she breathed. "Tell me something, can I go back to bed and have this entire day be a do-over?"

He let out a short laugh. "Sorry, no do-overs."

She gave him a peeved glare. "Boy, you're just all chock-full of comfort, aren't you?"

He didn't respond.

Cassandra watched the oncoming cars as she tried to think of what she should do. Where she should even begin to try to understand what had happened tonight.

Wulf drove them out of the city to a massive estate outside of Minnetonka. All the homes in the area were owned by some of the richest people in the country.

Wulf turned into a driveway that was so long, she couldn't see where it ended. Of course the five-foot-high snowbanks didn't help with that.

He pressed a tiny button in his visor.

The iron gates opened wide.

Cassandra let out a slow, appreciative breath as they proceeded down the driveway and she caught sight of his "house." "Palace" would be much more apropos, and given the fact that her father's house wasn't exactly small potatoes, that said a lot.

It looked very turn-of-the-century with large Greek columns and gardens that still appeared sculpted even in the deep winter snow and frost.

He drove them up the winding driveway to a five-car garage that was designed to look like a stable. Inside, it held Chris's Hummer (it was hard to miss his vanity plate, VIKING), two vintage Harleys, a sleek Ferrari, and one really cool Excalibur. The garage was so clean inside that it reminded her of a showroom. Everything from the ornate crown moldings to the marble floor said "wealthy beyond your wildest dreams."

She arched a brow at that. "You've come a long way from your little stone cottage by the fjord. You must have decided riches weren't so bad after all."

Parking the SUV, Wulf turned to face her with a scowl. "You remember that?"

She ran her gaze from the top of his gorgeous head to the toe of his black biker boots. Even though she was still angry at him, she couldn't suppress the warm tingle of sexual awareness she felt at being so close to such a hot man. He really was scrumptious, for an ass.

And speaking of that, he had a mighty fine one of those too.

"I remember all the dreams about us."

His scowl darkened. "Then you really were screwing with my head."

"Hardly!" she snapped, offended by his tone and the accusation. "I didn't have anything to do with it. For all I know, it was *you* messing with *me*."

Wulf got out of the truck and slammed the door.

Cassandra followed suit.

"D'Aria!" he shouted up at the ceiling. "Get your butt down here. Now!"

Cassandra was stunned when a light blue mist shimmered beside Wulf and a beautiful young woman appeared. With jet-black hair and pale blue eyes, she looked almost like an angel.

Her face emotionless, D'Aria stared eye to eye with him. "I have been told that that was rude, Wulf. If I had feelings, you would have hurt them."

"I'm sorry," he said contritely. "I didn't mean to be curt, but I needed to ask you something about my dreams."

D'Aria looked from him to Cassandra and it was then Cassandra understood. This was one of the Dream-Hunters she had read about on the Dream-Hunter.com Web site. All of the Dream-Hunters possessed black hair and pale eyes. These Greek gods of sleep had once been cursed by Zeus so that none of them were capable of feeling emotions.

They really were beautiful. Ethereal. And even though D'Aria was solid, there was something about her that was also shimmery. Something that let you know she wasn't as real as everything else in the room.

Cassandra felt a sudden, almost childish impulse to reach out and touch the dream goddess to see if D'Aria was made of flesh or something else.

"You two met in your dreams?" D'Aria asked Wulf.

Wulf nodded. "Was it real?"

D'Aria cocked her head slightly as she thought about that. Her pale eyes held a faraway, fragile look to them. "If you both recall it, then yes." Her gaze sharpened as she looked up at Wulf. "But it wasn't from any of us. Since you are under my care, none of the other Oneroi would have interfered with your dreams without telling me."

"Are you sure?" he asked emphatically.

"Yes. It's the one code we are all careful to follow. When a Dark-Hunter is given over to one of us to care for, we never trespass without a direct invitation."

That all too familiar frown creased Wulf's brow. Cassandra was beginning to wonder if the "real" Wulf was capable of any other expression than that sinister, intense look. "Since I'm under your care, how is it that you didn't know about the dreams I've had with her?"

D'Aria shrugged in a gesture that looked rather awkward for her. It was obvious the shrug was a practiced expression. "You didn't summon me to your dreams, nor were you hurt or in need of my healing. I don't spy on your unconscious mind without cause, Wulf. Dreams are private matters and only the evil Skoti go where they're not invited."

D'Aria turned to look at her. She held her hand out. "You may touch me, Cassandra."

"How do you know my name?"

"She knows all about you," Wulf said. "Dream-Hunters can see right through us."

Cassandra tentatively touched D'Aria's hand. It was soft and warm. Human. Yet there was a strange electrical field around it that was similar to static electricity, only different. It was oddly soothing.

"We are not so different in this realm," D'Aria said quietly.

Cassandra withdrew her hand. "But you have no emotions?"

"At times we can, if we have been recently inside a human's dream. It's possible to continue to syphon emotions for a brief time."

"Skoti can syphon for longer periods," Wulf added. "They're similar to Daimons that way. Instead of feeding off your soul, the Skoti feed off your emotions."

"Energy vampires," Cassandra said.

D'Aria nodded.

Cassandra had read about the Dream-Hunters extensively. Unlike the Dark-Hunters, there was a ton of ancient literature that survived about the Oneroi. The gods of sleep appeared throughout Greek literature, but there was seldom a mention of the evil Skoti who preyed on people while they slept.

All Cassandra knew about them was that they were highly feared in ancient civilizations. So much so that many ancient humans were afraid to even mention the

Skoti by name lest they incur a midnight visit from the sleep demons.

"Would Artemis have done this to us?" Wulf asked D'Aria.

"Why would she?" D'Aria countered.

Wulf shifted slightly. "Artemis seems to be protecting the princess. Could she have sent her into my dreams for that purpose?"

"I suppose most anything is possible."

Cassandra seized on D'Aria's words with zeal and a rare glimmer of hope. "Is it possible that I don't have to die on my next birthday?"

D'Aria's emotionless gaze held no more promise than her words. "If you are asking me for prophecy, child, that I cannot give you. The future is something each of us must meet on his or her own. What I say now may or may not be truth."

"But do all half-Apollites have to die at twenty-seven?" Cassandra asked again, desperate for an answer.

"That, too, is an Oracle question."

Cassandra closed her eyes in frustration. All she wanted was some hope. A little guidance.

One more year of life.

Something. But apparently she was asking too much.

"Thank you, D'Aria," Wulf said, his voice deep and strong.

The Dream-Hunter inclined her head to them, then vanished. There was no trace of her. No sign.

Cassandra looked around the elegant garage of a man who had lived for untold centuries. Then she looked at the small signet ring she wore on her right hand that her mother had given her just days before she died. A ring that had been handed down through her family since their first ancestor had prematurely crumbled to dust.

All of a sudden, Cassandra burst out laughing.

Wulf appeared bemused by her humor. "Are you all right?"

"No," she said, trying to sober. "I think I snapped a wheel at some point tonight. Or at the very least stepped over into the realm of Rod Serling's *Twilight Zone*."

His frown deepened. "How do you mean?"

"Well, let's see . . ." She looked at her gold Harry Winston watch. "It's only eleven o'clock and tonight I have gone to a club that seems to be owned by shape-shifting panthers, where a group of vampire hit men and one possible god attacked me. Went home only to be attacked again by said hit men, god, and then a dragon. Had a Dark-Hunter save me. My bodyguard may or may not be in the service of a goddess and now I just met a sleep spirit. Hell of a day, huh?"

For the first time since meeting him in the flesh, she saw a hint of a smile on Wulf's roguishly handsome face. "Just a typical day in the life from where I'm standing," he said.

He moved closer to her and examined her neck where Stryker had bitten her. His fingers were warm against her skin. Soothing and gentle. The scent of him filled her head and made her wish for a moment where they could go back and just be friends again.

There was very little blood on her shirt. "It looks like it's closed up already."

"I know," she said quietly. There was a coagulating gel in Apollite saliva, which was why they had to continually suck for blood once they opened a wound. Otherwise the wound would close before they had a chance to eat. The gel they secreted could also blind humans if an Apollite spat in their eyes.

She was just grateful that the bite didn't unite her with Stryker in any way. Only Were-Hunters had that ability.

Wulf stepped back from her and led her into his house. He wasn't sure why he had been given the task of seeing to her safety, but until Acheron told him otherwise, he would do his duty. Feelings be damned.

As he opened the door, his cell phone rang.

Wulf answered it to find Corbin on the other end. "Hey, did you find Kat?"

"Yeah," Corbin said. "She told me she only went to take out the garbage and came back to find Cassandra gone."

He relayed the information to Cassandra, who looked confused by it.

"What do you want me to do with Kat?" he asked Cassandra.

"Can she come here?"

Yeah. When the equator freezes. He wasn't about to let Kat near Chris or his home until he knew more about her and her loyalties. "Hey, Bin, can she stay with you?"

Cassandra narrowed her green eyes at him with malice. "That's not what I said."

He held his hand up to silence her. "Yeah, okay. I'll call you once we get settled." He hung up.

Cassandra bristled at his high-handed manner. "I don't like being shushed."

"Look," he said, clipping his phone back on his belt. "Until I know more about your friend, I'm not inviting her into my home, where Christopher lives. I don't mind wagering with my life, but I'll be damned again before I wager with his. Got it?"

Cassandra hesitated as she remembered what he had told her in their dreams about Chris and how much Chris meant to him. "I'm sorry. I didn't think about that. So he lives here too?"

He nodded as he turned on a light in the back hallway. To her right was a staircase and on the left was a small bathroom. Farther down the hallway was the kitchen. Large and airy, it was scrupulously clean and very modern in design.

Wulf hung his keys on a small rack by the stove. "Make yourself at home. There's beer, wine, milk, juice, and soda in the fridge."

He showed her where the glasses and plates were kept above the dishwasher.

They left the kitchen and he turned the lights off before leading her into an open, inviting living room. There were two black leather sofas, a matching armchair, and an ornate silver box of medieval design for a coffee table. One wall held an entertainment center, complete with large-screen TV, stereo, DVD and VHS players, along with every game system known to mankind.

She cocked her head at the sight as she imagined the large, cumbersome Viking warrior playing games. It seemed completely out of character for him and his overly serious attitude. "You play?"

"Sometimes," he said, his voice low. "Chris plays mostly. I prefer to veg in front of my computer."

She refrained from laughing at the image she had of that. Wulf was far too intense to simply "veg."

Wulf shrugged off his coat and draped it over his couch. Cassandra heard someone coming down the hallway toward the living room.

"Hey, Big Guy, did you see . . ." Chris's voice trailed off as he entered the room wearing navy flannel pajama bottoms and a white T-shirt.

His mouth fell open.

"Hi, Chris," Cassandra said.

Chris didn't speak for several minutes while he looked back and forth between them.

When he finally spoke, his voice was a cross between aggravation and anger. "No, no, no. This ain't right. I finally find a woman who'll actually let me into her place and you bring her home for you?"

Chris's face went pale as if he had another thought. "Oh, please tell me you brought her home for you and not for me. You didn't pimp me out again, Wulf, did you? I swear I'll stake you in your sleep if you did."

"Excuse me," Cassandra said, interrupting Chris's tirade, which appeared to amuse Wulf. "I happen to be standing right here. Just what kind of woman do you think I am?"

"A very nice one," Chris said, instantly redeeming himself, "but Wulf is extremely overbearing and tends to bully people into doing what he wants them to."

Wulf snorted at that. "Then why can't I bully you into procreating?"

"See!" Chris said, raising his hand in triumph. "I'm the only human in history to have a Viking yenta of his very own. God, how I wish my father had been a fertile man."

Cassandra laughed at the image Chris's words conjured in her mind. "Viking yenta, huh?"

Chris let out a disgusted breath. "You've no idea . . ." He paused and then frowned at the two of them. "And why is she here, Wulf?"

"I'm protecting her."

"From?"

"Daimons."

"Big bad ones," Cassandra added.

Chris took that better than she would have imagined. "She knows about us?"

Wulf nodded. "She knows pretty much everything."

"Is that why you were asking about Dark-Hunter.com?" Chris asked Cassandra.

"Yes. I wanted to find Wulf."

Chris was immediately suspicious.

"It's okay, Chris," Wulf explained. "She'll be staying with us a while. You don't have to hide anything from her."

"You swear?"

"Yes."

Chris looked very pleased by that. "So you guys fought some Daimons, huh? Wish I could. Wulf goes nuts if I even pick up a butter knife."

Cassandra laughed.

"Really," Chris said sincerely. "He's worse than a mother hen. So how many Daimons did you two kill?"

"None," Wulf muttered. "These were a lot stronger than the average soul-sucker."

"Well, that ought to make you happy," Chris said to Wulf. "You finally have someone who can fight you until you're bloody and blue from it." He turned back toward Cassandra. "Has Wulf explained his little problem to you?"

Cassandra's eyes widened as she tried to think of what "little" problem Wulf could possible have.

Unconsciously, her gaze dropped to his groin.

"Hey!" Wulf snapped. "That has *never* been my problem. That's *his* problem."

"Bullshit!" Chris snapped. "I haven't got any problems there either. My only problem is *you* yenting at me all the time to go get laid."

Oh, Cassandra really didn't want to go where this conversation was leading. It was way too much information about both men.

"Well, then, what problem were you talking about?" she asked Chris.

"The fact that if you walk out of the room, by the time you get to the end of the hallway, you won't remember him."

"Oh," she said in understanding. "That."

"Yeah, *that*."

"It's not a problem," Wulf said as he crossed his arms over his chest. "She remembers me."

"Ah, man," Chris said, his face contorted by disgust. "I've been making moves on a relative? That's so sick."

Wulf rolled his eyes. "She's not related to us."

Chris looked relieved for about half a second, then he looked ill again. "Well, then, that sucks even more. I finally find a woman who doesn't think I'm a total loser and she's here for you? What is wrong with this picture?"

Chris paused. The light came back to his face as if he'd had an even better thought. "Oh, wait, what am I saying? If she remembers you, I'm off the hook! Wahoo!" Chris started dancing around the couch.

Cassandra stared at his chaotic, off-rhythm movements. Wulf really needed to let the boy out more.

"Don't get too excited, Christopher," Wulf said, dodging him as he came around the couch and tried to include Wulf in the dance. "She happens to be an Apollite."

Chris froze, then settled down. "She can't be, I've seen her in the daylight and she has no fangs."

"I'm *half*-Apollite."

Chris stepped behind Wulf as if suddenly afraid she might start feeding on him. "So what are you are going to do with her?"

"She's my house guest for a while. You, on the other

hand, need to get your bags packed." Wulf pushed him toward the hallway, but Chris refused to budge. "I'm calling the Council to evacuate you."

"Why?"

"Because we have a nasty Daimon after her who has some unusual powers. I don't want you caught in the cross fire."

Chris gave him a droll look. "I'm not a baby, Wulf. You don't have to hide me at the first sign of something not boring."

In spite of Chris's words, Wulf held the look of a patient parent dealing with a toddler. "I'm not taking a chance with your life, so go pack."

Chris let out a disgusted growl. "I curse the day Morginne gave you the soul of an old woman and made you worse than any mother could ever be."

"Christopher Lars Eriksson, move!" Wulf barked in a tone so commanding that Cassandra actually jumped.

Chris just gave him a bored, blank stare. Sighing heavily, he turned and walked back down the hallway he'd emerged from.

"I swear," Wulf growled in a tone so low she barely heard him, "there are times when I could choke the life out of him."

"Well, you do talk to him like he's four."

Wulf turned on her with a glare so menacing that she actually stepped back from his wrath. "That is none of your business."

Cassandra held her hands up and returned his glare with one of her own. "Excuse me, Mr. Bad-Ass, but you will take another tone to me. I'm not your bitch to heel when you snap. I don't have to stay here."

"Yes you do."

She gave him an arch look. "I don't think so, and unless you take that anger out of your voice when you speak to me, all you're going to see is my heinie as it goes out that door." She pointed to the front door.

The smile he gave her was wicked and cold. "Have you ever tried to run from a Viking? There's a damned good reason why the western Europeans wet themselves whenever our names were mentioned."

His words made her shiver. "You wouldn't dare."

"Feel free to try me."

Cassandra swallowed. Maybe she shouldn't be so cocksure.

Oh, screw that. If he wanted a fight, she was more than ready. A woman who had spent her life fighting Daimons was more than apt to take on any Dark-Hunter.

"Let me remind you of this, Mr. Viking-Warrior-Barbarian-Hoodlum, while your ancestors were scrounging for fire and food, mine were commanding the elements and building an empire that not even the modern world can touch. So don't you dare threaten me with what you're capable of. I'm not about to take that from you or anyone else. Got that?"

To her surprise he laughed at her words and moved to stand in front of her. His eyes were dark, dangerous, and they made her hot in spite of how angry she was at him. The heat of his body incinerated hers.

She was even more breathless now.

More aware of him and that raw, unsettling masculinity that made every feminine part of her pant.

He placed his hand on her cheek. One corner of his mouth was turned up in amusement. The look of him watching her was totally devastating. "In my day, you would have been worth more than your weight in gold."

Then he did the most unexpected thing of all, he dipped his head down and kissed her.

Cassandra moaned at the feral taste of him. His breath mixed with hers as he plundered her mouth, making her hot and throbbing for him.

But then, that wasn't hard. Not when he was so scrumptiously perfect. So manly and fierce.

Her entire body sizzled at his nearness. At the taste of his tongue dancing with hers as he growled low in his throat.

He pulled her closer to him. So close that she could feel the bulge of his cock against her hip. He was hard already and she knew firsthand just how capable a lover he was. That knowledge made her even more breathless. Needy. He ran his hands down her back until he could cup her bottom and press her even closer to him.

Her anger melted under the desire she felt for this man.

"You taste even sweeter now than before," he breathed against her lips.

She couldn't speak. It was true. This was far more intense. Far more scintillating than anything in her dreams. All she wanted to do was strip his clothes off, throw him on the ground, and ride him until they both were sweaty and sated.

Every part of her cried out for her to make that fantasy real.

Wulf couldn't breathe as he felt her womanly curves against him and in his hands.

He wanted her madly. Desperately. Worse, he had taken her enough times in their dreams to know exactly how passionate she was.

She's an Apollite. The highest form of forbidden fruit.

The voice of sanity rushed through his mind.

He didn't want to listen.

But he had no choice.

Releasing her, he forced himself to step away from her and the need she created inside him.

To his surprise, she didn't let him go. She pulled him back to her lips and ravished his mouth with hers. He closed his eyes and hissed in pleasure as she permeated every sense he possessed. Her scent of roses and powder made him drunk.

He didn't think he could ever get enough of that smell. Of her body grinding against his.

He wanted her more than he had ever wanted anything.

She pulled away and looked up at him. Her green eyes were bright, her cheeks flushed by her passion. "You're not the only one who wants something impossible, Wulf. As much as you hate me for what I am, imagine how I feel knowing I've dreamt of a man who has slaughtered my people for how many centuries now?"

"Twelve," he said before he could stop himself.

She winced at his words. Her hands dropped away from his face. "How many of us have you killed? Do you even know?"

He shook his head. "They had to die. They were killing innocent people."

Her eyes darkened and turned accusatory. "They were surviving, Wulf. You never had to face the choice of being dead at twenty-seven. When most people's lives are just beginning, we are looking at a death sentence. Have you any idea what it's like to know you can never see your children grow up? Never see your own grandchildren? My mother used to say we were spring flowers who are only meant to bloom for one season. We bring our gifts to the world and then recede to dust so that others can come after us."

She held her right hand up so that he could see the five

tiny pink teardrops tattooed on her palm in the shape of a flower's petals. "When our loved ones die, we immortalize them like this. I have one for my mother and the other four are my sisters. No one will ever know the beauty of my sisters' laughter. No one will remember the kindness of my mother's smile. In eight months, my father won't even have enough of me left to bury. I will become scattered dust. And for what? For something my great-great-great-whatever did? I've been alone the whole of my life because I dare not let anyone know me. I don't want to love for fear of leaving someone like my father behind to mourn me.

"I will be a vague dream, and yet here you are, Wulf Tryggvason. Viking cur who once roamed the earth raiding villages. How many people did you kill in your human lifetime while you sought your treasure and fame? Were you any better than the Daimons who kill so that they can live? What makes you better than us?"

"It's not the same thing."

Disbelief went through her that he couldn't see what was so obvious. "Isn't it? You know, I went to your Web site and saw the names listed there. Kyrian of Thrace, Julian of Macedon, Valerius Magnus, Jamie Gallagher, William Jess Brady. I've studied history all my life and know each of those names and the terror they wrought in their day. Why is it okay for the Dark-Hunters to have immortality even though most of you were killers as humans, while we are damned at birth for things we never did? Where is the justice in this?"

Wulf didn't want to hear her words. He'd never given any thought to the Daimons and why they did what they did. He had a job to do and so he killed them. The Dark-Hunters were the ones who were right. They were human protectors. The Daimons were the predators who deserved to be stalked and killed. "The Daimons are evil."

"Am I evil?"

No, she wasn't. She was . . .

She was things he dared not name.

"You're an Apollite," he said forcefully.

"I'm a woman, Wulf," she said simply, her voice filled with emotion. "I cry and I mourn. I laugh and I love. Just like my mother did. I don't see a difference between me and anyone else on this planet."

He met her gaze and the fire in his eyes scorched her. "I do, Cassandra. I see the difference."

His words cut her to the quick. "Then we have nothing more to talk about. We are enemies. It's all we can ever be."

Wulf took a deep breath as she spoke a truth that couldn't be changed. Since the day Apollo had cursed his own children, Dark-Hunters and Apollites had been mortal enemies.

"I know," he said softly, his throat tight with that realization.

He didn't want to be enemies, not with her.

But how could they ever be anything else?

He hadn't chosen this life on his own, but he had given his word to live it now.

They were enemies.

And it killed him inside.

"Let me show you where you can sleep." He led her to the wing opposite Chris's where she could have all the privacy she wanted.

Cassandra didn't say anything as Wulf turned over a large, comfortable bedroom to her. Her heart was heavy, aching for things that were foolish and stupid. What did she want of him?

There was no way to prevent him from killing her people. It was the way of the world and no amount of argument would change that.

There was no hope of having a relationship with him or any other man. Her life was all but over now. So where did that leave them?

Nowhere.

So she resorted to the humor that had seen her through the tragedies of her life. It was all she had. "Tell me, if I get lost in this place, do you have a search party available to find me again?"

He didn't laugh. There was a solid wall between them now. He had completely closed himself off from her. It was just as well.

"I'll go get you something to sleep in." He started away from her.

"You won't even trust me to see where you sleep, huh?"

His look was piercing. "You've already seen where I sleep."

Her face turned red as she remembered the most erotic of her dreams. The one where she had watched his tawny body sliding against hers in the mirrors while he made slow, passionate love to her. "The black iron bed?"

He nodded, then left her.

Alone, Cassandra sat on the mattress and pushed her thoughts away. "What am I doing here?" Part of her said to screw it and just take her chances with Stryker.

But another part of her wanted to go back to her dreams and just pretend this day hadn't happened.

No, what she wanted was the one thing she knew she could never have . . .

She wanted a forbidden fantasy—a man of her own to have and to hold. One she could grow old with. One who could hold her hand as she brought his baby into the world.

It was so impossible that she had buried those dreams years and years ago.

Up until now, she'd never met anyone who made her ache for the things that were denied her. Not until she had stared into a pair of black eyes and listened to a Viking warrior talk about keeping a boy safe.

A man who felt guilt for his past.

She yearned now. And it was an impossible desire.

Wulf could never be hers, and even if he was, she would be dead in a matter of months.

Hanging her head in her hands, she wept.

Chapter 7

"Take me to Cassandra," Kat snarled at the auburn-haired Dark-Huntress in the car beside her. It wasn't in her nature to let anyone have control of her or her environment. "I'm the only one who can protect her."

"Yeah," Corbin said as she pulled into the driveway of her mansion. "You did a great job protecting her from what . . . the garbage, was it?"

Kat saw red at that. The urge to blast the Huntress into dust went through her—a byproduct of her mother's nasty temper that she had inherited. Luckily for Corbin, Kat had more of her father in her and had learned long ago to take deep breaths and not give in to her childish impulses.

Getting angry wouldn't accomplish anything. She had to find Cassandra, and if she used her powers to do it, Stryker would be able to locate Cass as well. That prick had learned long ago how to follow the subtle nuances of Kat's powers and use them against her. It was why she hadn't fought him in the bar. Like it or not, Stryker was more powerful than she was. Mostly because he didn't care who he hurt to get his way.

Which meant she needed the Huntress to take her to Cass.

Kat had teleported out of their apartment for no more

than five minutes so that she could go to the Destroyer and tell her to leave Cassandra alone.

How was she to know the Destroyer would use that distraction to send in Stryker and his men while she was away?

She felt so betrayed she couldn't breathe. After all these centuries, she had dutifully served both Apollymi and Artemis. Now the two of them were using her against each other and she didn't like it in the least.

And they both wondered why her father didn't want to play their reindeer games. He was far wiser than Kat since he had always managed to keep himself out of these situations. Only he seemed to understand both goddesses.

How she wished she could call him. He could probably end this in a matter of seconds. But involving him would only make things worse.

No, she had to handle this on her own.

Besides, she no longer cared what either goddess wanted. She had grown extremely fond of Cassandra these last five years and she didn't want to see her friend used, let alone hurt.

It was time for all of them to just leave Cassandra alone.

Corbin got out of the car.

Kat followed her into the garage, then stopped as Corbin unlocked the door to her house. "Look, we're all on the same team."

The Huntress looked at her as if she were insane. "Sure we are, hon. Now come inside so I can keep an eye on you and make sure you don't do anything like leave Cassandra to her enemies again."

Kat used enough of her powers to hold the door shut. Corbin rattled the knob and smacked the wood with her hand.

"You know," Kat said angrily, "if I wanted Cassandra

dead, don't you think in the last five years I could have killed her? Why would I wait until now?"

Corbin turned away from the door. "How do I know you've known her for five years?"

Kat laughed sarcastically at that. "Ask her and you'll see."

Corbin looked at her thoughtfully. "Then why did you leave her unprotected tonight?"

Kat locked gazes with her so that Corbin could see her sincerity. "I swear to you, had I known those homicidal loons were going to show up, I wouldn't have stepped one foot out of that apartment."

Still, Corbin's gaze doubted her. On the one hand, Kat admired the woman's protectiveness. On the other, she wanted to strangle her.

"I don't know," Corbin said slowly. "Maybe you're being honest and maybe you're full of shit."

"Fine." Kat threw her hands up in frustration. "You want proof?"

"You got any?"

Turning around, Kat lifted the hem of her shirt and showed Corbin the skin just above her left hip where her own double bow-and-arrow mark resided. That brand was the mark of Artemis.

Corbin's eyes widened. "I know you're not a Dark-Hunter. What are you?"

"I'm one of Artemis's handmaidens, and just like you, I've been charged with seeing Cassandra safe. Now take me to her."

Wulf knocked briefly, then pushed the door open to find Cassandra wiping her eyes. He froze at the sight. "Are you crying?"

"No," she said, clearing her throat. "I had something in my eye."

He knew she was lying, but he respected her strength. It was nice to find a woman who didn't use tears to manipulate men.

He entered the room hesitantly. The thought of her crying made his own chest ache. Worse, he felt an insane need to pull her into his arms and comfort her.

He couldn't. He needed to keep his distance from her.

"I . . . um . . . I borrowed these from Chris." He handed her the sweatpants and T-shirt in his hand.

"Thanks."

Wulf couldn't tear his gaze away from her. Her long strawberry-blond hair was pulled back from her face. Something about her reminded him of a scared little girl and at the same time there was something that was rock-solid and determined.

He cupped her cool cheek in his hand and tilted her head so that she was looking up at him. In his dreams, he would be laying her back on her bed and tasting her lips.

Unbuttoning her shirt . . .

"Have you been fighting like this all your life?"

She nodded. "Both Daimons and Apollites hunt my family. At one time, there were hundreds of us and now it's down to me. My mother always told us that we must have more children. That it was up to us to continue the line."

"Why didn't you?"

She sniffed daintily. "Why should I? If I die, then they will see that there is no truth to the myth that says our death will free them."

"So you've never thought of going Daimon then?"

She pulled away from him and he saw the truth in her eyes.

"Could you do it?" he asked her. "Could you kill an innocent person to live?"

"I don't know," she said, moving away from the bed to place the shirt and pants on the dresser. "They say it gets easier after the first one. And once you have a foreign soul in you, it changes everything about you. You become something else. Something evil and uncaring. My mother had a brother who turned. I was only six when he came to her and tried to make her a Daimon as well. When she refused, he tried to kill her. In the end, her bodyguard killed him while my sisters and I hid in a closet. It was terrifying. Uncle Demos had always been so good to us."

The sadness in her eyes as she spoke wrapped around his heart and squeezed it tightly. He couldn't imagine how much horror she had seen in her young life.

But then his childhood hadn't been easy either. The shame, the humiliation. Even after all these centuries, he could still feel the sting of it.

Some pains never eased.

"What about you?" she asked, looking at him over her shoulder since he didn't cast a reflection in the mirror. "Did you find it was easier to kill a man after you took your first life?"

Her question angered him. "I never murdered anyone. I only protected myself and my brother."

"Ah, I see," she said quietly. "So you don't think it's murder when you barge into someone's home to rob them and they fight you rather than submit to your brutality?"

Shame filled him as he remembered a few of his early raids. Back then, his people had traveled far and wide, attacking villages in the middle of the night to raid other people, other lands. They weren't after the kill, but rather wanted to leave as many alive as they could. Especially when they were after slaves they could sell in foreign markets.

His mother had been horrified when she learned that he and Erik had started raiding with the other sons of their neighbors.

"My sons are dead to me," she had snarled before she threw them out of their squalid home. *"I never want to see either of you again."*

And she hadn't. She'd died the following spring of a fever. His sister had paid one of the young village men to find them and deliver the news.

Three years passed before they were able to return home to pay their respects. By then his father had been slain and his sister taken by invaders. Wulf had gone to England to free her and it had been there that Erik had died after they left her village.

Brynhild had refused to leave with them. *"I reap what you and Erik have sown. It is God's will that I be a slave to serve as those whom you and Erik have sold are forced to do. And for what, Wulf? For profit and glory? Leave me, brother. I want no more of your warring ways."*

Like a fool, he had left her and she too had been slain a year later when the Angles invaded her small village. Life was death. It was the only thing that was inevitable.

As a human, he'd been well acquainted with it. As a Dark-Hunter he was an expert.

He turned away from Cassandra. "Times were different then."

"Really?" she asked. "I never heard before that people in the Dark Ages were supposed to be sheep to be butchered."

Cassandra cringed as Wulf turned on her with a fierce growl. "If you are looking for me to apologize for what I did, I will not. I was born to a race that respected nothing but the strength of one's sword arm. I grew up mocked and ridiculed because my father wouldn't fight. So when I was old enough to prove to them that I wasn't like him, that I could and *would* stand by them in battle, I took it.

"Yes, I did things I regret. What person hasn't? But I never once killed or raped a woman. I never hurt a child, nor a man who couldn't defend himself. *Your* people prize the death of a child or pregnant woman above all else. They stalk them for no other purpose than to elongate their putrid lives. So don't you dare preach to me."

She swallowed, but admirably held her ground. "Some do. Just as some of *your* people lived to rape and pillage. Didn't you tell me your own mother was a slave who had been captured by your father? It may come as a surprise to you, Wulf Tryggvason, but some of my people only prey on people like yours. Murderers. Rapists. There is an entire branch of Daimons called the Akelos who have all taken an oath to kill only the humans who deserve it."

"You lie."

"No," she said, her tone sincere, "I don't. Funny, when I first met you, I thought you might know more about my people than I do since you hunt us. But you don't, do you? We're just animals to all of you. Not even worth the trouble of talking to one of us to find out the truth."

It was true. He had never given any thought to the Daimons other than the fact that they were killers who needed to die.

As for Apollites . . .

He hadn't thought of them at all.

Now he had a "human" face to go with the term "Apollite."

Not just a face . . . he had a touch.

A lover's gentle whisper.

But what did it change?

Nothing. At the end of the day, he was still a Dark-Hunter and he would still pursue the Daimons and slay any of them he found.

There was nothing more to be said between them. This was one obstacle neither of them could ever overcome.

So, he withdrew from the conflict. "You have free run of the house at night and the grounds during daylight."

"And if I want to leave?"

He scoffed. "Ask Chris how easy that is."

That familiar light came into her emerald eyes. The one that challenged him and told him he didn't have any real power over her. It was one of the things he admired most in her—that fire and strong will. "You know, I'm used to getting out of impossible situations."

"And I'm used to tracking and finding Apollites and Daimons."

She arched one brow. "Are you challenging me?"

He shook his head. "I'm only stating fact. You leave and I will bring you back here. In chains if need be."

She gave him a suddenly droll look that reminded him of Chris. "Will you punish me too?"

"I think you're a little old for that. I also think you're smart enough to know how stupid it would be for you to leave here while Stryker and his men are salivating to find you again."

Cassandra hated the fact that he was right. "Can I at least call my father and tell him where I am so he won't worry?"

He pulled the cell phone off his belt and handed it to her. "You can leave it in the living room when you finish."

He turned and opened the door.

"Wulf," she said before he could leave.

He faced her.

"Thank you for saving me again when I know it must burn every part that you did so."

His look softened. "It doesn't burn every part of me, Cassandra. Only you do that."

Her jaw went slack as he left the room and closed the door behind him.

She stood dumbstruck as those words whipped through her. Who would have thought her Viking warrior could have a more tender side? But then she ought to know the truth. She had seen his heart in their dreams.

Dreams that were real. In those few precious hours, she had glimpsed the man's heart. His fears.

Things he kept guarded and secret from everyone, except for her . . .

"I must be out of my mind," she breathed. How could she feel any tenderness toward a man who made no bones about the fact that he killed her people?

And in the back of her mind, she wondered whether Wulf would kill her, too, if she turned Daimon.

Wulf let out a long, tired breath as he entered the living room where Chris was lounging on the couch. Just what he needed, one more person tonight who couldn't do what he'd been told.

Thor, didn't any of them have a lick of sense?

"I thought I told you to pack."

"Go pack, brush your teeth, get laid. All you do is tell me what to do." Chris flipped through the channels on the TV. "If you would look at my feet, you will see that I'm all packed and am just waiting on my next order, thank you very much."

Wulf looked down to see a black backpack in front of the couch. "That's all you're taking?"

"Yeah. I don't need much, and whatever else I need I'm sure I can buy since the Council knows that I am the charmed one who has to be humored lest the big bad Norseman go a Viking on their heads."

Wulf tossed one of the cloth sofa cushions at him. Gently.

Chris tucked the pillow behind his back and didn't respond as he continued to flip channels.

Wulf sat down on the other sofa, but his thoughts kept drifting back to the woman he'd left in his guest wing. He was so confused where she was concerned, and confusion wasn't something he had much experience with. He'd always been a basic man. If he had a problem, he eliminated it.

He couldn't eliminate Cassandra per se. Well, he could in theory, but that would be wrong. The closest he could come would be to toss her out the door and let her fend for herself or hand her off to Corbin.

But Ash had charged him with her care and he didn't believe in passing his obligations off. If Ash wanted him to watch her, there must be a reason for it. The Atlantean never did anything without a damned good reason.

"So how much does Cassandra know about us?" Chris asked.

"It appears everything. Like she said, she's an Apollite."

"Half."

"Half, whole, what's the difference?"

Chris shrugged. "The difference is I really like her. She's not snotty like most of the other rich hos in my college."

"Don't be so disrespectful, Christopher."

Chris rolled his eyes. "Sorry, I forgot how much you hate that term."

Wulf propped his head against his hand as he watched the TV. Cassandra *was* different. She made him feel human again. Made him remember what it was like to be normal. To feel welcomed.

Those were things he hadn't felt in a long time.

"Good grief. You two look like Village of the Sofa Damned."

Wulf leaned his head back to see Cassandra standing in the doorway. Shaking her head at them, she came forward and handed him the phone.

Chris laughed and turned the sound down. "You know, it freaks with my head to see you here in my house."

"Believe me, it freaks with my head to be here in your house."

Chris ignored her comment. "Not to mention how weird it is that you remember him when you come back into the room. I keep feeling the deep need to introduce the two of you."

Wulf's phone started playing Black Sabbath's "Ironman." He picked it up and flipped it open. Cassandra walked over to sit near Chris while Wulf answered it.

"What is she doing here?"

Cassandra frowned at Wulf's gruff question.

"It's security calling," Chris told her.

"How do you know?"

"The song. Wulf thinks it's funny that it plays 'Ironman' for my escorts. They live in the security house that's down the estate not far from the gate. Someone must have pulled in to the driveway and buzzed for entry."

And she thought her father was paranoid about security. "What is this place, Fort Knox?"

"No," Chris said earnestly. "You might actually break in or out of Knox. The only way out of here is with at least two guards trailing you at all times."

"You sound like you've tried to go over the wall."

"More times than you can count."

She laughed as she remembered what Wulf had told her in her room. "Wulf said it was useless."

"It is. Believe me, if there was a way out of here, I'd have found it and used it by now."

Wulf hung up and rose to his feet.

"Is it for me?" Chris asked.

"No, it's Corbin."

"She's the one with Kat?" Cassandra asked Wulf.

He nodded as he went to the front door.

Cassandra followed after him in time to see a sleek red Lotus Esprit pulling up in front of the house. The passenger door opened to show her Kat, who got out of the car and rushed up to the house.

"Hey, kid, you all right?"

Cassandra smiled. "I'm not sure."

"Why is she here?" Wulf asked Corbin as the Dark-Huntress drew near him.

The Huntress tucked her hands in her pockets as she drew closer to Wulf. "She's in Artemis's service too. Her job is to protect Cassandra, and I thought it wise to let her help you."

Wulf looked suspiciously at Kat. "I don't need any help."

Kat bristled. "Relax, Mr. Macho, I won't rain on your parade. But you do need me. I happen to know Stryker personally. I'm the only shot you have at deflecting him."

Wulf wasn't sure if he should put any faith in those words. "You said you didn't know him at the club."

"I didn't want to blow my cover, but that was before you guys separated us and I had to convince Corbin to return me to Cassandra before Stryker finds her again."

"Do you trust her?" he asked Corbin.

"About as much as I trust anyone. But she pointed out that she's been with Cassandra for five years and Cassandra ain't dead yet."

"It's true," Cassandra said. "I've trusted her implicitly all this time."

"All right," Wulf said reluctantly. He met Corbin's gaze. "Keep your phone on and I'll be in touch."

Corbin nodded, then headed back to her car.

"We haven't met formally," Kat said, holding out her hand to Wulf as Corbin drove off. "I'm Katra."

He shook her hand. "Wulf."

"Yes, I know." Kat led them into the house, back to the living room where Chris was still sitting on the sofa.

Wulf locked and bolted the door behind them.

"By the way, Wulf," Kat said as she paused by Chris's backpack. "If you're thinking of sending Christopher away in order to protect him, I'd urge you to reconsider it."

"Why?"

She indicated the TV with her thumb. "How many times have you seen the 'let's kidnap the good guy's sidekick and hold him for ransom' episode?"

Wulf snorted at that. "Trust me, no one would be able to get him free of the Squire's Council."

"*Au contraire,*" Kat said sarcastically. "Stryker won't have a bit of a problem finding him. The minute you let him out of this house, Stryker and his Illuminati will be on him like white on snow. He'll never make it into another protected area without them having him. Literally."

"They wouldn't dare kill him, would they?" Cassandra asked.

"No," Kat said. "That's not Stryker's style. He's into punishment and hitting people where it hurts the most. He'll send Chris back, all right. The kid just won't be intact any longer."

"Intact how?" Chris asked nervously.

Kat lowered her gaze to his groin.

Chris immediately covered himself with his hands. "Bullshit."

"Oh, no, baby doll. Stryker knows how much Wulf values your ability to procreate. It's the one thing he'd take from both of you."

"Chris," Wulf said sternly, "go to your room and lock the door."

Chris ran from the room without hesitation.

Wulf and Kat glared at each other. "If you know this Stryker so well, then how do I know you're not working for him?"

Kat snorted at that. "I don't even like him. He and I have a mutual friend who has caused us to run into each other a few times over the centuries."

"Centuries?" Cassandra asked. "As in *centuries*? What are you, Kat?"

Kat patted her comfortingly on the arm. "I'm sorry, Cass. I should have told you before, but was afraid you wouldn't trust me if I did. Five years ago when Stryker almost killed you, Artemis sent me in to make sure he didn't get that close to you again."

Cassandra's head swirled at the disclosure. "So you *were* the one who opened the portal in the club?"

She nodded. "I'm breaching nine kinds of oaths here, but the last thing I want is to see you hurt. I swear it."

Wulf moved forward. "Why all this trouble to keep her safe when she's only going to die in a few months anyway?"

Kat took a deep breath and stepped back. She looked at each of them in turn before she finally spoke. "I'm no longer here to keep *her* safe."

Wulf put himself between Kat and Cassandra. He

tensed as if ready to do battle. "What do you mean by that?"

Kat tilted her head so that she could meet Cassandra's gaze behind Wulf's back. "I'm here now to make sure the baby she carries is born healthy."

Chapter 8

"M-m-my what?" Cassandra asked, floored by Kat's words. She couldn't have heard that correctly. There was no way she was pregnant.

"Your baby."

Obviously her hearing was fine. "What baby?"

Kat took a deep breath and spoke slowly, which was a good thing since Cassandra was having a hard time following all this. "You're pregnant, Cass. Only just, but the baby will survive. I'll make double damn sure of that."

Cassandra honestly felt as if someone had slugged her with a stunning blow. Her mind could barely conceive of what Kat was telling her. "I can't be pregnant. I haven't been with anyone."

Kat's gaze went to Wulf.

"What?" he asked defensively.

"You're the father," Kat said.

"Oh, like hell. I hate to break it to you, baby, but Dark-Hunters can't have children. We're sterile."

Kat nodded. "True, but you're not really a Dark-Hunter now, are you?"

"Then what the hell am I?"

"Immortal, but unlike the other Dark-Hunters you didn't die. Ever. The others become sterile because their bodies were dead for a time. Yours, on the other hand, is every bit as intact now as it was twelve hundred years ago."

"But I didn't touch her," Wulf insisted.

Kat arched a brow at that. "Oh, yes you did."

"That was a dream," Wulf and Cassandra said in unison.

"A dream you both remember? No, you were put together so that you could renew Cassandra's bloodline, and I ought to know since I was the one who drugged Cassandra earlier so that she could be with you."

"Oh, I'm going to be sick," Cassandra said, stepping back to lean on the sofa arm. "This can't be happening. It's just not possible."

"Oh, well," Kat said sarcastically, "let's not have reality intrude now, shall we? I mean, hey, you're a mythological being descended from mythological beings and you're in the house of an immortal guardian no human can remember five minutes after they leave his presence. Who's to say that you can't get pregnant in a dream by him? What? We're jumping into the realm of reality now?"

She gave Cassandra a penetrating stare. "Tell you what, I'll believe in the laws of nature when Wulf here can go out in the daylight and not spontaneously combust into flames, or better yet, when you, Cass, can actually go to a beach and get a tan."

Wulf was so stunned that he couldn't move as Kat continued to rail. Cassandra was pregnant with his child? This was something he had never, ever even dared to think about or hope for.

No, he couldn't believe it. He just couldn't.

"How could I have made her pregnant in a dream?" he asked, interrupting Kat.

She calmed down a bit and actually explained it to them. "There are different kinds of dreams. Different realms for them. Artemis had one of the Dream-Hunters pull both of you into a semiconscious state so that you could, shall we say, get together."

Wulf frowned at that. "But why would she do that?"

Kat indicated Cassandra with her hand. "She wouldn't sleep with anyone else. In the five years I've been with her, she hasn't so much as even looked at a guy with lust in her eyes. Not until the night you stepped into the club to kill the Daimons. She lighted up like a firefly. After she ran out after you, I thought we'd finally found her someone she would happily sleep with.

"But did you two do the normal, natural thing and go back to your place and mate like bunnies? No. She comes strutting back in like nothing had happened. Sheez. You are both hopeless." Kat sighed. "So Artemis figured she could use that momentary connection you two had on the street to put Cass into your dreams so that you could impregnate her that way."

"But why?" Cassandra asked. "Why is it so important that I be pregnant?"

"Because the myth you laugh at is true. If the last of Apollo's direct bloodline dies, the curse is lifted."

"Then let me die and free the Apollites."

Kat's face turned dark with warning. "I never said they would be free. See, the fun thing with the Fates is that nothing is ever easy. The curse is lifted because Apollo will die with you. Your blood and life are linked to his. When he dies, the sun dies with him as does Artemis and the moon. Once they are gone, there is no world left. All of us are dead. *All* of us."

"No, no, no," Cassandra breathed. "This can't be right."

There was no reprieve in Kat's expression. "It's right, hon. Believe me. I wouldn't be here otherwise."

Cassandra looked at her while inside she struggled to make sense of it all. It was so overwhelming. "Why didn't you tell me before?"

"I did and you freaked out so badly that Artemis and I decided to erase it from your memory and start over more slowly."

Fury lanced through her. "You did what?"

Kat turned defensive. "It was for your own good. You were so angry at the prospect of being forced into pregnancy that Artemis decided you would need a father and a baby in order to cope with the reality of it. When I explained it to you, you were gung-ho to toss yourself under a bus rather than use a man and leave behind a baby to be hunted down. So it's great now that you found Wulf, right? With his powers, the Apollites and Daimons can't come near him without dying."

Cassandra started for Kat only to find Wulf pulling her back so that she couldn't reach her. "Don't, Cassandra."

"Oh, please," Cassandra begged him. "I just want to choke her for a few minutes." She raked an angry glare over the woman she had mistakenly thought of as a friend. "I trusted you and you used me and lied to me. No wonder you kept trying to set me up with guys."

"I know and I'm sorry." Her eyes said Kat meant that, but Cassandra had a hard time believing it at the moment. "But don't you see how it all works out for the best? Wulf is afraid of losing his last blood link to the world. Through you he has another line that will remember him while you have someone immortal who can tell your child and grandchildren about you and your family. He can watch over them and keep them all safe. No more running, Cass. Think about it."

Cassandra didn't move as Kat's words sank in. She would be remembered and her children would be safe. It was all she had wanted. It was why she'd never considered having children before now.

But dare she believe in this?

Apollites gestated their babies in a little over twenty weeks. Half the time of humans. Since they had such an abbreviated life span, there were several weird physiological differences. Apollites reached adulthood at age eleven and often married between the ages of twelve to fifteen.

Her mother had only been fourteen when she married her father, but her mother had looked like any human woman in her mid-twenties.

Cassandra looked at Wulf, whose face was unreadable. "What do you think about all this?"

"Honestly, I don't know what to think. Yesterday my number one concern was getting Chris laid. Now it's the fact that if Kat isn't on drugs or delusional, you are carrying a part of me that holds in his or her hand the fate of the entire world."

"If you doubt any of this, call Acheron," Kat said.

Wulf narrowed his gaze on her. "He knows?"

Kat hedged a bit and appeared nervous for the first time. "I seriously doubt Artemis told him any of this particular plan to put you two together and make a baby. He tends to get rather upset at her whenever she interferes with free will, but he can easily verify everything I've told you about the prophecy."

Cassandra let out a bitterly amused half-laugh upon hearing that her "friend" actually knew one of the men they had read about on the Web site. Not to mention the fact that Kat also knew Stryker and his men. "Just out of curiosity, is there anyone you don't know?"

"No, not really," Kat said a bit uneasily. "I've been with Artemis a l-o-n-g time."

"And just how long is that?" Cassandra asked.

Kat didn't answer. Instead, she stepped back and clapped her hands together. "You know what? I think I should give you two a few minutes to talk to each other alone. I think I'll go scope out Cass's room."

Without another word, Kat bolted for the hallway that led to Cassandra's wing. Though how she knew that was the right way to go, Cassandra couldn't imagine. Then again, Kat wasn't exactly human either.

Wulf didn't move until Kat had vanished. He was still trying to come to terms with everything Kat had told them.

"I didn't know about any of this, Wulf. I swear it."

"I know."

He stared at her, the mother of his child. It was incredible, and despite the confusion he felt, the one truth he knew was that a part of him wanted to shout out in delight. "Do you feel all right? Do I need to get you anything?"

She shook her head, then looked up at him. Her green eyes scorched him with need. "Actually, I don't know about you, but I could use a hug right now."

Mentally, he didn't think that it would be wise to get attached to her. To open himself up to a woman who came with a short expiration date, but he found himself pulling her into his arms anyway, and he had to tense to keep himself from falling victim to the sensation of her body against his. Her breath tickled the skin on his neck as she wrapped her arms around his waist.

She felt so good here. So right. In all these centuries, he'd never known anything like this feeling of warmth.

What was it about her that made him tremble? Made him hot and aching?

Closing his eyes, he held her close and let her scent of powder and roses lull him into forgetting they should be enemies.

Cassandra closed her eyes, too, and let Wulf's warmth seep into her.

It felt so wonderful to be touched like this. This wasn't sexual, it was the kind of touch that soothed. One that bound them a lot closer than the intimacies they had already shared.

How can I feel comforted by someone who has already told me he has no use for my people?

Yet there was no denying that she did.

Then again, feelings seldom made sense.

As she stood there, one horrible thought disturbed the peace she felt. "Will you hate my baby, Wulf, because it will be part Apollite?"

Wulf grew tense in her arms as if he hadn't thought of that. He stepped away from her. "How Apollite will it be?"

"I don't know. For the most part, my family has been pure-blooded. My mother broke with the custom because she thought a human father could protect us better." Her stomach tightened as she remembered the secrets her mother had imparted to her not long before she died. "She figured he would at least outlive his children and grandchildren."

"She used him."

"No," she said breathlessly, offended that he would think that for even a minute. "My mother loved him, but like you, she was doing her duty to protect us. I guess since I was so young when she died, she didn't really have time to tell me how important my role would be if all of us died without children. Or maybe she didn't know either. She only said that it was every Apollite's duty to carry on our lineage."

Wulf moved to turn off the TV, but he didn't look at her now. He kept his attention on the mantel where an old sword rested on its side on a pedestal. "How Apollite are you? You don't have fangs and Chris said you can walk in daylight."

Cassandra wanted to go over and touch him again. She needed to feel close to him, but she could tell he wouldn't welcome her.

He needed time and answers.

"I had fangs as a child," she explained, not wanting to hold anything back from him. He deserved to know what their child might need in order to survive. "My father had them filed off when I was ten to better hide me among the humans. Like the rest of my people, I need blood to live, but it doesn't have to be Apollite, nor do I have to drink it or have it daily."

Cassandra paused as she thought about the necessities of her life and how much she wished she had been born human. But all in all, she had been much more fortunate than her sisters, who had tended to be more Apollite than she was. All four of them had been envious of how much easier life had been for Cassandra, who could walk in daylight.

"I usually go to the doctor for a transfusion every couple of weeks," she continued. "Since my father has a team of research doctors who work for him, he fabricated tests to say that I have a rare disease so that I can get what I need without alerting other doctors that I'm not quite human. I only go whenever I start to feel weak. And I haven't aged as quickly as most Apollites either. I hit my puberty just like a human female."

"Then maybe our child will be even more human." She couldn't miss the hopeful note in his voice as he spoke those words, and, like him, she prayed for the same thing. It would really be a miracle to have a human baby.

Not to mention the joy she felt that Wulf referred to the baby as theirs. At least that boded well.

For the baby anyway.

"You don't deny the baby?" she asked.

His look blistered her. "I know I was with you in our dreams and as Kat said I'm living proof of what the gods are capable of. So, no, I don't doubt the reality of this. The baby is mine and I will be a father to it."

"Thank you," she breathed as tears welled in her eyes. It was so much more than she had ever dared hope for.

She cleared her throat and banished her tears. She wouldn't cry. Not over this. Cassandra was lucky and she knew it. Unlike others of her kind, her child would have a father to keep him safe. One who could watch him grow up. "Look on the bright side, you only have to tolerate me for a couple of months and then I'm out of your hair forever."

He gave her a look so feral that it made her step back. "Don't ever treat death lightly."

She remembered what he had said in his dreams about watching his loved ones die. "Believe me, I don't. I'm very much aware of just how fragile our lives are. But maybe the baby will live longer than twenty-seven years."

"And if it doesn't?"

His hell would continue, only worse now because they would be his direct heirs.

His child.

His grandchildren. And he would be forced to watch them all die as young adults.

"I'm so sorry you got dragged into this."

"So am I." He stepped past her, and headed for a set of stairs that led downward.

"At least you will get to know the baby, Wulf," she called after him. "He or she will remember you. I will only have a few weeks with the baby before I have to die. He'll never know me at all."

He stopped dead in his tracks. For a full minute he didn't move.

Cassandra watched for any telltale emotions. His face was impassive. Without a comment, he continued on his way downstairs.

She tried to push his dismissal out of her thoughts. She had other things to focus on now, like the tiny baby that was growing inside her.

Heading for her room, she wanted to start making preparations. Time for her was all too critical and way too short.

Wulf entered his room and closed the door. He needed a little time alone to digest everything he'd been told.

He was going to be a father.

The child would remember him. But what if the child was more Apollite than Cassandra? Genetics was a weird science and he had lived long enough to see just how bizarre it could be. Look at Chris. No one had looked so much like Erik since Erik's son had died more than twelve hundred years before. Yet Christopher was the very image of Wulf's brother.

Chris even possessed Erik's temperament and bearing. They could be the same man.

And what if his child turned Daimon one day? Could he hunt and kill his own son or daughter?

The thought made him cold inside. It terrified him.

Wulf didn't know what to do. He needed advice. Someone who could help him sort through this. Picking up his phone, he called Talon.

No one answered.

Cursing, he only knew of one other person who might help. Acheron.

The Atlantean answered on the first ring. "What happened?"

He scoffed at Ash's cynicism. "No 'hi, Wulf, how's it going'?"

"I know you, Viking. You only call whenever there's a problem. So what's up? You have trouble hooking up with Cassandra?"

"I'm going to be a father."

Total silence answered him. It was nice to know the news stunned Ash as much as it had stunned him.

"Well, I guess the answer to my question is a big no, huh?" Ash asked finally. He paused again before asking. "Are you okay?"

"So you're not surprised at the fact that I made a woman pregnant?"

"No. I knew you could."

Wulf's jaw went slack as rage gripped him tightly. Ash had known all this time? "You know, that information could have been vital to me, Ash. Damn you for not telling me this before now."

"What would it have changed had I told you? You would have spent the last twelve centuries paranoid of ever touching a woman for fear of making her pregnant and then her not remembering you as the father. You've had enough on you as it is. I didn't see the point in adding that too."

Wulf was still angry. "What if I made someone else pregnant?"

"You haven't."

"How do you know?"

"Believe me, I do. Had you ever made anyone pregnant, I would have told you. I'm not so big an ass as to withhold something *that* important."

Yeah, right. If Ash would withhold this, then there was no telling what other vital things the Atlantean had failed to mention. "And I'm supposed to trust you now after you've just admitted lying to me?"

"You know, I think you've been talking to Talon too much. Suddenly you two sound like the same person. Yes, Wulf, you can trust me. And I never lied to you. I just omitted a few facts."

Wulf didn't say anything in response. But he would love to have Ash in front of him long enough to beat the hell out of him for this.

"So how's Cassandra dealing with her pregnancy?" Ash asked.

Wulf went cold. There were times when Ash was truly spooky. "How did you know Cassandra was the mother?"

"I know lots of things when I apply myself."

"Then perhaps you should learn to share some of these details, especially when they involve other people's lives."

Ash sighed. "If it makes you feel better, I'm not happy with the way all this went down any more than you are. But sometimes things have to go wrong in order to go right."

"What do you mean?"

"You'll see one day, little brother. I promise."

Wulf ground his teeth. "I really hate it when you play Oracle."

"I know. All of you do. But what can I say? It's my job to annoy you."

"I think you should find a new occupation."

"Why? I happen to enjoy the one I have." But something in Ash's voice told Wulf the Atlantean was lying about that too.

So Wulf decided on a change of venue. "Since you don't want to give me anything helpful, let me change the subject for a minute. Do you happen to know one of Artemis's handmaidens named Katra? She's here and she claims to be on our side. She says she's been protecting Cassandra for five years, but I'm not sure if I should trust her or not."

"I don't know the handmaidens by name, but I can ask Artemis about it."

For some bizarre reason that actually made him feel better. Ash wasn't completely omniscient after all. "Okay. Just let me know immediately if she's not friendly."

"I will definitely do that."

Wulf moved to hang up.

"By the way," Ash said as soon as he pulled the phone away.

Wulf replaced it to his ear. "What?"

"Congrats on the baby."

Wulf snorted at that. "Thanks. Maybe."

Cassandra wandered around the huge house. It was like walking through a museum. There were Old Norse artifacts everywhere. Not to mention oil paintings she'd never seen before by famous artists that she was sure were authentic.

There was one in particular outside her room by Jan van Eyck, of a dark-haired man and his wife. In some ways it reminded her of the famous Arnolfini portrait, but the couple in this one looked entirely different. The blond woman was dressed in vibrant red and the man in navy.

"It's the wedding portrait for two of my descendants."

She jumped at the deep sound of Wulf's voice behind her. She hadn't heard him approach. "It's beautiful. Did you commission it?"

He nodded and indicated the woman in the picture. "Isabella was quite an admirer of van Eyck's work so I thought it would be a perfect wedding present for them. She was the eldest daughter of another Squire family who had been sent to marry my Squire Leif. Chris is descended from their third daughter."

"Wow," she breathed, impressed. "All my life, I have struggled to find out something about my heritage and lineage, and here you are, a walking textbook for Chris. Does he have any idea how lucky he is?"

He shrugged. "I've learned that at his age, most people aren't interested in their past. Only their future. He'll want to know as he gets older."

"I don't know," she said, thinking of the way Chris's eyes lit up whenever he tried to teach her Old English. "I think he knows a lot more about it than you realize. He's a star student in class. You should listen to him go. When we were studying, he seemed to know just about everything about your culture."

Wulf's features softened, turning him into the gentler man she'd seen in her dreams. "So he does listen."

"Yes, he does." Cassandra started for her room. "Well, it's getting late and it's been a really long night. I was going to go to sleep."

Wulf took her hand and pulled her to a stop. "I came to get you."

"Why?"

He stared at her intently. "Since you're now pregnant with my baby, I don't want you to sleep up here where I can't get to you, should you need protection. I know I told you you could come and go in the daylight, but I'd rather you didn't. The Daimons have human helpers just as we do. It would be too easy for one of them to get to you."

Her first reaction was to tell him to stuff it, but something in her refrained. "Are you ordering me?"

"No," he said quietly. "I'm asking you. For your safety and for the baby's."

She smiled at that and at the edge in his voice that told her he wasn't accustomed to asking anyone for anything. She'd heard him bark enough orders at Chris to know Wulf and free will weren't exactly synonymous.

"Okay," she said, giving him a small smile, "but only because you asked me."

His features relaxed. Good grief, the man was gorgeous when he looked like that. "Is there anything you need from your apartment? I can send someone after it."

"Clothes would be nice. Makeup and a toothbrush even more so."

He pulled his phone out and dialed it. Cassandra listened to him introduce himself to his security men as she opened the door and he followed her inside her room. Kat, who was sitting in a chair reading, looked up without comment.

"Hang on." He handed the phone to her. "Here, tell them what you need and where you live."

"Why?"

"Because if I tell them, they'll forget within five minutes what I said and won't leave the premises. I always have to have someone, usually Ash, Chris, or my friend

Talon, tell them what I need done, or I e-mail them. And right now e-mail or text-messaging would take too long."

Was he serious?

"I can go with them," Kat offered as she set her book aside. "I actually know what she uses and I want to grab a few things of my own."

Wulf relayed the message to his guards and then had Cassandra repeat every word of it.

Once she finished talking to the guard, she hung up the phone. Lord have mercy, and she had thought her life was screwed up. "So are you telling me that humans can't even remember a conversation with you?"

"No, never."

"Then how do you keep Chris under wraps? Can't he just tell them you said it was okay for him to leave?"

Wulf laughed. "Because any order concerning his safety has to be cleared through Ash first and Chris knows it. The security guards would never move without direct orders from Ash."

Wow, the man was strict.

Kat gave Cassandra a gentle smile as Cassandra picked up the clothes Wulf had given her from the dresser. "I'm glad you handled this so well this time. And Wulf too. It makes things a lot easier."

Cassandra nodded. It did indeed.

If only Wulf could accept her heritage as easily as he had the baby. But then what good would it do when she was destined to die?

Perhaps this was the best way for it to work out. This way he wouldn't mourn her.

No, the voice in her head said. She wanted more than that from Wulf. She wanted what they had shared in her dreams.

Stop being selfish.

Cassandra swallowed at the thought. She was right. It would be kinder to stay away from Wulf. The last thing she wanted was to know he would grieve for her.

The fewer people mourning her, the better. She hated the thought of people hurting for her the way she hurt for her mother and sisters. There wasn't a day that went by where they weren't in her thoughts. Where a part of her didn't ache that she could never see them again.

Once she had the T-shirt and sweatpants in her arms Wulf walked with her back through his house. His powerful presence touched something deep inside her. She'd never imagined feeling like this.

"You know, you have quite a place here," she said.

He looked around as if he hadn't noticed it in a while. "Thanks. It was built at the turn of the century by Chris's great-great-grandmother. She had fifteen boys and wanted enough room to raise them and their children." There was a tender note in his voice whenever he talked about his family. It was obvious he had loved every one of them deeply.

"So what happened to them that Chris is the only one left?"

Sadness darkened his eyes and it made her heart ache for his grief. "The eldest son went down with several of his cousins and uncle as passengers on the *Titanic*. The influenza plague of 1918 killed three more and made two more sterile. The war took four more. Two died as children and one died in a hunting accident as a young man. The other two, Stephen and Craig, married. Stephen had one son and two daughters. The son died in World War II and one daughter of illness at age ten, the other in childbirth before the baby could be born."

Cassandra winced at his words and at the pain she heard in his voice. It was so obvious he had loved each of them dearly.

"Craig had four sons. One died in World War II, one as an infant, one in a car accident with his wife, and the other was Chris's grandfather."

"I'm sorry," she said, touching his arm in sympathy. No wonder he guarded Chris so zealously. "I'm amazed you let so many go to war."

He covered her hand with his. The look in his eyes told her how much he appreciated her touch. "Believe me, I tried to stop them. But there's only so much you can do to keep a stubborn man home. I finally understand how my father felt when Erik and I left home against his wishes."

"But you don't understand why your mother refused to welcome you home."

He paused mid-step at that. "How did you know that?"

"I . . ." She paused as she realized what she had just done. "I'm sorry. Every now and again I can read passing thoughts. I don't mean to and I have no control over it, it just happens."

His eyes were stormy again.

"You know." She tried again, hoping to comfort him a little. "Sometimes people say and do things in the heat of anger that they later regret. I'm sure your mother forgave you."

"No," he said, his voice low and deep. "I had forsaken the very things she had raised me to believe in. I doubt she ever got over it."

Cassandra pulled at the silver chain around his neck until she held his necklace in her hand. Just as in the dream, it held Thor's hammer and a small crucifix. "I don't think you have forsaken everything. Why else do you wear this?"

Wulf looked at her fingers that cradled his mother's cross and his uncle's talisman. Ancient relics he had worn for so long that he barely remembered their presence.

They were the past and she was his future. The dichotomy reached deep inside him. "It's to remind me that words spoken in anger can never be recalled."

"And yet you speak so often in anger."

He snorted. "Some faults can't be broken."

"Perhaps." She rose up on her tiptoes and kissed him, intending it as a friendly gesture.

Wulf growled at the taste of her as he pulled her close and held her tightly against his chest so that he could feel every inch of her feminine body.

How he wanted her. Wanted to tear her clothes off her and sate the burning ache in his loins that he felt every time she looked at him. It felt so good to have a woman who knew him.

One who remembered his name and whatever he told her.

It was priceless to him.

Cassandra moaned deep in her throat at the sensation of his lips on hers. At his fangs gently grazing her lips, his tongue spiking against hers.

She felt his muscles flexing under her hand, felt the coiled steel of a body that was finely honed and ruggedly dangerous.

He was so overwhelming. So fierce and yet strangely tender. A part of her didn't want to ever let go of him.

A part of her demanded that she do so.

Aching at the thought of it, she deepened their kiss, then pulled away reluctantly.

Wulf wanted nothing more than to pull her into his arms again. He stared at her as his heart raced, his body burned. Why hadn't he found her as a human man?

What would it have mattered? She would still be an Apollite and he another species.

Theirs was an impossible relationship and yet they were joined together by a conniving goddess. He was captivated by Cassandra's spirit and passion. Her voice, her scent. Everything about her spoke to him.

Their relationship was damned from the beginning.

She's going to die.

The words sliced through him. He'd been alone for so long, his heart bruised and bloodied by loss. And she was going to be another scar there. He knew it. He could feel it.

Wulf only hoped that this one would heal, but something told him it wouldn't. Her presence would linger within him just as the rest had.

Her face would haunt him . . .

Forever.

In that moment, he hated Artemis for her interference. Hated her for forcing him into this life and for giving him a woman he had no choice except to lose.

It wasn't right.

And for what? Because Apollo had become angry and cursed his own people?

"Bloodlines are so fragile." He didn't realize he'd spoken out loud until Cassandra nodded.

"It explains why you protect Chris the way you do."

She had no idea.

He led her down the steps that descended into his rooms. "I have to admit that I'm surprised Apollo hasn't taken better care of his own. Especially considering how important it is."

"Like you, we started out as many and quickly dwindled down to me. Of course it didn't help any that we've been hunted to extinction."

Wulf paused outside his locked door, which had a keypad on the wall next to it.

"Paranoid?" Cassandra asked.

He smiled slightly in wry amusement as he entered the code. "We have a lot of servants who work here during the daylight and they know nothing of me since they can't remember my existence. This way, they don't stumble into my room and scream out that they have an intruder while Chris is at school."

That made perfect sense to her. "What's it like to be so anonymous?"

He opened the door and turned on a dim overhead light. "It's like being invisible sometimes. What's so strange to me is being able to see you and Kat again and not have to reintroduce myself to you."

"But Acheron and Talon remember you too."

"True. Dark-Hunters and Katagaria Were-Hunters can remember me, but I can't be in the physical presence of other Dark-Hunters for long and the Were-Hunters get nervous and cranky whenever I come near them. They don't like the idea of someone being around them who isn't one of their own."

Cassandra looked about as he moved toward his bed. The room was huge. There was a computer station against one wall that reminded her of NASA, right down to the silver Alienware computer on the black contemporary desk.

But what startled her was the large black bed in the far right corner. It was exactly as it had been in her dream. The walls around them were a black marble so shiny that it reflected, but unlike her dreams, Wulf cast no reflection in them now. Nor were there any windows.

On the wall to her left were more portraits and a long, mahogany buffet stood below them. The top of the buffet was littered with hundreds of silver picture frames. A black leather sofa and recliner like the ones upstairs were set before it along with a big-screen TV.

Looking at the myriad of faces from the past, she thought of the woman upstairs in the portrait outside of what was now Kat's room. Wulf had known a lot about her and it made her wonder how much he knew about every face on that wall and buffet. Faces of people who most likely had had little knowledge of him. "Did you have to reintroduce yourself constantly to Isabella?"

He closed and locked the door behind him. "With her it was a little easier. Since she was from a Squire's family, she understood that I was the cursed Dark-Hunter so whenever she met me, she would smile and say, 'You must be Wulf. Nice meeting you again.' "

"So all their spouses know about you?"

"No, just the ones who are from the Squire families. You can't exactly explain to the average human that there's an immortal Viking living in the basement who they won't remember seeing or speaking to. So the ones like Chris's mother never know I exist."

She watched as he sat down and pulled off his boots. The man had exceptionally large feet . . .

"Chris's mother isn't a Squire?" she asked, trying to distract herself from the fact that those bare feet made her long to see more bare parts of him.

"No. His father met her while she was working at a local diner. He was so in love with her that I didn't interfere."

"Why did they only have Chris?"

He sighed as he placed his boots under his desk. "She couldn't carry children very easily. She had three miscarriages before his birth. Even Chris was born seven weeks premature. Once he was born, I told his father that I didn't want either of them to go through another pregnancy."

She was surprised by that, given how important his lineage was to him. "Did you really?"

He nodded. "How could I ask them to keep doing that? It almost killed her to give birth and the miscarriages always broke her heart."

It was an admirable thing he'd done. She was glad to know he wasn't truly the barbarian she had feared him to be earlier. "You're a good man, Wulf. Most people wouldn't have thought of someone else."

He snorted. "Chris would disagree with you."

"I think Chris would disagree with a signpost."

She was rewarded with a real laugh from him. It was deep and pleasing, and sent a raw shiver through her. She really loved the sound of his accented voice.

Oh, don't go there . . .

She had to do something to keep her thoughts off how delectable he was.

"Well," she said, yawning, "I'm tired, barely pregnant, and really could use a good night's sleep." She indicated the closed door behind her. "Bathroom?"

He nodded.

"Okay. I'm going to change and then go to sleep."

"There's a new toothbrush in the medicine cabinet."

"Thanks."

Cassandra left him to get ready for bed. Alone in the bathroom, she opened the cabinet and paused. Inside were all manner of medical supplies, including a scalpel and sutures. Wulf must not be able to go to a doctor any more than she could.

As she reached for the new toothbrush, she remembered the shots the Daimons had fired into him.

Her gaze went back to the supplies.

He must have had to tend his own injuries. Alone. He hadn't even said a word about them. Nor had they existed in her dreams.

Then she thought of the way Stryker had healed when she stabbed him and wondered if Wulf's body had the same regenerating ability.

"Poor Wulf," she breathed as she changed her clothes.

It was so strange to be here. With him in his domain. Not once had she spent the night with a man. The few guys she'd slept with had been momentary flings and she had left their places as soon as she could. There was no need to stay and have them become attached to each other.

But she was attached to Wulf. A lot more than she should be. Or was she? He was the father of her baby. Shouldn't they have some degree of closeness?

It only seemed right.

She left the bathroom to find him sitting fully clothed, except for his bare feet, in the recliner in the sitting area.

"You can take the bed," he said. "I'll take the sofa."

"You don't have to, you know. It's not like you can make me pregnant or anything."

He didn't look amused by her words.

Cassandra closed the distance between them and took him by the hand. "C'mon, Big Guy. There's no need for you to wedge that extremely tall body into a small couch when you have a perfectly good bed waiting for you."

"I've never gone to bed with a woman before."

She arched a brow at that.

"To sleep," he clarified. "I've never spent the night with one."

"Never?"

He shook his head.

Boy, they were a lot more alike than she would ever have imagined. "Well, you're never too old for new experiences. Well, maybe *you* are, but in most cases that's a true statement."

His scowl deepened to that familiar level. "Is everything a joke to you?"

"No," she said honestly as she led him toward the bed. "But humor is how I get through the horrors of my life. I mean, come on. It's laugh or cry and crying just takes too much energy that I need to make it through the day, you know?"

She let go of him to braid her hair.

Wulf took her hands in his and stopped her from plaiting it. "I don't like for you to do that."

She swallowed at the hungry look in his midnight eyes. She had an odd sense of déjà vu here in his room with that look on his face. Even though she shouldn't, she liked to see the fire in his dark gaze. Liked the sensation of his hands on hers.

Or better yet, the sensation of his hands on her body . . .

Wulf knew he had no business being with her, no business sharing a bed or anything else, and yet he couldn't keep himself from it.

He wanted to touch her skin for real this time. Wanted to have her legs wrapped around him as he let the heat of her body soothe his weary heart.

Don't.

The command was so strong that he almost heeded it, but Wulf Tryggvason had never been the kind of man to listen to orders.

Not even his own.

He tilted her head up so that he could see the passionate heat in her green eyes. It scorched him. Her lips were parted, welcoming.

He skimmed his fingers down the line of her jaw until he buried them in her strawberry-blond hair. Then he took possession of her mouth. She tasted of warmth.

She pulled him close, her arms tight and demanding as she ran her hands over his back. His body stirred, his cock hardened immediately.

Groaning, he picked her up in his arms. To his surprise, she lifted her legs and wrapped them around his waist.

He laughed at her response even as the heat of her body stung him. Her core was pressed against his groin, making him well aware of how close that part of her was to him.

Her eyes dark with passion, she tugged his shirt off over his head.

"Hungry, *villkat*?" he mumbled against her lips.

"Yes," she breathed to his delight.

Wulf laid her on his bed. She reached down between their bodies and unzipped his pants. He growled deep in his throat the instant her eager hand reached down and touched him. The sensation of her fingers stroking his shaft shook every part of him. She even remembered how he liked to be touched. Stroked.

He almost felt like weeping from the miracle of that. Maybe he should have taken an Apollite or Were lover centuries ago.

No, he thought as he buried his lips against the column of her throat and inhaled her rose scent. They wouldn't have been Cassandra, and without being her, they, too, would be lacking what he needed.

There was something about this woman that filled him. That made him burn in a way no other ever had.

Only for her would he breach the code that forbade

him to take an Apollite to his bed.

Cassandra lifted her arms as Wulf pulled the T-shirt over her head. She moaned at how good the heat of his naked body felt pressed against hers. All that gloriously male skin was a divine feast for her eyes.

He ran the back of his fingers over her breasts, making them tight and aching. He took the right one into his mouth and savored her in a way that made her heart pound. His tongue was light and gentle as he flicked it back and forth. Her stomach fluttered in response to the intense pleasure he gave her.

Then, he trailed his kisses lower, over her abdomen. He stopped to nibble her hipbone while his hands slid the sweatpants down.

Cassandra lifted her hips so that he could slide them off. He dropped them on the floor, then used his hands to spread her legs wide.

She stared at him in needful expectation as he looked at the most private part of her body. He looked feral and hungry. Possessive. And it sent an electrical surge through her.

She hissed as he ran his fingers down her cleft. His touch teased and excited her. His touch was divine. Sating and inciting.

Wulf watched the pleasure on her face as she rubbed herself against his hand. He loved the way she responded to him. The way she was completely open and unguarded.

Climbing up on the bed, he laid his body over hers, then rolled over with her. She wrapped her body around his as they kissed hungrily. Her skin slid against his in a sensuous symphony that ignited him even more. Wulf sat up with her in his lap. She wrapped her long legs around his waist while her hands caressed his scalp, her fingers tangling in his hair.

He was honestly afraid of what he felt as she lifted

herself up and took him into her body. She rode him hungrily, her body milking his as she took what she needed and gave him what he craved.

He didn't want to let her go. Didn't want to ever leave this bed again.

Cassandra bit her lip at the ecstasy of having Wulf deep inside her for real. He was so hard and thick. He felt even better in the flesh than he had in her dreams.

The light hairs on his chest teased her sensitive breasts while he cupped her bottom and urged her movements. She stared at his eyes, which were dark with passion.

Their breathing was synchronized as she slammed her hips against his groin over and over again.

She'd never made love to a man like this. In his lap, their bodies wrapped together. It was the most intimate thing she'd ever experienced.

She leaned her head back as Wulf suckled her. Cradling his head, she felt overwhelmed by pleasure.

And when she came, she cried out loud.

Wulf lifted his head to watch her face as she orgasmed. She was so beautiful to him. He laid her back on the bed without leaving her body, then took control. Closing his eyes, he thought about nothing except the feel of her warm and wet underneath him.

There was no past, no tomorrow. No Dark-Hunter. No Apollites.

It was just the two of them. Her hands on his back, her legs entwined with his, as he thrust himself deep inside her.

Needing this more than he had ever needed anything else, he buried his face in her hair and released himself deep inside her.

Cassandra held Wulf tight as she felt him convulse. His breath tickled her neck. His body was damp from perspiration and his long black hair teased her skin. Neither of them moved as they breathed raggedly in the afterglow.

She took comfort in his weight pressing down on her. The feeling of his rough, masculine body prickling hers. She ran her hands over his muscular back, over his scars, then she idly traced the tattoo on his shoulder.

He lifted himself up so that he could look into her eyes. "I think I'm addicted to you."

She smiled at his declaration even though it made part of her sad to hear it. His hair fell around his face, which was soft and tender in the dim light. Tucking his hair behind his ears, she kissed him.

His arms tightened around her. She loved that feeling. It made her feel protected. Safe.

Sighing dreamily, she pulled back. "I need to go clean up."

He didn't release her. "I don't want you to."

She cocked her head at him in confusion.

"I like the sight of my seed on you, Cassandra," he said raggedly in her ear. "My scent on your skin. Yours on mine. Most of all, I like knowing that in the morning you'll remember what we did tonight and you'll still know my name."

She laid her hand on his whiskered cheek. The pain in his eyes touched her deeply. She kissed him lightly, then snuggled against him.

He withdrew only enough so that he could spoon himself behind her. She rested her head on his biceps as he cradled her tenderly. Her heart pounding with joy, she listened to him breathe.

He lifted his head, kissed her cheek, then settled down with one hand buried in her hair.

Within a few minutes, he was sound asleep. It was the most peaceful moment of her life. Deep in her heart she knew that tonight Wulf had shown her a side of himself that he had let no one else see.

He was gruff and stern. But in her arms, he was a tender lover. And in the back of her mind was the thought that she could learn to love a man like this. It wouldn't be hard.

Cassandra lay quietly in the stillness of the early morning. She wasn't sure what time it was, only that Wulf warmed a part of her she hadn't realized was cold until now.

She wondered as she lay there how many centuries Wulf had been confined to an area like this one. He had told her that this house was only a little over a hundred years old.

Looking around, she tried to imagine what it would be like to be here alone, day after day, decade after decade.

It must be lonely for him.

She reached down and placed her hand on her belly as she tried to imagine the baby there. Would it be a boy or girl? Fair in color like her or dark like its father?

She would most likely never know the baby's real hair color. Most children's baby hair fell out and it wasn't until they were toddlers that you could tell.

By then she would be dead. Dead before its first tooth. Its first step or word.

She would never know her child at all.

Don't cry . . .

But she couldn't help it.

"Cassandra?"

She didn't answer Wulf's sleepy call. Her voice would betray her if she did.

He rolled her over as if he knew she was crying and pulled her into his arms. "Don't cry."

"I don't want to die, Wulf," she sobbed against his

chest. "I don't want to leave my baby. There's so much I need to tell him. He won't even know that I ever existed."

Wulf tightened his grip on her as he heard those heartfelt words.

How he wished he could tell her how foolish her fears were, but they weren't. She cried over a fate neither of them could change.

"We have time, Cassandra. Tell me all your stories about you, your mother, and your sisters, and I'll make sure the baby knows every one of them. And every baby after this one. I won't let them forget you. Ever."

"Promise?"

"I swear to you, just as I swear I'll keep them safe forever."

His words seemed to calm her. Rocking her gently in his arms, Wulf wondered which of them had it worse. The mother who wouldn't live to see the baby grow, or the father who was damned to watch the baby and all those after him die.

Chapter 9

For three solid weeks, Wulf kept Chris and Cassandra under house arrest. But as time went by and no Daimons showed, he began to wonder if maybe he wasn't overreacting a bit.

Thor knew Chris accused him of it at least five times an hour.

Cassandra had withdrawn from school entirely even though she hated to. She was only about three weeks along, but looked more like three months. Her stomach was rounding out, letting them all know that there really was a child inside her.

It was the most beautiful thing Wulf had seen, even as he struggled to keep himself emotionally distant from her.

But it was hard. Especially as they spent so much of their time together taping her for their baby. Most of the time, she was perfectly calm as she told the baby about her past, her mother and sisters. Her father. With every fond memory she shared with the baby, he felt himself growing closer to her.

"See, this," she said, as she showed her hand with the signet ring on it to the small camcorder he held. Wulf focused the lens on it. "My mother told me that this was the actual wedding ring the Atlantean kings used when they married."

Cassandra looked at it sadly. "I'm not sure how it survived all these centuries. My mother gave it to my father so that he could give it to me. I'll make sure your father has it to give to you too."

Whenever she talked about the baby's future without her, it killed a part of him. The injustice of it tore his heart into pieces.

The pain in her eyes, the regret.

And whenever she cried, it hurt him even more. He would soothe her as best he could, but in the end they both knew what the outcome of all this would be.

There was no way to stop it.

Her father came often during the daylight hours to meet with her. Cassandra didn't have her father meet Wulf since her father wouldn't remember him anyway.

For that he was truly grateful.

Instead, Cassandra introduced her father to Chris and they made plans for the two of them to stay in touch after the baby came.

Acheron had called on Mardi Gras night and put Wulf on an immediate leave from his Dark-Hunter duties to watch over Cassandra and protect the baby. Two more Dark-Hunters had been transferred to St. Paul to take over Wulf's usual patrols and to help keep watch should Stryker or the others come after them.

Ash had also given him the name of an Apollite Dark-Hunter named Spawn who might be able to help them with what Cassandra needed for her pregnancy. Wulf had called every night to leave a message at Spawn's house, but Spawn had yet to respond.

Nor had he been able to reach Acheron again.

His phone rang.

Cassandra watched as Wulf pulled his phone out of his pocket and answered it. She knew he was worried and not just about her and Chris. His best friend, Talon, had vanished and none of the Dark-Hunters had had any contact with him in weeks.

Even more concerning, Acheron had also gone MIA. Wulf kept telling her it was a bad omen, even though Kat told them not to worry about it. Apparently Acheron was rather famous for having times when no one could reach him.

Kat had assured them that Artemis would never allow anyone to hurt Acheron. If he had been harmed, they would all know it.

Cassandra sat on the floor with Chris and Kat, playing Life. They had tried to play Trivial Pursuit earlier only to learn that a Dark-Hunter and an immortal handmaiden to a goddess had a decidedly unfair advantage over Cassandra and Chris.

In Life, the only thing that mattered was luck.

"Well, I'll be damned," Wulf said a few minutes later after he hung up the phone and rejoined the game.

"Something happen?" Cassandra asked as she moved her piece.

"Talon got his soul back."

"No friggin' way," Chris blurted out, sitting back on the floor in shock. "How'd he do that?"

Wulf's face was impassive, but Cassandra had grown to know him well enough to see the tenseness of his features. He was happy for his friend, but she could tell he was also a bit envious. Not that she blamed him.

"He met an artist and they fell in love," Wulf said as he sat back down beside her and adjusted his play money. "On Mardi Gras, she got his soul back and freed him."

Chris made a disgusted noise at Wulf's announcement. "Oh man, that sucks. Now he's going to have to join Kyrian on the geriatric patrol."

"Chris!" Cassandra gasped with an inappropriate laugh. "That's a horrible thing to say."

"Yeah but it's true. I can't imagine trading immortality for a woman. No offense, ladies, but something ain't right with that."

Wulf kept his attention on the game board. "Talon didn't trade his immortality. Unlike Kyrian, he got to keep his."

"Oh," Chris said. "That's cool then. Good for him. Man, must be nice to have your cake and eat it, huh?"

Chris's face flushed as he looked back and forth between them and realized what he'd just said. "I mean—"

"It's okay, Chris," Wulf said charitably. But his eyes betrayed the hurt he felt.

Kat took her turn.

Cassandra reached over and laced her fingers with Wulf's. "I didn't know Dark-Hunters could go free."

"It's rare," Wulf said, tightening his grip on her hand. "At least it was up until this last year. Talon and Kyrian make two we know."

"Three," Kat added as she moved her piece on the board.

"Three?" Wulf asked. He looked shocked.

Kat nodded. "Three Dark-Hunters have been freed. I heard the other handmaidens talking about it last night when I went to check in with Artemis."

"I thought you didn't get a chance to talk to her," Cassandra said, remembering what Kat had told them after her return last night.

"Oh, I didn't. She has the big Do Not Disturb sign on her temple door. There are definite times when no one but

Apollo dares to barge into her domain. But I did hear the other *koris* gossiping about it. Apparently, Artemis wasn't real happy over the matter."

"Hmm . . ." Cassandra said as she thought about that.

"Who else was freed?" Wulf asked.

"Zarek of Moesia."

Wulf's jaw went slack as Chris looked at Kat as if she'd sprouted a new head.

Chris snorted. "Now I know you're full of it, Kat. Zarek is marked for death. There's no way."

Kat looked over at him. "Yeah, well, he didn't die and ended up going free instead. Artemis has threatened everyone's head if she loses another Hunter."

Those words weren't comforting to Cassandra. She could only imagine how much less so they were for Wulf.

"I never thought I'd see the day when they would set Zarek free," Wulf said under his breath. "He's so psychotic they've had him under exile for almost as long as I've been a Dark-Hunter."

Cassandra took a deep breath at that. It didn't seem right that someone like this Zarek could be free while Wulf was cursed the way he was.

"I wonder what Nick'll be doing for a Dark-Hunter now that Talon's free," Chris said as he grabbed the canister of Pringles from Kat. "I can't imagine he'd ever serve Valerius."

"No doubt," Wulf said. He explained to Cassandra that Valerius was the grandson of the man who had ruined Kyrian's family and crucified the Greek general. Since Nick was Kyrian's former Squire and a personal friend, Nick would never serve the man whose family had done that to Kyrian.

Wulf, Kat, and Chris continued to discuss the Dark-

Hunters, while Cassandra thought over what she'd learned tonight.

"Could I free you?" Cassandra asked Wulf.

A strange look darkened his eyes. "No. Unlike the other Dark-Hunters, I don't have an out-clause."

"Why?"

Wulf let out a tired breath as he spun the wheel for his turn. "I was tricked into serving Artemis. Everyone else volunteered."

"Tricked how?"

"That was *you*?" Kat interrupted before Wulf could answer her question.

Cassandra turned toward Kat. "You know about it?"

"Well, yeah, there was a big brouhaha at the time it happened. Artemis is still steamed that Morginne beat her out. The goddess doesn't like anyone getting the better of her and most especially not when it's a mortal she owns."

"How did she do it?" Cassandra asked.

Kat took the Pringles back from Chris before he could polish them off. That boy liked to eat. They had yet to figure out how he managed to stay so skinny eating the way he did.

Grousing, he got up and headed to the kitchen, no doubt to get more snacks.

Kat set the canister down by her leg. "Morginne made a pact with the Norse god Loki. He used a thistle from the Norns that is said to be able to let someone swap places with someone else for a day."

Wulf frowned at her words. "Then how did they make it last?"

"Loki's blood. The Norse gods have some weird rules and he wanted Morginne for himself, so he swapped her soul for yours in order to keep her. Artemis didn't feel like going to war with him to get Morginne back. She figured you would be a better Hunter anyway."

Wulf's eyes narrowed.

Kat gave him a sympathetic pat on the arm. "If it makes you feel any better, he's still torturing Morginne for it and with him she has no out-clause either. Even if she did, Artemis would kill her. The only reason she hasn't is because Loki still protects her."

"It doesn't make me feel any better."

"No. I guess it wouldn't."

Stryker paced the floor of the dimly lit banquet hall, wanting blood. For three weeks now they hadn't been able to find a trace of Wulf or Cassandra.

They couldn't even get to her father to help draw her out.

Damn it all.

He had his son Urian working on it now, but it seemed useless.

"How hard can it be to find where a Dark-Hunter lives?"

"They are crafty, *kyrios,*" Zolan said, using the respectful Atlantean term for "lord."

Zolan was his third in command and one of Stryker's most trusted soldiers. He'd been promoted through the Spathi ranks for his ability to murder ruthlessly and show no mercy to anyone. He'd reached the coveted "general" status more than ten thousand years ago.

Like Stryker, he chose to dye his hair black and wore the Spathi symbol of a yellow sun with a dragon in its center—the emblem of the Destroyer.

"If they weren't," Zolan continued, "we'd be able to track and kill them through our servants while they slept."

Stryker turned on Zolan with a glare so malevolent that the Daimon shrank away from him. Only his son held enough courage to not flinch from his anger. Urian's bravery knew no equal.

The demon Xedrix appeared before him in the hall. Unlike the Daimons, Xedrix didn't bow or acknowledge Stryker's elevated stature in their world. Most of the time, Xedrix treated him as more of a servant than a master. It was something that angered Stryker even more.

No doubt the demon thought his place in the Destroyer's esteem was enough to protect him, but Stryker knew the truth. His mother loved him absolutely.

"Her Benevolent Grace wishes a word with you," the demon said in a low, even tone.

Benevolent Grace. Every time Stryker heard that title, he wanted to laugh, but knew better. His mother didn't really have a sense of humor.

He pushed himself up from his throne and willed himself into her private chambers.

His mother stood over a pool where water flowed backward up a glittering pipe from this world into the human realm. There was a fine rainbow mist and vapors around the water. It was here the goddess could scry so that she knew what was happening on earth.

"She is pregnant," the goddess announced without turning around.

Stryker knew the "she" that the goddess referred to was Cassandra.

"How can that be?"

The goddess lifted her hands and drew a circle in the air. Water from the pool formed like a crystal ball. Even though nothing but air held it, it swirled about until it held an image of the woman they both wanted dead. There was nothing in the ball to give him any indication of how to find Cassandra.

Apollymi dragged one fingernail through the image, causing it to shake and distort. "Artemis is interfering with us."

"There is still time to kill both mother and child."

She smiled at that. "Yes, there is." She opened her hands and the water arced from the ball, back into her pool. "Now is the time to strike. The Elekti is being held by Artemis. He can't stop you. He won't even know when you attack."

Stryker flinched at the mention of the Elekti. Like the Abadonna, Stryker was forbidden to attack him.

He hated restrictions.

"We don't know where to attack," he told his mother. "We've been searching—"

"Take one of the ceredons. My pets can find them."

"I thought they were forbidden to leave this realm."

A cruel half-smile curved his mother's lips. "Artemis broke the rules; so shall I. Now go, *m'gios*, and do me proud."

Stryker nodded and turned about sharply. He took three steps before the Destroyer's voice made him pause.

"Remember, Strykerius, kill the heiress before the Elekti returns. You are not to engage him. Ever."

He stopped but didn't look back. "Why have I always been forbidden to touch him?"

"Ours is not to question why. Ours is but to live or to die."

He ground his teeth as she gave him the distorted human quote.

When she spoke again, the coldness in her tone only angered him more. "The answer to that is how much do you value your life, Strykerius? I have kept you close all these centuries and I have no desire to see you dead."

"The Elekti can't kill me. I am a god."

"And greater gods than you have fallen. Many of them to my wrath. Heed my words, boy. Heed them well."

Stryker continued on his way, pausing only long enough to unleash Kyklonas, whose name meant "tornado." Once unleashed, the ceredon was a deadly menace. Much like Stryker.

It was close to midnight when Wulf's phone rang again. Answering it, he heard a gruff Greek accent that he didn't recognize.

"This is Spawn, Viking. You rang a few hundred times while I was gone?"

Wulf ignored the man's aggravated tone. "Where have you been?"

Spawn's response came out as a low growling challenge. "Since when the hell do I answer to you? I don't even know you, hence it's none of your damned business."

Well, someone hadn't taken his personality pills for the night. "Look, I don't personally have a beef with you, Daimon—"

"I'm an Apollite, Viking. *Big* difference."

Yeah, right. "Sorry. Didn't mean to offend."

"To quote you, Viking, *yeah, right.*"

Holy shit!

"And yes, I heard that too."

Wulf tamped down his anger and blanked out his mind. The last thing he wanted was to betray himself to a stranger who could be every bit as lethal as the Daimons after Cassandra. "If you know so much, then you should know why I was calling."

Silence answered him.

After a brief pause, Spawn laughed deep in his throat.

"You can't blank your thoughts from me, Wulf. There's no way to shield yourself from me so long as I have direct contact with you, such as the phone you're holding. But don't worry. I'm not your problem. I'm just surprised Apollo really does have an heiress to protect. Congratulations on the baby."

"Thanks," Wulf said less than sincerely.

"And to answer your question, I don't know."

"Know what?"

"If halflings live past twenty-seven. But then anything is possible. I say in a few months we should pop us some Orville Redenbacher's, then sit back and enjoy the show."

It enraged him that the Apollite would make light of something so tragic. "Shut up, Spawn. I don't find you funny at all."

"More's the pity then. I happen to think I'm quite the comedian."

Wulf wanted nothing more than to tear the Apollite Dark-Hunter apart.

"Then it's a good thing I live in Alaska where you can't reach me, huh?"

"How can you do that?"

"I'm a telepath. I know your thoughts even before you do."

"Then why are you being such an asshole?"

"Because I'm a telepath, not an empath. I couldn't care less how you feel, only what you think. But since I also had a message from Ash telling me to help you two, I suppose I will."

"Mighty big of you," Wulf said sarcastically.

"Yes, it is, especially given how much I detest most of you. But since Cassandra is one of my people, I'll try and play nice. If I were you, I'd go find her an Apollite midwife to help birth your son."

Wulf's heart clenched at his words. "It's a boy?"

"Not quite yet, but he will be when he forms a little more."

Wulf smiled at the thought, though to be honest, a small part of him wished for a daughter. One who could remind him of her mother once Cassandra was gone.

Squelching that thought before it led him somewhere he didn't need to go, he listened to Spawn's list of things Cassandra would require.

"My people are a little different from humans. There are special dietary concerns and environmental changes."

"I know Cassandra needs a transfusion," Wulf said, thinking of how pale she'd looked for the last two days. "She told me earlier she was feeling weak."

"Trust me, she needs more than that."

"Such as?"

Spawn ignored the question. "I'll make a few calls and see if I can find someone who is willing to help you two. If we're lucky, there might even be a colony to take you in. I can't make any promises. Since I'm now batting for the other team, my people have a bad tendency to hate my guts and want to kill me whenever I try to contact them."

"I appreciate it, Spawn."

"Yeah, and I appreciate your lying to me for the sake of politeness when we both know better. The only reason you're tolerating me right now is Cassandra. Good night, Wulf."

The phone went dead.

"I take it that didn't go well."

He looked over his shoulder to see Cassandra standing in the doorway of his room. His thoughts had been focused on Spawn's caustic personality, and he hadn't heard her come in. "About like walking into a bear cave coated in honey."

She smiled at that as she drew near him. "Interesting image."

He thought over what Spawn had said about her needs. She'd been pregnant for almost a month now. Was she okay? "How are you feeling?"

"Very, very tired. I came down to go to bed early."

He gave a halfhearted laugh at that. "Only in our world would midnight be considered early." He pulled her gently into his lap.

She settled across him easily and he realized just how comfortable he'd become with her.

"Yeah, I know," she said as she tucked her head under his chin and leaned against his chest. "The joys of being nocturnal."

She sighed. "When I was a little girl, I used to try and bring sunshine to my mother. I felt so bad that she had never really seen or felt it. So I would try and catch it in jars. When that failed, I captured jars and jars of lightning bugs and told her that if we could catch enough of them, then it would look like the sun. She'd laugh, hug me, and then set them free and tell me that nothing should have to live its life in a cage."

Wulf smiled. He could just imagine her bringing her jars to her mother. "I'm sure it pleased her."

She ran her hand over his forearm, raising chills on his entire body as she idly stroked his skin. "My older sister was like her. She couldn't tolerate the sun at all. If she was in it any more than three minutes, she would burn to a crisp."

"I'm sorry."

The two of them fell silent while Wulf closed his eyes and let her scent of roses permeate him. She was so soft against him. Her curves lush and full from her pregnancy.

All he wanted was to taste her.

"Do you think dying hurts?" she asked, her voice nothing more than a breathless whisper.

Pain lacerated him at the thought. "Baby, why do you do this to yourself?"

"I try not to," she whispered. "I really do, but I can't seem to stop myself from thinking about the fact that in seven months I will never see the sunshine again." She looked up at him with her eyes bright and shining from unshed tears. "Never see you. Kat. This ratty old cellar."

"My rooms are not ratty."

She gave him a bittersweet, winsome smile. "I know. I guess I should count my blessings. At least I have the benefit of knowing when I'll die. This way I can put everything in order."

No, she couldn't, because as he spent more and more time with her, he was drawn closer to her.

These last three weeks had been so incredible. He'd learned to feel almost normal. It was so nice to walk upstairs and not have to introduce himself to her and Kat.

To wake up at dusk and find her lying beside him, knowing him, his touch . . .

Sighing, she pushed herself out of his lap and headed toward the bed.

She took a step and stumbled.

Wulf moved with lightning speed to scoop her up into his arms before she fell. "You okay?"

"Dizzy spell."

She'd been having those for the last week. "Do I need to send for blood?"

"No. I think that one was pregnancy related."

He carried her to the bed and laid her down gently.

Cassandra smiled at the sight of her Viking warrior and his care. Whatever she needed or wanted, he sent someone for it or he went and got it himself.

As he started to pull away, she kissed his lips. His reaction startled her as he kissed her back desperately. He was like a wild animal as he explored every inch of her mouth. His tongue danced with hers, and when she brushed against his fangs, she shivered.

She felt the predator inside him, the barbarian. He tasted of bloodlust and mercy. Growling, he lifted her shirt up so that he could cup her breast in his hand.

Cassandra sighed at his demanding touch. He was normally so tender but tonight his touch was feral. He pulled her pants and panties off together so quickly that she barely felt the denim and silk leave her.

He didn't even bother removing his pants all the way. Instead, he shoved them down just below his hips, enough so that he could enter her.

Cassandra moaned as he filled her with such sweet bliss that she wanted to weep. He was so wild as he thrust himself against her, and she took delight in every deep, penetrating stroke.

Wulf couldn't breathe. He had no business with her. No business letting her inside his defenses when he had no choice except to let her go, but he couldn't help himself.

He needed to feel her in his arms. Needed to feel her body under him.

She sank her nails into his skin as she arched her back and came for him. He waited until she had finished shuddering before he joined her in that blissful place.

He laid himself carefully down over her body so as not to hurt her or the baby. All he wanted was to feel her entwined with him, her bare legs cradling his body.

"Are you all right?" she asked quietly. "It's not like you to be in such a hurry."

Wulf closed his eyes as her words tore through him.

Only Cassandra had ever known him. His habits. His likes and dislikes. And she remembered them. In all these centuries, she was the only lover who had learned those things.

What was he going to do without her?

A knock sounded on the door.

"Hey, Cass?" Chris called. "If you're still up, I ordered a pizza for you since you said you wanted one. It should be here in a few minutes."

She giggled at that as Wulf frowned at her. Their bodies were still joined. "I told him after you came down here that I would kill for one slice of pepperoni pizza," she explained. Raising her voice, she said, "Thanks, Chris. I'll be back up in a few minutes."

Wulf's frown deepened. "If you need to rest . . ."

"Are you kidding? I meant it when I said I'd kill for pizza."

"You should have said something earlier. Chris would have had the cook make you one."

"I know, but by the time I went upstairs, Marie had already started on the chicken and I didn't want to hurt her feelings. She's a really nice lady."

"I know."

She saw the stricken look on Wulf's face.

Marie had been working there for almost eight years and she mistakenly thought Chris was her boss. Marie had given Cassandra the whole story of how Chris's father had hired her and then three years ago, after Chris's father's heart attack in the living room, Chris's mother had moved to a new home across town so that she wouldn't have to relive her husband's death every time she walked through the house.

His mother had tried to get Chris to leave as well, but

for an obvious reason, he'd stayed behind with Wulf. The house had been left in trust to Chris by his father, so Chris's mother couldn't sell it and force him to move.

There was no telling how many times in the last eight years Wulf had met Marie.

"I'm sorry, Wulf."

"Don't be, I'm used to it."

He withdrew from her and dressed, then helped her back into her clothes. But he wouldn't let her walk back up the stairs for fear of her stumbling.

Instead, he carried her to the sofa and made her lie down while he fetched a pillow and blanket for her.

Cassandra smiled at his kindness as he returned and tucked the blanket around her, then snatched the remote from Chris.

"Hey!" Chris snapped indignantly.

"You're not pregnant, Chris." He handed it to Cassandra.

"Fine," Chris said sullenly. "See if I ever have a baby for you."

"Yeah, right. By the time you get around to it, my child will have grandchildren."

Chris was aghast. "Oh, oh, oh, I don't want to hear it from you, hornhead." That was a familiar insult Chris used to nettle Wulf. Cassandra hadn't understood it until Chris explained that it stemmed from the mistaken belief that Vikings wore horned helmets in the Middle Ages.

"That's it," Chris continued, "I'm switching schools to Stanford. I'm tired of all this snow anyway. I might not get laid there either, but at least the women in class won't be dressed in parkas."

Kat entered the room and rolled her eyes. "Is it just me or do these two argue like two little kids every time they get together?"

"They argue like kids," Cassandra said. "I think they're trying to make needling other people an Olympic sport."

Chris opened his mouth at the same time the door buzzed. "Pizza," he said, getting up.

A strange tremor went through Cassandra. Rubbing the back of her neck, she looked around.

"You okay?" Kat asked.

"I think so." She just felt . . . odd . . .

She leaned her head back against the sofa to see Chris with the pizza in his hand and the delivery guy outside. Chris paid him.

"Hey," the guy said as Chris pulled back. "Do you mind if I come in for a sec and use the phone? I need to call the store about the next delivery."

Chris cocked his head. "How about I bring you a cell phone for the porch?"

"C'mon, man, it's cold out here. Can't I come in to make a call?"

Wulf was on his feet, quickly heading for the door, as Chris pulled back even more.

"Sorry, dude," Chris said more sternly. "No one unknown comes into this house, *capische*?"

"Chris," Wulf snapped, his voice low and steely. "Get back."

For once Chris didn't argue.

Wulf grabbed a sword from the wall at the same time the Daimon on the porch pulled two huge daggers out from the insulated pizza bag.

The Daimon tossed one dagger at Chris, then turned to engage Wulf. Chris staggered back, his face pale as he fell to the floor.

Cassandra was on her feet headed for Chris when Kat caught her. "Think of the baby. Stay put."

She nodded as Kat jumped the couch to go help Chris.

Cassandra grabbed another sword off the wall, ready for battle, just in case.

Luckily, Chris was back on his feet unharmed by the time Kat reached him. The pizza, on the other hand, was DOA. Thank God the box had deflected the dagger.

Wulf and the Daimon continued to fight on the porch.

"Holy shit," Chris breathed, running toward Cassandra with Kat behind him. "There are a shitload more of them headed for the house."

"What?" Cassandra asked, her knees going weak with the thought of it.

Wulf killed the one on the porch and slammed the door shut.

"Dammit to hell, Chris, are you all right?"

Chris nodded.

Wulf crossed the room and inspected him anyway, then pulled him into his arms and held him fiercely.

"Hey, get off me, you homo." Chris bristled. "You're grossing me out. If you want to hug something, hug Cassandra."

She saw Wulf clench his teeth an instant before he mostly let go. He kept one hand fiercely locked on Chris's shoulder as he lowered himself to look the boy eye to eye. "You *ever* answer that door again, Christopher Lars Eriksson, and I'll rip your fool head off." He shoved Chris toward the hallway. "Go lower the shields."

"What is this, the *Enterprise*?" Kat asked as Chris sprinted to do Wulf's bidding.

"No, we have bulletproof metal security shutters. I don't know what the Daimons are up to, but I don't want them to be able to toss a Molotov cocktail or anything else through a window."

"Good thinking," Kat breathed.

The whole house shook as Chris lowered the steel shutters.

Wulf was quaking in anger as he called security to check on them.

"Hello?" The voice was not only unfamiliar, but heavily accented. Granted, the guards never remembered him, but Wulf knew each member of the security force that the Council had sent to protect Chris.

Wulf had a bad feeling. "Who is this?"

"Who do you think it is, Dark-Hunter? My compliments to whomever sent out for pizza. We enjoyed the midnight snack."

Wulf tightened his grip on the phone. "Where are my guards?"

"Oh, one is right here, but he's not feeling very talkative. Death has a way of making even the chattiest of people rather quiet. As for the other . . . he's . . . oh, wait, dead now. My boys just finished him off."

"You are going to pay for that."

"Well, then, why don't you come out here and hand me the bill?"

"I'm on my way." Wulf hung up and headed for the door, intent on skewering Stryker.

Kat caught him before he could reach the door. "What do you think you're doing?" she asked indignantly.

He glared angrily at her. "I'm going to finish this."

She gave him an arch look. "You can't. He'll kill you the minute you leave here."

"Then what do you want me to do?"

"Guard Chris and Cassandra. I'll be right back."

Kat flashed out of the house.

Kat honed into Stryker's energy and found him in the guardhouse. She winced as she saw the two dead men on the floor. There were at least a dozen Daimons outside, opening boxes and preparing for an attack.

Only four Daimons were inside the guardhouse. Stryker, Urian, Icarus, and Trates.

Trates looked up from the monitors and went pale.

"How did you get in here?" Kat demanded.

Stryker turned slowly, methodically, around to face her with a sardonic grin. There was no fear in him, only wry amusement. "The guards came outside when we ate the pizza deliveryman and tried to stop us. We dragged them inside after they were dead."

His words and lack of regard for what they'd done sickened her, but not half as much as when she caught sight of the ceredon with them on one of the monitors.

So Apollymi had changed the rules on her. Damn.

"You are so evil," she said between clenched teeth.

He smiled as if her words complimented him. "Thank you, love, I pride myself on that."

Kat opened the portal back to Kalosis. "It's time for you to all go home."

Stryker looked at the opening, then laughed. " 'Fraid not, sweetie. Mama likes me better at the moment. So you can shove that portal up your very attractive ass. Me and my boys have work to do. Either join us or leave."

For the first time in her life, Kat felt a tremor of fear. "You *have* to go. Those are the rules. The portal opens and you have to walk through it."

Stryker came forward, his eyes sinister and cold. "No, we don't."

The portal closed.

She gasped as realization dawned. The Destroyer had given him a key, too, and placed him in control.

Stryker stood so close to her that it sent a shiver over her. He cupped her face with his hand. "It's a pity she protects you so. Otherwise I would have had a taste of you centuries ago."

She glared at him in fury. "Get your hand off me or lose it."

To her surprise, he obeyed, but not before he kissed her rudely.

Kat shrieked and slapped him.

He laughed. "Go home, little girl. If you stay here, you might get hurt."

Her body shaking, Kat flashed back into the house. Cassandra was in the center of the living room while Wulf was arming himself from a cabinet against the wall.

"What do you have that I can use?" Kat asked, joining him at the armoire.

Wulf looked at her drolly. "I take it things didn't go well."

"No. In fact, we need to batten down the hatches. Things are about to get really ugly."

Chris came running into the room, his head covered by a football helmet.

"What the hell is wrong with you?" Kat asked as she caught sight of him.

Wulf looked over and frowned. "*Now* you wear the helmet?"

"Yes," Chris said as he stuffed a pillow down the front of his sweatpants. "Now I wear the helmet. In case neither of you have been paying attention, our little Daimons are busy on the lawn."

"We know."

"Ah," Chris said as he went to the armoire and pulled out a flak jacket. "So I have one question. I know the shutters can withstand fire and bullets. How are they against a LAWS rocket and dynamite?"

Before Wulf could answer, an explosion rocked the house.

Chapter 10

"Careful," Stryker warned his men as they fired another round at the house. "Not that it's likely, but give them a chance to come out before you blow the house apart."

"Why?" Trates asked. "I thought the objective was to kill the heiress."

Urian gave the man an irritated look that said, "Are you totally stupid?" "Yes, but if we hurt the Abadonna in the process, we're going to find out what it feels like to be turned inside out. Literally. Like most beings, I actually like the fact that my skin is outside my body."

"She's immortal," Trates argued. "What's a bomb to her?"

"Immortal like us, bone-head." Urian snatched the rocket launcher from Trates's hand and handed it to Icarus. "Blow her body apart and she *will* die. None of you want to know what the Destroyer would do to us if that happens."

Icarus aimed more carefully.

Stryker nodded his approval to his son, then projected his thoughts to the rest of his team. "Watch the exits. I know the Dark-Hunter will have a back way out of this place. When they run, you'd better catch them. Stand ready."

• • •

Cassandra frowned as Chris packed another pillow down the front of his sweatpants. "What are you doing?"

"Protecting my assets. After what Kat said about Stryker and that near miss with the pizza knife, I don't want to take a chance with my prized jewels."

"Hallelujah," Wulf said under his breath. "The boy finally developed some brains."

Chris directed a sullen stare at him that Wulf ignored.

Wulf turned the TV on and switched it to the parameter cameras so that they could see the Daimons' positions. Several of them were running across the lawn.

"It looks like that blast took out some of the east wing," Wulf said quietly.

Another blast went into the garage.

Chris let out an excited whoop. "I think they just nailed the Hummer. Yes!"

"Christopher!" Wulf snapped at him.

"I can't help it," Chris said, calming a degree. "I really hate that thing. Besides, I told you it wouldn't protect me from everything. See. It was worthless against the grenades."

Wulf shook his head at his Squire, then noticed Cassandra picking up weapons from the armoire. "What are you doing?" He moved toward her lightning-fast to keep her from touching the weapons.

She let out an irritated breath. "Arming myself."

"Like hell. Your job is—"

"To stay alive," she said, her face determined. She touched him gently on the arm in a light caress that sent chills over his chest. She was so beautiful standing there, ready to take on the world.

"Don't worry, Wulf, I'm not stupid. I'm not going to

engage them and take a chance on one of them kicking me in the stomach. Likewise, I'm not going to just stand here and let them take me without something to fall back on. I'm no more used to being without a weapon than you are."

"She's right about that," Kat said, moving to stand behind Cassandra. "Her teddy bear is a six-inch retractable knife and a snub-nosed .38 Special."

Wulf stared at Cassandra and the raw determination in her eyes. He admired her more in that moment than he ever had anyone else.

Stepping back, he took her to the cabinet and fastened wrist blades on each of her arms. He showed her the release for the blades and how they swung out.

"And this one . . ." He pulled out a small-caliber Beretta Panther. He slid the fully loaded clip into the handle and switched the safety on. "Is just to get their attention."

He placed it in a concealed holster, then fastened it to her hip.

Cassandra's face softened as she looked up at him. For some reason, that look made his entire body hot. "So what's the plan?"

"Run for it."

"Run where?" Chris asked. "If we head to another Dark-Hunter's house, it'll just drain your power and theirs. No offense, but I think these guys are a little stronger than the average Daimon and I don't want to see your butt kicked. At least not tonight while I got things to protect."

Another explosion shattered the glass windows that were covered by the shields.

"We don't have a choice, Chris," Wulf said as he put

more distance between Cassandra and the windows. "They're not going to wait until morning and give us a chance to evacuate in the daylight, and if we don't leave, they'll blow the house apart around us. We'll just have to have an open evacuation plan."

Chris appeared less than convinced. "I really, really don't like this open evacuation plan idea. Anyone got something better?"

They looked at Kat, who stared back bemused. "I'm not of this world. I have no idea where to hide. I say we go with Wulf."

"What about Artemis?" Cassandra asked. "Will she help us?"

Kat shook her head. "Sorry. She's occupied at the moment and honestly couldn't care less if the world did end. If I disturb her over this, she'll have a raging tantrum."

"All right then," Wulf said. "I suggest everyone get their heaviest clothes on and be prepared to jump ship as soon as possible."

Stryker watched the security cameras closely. He knew the heiress and her guards wouldn't stay inside much longer. His men had already blown up the entire garage and were now slowly shooting into the house, section by section. There was a lot of exterior damage, but he couldn't really tell how much was being done internally.

Not that it mattered. If this didn't work, they'd burn it down. He already had the flamethrowers on standby.

Anyone worth his salt would have exit tunnels. And Wulf was certainly worth his salt.

Urian had found several exits so far.

His son just had to make sure they had found them all *before* their prey left the premises.

"Urian?" he asked his son telepathically. "Are you in position?"

"Yes. We have all of the exits covered."

"Where are you?"

"The back lawn. Why? Is something going wrong?"

"No, I just want to make sure we can get to them."

"They're ours, Father. Relax."

"I will *after* she's dead."

Wulf took one last inspection of his charges. They were bundled up and ready. He, on the other hand, was scantily clad. He needed to be able to move freely in case he had to fight more.

"Okay, children," he said in warning. "Remember, we have to move silently. They can see better at night than . . ." He paused as he realized who he was talking to. "Well, better than Chris can anyway. I'll lead the way. Kat, you pull up the rear and, if anything happens, shout and don't vanish on us."

"You got it."

Wulf offered Cassandra an encouraging smile. He took her hand into his and kissed her knit glove, wishing he could feel her skin under there.

She smiled back, then covered her face with her muffler.

Reluctantly dropping her hand, he led them to his bedroom. There were more explosions upstairs.

Wulf growled at the sound of things shattering. "I swear I'm going to take all this out of Stryker's hide."

"I just want to know where the cops are," Cassandra said. "Surely someone has heard all that."

"I don't know," Chris added. "We're pretty far out. No one probably knows."

Another blast shook the house.

"Someone has to hear *that*," Cassandra said. "They've turned it into a war zone."

"Well, let's hope the cops don't come," Kat added from behind her.

Cassandra looked at her from over her shoulder. "Why?"

"Because if they do, all they'll be is another midnight snack for the Daimons."

Cassandra curled her lip at the thought. "Oh, God, Kat, that's awful!"

"But all too true," Wulf said as he led them past his bed, into his closet, which was the size of most people's bedrooms. "In spite of what you think, Cassandra, Daimons are nothing more than rabid animals in need of a mercy killing."

She stiffened, but for once didn't argue with him.

Cassandra cocked a brow at his wardrobe as they walked through the closet. Everything from the hanging items to every pair of shoes lacked color. It looked like a great black hole. "Like black, do you?"

One corner of his mouth quirked up. "It serves its purpose. It's hard to look intimidating in pastels."

She laughed at that and started to make a comment about how he looked best naked, but then refrained. It wasn't like Chris and Kat didn't know they were lovers, but it still didn't feel right to say that out loud around them.

Wulf pressed a series of codes into the keypad and opened a secret door in the back that led into his own private catacombs he had had built under the house and grounds in case of emergency.

Though to be honest, Daimons bombing his home hadn't been one of the things that had entered his mind when he'd had this built.

He'd been thinking more along the lines of a house fire during daylight or maybe a home invasion by more normal, nonfanged terrorists.

Who knew?

Following true medieval fashion, the corridor was long and narrow in order to keep more than one person from going through it at a time and to make it easy to block it should anyone be chasing after them.

Sometimes it paid to be paranoid.

Wulf grabbed a flashlight and led them single file into it.

They walked for several minutes before they came to a five-way split.

"Wow," Chris said as he peeped around Cassandra and Wulf. "Where do all of these go?"

Wulf indicated the one on the far right with the light. "That one goes to the garage, the next one over goes to the field just beyond the south gate, the middle one is for a bomb shelter farther underground. The next one leads to the street outside the main gate and this one"—He indicated the one on his left—"leads to the boathouse."

"Man, I wish I'd known about this when I was a kid, I could have had a ton of fun down here."

"Yeah, and you could have gotten lost or hurt and no one would know."

Chris blew him a raspberry.

Ignoring him, Wulf led them down the long, winding tunnel that ran the length of his property. The boathouse was set off to the side so that, to people who didn't know better, it would look like it wasn't part of his holdings.

That, along with the design of the boathouse, had been intentional.

More than five thousand square feet in size, the boat-house looked like a home from the water, with the first level of it housing his collection of boats. The second floor had four bedrooms, a kitchen, living, dining, and game rooms. Over the years this had served as guest accommodations for Acheron whenever he came to town.

Wulf only hoped Stryker wasn't bright enough to figure out he had an escape route this far down his property.

At the end of the tunnel, there was a steel ladder leading up to a trapdoor that opened in the back of the boat-house inside a storage closet.

Wulf went first, ready for anything. The lock on this door was manual in case of fire. Wulf spun the combination, then waited for the release to sound.

Slowly, he pushed the door open, expecting the worst.

There was no motion in the room or outside it. No sound of someone or something walking about. He listened for several minutes, but all he could hear was the creaking of the ice and the howl of the winds.

All seemed right . . .

Lifting himself through the trapdoor, he reached down to help Cassandra up. She drifted a small distance away in the closet while Chris and then Kat climbed up.

"Okay," Wulf whispered to them. "It looks good so far. I want you," he said to Cassandra, "and Chris to stay back. If anything happens, you two dodge back into the tunnels and press the red button to lock the door behind you."

"What about you and Kat?" Cassandra asked.

"We'll take care of ourselves. You and Chris are the important things."

Cassandra's eyes told him she didn't agree.

"It'll take a couple of minutes to lower the airboat from its harness down to the ice," he explained to her. "Let's hope the Daimons don't hear it."

Cassandra nodded and kissed him lightly. "Be careful."

Wulf hugged her gently, then opened the door. He took a step out, then hesitated as his foot collided with something large and solid on the floor.

No, wait.

It was left-behind clothing. Something that reminded him of Daimon remains.

Wulf pulled his retractable sword from his boot at the same time a slight shadow moved toward him. He prepared to attack.

"It's okay," a feminine voice whispered. "I'm a friend."

Wulf was far from placated.

He heard Cassandra gasp in alarm. Glancing toward her, he saw she was hesitating in the doorway as if unsure of what to do.

"Phoebe?" she breathed. "It is really you?"

Phoebe was the name of one of her sisters who had died with her mother.

The shadow stepped into the light so that they could see her face, which was strikingly similar to Cassandra's. The only difference was their hair. Phoebe's was golden blond and straight and Cassandra had tight strawberry-blond curls. Phoebe wore a black pantsuit and didn't appear to have any weapons on her. "It's me, Cassie. I'm here to help you."

Cassandra stepped back and collided with Chris, who eyed the newcomer suspiciously. Even Kat was tense.

Cassandra gave her sister a disbelieving once-over. "You're supposed to be dead."

"I am dead," Phoebe whispered.

"You're a Daimon," Wulf said accusingly.

Phoebe nodded.

"Oh, Phoebe," Cassandra said, her voice thick with disappointment. "How could you?"

"Don't judge me, little sister. I had my reasons. Now we have to get *you* to safety."

"Like I'm going to trust you," Cassandra said, stiffening. "I remember Uncle Demos."

"I'm not Uncle Demos and I have no intention of turning you into me." Phoebe took a step toward her, but Wulf prevented her from getting any closer to Cassandra until he knew the truth of her intentions.

Phoebe gave him an irritated glare, then looked back at her sister. "Please, Cassie, you have to believe me. I would never, ever harm you. I swear it on Mother's soul."

Another Daimon came through the door. A male. He was tall and blond and Wulf remembered him well from the club. The Daimon had kicked the crap out of him.

This had been the Daimon who referred to Stryker as his father.

Kat gasped.

"Hurry, Phe," the Daimon said to Cassandra's sister. "I can't keep this covered much longer." He paused long enough to meet Wulf's gaze without flinching. The anger and hatred of the two men was tangible enough to make Cassandra shiver. She half-expected one of them to attack the other at any second.

"Why are *you* helping us?" Wulf demanded.

The Daimon curled his lip in repugnance. "Like I give a rat's ass about you, Dark-Hunter. I'm only here to help my wife protect her baby sister. Which I still think is a stupid idea." He looked at Phoebe who looked back at him irritably.

"You'll feel better tomorrow about this," Phoebe said.

The Daimon snorted. "It's a good thing I love you."

Kat gaped. "Urian has a heart? Who knew?"

Urian glared at her. "Shut up, Abadonna."

Cassandra saw the love on Phoebe's face as Urian neared her. "Urian is the one who saved me when Mom died," Phoebe explained. "He pulled me from the car after the bomb exploded and hid me. He tried to save Mom and Nia too, but couldn't get to them in time."

Cassandra didn't know what to think about that. It didn't make sense that a Daimon, let alone one related to Stryker, would help them when all their lives they had been pursued by Urian's kind. "Why?"

"There's no time for this," Urian hissed. "My father isn't a stupid man. He'll catch on quickly when he doesn't hear from the two dead men."

Phoebe nodded, then turned back to Cassandra. "I'm asking you to trust me, Cassie. I swear you won't regret it."

Cassandra exchanged frowns with Wulf and Kat. "I think we can trust her."

Wulf glanced to Urian, then to Kat. "You said they were sadistic. Any chance they're playing with our heads?"

Urian gave a low, bitter laugh at that. "You have no idea."

Phoebe smacked her husband in the stomach. "Behave, Uri. You're not making this any easier."

Scowling at his wife, Urian rubbed his stomach where she'd hit him, but didn't say anything else.

"Go for it," Kat said. "If he's lying, I now know how to hurt him." Her gaze went meaningfully to Phoebe.

Urian went ramrod stiff. "Destroyer or no, you *ever* touch her and I will kill you, Katra."

"Then we understand each other," Wulf said. "Because if anything happens to Cassandra, Kat is the least of your problems."

Urian stepped forward, but Phoebe forced him back. "You said we have to hurry."

Urian's rigid features softened as he looked at Phoebe and nodded. Without another word, he led them toward a black airboat that was already on the ice, waiting for them.

Chris climbed on board first, followed by Kat.

Cassandra followed suit. "Is this the same boat the Canadian Mounties use for search and rescue?" she asked Wulf.

Wulf cleared his throat as if offended. "Same company makes both, but I'd like to think mine is a bit nicer."

And it was too. Plush to the extreme, right down to the padded chairs.

"Yeah," Chris said as he took a seat and strapped himself in. "Dudley Do-Right is us."

Cassandra smiled at him as Wulf took the helm. Her sister jumped in, then paused when she realized her husband had stayed on the dock and wasn't making any moves to join them.

Phoebe's face was even paler. "Come with us, Uri," she begged, reaching up to take his hand into hers. Her voice was filled with strain and worry.

Cassandra stared at their joined hands that showed how much each one wanted to hold on and never let go.

"They'll slaughter you if they find out about this."

The pain on Urian's face as he stared longingly at Phoebe made Cassandra ache for both of them. "I can't, baby, you know I can't. I have to stay and cover your tracks, but I promise I'll be in touch as soon as I'm able."

He kissed Phoebe passionately, then kissed her hand and let her go. "Be safe."

"You too."

He nodded, then removed the last bit of harness rigging. "Take care of my wife, Dark-Hunter."

Wulf glanced at Phoebe and nodded. "Thanks, Daimon."

Urian scoffed. "Bet you never thought you'd utter those words."

Urian raised the doors to the dock at the same time a group of Daimons broke into the boathouse.

Phoebe gasped and started for her husband. Chris pulled her back as Wulf gunned the engine and flew north over the ice. Luckily, the wind was with them and they accelerated quickly.

"No!" Phoebe shrieked as they sped across the lake. "We can't leave him."

"We have no choice," Chris said. "I'm sorry."

Cassandra saw the despair on her sister's face, but Phoebe didn't cry. She merely stared behind them where the boathouse was quickly drifting out of sight, her eyes filled with horror.

Cassandra held on tightly to her seat belt, her heart pounding. "How fast are we going?" she asked Chris.

"Over a hundred at least," he answered. "These things can move as fast as one hundred forty with the wind, but only about forty against it."

Wow. She looked over at her sister, who still hadn't stopped looking behind her even though the boathouse had already faded from sight.

"He'll be okay, Phoebe," Kat said. "His father wouldn't really hurt him. Stryker may be psychotic, but he loves Urian."

Phoebe's face showed every bit of her doubt.

"Keep going north," Phoebe said to Wulf. "We have a safe place where we can hide all of you."

No sooner were the words spoken than Cassandra heard the fierce shriek of something that sounded like it came from Hollywood. It was followed by the distinct sound of wings flapping.

Looking up, she saw the dragon headed for them.

"Oh, my . . ." She couldn't finish the words as horror choked her.

Kat reacted instantly. She threw herself over Cassandra.

The dragon shrieked louder as if frustrated by her actions. Fire blew across the prow of the boat.

Wulf didn't slow down at all. He pulled his gun out and fired up at the dragon.

The dragon dove straight for them, screaming as it came. Cassandra could see when the bullets struck it. The dragon recoiled, but didn't really slow or veer off.

It continued toward them with a single-minded determination.

Closer.

Closer . . .

It swooped in so close she could feel the dragon's hot breath.

Wulf reloaded his clip and fired more rounds.

Just as Cassandra was sure it would devour them, the dragon vanished instantly.

For a full ten seconds, no one moved.

"What happened?" Chris asked.

"He must have been recalled," Kat answered. "It's the only thing that could have stopped him like that."

Wulf finally slowed a degree. "Recalled by whom?"

"The Destroyer," Phoebe said. "She won't let him hurt Kat."

"And just why is that, Kat?" Wulf asked.

Kat appeared uncomfortable with that question. "Like Stryker, I'm one of her servants."

"I thought you served Artemis," Cassandra said.

"I serve them both."

Cassandra tilted her head as she looked at her friend. Someone she had thought she'd known for years, and now she realized she really knew nothing at all about Kat.

"Question," Cassandra said, her heart pounding in fear. "What happens when you have a conflict of interest? Which one of them will you follow then, Kat?"

Chapter 11

Kat glared at her indignantly. "I think the answer to that is quite obvious. I'm here, aren't I?"

"Are you?" Cassandra asked, her anger erupting. "Every time I turn around there seems to be a Daimon on my tail. Now every other day I'm learning a vital fact about you that you have conveniently neglected to tell me in the past . . . oh . . . *five* years. How do I know I can trust anyone at this point?"

Kat looked hurt as she pulled away from Cassandra. "I can't believe you would doubt me."

"Cassie—"

"Don't Cassie me, Phoebe," she said, snapping at her sister. "Why didn't you ever bother to tell me you were alive? You know a postcard wouldn't have killed you. No pun intended."

Phoebe raked an angry glare over her. "Don't you dare take that tone with me! Not after Urian and I have risked everything for you. For all I know, right now, they're back there killing him."

The tremor in her sister's voice brought Cassandra back to her senses and calmed her down. "I'm sorry, Phoebe. Kat. I'm just scared."

Kat helped her to her feet, but instead of going back to

her seat, Cassandra headed to Wulf's chair. He slowed the boat only enough so that she could sit safely in his lap.

At least there she felt sheltered. Secure. She trusted him implicitly.

"You'll be okay, Cassandra," he said against her hair, over the roar of the boat.

She snuggled closer to him and inhaled his warm, masculine scent. Cassandra held tight as he sped them into a future that terrified her.

Dawn was coming. Cassandra could feel it as she rode silently in the custom-built, heavily modified Land Rover next to Wulf. She was immune to the rays, but she knew Wulf and her sister weren't. Chris was asleep in the back seat, sitting between Kat and Phoebe with his head on Kat's shoulder, while Kat looked out the window nervously.

They had left the boat behind well over an hour ago and were now in a multiterrain Land Rover racing for a destination Phoebe wouldn't name. She just gave them directions.

"How much longer?" Cassandra asked.

"Not much farther." The uncertain apprehension in Phoebe's voice belied her words.

Cassandra took Wulf's hand into hers. He squeezed her fingers reassuringly, but didn't speak.

"Will we make it before sunrise?" she asked her sister.

"It's going to be close." Then under her breath, Phoebe mumbled the words, "Real close."

Cassandra watched Wulf as he drove. He had his sunglasses on to help with the glare from the snow, but the night was so dark, she wasn't sure how he saw at all. His whiskered jaw was set and rigid. Even though he didn't say anything, she noted the way he kept glancing at the clock on the dashboard.

She offered a prayer that they made it to their destination before the sun killed him.

Forcing her fear away before it overwhelmed her, she looked down at their joined hands. Her hand was covered by her black knit gloves. His bare fingers were long and manly. The hands of a protective warrior.

Who would ever have thought that she would find a friend and lover born to a race that was the sworn enemy of her own?

And yet here she sat, knowing he was the only thing that could save and protect her baby. Knowing he would willingly die to protect her child. Her heart ached with that knowledge and with the nervousness she felt as the sky lightened.

He couldn't die. Surely the Fates wouldn't be so cruel.

Cassandra let go of his hand long enough to pull her glove off, then took his hand again into hers. She needed that physical connection to him.

He glanced at her and offered her an encouraging smile.

"Turn right there," Phoebe said, leaning forward between them to point at a small trail where there was no road.

Wulf didn't question it. There wasn't time. Instead, he turned as she indicated.

He was an idiot for trusting her, he knew that. But there wasn't any choice. Besides, Phoebe hadn't betrayed them yet.

Even if she did, he would make sure she paid for it. Along with anyone else who dared to come after Cassandra.

They crashed through the woods, the armor plating of

the SUV making it relatively easy to plow through smaller trees and travel over the snow, ice, and debris. Wulf cut the lights off so that he could see better as the Land Rover bounced over the uneven terrain.

Chris came awake with a curse. "Is Stryker back?"

"No," Kat told him. "We had to leave the road."

Wulf slowed a bit so as not to throw one of the tank tracks that had replaced the SUV's tires. They were a lot sturdier in this climate, but were still a far cry from being infallible, and the last thing he needed was to be stranded out in the open with daylight so close.

Just as the sun was appearing over the mountain, he broke through the trees and came to a cave.

There were three Apollites standing outside of it. Waiting.

Cassandra hissed and released his hand.

"It's okay," Phoebe said as she opened her door and sprang from the truck.

Wulf hesitated as he watched Phoebe run to the men and point back at them.

"Well," he breathed, watching the sun starting to creep over the peaks. "It's a moment of truth. We can't run from them now."

"I'm with you to the end," Kat breathed from the back seat.

Chris nodded. "Me too."

"Stay here," Wulf said to Cassandra and Chris before he slid out, his hand on the hilt of his sword.

Kat got out with him.

Chris leaned forward so that his head was almost even with hers. "Are those what I think they are?"

"Yes," Cassandra said, holding her breath. "Those are Apollites and they don't look happy to see us."

The Apollites eyed Kat and Wulf suspiciously. The hatred between them was even more fierce than when Urian had faced Wulf in Wulf's boathouse.

It made Cassandra's blood run cold.

Phoebe motioned to the cresting sun and said something to the men. Still they didn't move.

Until Wulf looked over his shoulder at Cassandra. His gaze met hers and he gave her a subtle nod.

His face unreadable, he handed over all his weapons.

Cassandra's heart pounded. Would they kill him?

She knew he would never have handed his weapons over to his enemies. He would have fought to the bitter end. But for her he had surrendered himself.

The Apollites led him inside with Phoebe while Kat came back for them.

"What's going on?" Cassandra asked.

Kat let out a tired breath. "They're taking Wulf into custody to make sure he doesn't hurt any of them. Come on, they have a doctor inside waiting for you."

Cassandra hesitated as she looked in the direction where they had vanished. "Do you really trust them?"

"I don't know. Do you?"

She thought about that and wasn't exactly sure of the answer. "I trust Phoebe. I think."

Kat laughed at that.

Cassandra scooted out of the truck and let Kat lead her and Chris into the cave where Wulf had been taken.

Phoebe met them just inside. "Don't be afraid, Cassie. We all know how important you and your baby are. No one here will hurt either of you. I swear it."

Cassandra could only hope her sister meant that. "Who are *we*?"

"This is an Apollite community," Phoebe said as she led them deep into the cave. "One of the older ones in North America."

"But why are you helping me now?" Cassandra asked. "It's not like you haven't known I've been hunted all these years."

Phoebe looked pained by the question. "I knew you lived and I was hoping you would carry on our line. I was afraid to tell you I was still existing for fear of how you would take it. I thought it would be easier this way."

"Then why change now?"

"Because an Apollite named Spawn called a few days ago and explained what was going on. Once I talked to Urian and knew what his father had planned, I realized I couldn't leave you alone anymore. We are sisters, Cassandra, and your baby has to live."

At the back of the cave, Phoebe placed her hand against one of the stones where a spring release opened an elevator door.

Chris gave an overexaggerated gape. "Holy Hand Grenade, Batman, it's a bat cave."

Cassandra cast him a droll look.

"Oh, come on," Chris said, "someone other than me has to see the humor in this?" He looked around at their three unamused faces. "Guess not."

Cassandra entered the elevator first. "What about the men I saw outside? Who are they?"

Phoebe entered next. "They are our ruling council. Nothing can be done here without their direct approval."

Kat and Chris joined them. The door to the elevator closed.

"Are there any Daimons here?" Chris asked as Phoebe pressed a button to start the elevator on its downward path.

"The only Daimon in this community is me," Phoebe said sheepishly. "They allow me to live here because they owe Urian for his help. So long as I don't draw attention to myself or their existence, I'm allowed to stay."

As the elevator continued downward, Cassandra didn't know what to expect from the Apollite colony. Or her sister. Long ago, she would have trusted Phoebe without hesitation, but that was a Phoebe who wouldn't have been able to take someone else's life to sustain her own.

This new Phoebe scared her.

Cassandra's ears popped, letting her know they were traveling far beneath the mountain.

When the doors opened, she felt like she had just stepped into some science fiction movie.

Everything was fashioned like a futuristic city. Made of steel and concrete, the walls were painted with brilliant murals depicting sunshine and beauty.

Her group stepped out into a central area that was probably the size of a football field. There were openings all around that showed more corridors leading to other areas.

There were all kinds of shops in this main area, except for food vendors—a service the Apollites would have no need of since they lived off each other's blood.

"The city is named Elysia," Phoebe explained as she led them past a handful of Apollites who had paused to stare at them. "Most of the Apollites here live their entire lives below ground. They've no desire to go topside and see the humans and their violence. Nor do they wish to see their kin hunted and slaughtered."

"I take exception to that," Chris said. "I'm not violent. At least I don't suck on other people."

"Keep your voice down," Phoebe warned. "Humans have never been kind to my people. They have hunted and persecuted us even more than the Dark-Hunters. Here you are a minority and if you threaten any of my people, they just might kill you without bothering to find out whether or not you're violent."

Chris clamped his mouth shut.

Cassandra saw the sneers and glares they collected as Phoebe led them toward a hallway on the left.

"What do they do with the Apollites who turn Daimon?" Chris asked as soon as they were away from the other Apollites.

"No Daimons are tolerated here since they require a steady diet of human souls. If an Apollite decides to go Daimon, they are allowed to leave, but they can never return here. Ever."

"Yet you live here," Kat said. "Why?"

"I told you, Urian protects them. He was the one who showed them how to build this place."

"Why?" Kat pressed.

Phoebe stopped and turned to give Kat a measuring stare. "In spite of what you might think of him, Katra, my husband is a good man. He only wants what's best for his people." Phoebe's gaze went to Cassandra. "Urian was the first child to ever be born a cursed Apollite."

Cassandra gasped at the news. "That would make him—"

"Over eleven thousand years old," Phoebe said, finishing her sentence for her. "Yes. Most of the warriors who travel with him are that old. They go back to the very beginning of our history."

Chris whistled low. "How is that possible?"

"The Destroyer protects them," Kat answered. "Just as the Dark-Hunters serve Artemis, the true Spathis serve her." Kat sighed as if the conflict pained her. "Artemis and Apollymi have been at war since day one. The Destroyer is in captivity because Artemis tricked her into it and she spends all her time plotting Artemis's torture and death. If she ever gets out, Apollymi will destroy her."

Cassandra frowned. "Why does the Destroyer hate Artemis?"

"Love. Why else?" Kat said simply. "Love, hatred, and revenge are the most powerful emotions on earth. Apollymi wants revenge on Artemis for killing the one thing she loved most in the universe."

"And that is?"

"I would never betray either one by saying it."

"Would you write it down?" Chris asked.

Kat rolled her eyes.

Cassandra and Phoebe shook their heads.

"Oh, yeah, like the two of you weren't thinking the same thing," Chris said.

Phoebe motioned them to follow her again. She led them down a corridor that was lined with doors. "These are apartments. You will be given a large unit with four bedrooms. Mine is down a separate hallway. I would have liked to have had you closer, but this was the only one available that was big enough to accommodate all of you and I didn't think it wise to break up your number."

Cassandra wished she were closer to Phoebe too. She had a lot of catching up to do with her sister. "Is Wulf already there?"

"No," Phoebe said, averting her gaze. "He was taken to a holding cell."

Cassandra was aghast, then angry. "Excuse me?"

"He's our enemy, Cassie. What would you expect us to do?"

"I expect you to release him. Now."

"I can't."

Cassandra stopped dead in her tracks. "Then show me the door out of here."

Phoebe's face mirrored her disbelief. "What?"

"You heard me. I will not stay here unless he's welcome. He has risked his life for me. His home was destroyed because of me and I will not live comfortably while the father of my baby is treated like a convict."

Someone behind them started clapping.

Cassandra turned to see a man who dwarfed her. Standing somewhere near seven feet in height, he was gorgeous. Blond and slender, he appeared to be around her age.

"Nice speech, princess. It changes nothing."

Cassandra narrowed her gaze on him. "Then how about a good ass-kicking?"

He actually laughed. "You're pregnant."

"Not that pregnant." She shot one of the daggers from her wrist at the man. It embedded in the wall just past his head.

His face lost all humor.

"The next one goes into your heart."

"Cassie, stop!" Phoebe commanded, grabbing her arm.

Cassandra shrugged off her hold. "No. I've spent the whole of my adulthood putting any Daimon or Apollite who made the mistake of coming after me out of his misery. If you think for one minute Kat and I can't tear down this place to free Wulf, then you need to think again."

"And if you die?" the man asked.

"Then we all lose."

He gazed at her thoughtfully. "You're bluffing."

Cassandra exchanged a determined look with Kat.

"You know I'm always itching for a good fight." Kat pulled her fighting staff out of her coat pocket and extended it.

The man's nostrils flared as he saw them preparing to engage him. "This is how you repay my kindness for sheltering you?"

"No," Cassandra said with a calmness she didn't feel. "This is how I repay the man who protects me. I won't see Wulf kept like this after all he's done."

She expected the man to fight, instead he stepped back and bowed his head respectfully toward her.

"She does have the courage of a Spathi."

"I told you so," Phoebe said, her face shining with pride.

The man offered them a slight smile. "Go inside with Phoebe, princess, and I will have your Dark-Hunter brought to you."

Cassandra eyed him suspiciously, not sure if she should trust him or not. "Promise?"

"Yes."

Still skeptical, Cassandra looked at her sister. "Can I put any faith in that?"

"You can. Shanus is our Supreme Councilor. He never lies."

"Phoebe," Cassandra said sincerely, "look at me."

She did.

"Tell me the truth. Are we safe here?"

"Yes, I swear it by everything I hold dear—even Urian's life. You are here because Stryker will never think to look in an Apollite commune for you. Every one of us here knows that if your baby dies, so does the world. And our lives, such as they are, are still precious to us. Twenty-seven years to the people here is better than none at all."

Cassandra took a deep breath and nodded. "Okay."

Phoebe opened the door behind her while Shanus excused himself and left them to explore their new home.

Cassandra stepped into an extremely nice living room. Probably four to five hundred square feet, it had everything a regular human home might have. A stuffed sofa and love seat, entertainment center complete with television, stereo, and DVD player.

"Does that stuff work?" Chris asked as he walked over to examine it.

"Yes," Phoebe said. "We have relays and uplinks that can bring the human world down to us."

Kat opened the doors to the bedrooms and bathroom that were off the main living area. "Where's the kitchen?"

"We don't have kitchens," Phoebe explained. "But the councilors are working on getting a microwave and refrigerator brought in for you. Along with groceries. There should be something here very soon for all of you to eat."

Phoebe showed them a small dark green box on an end table. "If you need anything, the intercom is here. Just press the button and one of the operators will help you. If you want to buzz me, just tell them you want Urian's wife and they'll know which Phoebe to put you through to."

A knock sounded on the door.

Phoebe went to open it while Cassandra stood back with Kat and Chris. "What do you guys think?"

"It seems okay," Chris said. "I'm not picking up any evil vibes, what about you two?"

Kat shrugged. "I agree with Chris. But there's still a part of me that doesn't trust them. No offense, Cass, but Apollites aren't known for being honest."

"Tell me about it."

"Cassandra?"

She turned to see a woman her age with Phoebe. The woman's blond hair was arranged in a bun and she wore a light pastel sweater with a pair of jeans.

"I'm Dr. Lakis," she said, extending her hand to Cassandra. "If you don't mind, I would like to examine you and see how the baby is doing."

Wulf sat in the cell wondering how the hell he had gotten himself into this. They could be killing Cassandra for all he knew and he had docilely allowed them to take him.

"I should have fought."

Cursing, he paced the small cell where they had incarcerated him. It was dim and dank, with only a bed and toilet inside. He'd never been inside a human jail, but from what he'd seen in movies and on TV, the Apollites had modeled this one after them.

He heard footsteps outside.

"I'm here for the Dark-Hunter."

"We were told he's to stay."

"The heiress wants him and she won't remain under our protection unless we release him."

Wulf smiled at those precious words. Leave it to Cassandra. Then again, she was extremely stubborn when it came to getting her way.

It was one of the things he loved most about her.

Wulf's heart stopped as that thought went through him. There were a lot of things about her that he liked.

Things he was going to miss . . .

"Are you mad?" the guard outside continued to argue. "He'll kill all of us."

"He's not allowed to kill Apollites, you know that. No Dark-Hunter can kill us until we go Daimon."

"Are you willing to bet your life on that?"

"No," Wulf said loudly so that they could hear him outside. "He's willing to bet yours on it. Now let me out of here so that I can make sure Cassandra hasn't been hurt."

The door opened slowly to reveal a man who was surprisingly taller than him. It wasn't often Wulf met such a person.

"So you do protect her," the man said quietly.

"Yes."

The Apollite gave him a strange look. "You love her." It was a statement, not a question.

"I barely know her."

The man gave a half-smile at that. "Time has no meaning to the heart." He held his hand out to Wulf who shook it reluctantly. "My name is Shanus and I'm glad to know you will do anything to keep her safe. Good. Now, come, she's waiting for you."

Cassandra was lying on the bed while a nurse prepared her blood transfusion. It was a good thing too. She'd been weak before tonight, but the added excitement of Stryker's attack had taken a lot out of her.

The doctor handed her a T-shirt to put on instead of the sweater so that they could hook her up to the machine. At first, they had balked at her refusing to drink blood. Apparently, Apollites weren't squeamish, but Cassandra had enough human in her to not want to do that.

So after a brief, heated debate, they had given in to her.

Cassandra exchanged shirts while the doctor prepared her for a sonogram.

"You will need more blood than normal to accommodate your baby," Dr. Lakis explained as Cassandra lay back down on the bed. The doctor lifted Cassandra's shirt, exposing her slightly rounded stomach. "It's a good thing you're here since Apollite blood is stronger and will have the nutrients in it your baby needs. You'll also need a lot more iron and calcium since you're part human. I'll make sure you have plenty of vitamin-enhanced food to eat."

Cassandra heard Kat say something outside the door. She lifted herself up on her elbows and cocked her head to listen but she couldn't make anything out.

Weird. Chris and Phoebe had both gone on to their rooms to sleep.

Cassandra was about to get out of the bed to go check outside when Wulf came through the door.

Relief flooded her at the sight of all six feet six inches of that well-muscled male form. He looked tired, but un-hurt. She drank in the gorgeousness of his body and face.

The doctor, however, looked at him suspiciously. "Are you the baby's father?"

"Yes," they said in unison.

Cassandra held her hand out to Wulf who took it, then kissed her knuckles.

"You're just in time," the doctor said as she rubbed an oily gel over Cassandra's belly. She placed the cool pad-dle against her.

The machine on the cart bonged and hissed.

Cassandra watched the screen anxiously until she saw the teeny-tiny infant that was kicking its feet.

Wulf's hand tightened on hers.

"There he is," the doctor said. "A fine healthy little boy all ready to take on the world."

"How can you tell it's a boy?" Cassandra asked breath-lessly as she watched her son flex. He looked much like a tadpole to her.

"Well, we actually can't really tell yet," Dr. Lakis said as she took measurements with the machine, "but I can feel him. He's strong. A fighter like both of his parents."

Cassandra felt a tear roll out from the corner of her right eye. Wulf kissed it away.

She looked at him and saw the happiness on his face. He was proud of his son.

"Everything looks fine so far," the doctor said as she printed out a small photograph of the baby. "You just need to rest a lot more and eat a better diet."

The doctor wiped the goo off her belly while Wulf and Cassandra looked at the tiny picture.

"He looks like an angel," Cassandra whispered.

"I don't know. I think he looks like a frog or something."

"Wulf!"

"Well, he does. Kind of."

"Dr. Lakis?" She waited until the doctor paused and looked at her. "Do you think the baby will . . ." She hesitated, unable to finish her sentence.

"Die like an Apollite?"

Cassandra nodded, her throat tight with apprehension.

Dr. Lakis's eyes were sympathetic. "I honestly don't know. We can run tests once he gets here and see, but genetics are a strange thing so there's really no way to predict."

Swallowing the lump in her throat, Cassandra forced herself to ask the other question she was desperate to have answered. "Is there a way you can tell if I'll live longer?"

"You already know the answer to that, Cassandra. I'm sorry. You are one of the lucky ones who has some human traits, but your genetics are strongly Apollite. The mere fact you're in the middle of a blood transfusion says it all."

Cassandra's eyes welled with tears as she felt the last of her hope dwindle.

"Isn't there something we can do?" Wulf asked.

"Her only chance to live longer is to turn Daimon and I somehow doubt you would allow her that option."

Cassandra clutched the picture of her baby as she wondered how Apollite he would be. Would he, too, be damned?

She didn't speak further while the doctor and nurse were in the room with them. It was only when she was alone with Wulf that she reached for him and held him close.

She held on to him tightly, afraid of tomorrow. Afraid of everything.

"It'll be okay, *villkat*," he whispered.

How she wished that were true. Still, she was glad he at least went through the motions of pretending they were a normal couple with normal concerns.

Someone knocked on the door.

Cassandra pulled away before Wulf went to answer it.

It was Phoebe. She ignored Wulf and moved to where Cassandra sat on the bed. "I thought you might want some fresh clothes."

Cassandra thanked her as Phoebe placed the bundle of clothes on the bed at her feet. "Have you heard anything from Urian?" she asked her sister.

Phoebe shook her head sadly. "But sometimes it takes a few days before he can talk to me. Sometimes a few months . . ."

Cassandra felt for her sister. She hadn't known Wulf very long and yet she couldn't imagine not being able to talk to him everyday. Not having him make her laugh at something he said. It must be much worse for her sister. "Why don't you live with him?"

Phoebe gave her a "duh" stare. "His father tried to kill me, Cassie. He knows what we"—she indicated herself and Cassandra—"look like. He would kill Urian if he ever caught us together."

Wulf moved to stand near Phoebe. "Since you're still alive and married, Apollo's lineage is safe, right?"

"No," Phoebe said wistfully. Her face was dark and sad. "Daimons can't have children. Like Dark-Hunters, we're walking dead. It's why I allowed my father and Cassie to think I was dead too. There was no need to make them even sadder about who and what I've become."

"Did it change you much?" Cassandra asked. "Is it like we always heard?"

"Yes and no. The craving for the kill is hard to resist. You have to be careful of the soul you take because a part of it blends with you too. I think it's different for Daimons who kill than for those like me."

"What do you mean 'those like you'?" Wulf asked.

"You're an Anaimikos Daimon," Cassandra said.

Phoebe nodded.

Wulf was completely confused now. He'd never heard that term. "What's that?"

"A Daimon who feeds from another Daimon," Phoebe explained. "I take my nourishment from Urian."

Wulf was stunned. "You can do that?"

"Yes."

Wulf moved back, away from the women, as he digested that. In his world there were only two kinds of Daimons. The regular ones who ran when they were chased and the Spathi who fought back. Since meeting Cassandra he'd learned of two more; the Agkelos, who only preyed on evil humans, and the Anaimikos, who preyed on other Daimons.

He wondered if any of the other Dark-Hunters knew of this and why no one had ever bothered to tell him about the different classifications.

"How did you meet Urian?" Cassandra asked as she put away some of the clothes Phoebe had brought for her in the large dresser by the door.

"Back when we lived in Switzerland, Urian was the one watching us. He was supposed to be gathering information to kill us, but he says that as soon as he saw me, he was in love." Her sister's face practically glowed. Cassandra was happy to see Phoebe so in love. "One night we met by accident when I was escaping the house after that big fight with Mom about college. I stepped right on top of him in his hiding place."

Cassandra remembered that night well. It wasn't often Phoebe and her mother fought, but that night had been a particularly nasty one. Phoebe had wanted to go off to take night classes in the semblance of being a normal teenager. Their mother had refused her request.

Phoebe sighed. "He was so beautiful. I knew he was a Daimon, but I wasn't afraid. I stayed with him for hours that night. We started meeting every night after that."

"So that's where you would sneak off to," Cassandra said, remembering the times she had covered for Phoebe's midnight escapes.

Phoebe nodded. "I'd only known Urian for about six months when his father grew impatient and bombed the car. I wasn't supposed to go that night. I was supposed to stay home with you, remember?"

Cassandra remembered that night well. Every detail of it was emblazoned on her memory with crystal clarity. She'd stayed at home that night only because she was sick and her mother had refused to let her out of bed.

"You wanted to go to the airport with Nia," Cassandra said, her throat tight. Their older sister had been going to take a charter flight to see their father in Paris. Nia had planned on staying a week there and then she and their father were supposed to fly back together to stay in Switzerland with the rest of them for a little holiday.

Phoebe nodded. "Urian pulled me out of the car and used his own blood to restore me."

Cassandra flinched at her sister's words. "He made you a Daimon against your will?"

"It was my choice. I could have died, but I didn't want to leave him."

Wulf cocked his head. "How did he make you a Dai-mon?"

Both of the women looked at him in disbelief.

"If an Apollite drinks the blood of a Daimon, it auto-matically converts them. Didn't you know that?" Cassan-dra asked.

"No, I didn't. I thought the only way to become a Dai-mon was to take a human soul."

"No," Phoebe said. "I've never killed a human. I doubt that I could."

Cassandra was glad to know that, but it was hard for a Daimon to live that way. Dangerous too. "What do you do if he's gone too long?"

"One of the Apollites gets word to him to come to me. He's so strong that I can go a long time between feedings and the infirmary keeps a pint of his blood in case of emergency. He always makes sure to replenish it with a new supply every time he visits."

"Does that work?" Cassandra asked. Unlike with Apol-lites, it wasn't blood that sustained Daimons, it was the life force or strength in the blood that kept them living.

"It won't last long, but it will tide me for an hour or two until he can get to me."

"So he kills for both of you?" Wulf asked.

She nodded, and took Cassandra's hands into hers. "Don't feel sorry for me, Cassandra. I have a man who loves me more than anything else on this earth. If he didn't, you would be dead now. I just wish you could know the love I have with him."

Phoebe kissed Cassandra on the cheek. "You need to rest now. It's been a long night. Would you like me to have someone bring you food?"

"No, thanks. I just need to sleep for a bit."

"Good day to you both." Phoebe left their bedroom.

Wulf locked the door behind her, then stripped his clothes off while Cassandra pulled on a dark green silk nightgown that Phoebe had brought to her. To her surprise, it fit perfectly, even over her slightly bulging belly.

Wulf climbed into bed and gathered her into his warm arms. "How are you doing for real, *villkat*?"

"I don't know. It's been an exciting, strange night." The events replayed through her mind. She'd learned a lot and had had one too many surprises. Now she was exhausted. "I'm very sorry about your house."

She felt him shrug. "Houses can be rebuilt. I'm just glad no one was hurt."

"Me too."

Wulf felt her relaxing as she closed her eyes and snuggled into him. He buried his face in her hair and inhaled the soft womanly scent of her. His mind whirled with everything that had happened tonight.

Most of all, it whirled with thoughts of the baby he had seen on the monitor. He laid his hand on Cassandra's stomach and imagined the baby thriving in there. His baby.

Their son.

A part of both of them. The child of a Dark-Hunter and an Apollite. Two beings who should never have united and yet here they were. No longer enemies, he wasn't sure what to call her. She was his lover. His friend.

He froze as realization dawned on him. She really was his friend. The first one he had made in centuries. He had laughed with her often these last three weeks. Listened to her stories, her fears. Her hopes for the baby's future.

And he was going to lose her.

Anger and pain swelled up inside him. Jealousy, too, as he thought of the other three Dark-Hunters who had been given a second chance.

He was glad Kyrian and Talon had found their wives. They were good men.

How he wished he could be granted such a blessing.

The pain of losing Cassandra would be excruciating, and he had to admit that he was selfish. He wanted Cassandra and his baby both.

Alive and healthy.

If only he knew of some way to make her live past her birthday.

There had to be something. The gods always made a loophole. This couldn't be the end of their relationship. No matter what it took, he was going to find that loophole.

The alternative was unacceptable to him.

Chapter 12

Cassandra didn't wake up until almost six o'clock in the evening. She was completely alone in the room. Getting up, she dressed in a pair of black wool maternity pants and a large gray sweater Phoebe had given her.

She opened the door and found Chris, Wulf, and Kat eating on the floor in the living room. Her jaw went slack at the feast they were consuming.

"Hungry?" Chris asked as he saw her hesitating in the doorway. "Jump in. Wulf said he hasn't seen anything like this since his days in a Norse mead hall."

Cassandra joined them at the coffee table that was set with dozens of dishes. She was amazed at the variety of foods the Apollites had provided for them. They had steak, fish, roasted chicken. Eggs, potatoes, bananas, apples, roasted and sliced. You name it.

Kat licked her fingers. "Shanus said they didn't know what or how much humans ate so they went a little overboard."

"A little?" Cassandra asked with a short laugh. There was enough food there for an entire Dark-Hunter army.

"Yeah, I know," Kat said with a smile, "but it's all *really* good."

Cassandra agreed as soon as she bit into a succulent leg of roasted lamb.

"Here's the mint jelly," Kat said, passing it over. "Wait until you taste that."

Wulf reached over and wiped at Cassandra's chin. "You have a bit of grease."

"Thank you."

He nodded warmly.

As soon as Cassandra was finished and stuffed, she wanted to go for a walk to help combat her overconsumption of food. Wulf walked with her, not wanting her to go alone just in case something happened.

They left the apartment and headed back toward the merchant part of the underground city so that she could window-shop. But as they walked past the Apollite townspeople, the animosity they directed toward Wulf was tangible.

And it wasn't like he could blend in among the tall, golden-blond race. There was no doubt Wulf didn't belong to them.

She was looking in one window at baby clothes when a young man who appeared the human age of sixteen, but was probably only eleven or twelve by real Apollite years, passed by.

"Excuse me," Wulf said, stopping him.

The boy's eyes were panicked.

"Don't worry, kid, I'm not going to hurt you," Wulf said, his voice gentle. "I just wanted to ask you about that emblem on your sweatshirt."

Cassandra turned to see the interlocking circle pattern in the center of his shirt.

The boy swallowed nervously as if he were terrified Wulf was one step away from hurting him. "It's the emblem for the Cult of Pollux."

Wulf's eyes darkened dangerously. "So you do hide Daimons here."

"No," the boy said, his face even more panicked.

"Is there a problem?"

Cassandra looked past the boy to see a woman her age approaching. She was dressed in a cream uniform that denoted an off-duty Apollite police officer. Though the term "police" didn't have quite the same meaning to them as it did to humans. Apollite police were only used to manage Daimons since Apollites rarely fought and never broke the laws of their people.

Phoebe had told her the Elysian police were paid to escort any Apollite about to go Daimon out of the city and to give them money and transportation for the human world.

"No problem," Cassandra said to the officer, who was eyeing Wulf coldly.

The boy ran off while the woman raked a sneer over Wulf. "I'm not a child to live in fear of you, Dark-Hunter. After tonight, there's nothing you can do to me anyway."

"Meaning?"

"I die tomorrow."

Cassandra's heart shrank at her words. "I'm sorry."

The woman ignored her. "So why were you scaring my son?"

Wulf's face was impassive, but Cassandra knew him well enough to know he hurt for the woman as much as she did. She saw the sympathy in his dark eyes, heard it in the tone of his voice when he spoke. "I only wanted to know about the emblem on his shirt."

"It's our emblem," she said, her lips still curled. "Every Apollite here takes an oath at their majority to uphold the Code of Pollux. Just like the ancient god, we are all bound to each other. We won't ever betray our community or our brethren. Nor will we be cowards. Unlike other Apollites, we don't practice ritual suicide the night before our birthdays. Apollo meant us to die painfully and so we don't argue with his decree. My son, along with all my relatives, is wearing the badge to honor me and the fact that I refuse to run from my heritage."

There was a suspicious glint in Wulf's eyes. "But I've seen that emblem outside of here. It was on a particularly vicious Daimon I killed about a year ago."

The officer's sneer faded into remorse. She closed her eyes and winced as if the news pained her. "Jason." She whispered the name. "I always wondered what became of him. Did he go quickly?"

"Yes."

The officer sighed raggedly at that. "I'm glad. He was a good man, but the night before he was to die, he ran from here, scared. His family tried to stop him, but he wouldn't listen. He said he refused to die when he had never even seen the surface world. My husband was the one who took him out and let him go. He must have been terrified up there alone."

Wulf scoffed. "He didn't seem terrified to me. Rather, he burned that emblem on every human he killed."

The officer tapped her chin three times with her first two fingers—an Apollite holy gesture. "Gods grant him peace. He must have been preying on evil souls."

"What do you mean?" Wulf asked.

"He's one of the Daimons who refuse to kill innocent humans," Cassandra explained, "And who prey on criminals instead. After all, criminal souls are full of power fueled by anger and hatred. The only problem is their souls are corrupted, and if the Daimon isn't strong enough, their venom can overtake them and make the Daimon every bit as evil as they were."

The officer nodded. "It sounds like Jason fell victim to that. By the time you killed him, he was probably wanting to die. It's sheer torture when the souls begin to possess and control you. Or at least that's what I've been told." She sighed. "Now if you'll excuse me, I'd like to spend as much time as possible with my family."

Cassandra wished her well.

With a nod, the officer left them and headed off after her son.

Wulf watched the woman leave, his eyes dark and sad. "So you weren't kidding me about the Daimons."

"Of course not."

Wulf thought about that. There was so much about them that the Dark-Hunters didn't know. It actually amazed him.

She'd been right. Since Dark-Hunters spent so much time annihilating the Daimons, they should have a better understanding of them.

Then again, maybe not. It was much easier to kill someone you didn't feel sorry for. Easier to think of things in terms of black and white.

Good and evil.

"Let's go see Phoebe," Cassandra said, taking his hand and leading him toward another corridor. "She told me I could drop in on her any time."

It didn't take long to reach her sister's apartment. Phoebe's side of the city was a lot busier than theirs.

Wulf stood to the side, watching the Apollites walk hurriedly past them while Cassandra keyed in the code for Phoebe's lock.

Cassandra was doing her best to not think about the future. Or to think about the officer who was spending her last night with her family. Just as she would do one day all too soon with Wulf.

How she needed to push him away. To keep him at bay so that her death wouldn't hurt him too much.

She focused instead on the fact that she still had one of her sisters with her.

The door slid open.

Cassandra started into the room, then froze. Phoebe was on her couch on top of Urian. Their bare skin was set off to perfection by the dull light of candles that had been set around the room.

Cassandra gasped to find them in flagrante delicto.

Phoebe jerked up, her mouth coated in blood.

Mortified, Cassandra stepped back and closed the door. "Oh, that was really bad timing."

"What?" Wulf asked as he turned toward her.

Grateful he hadn't seen them and gone berserk over the way most Apollites fed, Cassandra grabbed his hand. "I think I'll talk to her later."

Wulf didn't budge easily. "What happened?"

Cassandra didn't want to share her experience with a Dark-Hunter who would judge her sister harshly for feeding.

The apartment door opened.

"Cassie?" Phoebe was now wearing a thick blue bathrobe. Her face and mouth were clean, but her hair was completely disheveled. "Is something wrong?"

"Nothing that can't wait," Cassandra hastened to assure her. "You go finish and I'll talk to you later."

Her face flushing, Phoebe went back inside.

Wulf burst out laughing. "Let me guess. Urian in there with her?"

Cassandra's face flamed even more than her sister's.

He laughed harder.

"It's not funny, Wulf," she snapped at him. "How would you feel if someone barged in on us?"

"I'd have to kill them."

"Well, there you go. I'm sure Urian feels the same way. Now let's go back so I don't have to think about the fact that the image of them naked together will give me nightmares for months."

As they headed down the corridor, a little girl came running up to Wulf. She craned her neck to look up at him accusingly. "Are you really going to kill my baby sister tonight because she didn't wash behind her ears?"

Both of them were aghast at her question.

"Excuse me?" Wulf asked.

"My mommy says Dark-Hunters kill little boys and girls when they don't behave. I don't want you to kill Alycia. She's not bad, she just doesn't like to get her ears wet."

Wulf knelt down in front of the little girl and brushed her hair back from her face. "Little one, I'm not going to hurt your sister or anyone else here. I promise."

"Dacia!" a man snapped as he rushed forward. "I told you never to talk to anyone with dark hair." He scooped his daughter up and ran off with her as if terrified that Wulf really would kill her.

"Hasn't anyone ever told you people that we don't hurt Apollites!" Wulf shouted after them.

"Sheez," he said under his breath. "And all this time, I thought Christopher was the only person I terrorized."

A passing man answered his words by spitting on Wulf's shoes.

"Hey!" Cassandra snapped, going after the man. "There's no need to be rude."

The man raked a repugnant glare over her. "How could you let something like him touch you? I say we should have left you to die by the Daimons. It's what a whore like you deserves."

His eyes darkening, Wulf slugged the Apollite. Hard. The Apollite staggered back, then charged him.

He caught Wulf about the stomach and slammed him back into the wall. Cassandra cried out at the sight, wanting to stop them, but she was too afraid of hurting the baby to try.

Suddenly, Apollites came out from all directions to break them apart. Even Urian came out of nowhere.

Urian was the one who pushed Wulf back. His skin tone was ashen and it was obvious Urian was extremely weak. Even so, he put himself between Wulf and the Apollite and kept a hand on each one.

"Enough!" Urian roared at the two of them.

"Are you all right?" Wulf asked him.

Urian released both men. The Apollite was taken off by the others, but he cast a parting malevolent glare at them.

"You need to stay out of sight, Dark-Hunter," Urian said, his tone much kinder than it had been earlier. He wiped a hand over his sweat-covered brow.

"You really don't look good," Wulf said, ignoring his warning. "Do you need something?"

Urian shook his head as if to clear it. "I just need to rest for a while." He curled his lip at Wulf. "Can you stay out of trouble long enough for that?"

"Uri?" Phoebe asked as she joined them. "Did I take too much?"

Urian's face softened instantly. He pulled her against his side and kissed the side of her head. "No, love. I'm just tired. I'll be fine."

He pulled away and started back for their apartment. He staggered.

"Bullshit," Wulf said. Before Cassandra knew what he

was doing, Wulf had Urian's arm slung over his shoulders and was headed back for their apartment.

"What are you doing?" Urian asked angrily.

"I'm taking you to Kat before you pass out."

Urian hissed at that. "Why? She hates me."

"So do I, but we both owe you."

Cassandra didn't speak as she and Phoebe followed after them all the way back to their apartment.

Kat and Chris were playing cards when they entered.

"Oh, jeez, what happened?" Kat asked as soon as she saw Urian.

"I think I took too much blood from him," Phoebe said, her beautiful face lined with worry.

Wulf laid Urian down on the couch. "Can you help him?" he asked Kat.

Kat pushed Wulf out of the way. She held up two fingers in front of Urian's face. "How many fingers do you see?"

"Six."

She popped him on the side. "Stop that. This is serious."

Urian widened his eyes and tried to focus his gaze on her hand. "Three . . . I think."

Kat shook her head. "We'll be back."

Cassandra watched in awe as Kat flashed them out of the room.

"Now why didn't she do that when we were being chased by Stryker?" Chris asked.

"She's taking him to Kalosis, Chris," Phoebe answered. "I doubt any of you want to go into a realm ruled by nothing but Spathi Daimons and one really pissed-off ancient goddess who is bent on destroying the entire world."

"You know," Chris said. "I really like it here. Not to mention, I can now look at Kat's hand." He picked up her cards and cursed. "I should have known she wasn't bluffing."

Cassandra watched her sister closely. In spite of the worry on her face, Phoebe looked a lot better than she had before. Her cheeks were pink, her skin bright.

"I'm so sorry I interrupted you two," Cassandra said, her face growing instantly warm again.

"Please don't be. I mean, don't make it a habit, mind you, but if you hadn't come in, I might have killed him. He has a bad tendency to not tell me when I've taken too much blood. It scares me sometimes."

Wulf crossed his arms over his chest. "So Daimons can die from blood loss?"

"Only when it's being sucked out of them," Cassandra answered.

Phoebe gave him an arch stare. "Are you planning on using that against us?"

Wulf shook his head. "I'd rather die myself than suck on another man's neck. That's disgusting. Besides, didn't you tell me that's how Apollites can be changed into Daimons? It begs the question that since Dark-Hunters have no souls, could they be made Daimon too?"

"Yeah, but DH blood is poisonous to the Daimons," Chris said as he shuffled his deck of cards. "Isn't the point of that so that no Daimon can feed off or convert you guys?"

"Perhaps . . ." Phoebe said. "But then disembodied souls can possess a Dark-Hunter, and since Uri and I share souls, it makes you wonder if perhaps a Daimon and Dark-Hunter could share one too."

"Let's hope we never find that one out," Wulf said as he moved to sit on the couch in front of Chris.

Phoebe turned back toward Cassandra. "So what did you want when you came to see me?"

"I've been putting together a memory box for the baby. Notes and pictures from me. Little mementos to tell him about our people and family, and I was wondering if you would mind putting something in there from you."

"Why do you need something like that when we'll be more than happy to tell him anything he wants to know?"

Cassandra hesitated, not wanting to hurt her sister's feelings. "He can't grow up here, Phe. He'll have to be with Wulf in the human world."

Her sister's eyes snapped fire. "Why can't he grow up here?" Phoebe insisted. "We can protect him just as well as Wulf. Probably more so."

Wulf glanced up as Chris dealt him a hand of cards. "What if he's even more human than Cassandra is? Would he be safe here?"

The indecision on Phoebe's face said it all.

No, he wouldn't be. They had seen enough of Wulf's treatment tonight to verify that. Apollites were no more tolerant of humans than humans were of Apollites.

At least they didn't tie each other to stakes anymore and set fire to them.

At least not often.

Wulf looked meaningfully at Phoebe. "I can protect him and his children a lot easier than you can. I think the temptation of having a human soul here would be way too much for some of your people to handle. Especially given how much they hate Dark-Hunters. What a coup. Kill my son, get a human soul, and take revenge on the very thing all of you despise most."

Phoebe nodded. "I suppose you're right." She took Cassandra's hand. "Yes, I would like to add some things to the box for him."

While Wulf and Chris played cards, Cassandra went to the bedroom and retrieved the large silver-inlaid box that Kat had brought with them from the house, along with paper and pens.

She and Phoebe wrote letters to the baby. After a while, Phoebe left her alone to run a quick errand.

Cassandra sat alone in her room, flipping through the pages of notes and letters she had made for her son. How she wished she could see him grow. She would give anything to glimpse her son as a grown man.

Maybe Wulf could contact a Were-Hunter and have one take her forward in time. Just for a quick glance. Just to let her see what she would miss.

But then that might be even worse. Besides, pregnant women couldn't travel through the time portals.

"I hope you look like your father," she said, rubbing her stomach gently as she imagined the little baby inside her. She could easily see him with dark, wavy hair like Wulf's. He'd be tall, hopefully muscular.

And he would be forced to grow up without a mother's love. Just as Wulf would be forced to watch her die . . .

A sob caught in her throat as she reached for another piece of paper. She wrote quickly, holding back her tears, telling her son just how much she did love him. Letting him know that even though she wasn't with him physically, she would be with him spiritually.

Somehow she would find a way to watch over him. Always.

She finished the letter, placed it in the box, then took it to the living room where the guys were still playing cards. She was afraid to be alone. Her thoughts had a nasty way of torturing her whenever she was by herself.

Chris and Wulf were champions at keeping her mind

off the future. At making her smile even when she didn't feel like it.

Chris had just dealt Cassandra into their game when Phoebe returned with a book.

"What's this?" she asked as Phoebe added it to the box on the couch next to her.

"It's a book of Apollite fairy tales," Phoebe said. "Remember the one Mom used to read to us when we were kids? Donita sells them in her shop so I went just now and bought one for the baby."

Suspicious, Wulf picked the book up and flipped through it with a frown. "Hey, Chris," he said, handing it to his Squire. "You read Greek, right?"

"Yeah."

"What's in here?"

Chris started reading silently, then burst out laughing. Hard.

Cassandra cringed as she remembered some of the things her mother had read to them when they were children.

Chris kept laughing. "I don't know if you want the baby to see this if you're the one raising him."

"Let me guess," Wulf said, narrowing his gaze on Phoebe. "He'll have nightmares that Daddy is going to hunt him down and rip his head off?"

"Pretty much. I am particularly fond of the one called: 'Acheron the Great Evil.'" Chris paused as he turned to another story. "Oh, wait . . . You'll love this one. They got the story of the nasty Nordic Dark-Hunter. Remember the story with the witch and the oven? This one features you with a furnace."

"Phoebe!" Wulf snapped, looking over at her.

"What?" Cassandra's sister asked innocently. "That's our heritage. It's not like you guys don't swap stories on

Andy the Evil Apollite or Daniel the Killer Daimon. You know, I see human movies and read their books too. They're not exactly nice to my people. They portray us all as soulless killers who have no compassion or feelings."

"Yeah, well," Wulf said, "*your* people happen to be soul-sucking demons."

Phoebe cocked her head with attitude. "You ever met a banker or a lawyer? Tell me who's worse, my Urian or one of them? At least we need the food; they do it just for profit margins."

Cassandra laughed at their banter, then took the book from Chris's hands. "I appreciate the thought, Phe, but could we find a book that doesn't paint the Dark-Hunters as Satan?"

"I don't think one exists. Or if it does, I've never seen it."

"Great," Wulf muttered, picking up another card, "just great. My poor son's going to have nightmares all of his childhood."

"Trust me," Chris said as he upped his bet against Wulf. "That book's going to be the least of your kid's problems with you as his father."

"What do you mean?" Cassandra asked.

Chris put his cards down and met her gaze. "You do know that as a small child, they actually carried me around on a pillow? I had a custom-made helmet that I had to wear until I was four."

"That's because you banged your head every time you got angry. I was afraid you were going to get brain damage from it."

"The brain is fine," Chris said. "It's my ego and social life in the toilet. I shudder at what you're going to do to that kid."

Chris dropped his voice and imitated Wulf's lilting Norse accent. "Don't move, you might get bruised. Oops, a sneeze, better call in specialists from Belgium. Headache? Odin forbid, it might be a tumor. Quick, rush him for a CAT scan."

Wulf shoved his shoulder playfully. "And yet you live."

"Ever the better to procreate for you." Chris met Cassandra's gaze. "It's a hell of a life." Then Chris dropped his gaze as if he were thinking about that for a minute. "But there are worse ones out there."

Cassandra wasn't sure which of them was most stunned by that confession. Her or Wulf.

Chris got up and went to the foyer where a trestle table was set with snacks and drinks. He poured himself more Coke and grabbed some chips before he and Wulf resumed their game of cards.

It was just before midnight when Urian rejoined them. He looked a lot better than he had earlier. His deep tawny skin had a healthy glow. His eyes were bright and for once he wore his long, blond hair down around his shoulders. Cassandra would give Phoebe credit. Her husband was extremely gorgeous.

When he was dressed completely in black, there wasn't much difference between Urian and a Dark-Hunter. Except for what they needed in order to live.

Phoebe smiled as Urian neared her.

Wulf didn't. In fact, the tension between the men was fierce.

"What's the matter, Dark-Hunter?" Urian asked as he draped his arm around Phoebe's shoulders. "You were hoping I'd succumb?"

"No, I was just wondering who you killed to reclaim your health."

Urian gave a short amused laugh at that. "I'm sure the cows you eat aren't exactly thrilled by their slaughter either."

"They're not people."

Urian sneered at that. "In case you haven't noticed, Dark-Hunter, there are a lot of people out there who aren't human either."

Taking Phoebe's hand, Urian led her toward the door. "C'mon, Phe, I don't have much time before I have to return to Kalosis and I don't want to spend it with my enemies."

As soon as Urian and Phoebe left, Chris headed off to bed.

Cassandra and Wulf were alone.

"You think Kat's okay?" Wulf asked as he picked up Chris's glass and closed the chips.

"I'm sure she is. She'll probably be back soon." Cassandra gathered her sister's letters for the baby and tucked them inside the box.

"After that book she bought, I shudder to think what your sister wrote in her letters."

"Hmmm," Cassandra said, glancing back at the box. "Maybe I should read them first . . ."

"Well, if they point to me as a horned demon, I would appreciate it."

Cassandra dropped her gaze down to his lap and to the bulge that was already there. "I don't know about that. From my experience you are a horny demon."

He arched a brow. "Am I?"

"Uh-huh. Horny to the extreme."

He laughed, then kissed her slowly, hotly. "You taste like lemon," he whispered against her lips.

Cassandra licked her lips as she remembered putting lemon juice on her fish.

Wulf tasted of decadence, wild, fierce decadence, and he made her heart race.

"Oh, oh, wait, I'm going blind!"

Wulf pulled back at the sound of Kat's voice.

Cassandra looked over her shoulder to see her friend standing in the open doorway.

Kat shut the door behind her. "Thank goodness no one's naked."

"Three more seconds and we would have been," Wulf teased.

"Ew!" Kat cringed. "More information than I needed."

She walked over to sit across from them. Her joking aside, Kat's features looked pinched.

Wulf was a bit disgruntled by her intrusion.

Cassandra pulled back from him and turned around to face Kat. "Something wrong?"

"Just a bit. Stryker isn't happy about your vanishing. The Destroyer was also pissed at me. A lot. Luckily, she hasn't rescinded the no-touch law where I'm concerned. It gives us some leeway, but I'm not sure how long Stryker will abide by it."

"Will you have any warning if they do rescind it?" Wulf asked.

"I don't know."

"What happened with Urian?" Cassandra asked. "Did they find out about his helping us?"

"No, I don't think so. But I'll tell you what. I'm afraid of what Stryker might do to him if he ever learned Urian was helping us. He wants you and the baby dead in the worst way."

Cassandra swallowed at that, then changed the subject. "So what did you two do?"

"I dropped Urian off at his house and left him there so that no one would know I was helping him. If anyone saw me near him, they'd be suspicious immediately. We haven't exactly been friends over the centuries. Hell, we haven't even been cordial."

"Why?" Cassandra asked. "He seems nice enough. A bit standoffish, but I can't really blame him for that."

"Trust me, hon, he's a different Urian here. He's not the same guy I've known for eleven thousand years. The Urian I've known wouldn't hesitate to kill anyone or anything at his father's command. I've seen him snap the neck of any Daimon who crossed them and you don't want to know what he does to Were-Hunters who betray them."

Wulf reached for his drink on the coffee table. "The Spathis are the reason Dark-Hunters never come out of bolt-holes, aren't they?"

She nodded. "The bolt-hole drops you front and center into the main banquet hall of Kalosis. Right in the heart of their city. Dark-Hunters are killed instantly. Weres are given a chance. They can swear allegiance to the Destroyer and be spared or they die."

"And Daimons?"

"Are welcomed so long as they train with the Spathis and uphold their warrior's code. The instant they show weakness, they die too."

Wulf let out a slow breath. "Hell of a place you come from, Kat."

"That's not my place. I come from Olympus."

"Then how did you get involved with the Destroyer?"

Cassandra was curious about that too.

Kat was sheepish. "I really can't go there."

"Why not?" Cassandra asked.

Kat shrugged. "It's something no one talks about, least of all me."

Well, that was just irritating and told her nothing. But

then Cassandra had other things on her mind. "Do you think Stryker will be able to find us here?"

"Honestly, I don't know. Stryker has a lot of spies in the Apollite and Were communities. It's how he found us before. Apparently one of the Weres at the Inferno works with him and contacted them as soon as we came in the door."

Wulf indicated the door that led out into the city. "So any one of the people out there could betray us?"

"I won't lie and say no. It is possible."

Cassandra swallowed as fear invaded her heart. "Is there any place safe?"

"At this time. No."

Chapter 13

Cassandra was getting ready for bed. Wulf was still outside with Kat, brainstorming escape plans in case they needed a quick exit from Elysia.

Personally, Cassandra was tired of running. Tired of being hunted.

Look on the bright side, it will all end on your birthday.

Somehow that thought was less than comforting to her. Sighing, she ran her hand through the letters in her memory box. Cassandra paused as she noticed a piece of sealed gray vellum paper that was different from the cream ones she used.

She hadn't added that one. Wulf's fears about what her sister might write made her more than curious.

A frown creasing her brow, she pulled the letter out and looked it over. She pried the seal up so as not to hurt it, then opened it.

Her heart stopped as she read the masculine, flowing script.

> *Dear son,*
>   *I would call you by name, but I'm waiting for your mother to decide. I only hope she is joking when she calls you Albert Dalbert.*

Cassandra paused to laugh at that. It was a joke between them, at least most of the time.

Sobering, she read on.

For weeks now I have watched your mother zealously gather her tokens for this box. She's so afraid of you not knowing anything about her, and it bothers me greatly that you'll never know her strength firsthand. I'm sure by the time you read this, you'll know everything I do about her.

But you'll never know her for yourself and that pains me most of all. I wish you could see the look on her face whenever she talks to you. The sadness she tries so hard to hide. Every time I see it, it cuts through me.

She loves you so much. You're all she talks about. I have so many orders from her for you. I'm not allowed to make you crazy the way I do your Uncle Chris. I'm not allowed to call the doctors every time you sneeze and you are to be allowed to tussle with your friends without me having a conniption that someone might bruise you.

Nor am I to bully you about getting married or having kids. Ever.

Most of all, you are allowed to pick out your own car at sixteen. I'm not supposed to put you in a tank. We'll see about that one. I refused to promise her this last item until I know more about you. Not to mention, I've seen how other people drive on the roads. So if you have a tank, sorry. There's only so much changing a man my age can do.

I don't know what our futures will hold. I only

hope that when all is said and done, you are more like your mother than you are like me. She's a good woman. A kind woman. Full of love and compassion even though her life has been hard and full of grief. She bears her scars with a grace, dignity, and humor that I lack.

Most of all, she has courage the likes of which I haven't witnessed in centuries. I hope with every part of me that you inherit all her best traits and none of my bad ones.

I don't really know what more to say. I just thought you should have something of me in here too.

Love,
Your father

Tears rolled down her cheeks as she read his words. "Oh, Wulf," she breathed, her heart breaking at the things he would never admit to aloud. It was so strange to see herself through his eyes. She never thought of herself as particularly brave. Never thought of herself as strong.

Not until the night she had met a dark champion.

As Cassandra folded up the note and resealed it, she realized something.

She loved Wulf. Desperately.

She wasn't sure when it had happened. It might have been the first time he took her into his arms. Or it might have been when he reluctantly welcomed her into his home.

No, she realized, it was none of those times. She had fallen in love with him the first time he had touched her belly with his strong, capable hand and called her baby his.

Dark-Hunter or not, he was a good, wonderful man for an ancient barbarian.

The door opened.

"Are you all right?" Wulf rushed forward to the bed.

"I'm fine," she said, clearing her throat. "It's these stupid pregnancy hormones. I cry at the drop of a hat. Ugh!"

He wiped her tears away from her cheeks. "It's okay. I understand. I've been around plenty of pregnant women in my day."

"Your Squires?"

He nodded. "I've even delivered a few of their babies."

"Really?"

"Oh, yeah. You have to love the days before modern roads and hospitals when I was up to my elbows in placenta."

She laughed, but then she always did around him. He had an incredible knack for making her feel better.

Wulf helped her put everything away. "You should probably go on to sleep. You didn't rest well last night."

"I know. I'm going, I promise."

He tucked her into bed after she had changed into her nightgown, then turned the lights off and left her alone. Cassandra lay in the dark, her thoughts wandering.

Closing her eyes, she imagined her and Wulf in his house, with a passel of children running around them.

Funny how she had never dared dream for a single child and now she wanted more time to have as many as possible.

For him.

For her.

But then, all of her people wished for more time on this earth. Her mother, even her sister.

You could go Daimon too.

Maybe, but then the man she loved would be honor bound to kill her.

No, she couldn't do that to either one of them. Like all the Apollites here, she would meet her death with the dignity Wulf had written of.

And he would be left behind to weep for her . . .

Cassandra winced at that. How she wished she dared run so that he would never see her die. Never know when she passed away. It was so cruel to him.

But it was too late for that. There was no way to escape him while she needed his protection. All she could do was try to keep him from loving her as much as she loved him.

For the next three days, Cassandra had the distinct feeling that something was up. Whenever she drew near Wulf and Kat when they were together, they would immediately become quiet and act nervous.

Chris had taken up with a group of young female Apollites that Phoebe had introduced him to when she'd taken him shopping to buy electronics that would keep him from being bored. The Apollite girls thought his dark coloring was "exotic" and they adored the fact that he was so into computers and technology.

"I have died and gone to Valhalla!" Chris had exclaimed the night he met them. "These women appreciate a man with a brain and they don't care that I don't tan. None of their people do either. It's great!"

"They're Apollites, Chris," Wulf had warned him.

"Yeah, so? You got an Apollite babe. I want one too. Or two or three or four of them. This is so cool."

Wulf had shaken his head and left Chris to them with

one last warning. "If they make a move on your neck, run."

By day five, Cassandra was really starting to worry. Wulf had been nervous since the moment she woke up. What's more, he and Kat had been gone for hours the night before and neither one of them would tell her what they'd been up to.

He reminded her of a skittish colt.

"Is there something I need to know?" Cassandra asked after she cornered him in the living room.

"I'm going to go find Phoebe or something," Kat said, shooting for the door.

She made a hasty exit.

"There's just something, I . . ." Wulf paused.

Cassandra waited.

"Well?" she prompted.

"Wait here." He left her to go to Chris's room.

A few minutes later, he came back with an old Viking sword. She remembered having seen it in a special glass case in his cellar. The two of them must have gone back to his place last night to retrieve it. But why they would take such a chance, she couldn't imagine.

Holding the sword in his hands between them, Wulf took a deep breath. "This isn't something I've thought about doing in more than twelve hundred years and I'm trying to remember everything, so give me a second."

She didn't like the sound of that. She drew her brows into a deep vee. "What are you going to do? Cut my head off?"

He gave her a peeved stare. "No, not hardly."

She watched as he took two gold bands out of his pocket and placed them on the blade. Then he presented them to her.

"Cassandra Elaine Peters, I would like to marry you."

She was dumbstruck by his proposal. The thought of marriage had never even entered her mind. "What?"

His dark eyes burned into hers. "I know our son had a strange conception, and will most definitely have an odd life, but I want him to be born the old-fashioned way—to married parents."

Cassandra covered her face with her hands as tears welled. "What is it about you that you make me cry all the time? I swear, I never wept until the day I met you."

He looked as if she had struck him.

"I don't mean it in a bad way, Wulf. You just do things that touch me so deeply in my heart that it makes me cry."

"So you'll marry me?"

"Of course, you silly man."

He moved to kiss her. The sword tilted and the rings went rolling across the floor. "Damn," he snapped as they scattered. "I knew I was going to botch this. Hold on."

He got down on his hands and knees and retrieved the rings from under the couch. Then he returned to her and kissed her lips hotly.

Cassandra savored the taste of him. He had given her so much more than she ever hoped for or dreamed of.

Nipping her lips, he pulled back. "In Norse custom, we did things backward. The couple exchanged plain bands at the betrothal. You'll receive your diamond ring when we get married."

"Okay."

He slid her smaller ring on her trembling hand, then handed her the larger one.

Cassandra's hand shook even more as she saw the intricate Norse design of a highly stylized dragon. She slid it onto his finger, then kissed the back of his hand. "Thank you."

He cupped her face gently and kissed her. Cassandra was instantly dizzy.

"I have everything planned for Friday night if that's okay with you," he said quietly.

"Why Friday?"

"My people always married on Fridays to pay tribute to the goddess Frigga. I thought we could combine the customs of your people with mine. Since the Apollites have no set day of the week, Phoebe said it wouldn't matter to you."

Cassandra pulled him back to her lips and kissed the devil out of him. Who knew an ancient barbarian could be so thoughtful?

The only thing that would make this more perfect would be to have her father present, but Cassandra had learned long ago not to ask for the impossible.

"Thank you, Wulf."

He nodded. "Now Kat and Phoebe need you to go shopping for a wedding dress."

He opened the front door only to have Phoebe and Kat spill into the room.

They both gave false smiles as they righted themselves.

"Oops," Kat said. "We just wanted to make sure everything was going as planned."

Wulf shook his head.

"Of course it is," Cassandra said. "How could it not?"

And before she knew it, they had whisked her away to a small shop down in the main part of the city while Wulf stayed in the apartment.

Cassandra hadn't really been back to the city after Wulf's "warm" reception and her horrifying discovery of Phoebe and Urian together.

Rather, she and Wulf had spent most of their time confined to their apartment where she was safe and didn't have to worry about anyone insulting him.

It was nice to be out now, even if the air was recycled rather than fresh. Phoebe took her into a dress store that was owned by a friend of hers who was expecting them. In fact, all the women in the store were surprisingly friendly toward her.

Cassandra had a suspicion most of that was because they owed so much to Phoebe's husband.

Melissa, the clerk assigned to help them, appeared around the age of twenty. She was a skinny blond woman no taller than five ten, which for a Daimon was tiny.

"This one could be easily altered by Friday," Melissa said, holding up a sleek, gauzy dress that shimmered in the faint light. It was an iridescent silvery white. "Would you like to try it on?"

"Okay."

As soon as Cassandra saw it in the full-length mirror, she knew there was no need to go any further. It was gorgeous and she felt like a fairy princess in it. The material was buttery soft and slid sensuously against her skin.

"You're so beautiful," Phoebe whispered as she stared at her in the mirror. "How I wish Mom and Dad could see you right now."

Cassandra smiled at her. It was hard to feel beautiful with her stomach sticking out a mile, but at least she had a good reason for being fat.

"You are lovely," Kat concurred as she helped to adjust the floor-length hem.

"What do you think?" Melissa asked. "I have more if—"

"I'll take it."

Smiling, Melissa moved forward and helped her out of

it, then took measurements for the alterations. Kat and Phoebe left the dressing room and went outside to look for accessories.

"You know," Melissa said as she measured Cassandra's waist, "I have to say that I admire you for what you've done."

Cassandra looked at her with consternation. "What do you mean?"

"Finding a Dark-Hunter to protect you," Melissa said as she made notes on a small PDA. "I wish I had someone like that to look after my little ones when I'm gone. My husband died three months ago, and though I have another two years, I can't help but worry about them."

Two years . . .

Melissa looked younger than that. It was hard to imagine the vibrant, healthy salesclerk dying of old age in such a short time.

The poor woman had lost her husband. Most Apollites married people within a few months of their own age for that reason. It was considered a bonus to find a spouse who shared your birthday.

"Is it . . . painful?" Cassandra asked hesitantly. She'd never seen an Apollite die of "natural" causes.

Melissa made another note. "We make a vow here to let no one die alone."

"You haven't answered my question."

Melissa met her gaze. Her eyes were filled with unspoken emotions, but it was the fear there that reached out and made Cassandra shiver. "Do you want the truth?"

"Yes."

"It's unbearable. My husband was a strong man. He cried like a baby all night long from the pain of it."

Melissa cleared her throat as if her own pain were too much to bear. "I sometimes understand why so many of our people kill themselves the night before. I even thought about moving my children to a new community so that they would have the choice, but up on the surface, we have too many predators to fight. Other Apollites, Daimons, Were-Hunters, humans, and Dark-Hunters who are looking for our brethren. My mother brought me here when I was just a child. But I remember the upper world well. It's so much safer here. At least we can live openly without fear of someone learning about us."

Cassandra couldn't breathe as thoughts tore through her. She had known it wouldn't be pleasant, but what Melissa described was so much worse than what she had imagined.

It would be bad enough for her to suffer . . . but what of the baby? He was so innocent. He didn't deserve such a fate.

But then who did?

"Oh, here now," Melissa said quickly, "I didn't mean to upset you."

"It's okay," Cassandra said past the lump in her throat. "I asked and I appreciate your honesty."

As soon as they were finished, Cassandra no longer felt festive, nor did she want to continue shopping. She needed to see Wulf.

She found him in the bedroom of their apartment, flipping channels on the TV. He turned it off the instant he saw her. "Is something wrong?"

She hesitated at the foot of the bed. He sat back against the pillows, his feet bare and one leg bent. The concern in his eyes meant the world to her, but it wasn't enough.

"Will you hunt my baby, Wulf?"

He scowled. "What?"

"If our son grows up and decides he doesn't want to die. Will you kill him for it?"

Wulf held his breath as he debated. "I don't know, Cassandra. I really don't. My honor commands it. But I don't know if I can."

"Swear to me you won't hurt him," she said, moving to stand beside him. She grabbed his shirt and held tight as fear and agony washed through her. "Promise me that when he's grown, if he turns Daimon you'll let him go."

"I can't."

"Then why are we here?" she shrieked at him. "What good is having you as his father if you're going to kill him anyway?"

"Cassandra, please. Be reasonable."

"You be reasonable!" she shouted. "I'm going to die, Wulf. Die! Painfully. And I'm almost out of time." She let go of him and paced back and forth, trying to breathe. "Don't you see. I won't remember anything after I'm dead. I'll be gone. Gone from all of this. From all of you." She looked around the room frantically. "I won't see these colors. Your face. Nothing. I'm going to die. Die!"

Wulf pulled her into his arms as she sobbed against his chest. "It's okay, Cassandra, I have you."

"Stop saying it's okay, Wulf. It's not okay. Nothing we can do will stop this. What am I going to do? I'm only twenty-six. I don't understand. Why do I have to do this? Why can't I see my baby grow up?"

"There has to be something to help you," he insisted. "Maybe Kat can talk to Artemis. There's always a loophole."

"Like you have?" she demanded hysterically. "You can't escape being a Dark-Hunter any more than I can escape being an Apollite. Why are we even getting married? What's the point?"

His gaze burned into hers. "Because I'm not going to let it end like this," he growled fiercely. "I have lost everything I cared about in my life. I'm not going to lose your or my child to this. Do you hear me?"

She heard him, but it changed nothing. "What's the solution?"

He pulled her roughly against his chest. "I don't know. But there has to be something."

"And if there's not?"

"Then I'll tear down the halls of Olympus or Hades or whatever I have to to find you. I'm not going to let you go, Cassandra. Not without a fight."

Cassandra held him close, but in her heart, she knew it was futile. Their days were finite, and with every passing hour, she was drawing irrevocably closer to the end.

Chapter 14

By the time Friday came, Cassandra was more than ready for the wedding to be behind her. Her sister and Kat had kept her busy and frantic the whole week. Wulf had stayed blissfully out of their way.

If they ever asked him his opinion on anything, his answer was always, "I know better than to get in between three women arguing. If you'll remember, the whole Trojan War was started over that."

Chris wasn't so wise and had finally learned to stay out of the apartment as much as possible. Or to run the minute he saw the three of them approaching him.

Now Cassandra stood in the bedroom, dressed in her wedding gown and waiting. Her long, strawberry-blond hair was left down around her shoulders as was the custom of Wulf's people. She wore a silver crown intertwined with fresh flowers—another Nordic custom. Chris had told her that the crown had been passed down from Wulf's sister-in-law through all the generations of his family.

It meant a lot to her to be wearing it now. To feel connected to Wulf's past.

Wulf would also be wearing his family sword for the

event, and when their baby married, he too would carry the sword strapped to his side.

The door opened slowly to reveal Urian on the other side. His long blond hair hung around his shoulders and he was dressed in an elegant black silk tuxedo. "Are you ready?"

They had decided after much debate to let him be her sponsor. Apollites didn't have the same customs as humans. Since there was a good chance the bride's parents were already dead, they chose a sponsor who would escort the bride down the aisle and deliver the customary words to unite the couple.

Cassandra wished they could have a minister for the event, but both she and Wulf had agreed that it would jeopardize the community too much to bring one in. So they would be married in true Apollite fashion.

At first, Urian had balked at the idea of being her sponsor, but Phoebe had quickly convinced him it would be in his best interest to play along with their wishes.

"You will do it and play nice with Wulf or you'll sleep on the couch. Forever, and considering your *age, that means something."*

"Is Wulf ready?" Cassandra asked Urian.

He nodded. "He and Chris are waiting for you in the main complex."

Kat handed her the single white rose that was wrapped with red and white ribbons. Another Apollite custom.

Cassandra took the rose.

Kat and Phoebe took their places in front of her and led the way. Arm in arm, she and Urian walked behind them.

The Norse custom was for weddings to be held outside. Since such a thing was even more dangerous than bringing in a minister, they had rented the open merchant area. Shanus and several council members had gone out of their way to bring hydroponic plants and flowers to simulate a garden center.

They had even constructed a small fountain.

Cassandra hesitated as they entered the complex.

Wulf and Chris stood in front of the hastily constructed waterfall that still managed to be beautiful. She had half-expected Wulf to be dressed in his Nordic clothes. Instead, he and Chris were in tuxedos that matched Urian's.

Wulf wore his hair long and loose, brushed back from his face. The silk of his tuxedo molded perfectly to his body, accentuating every muscled curve. Never in her life had she seen a more handsome man.

He was completely gorgeous.

"I'll take it from here."

Cassandra gasped as she heard her father's voice behind her.

"Daddy?" she said, whirling to find him there with a wide smile on his face.

"You didn't really think I'd miss my baby getting married, did you?"

She ran her gaze over his body, her heart hammering. She couldn't believe he was here with her. "But how?"

He indicated Wulf with a nod. "Wulf came to the house last night and brought me here. He said it wouldn't be a wedding for you unless I came. And he told me about Phoebe. I spent last night in her apartment with her so that we could catch up and then surprise you." His eyes welled with tears as he stared at her stomach. "You look beautiful, baby."

She threw herself into his arms, or at least as close as she could, given her distended belly, and held him tight. It was the best present Wulf could have given her.

She was blubbering like a child.

"Should we call the wedding off before you drown us in tears?" Kat asked.

"No!" Cassandra said, pulling herself together with a sniff. "I'm fine. Really."

Her father kissed her cheek, tucked her hand into the crook of his arm, and led her to Wulf. Kat and Phoebe moved to stand behind Chris while Urian took his place by Phoebe's side. The only other person present was Shanus, who stood back but watched them with a friendly expression that said he was more than happy to bear witness to the event.

"Thank you," she mouthed to Wulf who gave her a small, heartrending smile.

In that moment, she felt the full depth of her love for him. He would make a good husband to her for the next few months and he would be a great father.

In spite of what Chris said.

Once they reached her soon-to-be husband, her father took her hand and placed it in Wulf's. Then her father took the red and white ribbons from the rose and wrapped it around their joined hands.

Cassandra stared at Wulf. His eyes were hot. Kind. They smoldered with his passion and with pride as he looked at her. It made her shiver. Made her hot.

His look touched every part of her body.

He tightened his hand on hers as her father began speaking the words to bind them together. "It is through night we are—"

"Light," Urian whispered loudly, interrupting him.

Her father's face flushed a bit. "I'm sorry. I had to learn this rather hastily." He cleared his throat and began again. "It is through light we are born and through . . . through . . ." Her father hesitated.

Urian came forward to whisper in her father's ear.

"Thank you," her father said. "This ceremony is nothing like ours."

Urian inclined his head and stepped back, but not before he gave Cassandra an uncharacteristic wink.

"It is through the light that we are born and through the night that we travel. The light is the love of our parents who greet us and welcome us into this world and it is with the love of our partner that we leave it.

"Wulf and Cassandra have chosen to be with each other, to ease their remaining journey and to comfort one another in the coming nights. And when the final night is upon them . . ." Her father stopped as his eyes welled up.

He looked at her. The misery and horror she saw in his eyes made her own well up.

"I can't," he said quietly.

"Daddy?"

He stepped back as a tear fell down his cheek.

Phoebe came forward and wrapped her arms around him.

Cassandra started toward him, but Phoebe stopped her. "Finish it, please, Uri."

Phoebe escorted their father off to the side.

Cassandra wanted to join them, but could tell her father was already embarrassed and upset that he had spoiled her wedding for her. So she stayed by Wulf's side.

Urian moved to stand with them. "When the final night is upon us, we vow to stand together and ease the one who travels first.

"Soul to soul we have touched. Flesh to flesh we have breathed. And it is alone that we must leave this existence, until the night comes that the Fates decree we are reunited in *Katoteros*."

Cassandra felt her own tears starting again as Urian spoke the Atlantean term for "heaven."

Urian stepped to the pedestal that held an elaborate gold cup. The three Fates were engraved on it. He brought it over to Cassandra. "Normally this would be the blood of both of you combined, but since neither one of you is particularly gung-ho for that, it's wine."

Urian handed the cup to Cassandra who took a sip, then gave it to Wulf who followed suit. Wulf handed the cup to Urian. As was the Apollite custom, Wulf bent down and kissed her so that the taste of wine was mingled with them.

Urian returned the cup to the pedestal and finished the ceremony. "Here stands the bride, Cassandra. She is unique in this world. Her beauty, grace, and charms are the legacy of those who have come before her and will be gifted to those who are born through her.

"This man, Wulf, on the other hand stands before us a product of . . ." Urian frowned as he paused. "Well, he's the product of a bitch who can't stand the thought of Apollo's children ruling the earth."

"Urian, behave!" Phoebe snapped from where she stood with their father.

He bristled at her command. "Considering the fact that I just bound a member of your family to one of the people I have sworn to annihilate, I think I'm being remarkably good."

Phoebe cast him a glare that loudly proclaimed he'd be sleeping alone for at least a week.

If not longer.

Urian curled his lip at Wulf. It was clear who he blamed for his wife's upset. "Fine. I'm glad I didn't say what I really thought," he muttered under his breath.

Louder, Urian returned to the ceremony. "It is your similarities that brought you together and your differ-ences that add variety and spark to your life. May the

gods bless and protect your union and may you be . . ."
He paused again. "Well, you already are blessed with fertility so we'll skip that."

Phoebe growled low in her throat while Cassandra gave him a glare of her own.

Urian cast another murderous look at Wulf. "May the two of you enjoy every minute left to you."

Then, Urian took the ribbons that combined their hands and tied them into a double knot. The ribbons would last for the night and in the morning they would be cut and buried for luck.

Chris and Kat led the way back to the apartment.

Her father came up to her and wrapped his arm around her waist. "I'm sorry I couldn't finish."

"It's okay, Daddy. I understand."

And she did. The prospect of saying good-bye to him hurt her too.

When they reached the apartment, Wulf, as was Norse custom, picked her up and carried her over the threshold. It amazed her because he had to do it with one arm since his other hand was still bound to hers.

Chris poured everyone drinks. "This is where Wulf's people would get drunk and party for a week. All hail the Vikings, forerunners to the frat boys!"

"You can party," Wulf said to him, "but I better not catch you drunk."

Chris rolled his eyes, then bent down and said to Cassandra's stomach, "Be wise, little guy, stay in there where Lord King Neurotic can't kill all your fun."

Wulf shook his head at him. "I'm surprised you're here without your newfound friends."

"Yeah, I know. I'm going to go find them shortly. Kyra is working on a new program and I'm going to test it."

Urian snorted at that. "That's one way of putting it."

Chris's face turned beet red. "And I thought he"—he indicated Wulf with his thumb—"was bad. What is it with you Peters women that you're attracted to losers?"

"I think I resent that," her father said.

Wulf laughed. "Boy, you better go find Kyra before you dig yourself in any deeper."

"Yeah, I think I agree." Chris excused himself and left.

Kat came up behind Cassandra and took the crown off her head. "I'll make sure and put it back in its case."

"Thanks."

Suddenly, it felt a bit awkward in the room.

"Daddy? You want to come back to our place with us?" Phoebe asked.

"Sure." He kissed Cassandra on the cheek. "Not much of a reception, but I think you two should be alone."

Kat joined them as they left.

They were alone now, and Wulf pulled a perfect single-carat diamond ring from his pocket and slid it over her finger. The band was a very delicate Nordic lattice pattern. She'd never seen anything more lovely.

"Thank you, Wulf," she breathed.

Wulf nodded. He stared at her in the pale light, her eyes glowing with warmth.

His wife.

The one thing he had never thought to have. At least not in the last twelve hundred years.

Normally a couple on their honeymoon would be thinking about their future together. How they were going to spend their lives . . .

He didn't want to think about the future. It was too bleak. Too painful. He should have kept her out of his heart. Every day he tried and every day he found her there even deeper than before.

"Cassandra Tryggvason," he whispered, testing her new name.

"It has a nice ring to it, doesn't it?"

He touched her lips with his fingers. Like her, they were soft and delicate. Inviting. "Are you happy?"

"Yes." And yet her green eyes were tinged by sadness. How he wished he could erase that from her forever.

Cassandra stood up on her tiptoes and kissed him. Wulf groaned at the taste of her. At the way her hand felt on the back of his neck while her long, graceful fingers tugged at his hair.

Her rose scent went through him, making him drunk and hot. "You are beautiful, my Cassandra."

Cassandra shivered at his low-voiced words. She loved it whenever he referred to her as his.

Taking her hand that was tied to his, he led her toward the bedroom.

Cassandra bit her lip as she watched him. He was so tall and devastating. He laid her carefully on the bed, then paused.

"How are we supposed to take off our clothes with this on our wrists?"

"My sleeves unzip."

"Mine don't."

"Then you're going to be wearing that tuxedo for the night. Ew!"

"Ew?" he asked playfully. "Suddenly I'm ew?"

She moaned as he cupped her chin and nipped her lips with his teeth. "Ew to the extreme," she teased breathlessly.

She felt him unzip the back of her dress slowly as if savoring the anticipation of her being naked with him.

"You know, in Viking tradition, we'd have had witnesses for this."

She shivered as his hot hand skimmed her bared skin. "No offense, I am so glad this isn't in your lifetime."

"Me too. I'd have to kill any man who saw just how beautiful you really are. If they saw you, I know they'd be dreaming of you, and that I could never allow."

She closed her eyes, savoring those words, as he pulled her dress from her.

He paused only long enough to kiss her bulging stomach. The minute his lips grazed her, she felt the light, fluttering movement inside.

"Oh, my God," she breathed. "I just felt the baby!"

He pulled back. "What?"

Her eyes welling up, she placed her hand over the spot his lips had touched, wanting to feel the baby again. "I felt him," she repeated. "Just now."

Pride shone brightly in Wulf's eyes as he dipped his head and kissed her stomach again. He nuzzled her bare skin with his whiskered cheek.

Cassandra should have felt embarrassed to have a man so perfectly formed nuzzling her when she was the size of a whale, but she didn't. It was so comforting to have him with her.

He was her champion. Not because he had saved her life, but because of the way he stayed with her now. The way he held her when she cried. The way he comforted her.

He was her strength. Her courage.

And she was so damned grateful to have him with her. She didn't want to face the end alone.

Wulf wouldn't let her. He would be there with her, even though it was going to kill him to see her die. He would hold her hand, and when she was gone, she would be remembered throughout time.

"I don't even know the name of my grandmother."

Wulf frowned. "What?"

"I don't know my grandmother's name. My mother died before I could ask. Phoebe said she'd never thought to ask either. I don't know what either she or my grandfather looked like. I only know my father's parents from pictures. I was just thinking that I will be only a picture to the baby. He will look at me as I used to look at them. Abstract people. Never really real."

His eyes sparked with intensity. "You will be real to him, Cassandra. I promise you."

How she hoped that was true.

He enveloped her in his arms and held her close. Cassandra held on, needing his warmth. She pushed the regret and pain out of her mind.

There was nothing she could do. Inevitable meant inevitable. At least she had this moment in time.

She burst out laughing and crying at the same time.

Wulf pulled back and stared at her in confusion.

"I'm sorry," she said, trying to control her emotions. "I was just thinking of that stupid song, 'Seasons in the Sun.' You know, 'we had joy, we had fun, we had seasons in the sun.' Good grief, I should be a mental patient."

He wiped her tears away and kissed her cheeks. His warm lips burned her skin. "You have more strength than any warrior I have known. Don't ever apologize to me again for those few times when you show your fear to me, Cassandra."

The love she felt for him ran through her, choking her up even more than her regrets. "I love you, Wulf," she breathed. "More than I think I have ever loved anything else."

Wulf couldn't breathe as he heard those heartfelt words. They tore through him like shattering glass.

"I love you too," he said, his throat tightening at the truth of it. He didn't want to let her go. Ever.

But there was nothing he could do to stop it.

Cassandra gasped as he kissed her passionately. He finished undressing her in a fever pitch. She unbuttoned his shirt and when they couldn't find a way to remove it or his jacket, Wulf tore them off.

She laughed at the sight of him. But the laughter stopped the instant he laid his hot, heavy body against hers and returned to her lips.

He rolled over onto his back and pulled her on top of him. He always took great care with her so as not to press against her stomach or hurt either her or the baby.

His eyes searing, he placed her on top of him.

They both groaned the minute he entered her. They made love furiously, each aware of the fact that for them the end was racing toward them.

Aware that as every day passed, they were nearing an outcome that neither of them could control or avoid.

It was frightening.

Cassandra cried out as she came in a wave of molten passion. Wulf pulled her against him as he joined her.

Their joined hands rested on the bed above their heads. Wulf laced his fingers in hers and made her a ragged promise.

"I will not let you go without a fight."

Chapter 15

The next few weeks went by in a blur as Cassandra finished the baby's memory box. For the first time in her life, she actually felt safe somewhere.

It was a glorious feeling.

Chris and Kyra, the so-called Apollite babe Chris had found, spent a lot of time in the apartment. Kyra was a pleasant woman who would often pretend that she couldn't remember Wulf just to annoy him.

The tall, thin Apollite would look at him guilelessly and ask, "Do I know you?"

It irritated Wulf but amused everyone else.

As the pregnancy progressed, Cassandra realized another reason why Daimons couldn't have children. She became increasingly needful of blood. Her biweekly transfusions turned into daily ones, and for the past two weeks, she'd needed two to three of them a day.

The increase worried her. Did it mean the baby would be more Apollite than human?

Dr. Lakis had told her it really had no bearing on the baby's biology and that she should relax. But it was hard for her.

All night long, Cassandra had been rather depressed

and too tired to move. She'd gone to bed early, even before dawn, wanting to rest and just be comfortable for a few minutes.

Wulf came in and woke her up long enough to ask her how she was.

"I'm sleeping," she snapped. "Leave me alone."

He'd held his hands up in surrender, laughed good-naturedly, and then curled up around her. She had to admit she loved the feeling of him there. The sensation of his hand on her stomach.

It always seemed like the baby knew when it was Wulf's hand on him. He would immediately become more active, as if wanting to say, "Hi, Daddy, can't wait to meet you."

He also reacted to his father's voice.

Closing her eyes, Cassandra tried to go back to sleep, but it wasn't easy since Little Bigfoot started dancing the fandango and decided to knee her in the ribs a few times.

She lay there for about an hour until the lower back pain set in. Within twenty minutes, she realized her contractions had stabilized and were steady.

Wulf was sleeping peacefully when Cassandra woke him up.

"The baby's coming," she gasped out.

"Are you sure?" But one look at her exasperated face and he knew the answer to that asinine question.

"Okay," he said, trying to wake up and clear the fog in his mind. "Stay here and I'll summon the troops."

He ran from the room to wake Kat and to send Chris for the doctor, then he ran back to the bedroom to be with Cassandra who was up, walking around.

"What are you doing?"

"I'm pacing to help with the pain."

"Yeah, but—"

"It's okay, hon," Kat said as she came through the door. "The baby won't be born on his head."

Wulf wasn't sure about that, but had learned not to argue with a pregnant Cassandra. She was rather tense and emotional, and could let blood with her tongue when she wanted to.

Better to just give her what she wanted.

"What can I get you?" Wulf asked.

Cassandra was panting. "How about someone else to have this kid for me?"

He laughed at that. At least until she gave him a murderous glare.

Sobering, he cleared his throat. "I wish I could."

By the time the doctor came, Wulf was standing behind her, holding her stomach and trying to help her breathe through the contractions. He could feel each contraction tighten against his palms and knew exactly when she was going to curse in pain from it.

He hated that she had to go through this. She was already sweaty from the exertion and she had barely begun the labor to bring their son into the world.

Hours went by slowly as they worked together and Cassandra screamed all manner of obscenities at him, all men in general, and the gods in particular.

Wulf would hold her hand and bathe her brow while the doctor directed them both on what to do.

It was just after five P.M. when his son was finally born.

Wulf stared at the tiny infant in the doctor's hands as the baby squalled with a set of lungs that had to come from a healthy child.

"He's really here," Cassandra sobbed as she held on to Wulf's hand and stared at the baby she had birthed.

"He's here," Wulf laughed, kissing her damp temple. "And he's beautiful."

The doctor cleaned and examined him, then handed the baby to his mother.

Cassandra couldn't breathe as she held her child for the very first time. His tiny fists were clenched as his screams let them all know he was here. His face was wrinkled like an old man's, but even so he was gorgeous to her.

"Look at his hair," she said, brushing the thick mat of black hair down. "He looks like his father."

Wulf smiled as the baby wrapped his tiny hand around his father's index finger. "He has your lungs."

"Oh, please!" she said indignantly.

"Trust me," Wulf said, meeting her gaze. "Every Apollite here now knows that my parents were unmarried at my birth, and that if you survive the night, you plan on making me a eunuch."

She laughed at him and then kissed him while she held their son.

"By the way, if you were serious about any of that, Cassandra," the doctor said, her eyes alight. "I do have a scalpel I can loan you."

Cassandra laughed again. "Don't tempt me."

Wulf took the baby from her and held him carefully in his large hands. His son. The joy and fear inside him was debilitating. He'd never known anything like it.

The baby was so incredibly tiny. A miracle of life. How could something so tiny ever survive? He knew he would kill or seriously maim anyone who ever threatened his child.

"What are you going to name him?" Wulf asked Cassandra. In all these weeks, he had purposely stayed out of her decision. He wanted the baby's mother to name him.

It would be her lasting legacy to their son, who would never really know her.

"How about Erik Jefferson Tryggvason?"

Wulf blinked in disbelief. "Are you sure?"

She nodded as he lightly touched the baby's cheek.

"Hi, Little Erik," he breathed. His heart clenched as he called him his brother's name. "Welcome home."

"The baby probably wants to nurse now," Dr. Lakis said as she finished cleaning everything up. "You might want to hand him back to his mother for a bit."

Wulf did as she suggested.

"Will you need a lactation nurse?" Dr. Lakis asked Cassandra. "Apollite babies generally won't take bottles or formula, especially when they have a mixed heritage. There's not really a safe formula we can try since we don't know how much Apollite or human is in him."

"I think the nurse would be a good idea," Cassandra said. "I don't want to mess this up and stunt his growth or turn him into a mutant or anything."

The doctor had a strange look on her face that basically said, "I thought your child *was* a mutant."

Wisely, she held her tongue.

Wulf walked the doctor out. "Thank you," he said as they entered the living room where Chris and Kat sat waiting.

"Ha!" Kat said as soon as she saw Wulf. "I told you he'd arrive unhurt."

"Damn," Chris muttered before he handed her a twenty. "I just knew he'd been neutered after all that."

They both rushed toward the bedroom to see the baby, while Wulf talked to the doctor.

She gave him a sad smile. "I suppose it's somehow fitting."

"What is?"

"The last baby I help into this world is the one who is destined to keep it safe."

Wulf scowled. "What do you mean, the last baby?"

Dr. Lakis sighed as if the weight of Armageddon were upon her. "My birthday is Thursday."

Wulf went cold at her words and what they meant. "Your twenty-seventh?"

She nodded. "Dr. Cassus will take over monitoring their health. She'll be the one who gives Cassandra her four-week physical and makes sure everything is progressing as it should."

Dr. Lakis started for the door.

"Doctor, wait."

She turned toward him.

"I'm—"

"Don't say you're sorry. I'm just another Apollite to you."

"No," he said sincerely. "You're not. You're the woman who kept my wife safe and who helped to birth my son. I won't ever forget that."

She offered him a tremulous smile. "I wish you luck with your son. I hope he grows up to be the man his father is."

Wulf watched her leave, his heart heavy. He had tried so hard to stay detached from everyone here. To not care and not see how very human his enemies were. But it was impossible. Just like staying away from Cassandra was impossible.

Against his will and common sense, they had all invaded his heart.

How could he ever go back to his role as a Dark-Hunter after all this?

How could he kill another Daimon when he understood them so well?

How?

Cassandra was exhausted by the time Wulf returned to her. Kat and the nurse had taken the baby to watch so that she could rest. Of course, they would have to wake her when it was time for his next feeding, but for a little while, Cassandra would be able to rest in comfort.

"Close your eyes," Wulf said.

Cassandra did as he asked without question and felt him place something around her neck. Opening her eyes, she saw an intricate, antique necklace. The design was obviously Norse. It had four square pieces of amber mounted on their sides in a diamond shape. In the center was a circular piece with another amber stone embedded in it, and dropping down from that was a tiny Viking ship that had its sail made of more amber.

"It's beautiful."

"Erik and I bought two of them from a Danish merchant in Byzantium. It reminded us of home. He gave his to his wife and I was going to give mine to my sister, Brynhild."

"Why didn't you give it to her?"

"She wouldn't take it. She was too angry at me for not being there when our father died, angry at me for raiding. She said she never wanted to see me again, so I left and have kept the necklace with me ever since. I pulled it out of my safe when Kat and I went back for my sword."

His sadness touched her. Over the past few months, she had learned just how much Wulf's siblings had meant to him. "I'm sorry, Wulf."

"Don't be. I like seeing it on you. It's as if it were meant to be there." He brushed his hand through her hair. "Do you want me to go sleep on the couch?"

"Why would I want that?"

"You said earlier that you weren't ever again going to let me near your bed."

She laughed lightly. "I don't even remember half of what I said."

"That's okay. I think Chris was recording it in the other room for posterity."

She covered her face with her hands. "I hope you're joking."

"No, not really."

Cassandra ran her hand through his silken hair and let the strands of it slide through her fingers. "Well, now that it's over, I'm much more tolerant of you. So, come and snuggle up. I think I could use it."

Wulf quickly obliged her.

Cassandra let out a long, tired breath and drifted off to sleep.

Wulf watched her as he let the warm softness of her body seep into his very heart. He took her hand in his and studied the delicate shape of it.

"Don't leave me, Cassandra," he whispered. "I don't want to raise our son without you."

But wishing for her to stay was as productive as wishing for his soul back.

On Thursday morning, Wulf couldn't sleep. Cassandra and Erik were both blissfully unconscious. But his thoughts wouldn't settle down long enough for him to rest.

Getting up, he donned his clothes and left the apartment. Since few Apollites were up and about, he didn't have to endure many sneers or glares.

He knew he had no business headed where he was, but he couldn't stop himself.

He had to say good-bye to Dr. Lakis. She had strangely become another member of their small troop over the weeks when she had kept vigil over Cassandra's and Erik's health.

Her apartment wasn't far away from Phoebe's.

Unsure of his reception, he knocked on her door.

A boy around the age of twelve answered it.

"Are you Ty?" he asked the boy, remembering Dr. Lakis talking about her oldest son.

"My mama's not going Daimon. You can leave her alone."

Wulf flinched at his angry words. "I know she's not. I just want to see her for a minute."

"Aunt Millicent," he yelled without letting him in. "The Dark-Hunter wants to see Mama."

A beautiful woman around Chris's age came to the door. "What do you want?"

"I want to see Dr. Lakis."

"He's going to kill her!" the boy said from behind her.

She ignored the boy. Narrowing her eyes, she stepped back and let Wulf enter.

Wulf took a deep breath in relief as she led him to a bedroom on his left. The door opened to show him a room with five small children and one more woman around Millicent's age. Dr. Lakis lay on the bed, but he barely recognized her. Instead of the young vibrant woman who had delivered his baby, she already looked as if she were fifty years old.

Millicent shooed the children and the other adult out.

"You only have five minutes, Dark-Hunter. We want to be with her as long as we can."

He nodded, and once he was alone with her, he knelt beside the bed.

"Why are you here, Wulf?" Dr. Lakis asked. It was the first time she had ever used his name.

"I'm not sure. I just wanted to thank you again."

She blinked her tear-filled eyes and appeared to age another ten years. "This isn't the bad part," she whispered. "That comes later when our bodies fall apart while we're still alive. If we're lucky, our organs fail quickly and we die. Otherwise it lasts for hours and is excruciating."

Her words tore through him as he thought about Cassandra going through this. Of her in even more pain than she had been in when Erik was born. "I'm so sorry."

Dr. Lakis didn't take pity on him. "Just answer me one question?"

"Anything."

Her gaze bored into his with its molten heat. "Do you understand?"

He nodded. Yes, he knew what they went through and he understood why Daimons became what they did. Who could blame them?

Dr. Lakis reached out and touched his hand with hers. "I hope your son is spared this. I really, really do. For his sake and for yours. No one should die like this. No one."

Wulf stared at the hand that now had wrinkles and age spots. A hand that had been as smooth as his just a few hours ago.

"Is there anything I can do for you?" he asked.

"Take care of your family and don't let Cassandra die alone. There's nothing worse than going through this on your own."

Her family returned to the room.

Wulf got up and left them to their loved one. As he reached the door, Dr. Lakis stopped him.

"In case you wanted to know, Wulf, my name is Maia."

"Safe journey to you, Maia," he said, his voice deep from his repressed emotions. "I hope your gods are far more merciful to you in the next life."

The last thing he saw was her son falling into her arms and weeping.

Wulf left the apartment and headed back to his own. By the time he reached it, his anger was smoldering. He entered his room to see Cassandra lying asleep with Erik beside her.

They looked so beautiful like that. She was a young woman who should have the rest of her life ahead of her. She had a baby who needed to know his mother.

Most of all, Wulf needed her.

It couldn't end like this. It couldn't.

He wouldn't let it.

Grabbing his cell phone, he went back to the living room and called Acheron.

To his surprise, Ash answered it on the first ring.

"Are you back?" Wulf asked.

"Apparently so."

He ignored Ash's usual sarcasm and went to the matter at hand. "Have you any idea what has happened while you've been gone."

"I know, Wulf," Ash said in a sympathetic tone. "Congratulations on your marriage and Erik."

He choked at the mention of his son. He didn't bother to ask Ash how he knew about either event. Ash wouldn't answer and everyone knew the man was a freak.

"Is there any . . ." Wulf couldn't even bring himself to ask whether or not they had any hope of a future together.

"You're not ready for the answer."

His anger exploded at that. "Fuck you, Ash. What do you mean, I'm not ready?"

"Listen to me, Wulf," he said in the patient tone of a parent dealing with an upset child. "Listen carefully. Sometimes to have what we want most, we have to give up everything we believe in. You're not ready to do that yet."

Wulf tightened his grip on the phone. "I don't even know what you're talking about. Why can't you ever answer a simple question?"

"Ask me a simple question and you will get a simple answer. What you ask me is extremely complicated. You've done what Artemis wanted you to do. You've saved your lineage and her brother's."

"Then why don't you sound happy about it?"

"I don't like to see anyone played with or used. I know you're in pain right now. I know you're angry. I understand it. You have every right to feel every emotion that's churning inside you. But this isn't over. When you're ready, I'll answer your question."

The bastard actually hung up on him.

Wulf stood there feeling even more betrayed. He wanted Ash's blood, but most of all he wanted Artemis's and Apollo's. How dare they screw with them like this, as if they were nothing.

The door to his bedroom opened to show him Cassandra standing there, her brow furrowed with concern.

"Hi," she said, looking very tired.

"You should be in bed."

"So should you. I was worried when I woke up to find you gone. Is everything okay?"

For some reason it was always okay whenever she was around him. It was what made it so hard being with her now.

He tried to imagine what it would be like holding her hand while she aged in front of him.

What it would be like when he watched her decay into dust . . .

Pain racked him so fiercely it was all he could do not to show it. Not to shout out until his anger shook the very halls of Olympus.

He wanted her then, wanted to be inside her so badly that he could barely think.

But it was too soon. She was still sore from birthing his son. And no matter how much he wanted the physical comfort of her body, he would never be so selfish.

Cassandra wasn't expecting Wulf to pick her up and pin her to the wall behind her. His lips covered hers as he kissed her as if he'd never have another chance to kiss her.

Breathless, she breathed in the scent of her ancient warrior. Let the feel of his arms holding her steal her away from the reality of what was inevitable.

She knew he needed her. He wouldn't admit it. She knew that too. He was too strong to ever admit he had a weakness. To ever say he was afraid, but how could he not be?

Neither of them knew if their son was human or Apollite. The preliminary test had been inconclusive. And it would be another three months before they would test Erik again to see which DNA was dominant in him.

Whatever the outcome, Wulf would be left alone to see to Erik's needs.

He let go of her.

Cassandra took his hand and led him back to the bedroom. She sat him on the bed, then forced him to lean back.

"What are you doing?" he asked.

She unzipped his pants. "After all these centuries, I

would think you would be able to recognize a woman seducing you when you saw it."

He sprang out into her hands. Cassandra ran her hand down the length of his cock. He was already hard and leaking. She traced the tip of him, letting his wetness coat her fingertips.

Wulf couldn't breathe as he watched her. He cupped her face with his hands as she bent down to tease him with her sweet mouth.

His breathing ragged, he watched as she licked her way up to his tip while her hand gently cupped his balls. It was so nice to make love to someone who knew him. Someone who remembered how he liked to be touched and caressed.

Someone who remembered him.

For centuries, he'd only had strangers touch him. None of them felt like this. None of them warmed the cold place inside his heart and made him weak from it.

Only Cassandra did that.

Cassandra felt his body relaxing more with every gentle suck and lick she gave him.

He came with a fierce growl.

After he was completely sated and drained, he lay on the bed, panting, his eyes closed while she straddled him and lay down over his chest. His arms enclosed her as she listened to his heart pounding.

"Thank you," he said softly, stroking her hair.

"You're welcome. You feel any better?"

"No."

"Well, I tried."

He gave a bittersweet half-laugh. "It's not you, love. It's really not you."

Suddenly Erik woke up crying. Wulf fastened his

pants while Cassandra picked the baby up and comforted him.

Wulf watched as Cassandra lifted her shirt up to suckle his baby. He stared in awe at the sight, which touched every feral male part of him. This was his wife and his son.

He felt primal around them. Protective. He would kill anyone who dared to threaten either one.

He sat back on the bed and cuddled Cassandra as she fed his son.

"We've started freezing my breast milk this morning," Cassandra said quietly.

"Why?"

"For Erik. Dr. Lakis said he would most likely need my milk until he's six months old. The Apollites have developed a way of preserving it since so many of their women die before their children are weaned."

"Don't," he whispered against her temple, unable to bear the thought of her dying. "I . . . I've been thinking about this. A lot."

"And?"

"I want you to go Daimon."

She leaned back to give him a shocked stare. "Wulf? Are you serious?"

"Yes. It makes perfect sense. That way—"

"I can't do that," she said, interrupting him.

"Sure you can. All you have to do—"

"Is kill innocent people." She looked horrified. "I can't."

"Phoebe doesn't kill anyone."

"But she feeds from someone who does and she has to suck *his* blood. No offense, yuck! Not to mention the small fact that I am no longer equipped to suck anyone's blood and the last person I want to bite into is Urian. And while we're at it, let's not forget that you and your cohorts will be after me if I ever step foot out of Elysia to hunt anyone else."

"No they won't," he said emphatically. "I won't let them. I can keep you safe, Cassandra. I swear it. You can stay in the cellar with me. No one ever has to know."

Her features softened. She laid her soft, warm hand against his cheek. "I would know, Wulf. Erik would know. Chris . . ."

"Please, Cassandra," he begged, thinking of Dr. Lakis and what she had looked like. How she had aged. The pain on her face. "I don't want you to die. Most especially not like—"

"Neither do I," she said, interrupting him. "Believe me on that one."

"Then fight for me. Fight for Erik."

She flinched. "That's so not fair. I don't want to die any more than you want me to, but what you're asking me is impossible. It goes against everything you have fought for and believed in. You would hate me."

"I could never hate you."

She shook her head in disbelief. "The divorce courts are full of husbands who thought that when they married their wives. How would you feel a year from now after I have taken several innocent lives?"

He didn't want to think about that. He only wanted to think about them. For once in eternity he wanted to be selfish. To hell with the world. For twelve hundred years he had defended the humans.

All he wanted was one year of happiness. Was that so much to ask, for all he'd done for humanity?

"Would you at least think about it for me?" he asked quietly, even though he knew she was right.

"Be careful what you ask for, you just might get it."
Talon's words haunted him.

"Okay," Cassandra whispered, but even as she said the words, she knew better.

They both jumped as the phone rang.

Thinking it was Ash since it didn't register a caller ID or number, Wulf pulled it off his belt and answered it.

"Hi, Viking."

His blood went cold at the sound of the thick Greek accent he remembered all too well. "Stryker?"

"Yes. Very good. I'm proud of you."

"How did you get my number?"

If Urian had betrayed them, so help him, Wulf would rip his Daimon heart out and feed it to him.

"Ah, that's an interesting question, isn't it? I'll give you credit. You have led me on quite a merry little chase around town. But I do have my resources. Luckily one of them lives right here in town."

"Who?" Wulf demanded.

Stryker tsked at him. "The anticipation must be killing you, no? Who do I have? What do I want? Will I kill this person I hold?" He paused to make a delighted noise. "Well, I'll have mercy on you. I think you're smart enough to know what I'm after."

"I won't give you Cassandra. I don't care who you hold."

"Oh, it's not Cassandra I want anymore, Viking. Use your head. She's as good as dead in a few weeks anyway. What I want is your son and I want him *now*."

"Fuck you!"

Again the Daimon tsked at him. "Is that your final answer? Don't you even want to know whose soul I'm going to devour?"

Not when compared to his son or Cassandra. It really

didn't matter. No one on earth was more important to Wulf. But he had to know. "Who do you have?"

The phone went silent for several seconds while Wulf held his breath. It couldn't be Cassandra, Erik, or Chris he held. Who was left?

The answer made his blood run cold.

"Wulf?"

It was Cassandra's father.

Chapter 16

Wulf hung up the phone, his thoughts whirling. He looked at Cassandra who had gone pale. "What did he say?"

Part of him wanted to lie to her, but he couldn't. Their relationship was beyond that. He'd never kept anything from her. He wasn't about to start now. She had a right to know what was going on.

"Stryker wants to exchange your father for Erik. If we refuse, your father dies."

What he didn't tell her was that her father would probably die anyway. Given what he knew about Stryker. It was pretty much a given.

But maybe Urian would be able to keep Jefferson Peters alive since he had a vested interest in the man's health.

Cassandra covered her mouth with her hand. Her eyes were large, terror filled. "What do we do? I can't let him kill my father and I damn sure can't give him my baby."

Wulf stood up and kept his voice calm so as to not alarm her any more. She had her own health and Erik's to worry over. He would take care of the rest. "There's only one thing I know to do. I'm going to go kill Stryker."

She looked less than convinced. "We've tried that. Remember? It didn't exactly work. I seem to recall he and his men cut a swathe through you, the Were-Hunters, and Corbin."

"I know, but the thing about us Vikings, we know how to take advantage of surprise attacks and disorient our opponents. He won't be expecting me to attack."

"Sure he will. He's not stupid and he knows who he's dealing with."

"Then what do you want me to do?" he asked in frustration. "You want me to give him Erik and say *bon appétit*?"

"No!"

"Then offer me another solution."

Cassandra tried desperately to think of something. But he was right. There was no other way.

Maybe if they could reach Urian, but he'd been gone for several days now and no one, not even Phoebe, had seen hide nor hair of him.

"When and where are you supposed to meet him?" she asked.

"Tonight at the Inferno."

"We'll think of something by then."

Wulf hoped so. The alternative was completely unacceptable to him.

"I'll go and help."

Both Wulf and Kat looked at Chris as if he'd lost his mind.

"What are we supposed to do with you, Chris?" Wulf asked. "Lob you at them?"

Chris bristled, offended. "I'm not a baby, Wulf. I happen to know how to fight. Hell, I've been sparring against you for years."

"Yeah, but I never really hit you."

Chris looked even more offended.

Kat patted him on the arm. "Don't worry, Chris. The day that Sony PlayStation attacks the world and threatens to destroy it, we'll give you a call."

Chris made a disgusted sound. "Why do I bother?"

Wulf took a deep breath as he fastened his sword on. "Your job is to protect Cassandra and Erik. I need you here, boy."

"Yeah, yeah. I'm ever useless."

Wulf grabbed Chris by the back of his neck and pulled him close. "You are *never* useless to me. I don't ever want to hear that out of your mouth again. You hear me?"

"Okay." Chris relented as he tried to shrug off Wulf's fierce grip. "I guess my baby-making abilities aren't completely defunct with the new heir, huh?"

Wulf ruffled his hair, then turned to Kat. "You ready?"

"I suppose. You do realize they'll just run from me?"

"Good. Keep them stirred up. If they're busy worrying about hurting you, then they can't concentrate on hacking me into pieces."

"Good point."

As he started for the door, Cassandra stopped him. She pulled him tight against her and held him close. "Come back to me, Wulf."

"I fully intend to. God and Odin willing."

She kissed him, then let him go.

Wulf took one last look at his wife and the baby who was sleeping on the floor completely oblivious to what was happening tonight. Oblivious that if Stryker had his way, Erik would die and the world would end.

How he wished he could be so ignorant.

But he couldn't. He had a job to do and too much to lose if he failed.

In the back of his mind was the one repeating thought . . . How had Stryker found out about Cassandra's father?

Could Urian have betrayed them? Would he?

Part of him wanted to believe it was a coincidence. The other part of him couldn't help wondering if Urian had changed his mind about helping Stryker after all. The man was his father . . .

He and Kat left the apartment and met Phoebe at the main entrance. She held out a necklace to him and placed it around his neck. "This will allow the door to Elysia to open when you return. I couldn't get in touch with Urian and that concerns me. I only pray they haven't learned of his helping us."

"He's all right, Phoebe," Kat soothed. "Believe me, he's a great actor. I had no idea he wasn't a complete asshole. I'm sure his father doesn't know either."

Phoebe looked peeved by her words.

"It was a joke, Phoebe," Kat said. "Lighten up."

Phoebe shook her head. "How can you be so nonchalant when you know what's at stake?"

"Unlike the rest of you, I know I'll live through the night, one way or the other. Unless the earth is destroyed or they hack me to pieces, I'm in no danger. My only fear is for all of you."

"Then make sure you stand close to me," Wulf said, only half-jokingly. "I need some Teflon-coated armor."

Kat shoved him toward the exit. "Yeah, yeah. Big Viking defender hiding behind me. I'll believe that one when I see it."

Wulf led the way out of the city, up to the surface. The truck they had arrived in had been moved to a nearby cave that housed several vehicles they kept just in case one of their people went Daimon and needed a link to the human world.

It was sick, but Wulf was grateful just this once for their "care" of the Daimons.

The spring thaw had started and the ground wasn't as frozen as it had been before.

Shanus had given him several sets of keys so that he could choose the automobile most likely to get them there quickly. Wulf chose the navy blue Mountaineer.

Kat got in first. He looked back the way they had come while his thoughts returned to his family.

"It'll be okay, Wulf."

"Yeah," he whispered. He knew it would be. He was going to make damn sure of it.

Wulf got in and drove them back toward the city. His first stop would be his house. Or what was left of it. He wanted to be fully armed for this conflict.

They drove for well over an hour before they reached his estate. Wulf pulled into his driveway and hesitated. There was no sign of battle here anymore. His garage, his windows were all intact.

Even the front gate was standing.

"Did Stryker repair it?" he asked Kat.

She burst out laughing. "Not his style. Believe me. He never repairs the damage he does. I have no idea what happened here. Maybe your Squires' Council?"

"No. They didn't even know about this."

Wulf keyed the lock for his gate, then pulled toward the house slowly, expecting the worst.

As he neared the front door, he stopped suddenly.

There in the shadows beside his house, he saw movement.

The mist from the lake was thick, swirling. He cut the

lights so that his vision wouldn't be impaired by them and reached for the retractable sword under his seat.

There were three very tall men dressed in black walking toward them slowly, arrogantly, as if they had all the time in the world. They were united in power and strength, and their eagerness to fight bled from every pore of them.

All of them were blond.

"Stay here," he warned Kat as he got out, ready for battle.

The fog swirled around the three men as they came closer.

Probably no more than six feet three, one of them was dressed in trousers, sweater, and wool overcoat. One side of the coat was pulled back to show an ancient scabbard and sword of Greek design. The one in the middle was two inches taller. He, too, wore wool trousers and a sweater along with a long black leather coat.

The third one had short hair, a shade darker than the other two. Dressed all in biker leather, he had two braids that fell down from his left temple.

And in that instant, Wulf remembered him.

"Talon?"

The biker broke into a wide grin. "From the way you're holding that sword, I was wondering if you were going to recall me or not, Viking."

Wulf laughed as his old friend drew near. They hadn't seen each other in over a century. He gladly shook the Celt's hand.

Wulf turned to the man in the middle and remembered him, too, from the brief time he had spent in New Orleans over one hundred years ago during Mardi Gras.

"Kyrian?" he asked. The ancient Greek general had changed quite a bit since the last time he had met him.

Back then, Kyrian's hair had been cropped short and he had worn a beard. Now it was shoulder length and his face was clean-shaven.

"Nice seeing you again," Kyrian said, shaking his hand. "And this is my friend Julian of Macedon."

Wulf knew the man only by reputation. Julian had been the one who had taught Kyrian everything he knew about fighting and battle. "Glad to meet you. Now what the hell are the three of you doing here?"

"They're your backup."

He turned to see Acheron Parthenopaeus joining their group. He didn't know what stunned him most, their presence or the sight of the infant Ash had strapped into a baby harness, facing his chest.

Wulf was aghast. "Kyrian? Is that your baby?"

"Hell, no," Kyrian said. "No way I would bring Marissa into this. Amanda would geld me first and then kill me if I even considered it." He inclined his head to Acheron. "That's Ash's baby."

Wulf cocked a brow at that. "Lucy," he said in a mock Ricky Ricardo accent, "you got some 'splaining to do."

Ash grunted. "Stryker isn't stupid. Your idea of going in with a plastic baby, while admirable, would never work. Stryker would smell the plastic in an instant." He turned the Snugli sack around to face Wulf so that he could see the tiny, dark-haired infant it contained. "So I give you a real baby."

"What if it gets hurt?"

The baby sneezed.

Wulf jumped as fire shot out of its nostrils and almost singed his leg.

"Excuse me," the baby said in a singsongy voice. "I almost made Dark-Hunter barbecue, which would be really sad 'cause I ain't got no barbecue sauce with me." The baby leaned its head back to look up at Ash. "You know fried Dark-Hunter isn't good plain. What you need—"

"Sim," Ash said in a warning tone under his breath, cutting the baby off.

The baby looked up at him. "Oh, I forgot, *akri*. Sorry. Goo, ga, goo."

Wulf rubbed his forehead. "What is *that*?"

"He told you, Simi's his baby . . . demon."

All five of them turned at the deep, sinister voice that was laced with a heavy Greek accent. Another man stepped out of the shadows. He was almost as tall as Acheron with black hair and vibrant blue eyes.

Ash arched a brow. "You came after all, Z. Glad you made the party."

Zarek snorted. "What the hell? I didn't have anything better to do. Figured I might as well come kick ass and take names. Not that I really give a damn about their names. I'm just in it for the bloodlust."

"So you're Zarek," Wulf said, eyeing the notorious ex-Dark-Hunter who had once been exiled to Fairbanks, Alaska.

His nasty attitude not only bled from every pore, but was apparent from the lip he kept perpetually curled. Billy Idol and Elvis had nothing on this man.

"Yeah," Zarek said, sneering even more. "And I'm freezing, so can we rush this little get-together so I can kill some assholes and get back to the beach where I belong?"

"If you hate it here so much," Talon asked, "why did you agree to come?"

In a subtle gesture of flipping Talon off, Zarek scratched his eyebrow with his middle finger, which was covered with a long, sharp metallic claw. "Astrid wants me to make friends. I don't know why. Some weird woman thing. She's trying to make me more sociable."

Ash let out a rare laugh at that.

Zarek passed an equally amused, knowing look at Acheron. "I don't want to hear it from you, O Great Ash. You're the one who got me into this in the first place." Then Zarek did the most surprising thing of all; he bent down and chucked the baby on the chin. "How you doing, little Simi?"

The baby jumped happily up and down in the harness. "Fine. You got any more frozen beans for me? I miss being in Alaska with you. It was fun."

"No time for food, Sim," Ash answered.

The baby blew him a raspberry. "Can I eat the Daimons then?"

"If you can catch them," Ash promised, making Wulf wonder what the man knew about the Daimons that he wasn't sharing.

"What's that mean?" Zarek asked for him. "You being vague again?"

Ash looked at him archly. "Always."

Zarek let out a sound of disgust. "Personally, I think we should get together and beat the hell out of you until you come clean."

Kyrian scratched his chin thoughtfully. "You know—"

"Don't even go there," Acheron said irritably. He turned to Wulf. "Go get your weapons. You have an appointment to keep."

Wulf paused by Ash's side. "Thanks for coming."

Ash inclined his head to him and stepped away as he cuddled the baby demon to his chest.

Wulf went back to the car to get Kat, but she was nowhere to be seen. "Kat?" he called. "Kat?"

"What's wrong?" Talon asked as he and the others joined Wulf by the car.

"Did you see the woman I was with?"

They shook their heads.

"What woman?" Talon asked.

Wulf frowned. "She's six feet four and blond. She couldn't have just van—" He paused as he rethought that statement. "Never mind, she's one of the few people who could have just gone poof."

"Is she your wife?" Kyrian asked.

"No, she's one of Artemis's handmaidens who's been helping us."

Ash scowled at that. "Artemis doesn't have a *kori* taller than her. Believe me. She doesn't let any woman look down on her. Literally."

Wulf looked at him as a feeling of dread went through him. "I hope you're wrong. Because if you're not, then Kat was working with Stryker all this time and is most likely off to tell him about our surprise party."

Ash cocked his head slightly as if listening for something. "I don't even sense her. It's as if she doesn't exist."

"So what do you think?" Kyrian asked.

Ash picked his baby up as she started kicking him in the groin and moved her to his hip. The baby played with his braid, then started chewing it.

Wulf furrowed his brow. If he didn't know better, he'd swear that baby had fangs.

"I don't know what to think," Ash said, pulling his hair away from the baby. "Kat bears the description of an Apollite or Daimon."

"But she walks in daylight," Wulf added.

Zarek cursed. "Don't tell me there's another Day-Slayer loose."

"No," Acheron said firmly. "I know for a fact Artemis hasn't created one. She wouldn't dare. At least not at the moment."

"What's a Day-Slayer?" Talon asked.

"You don't ever want to know," Julian answered.

"Yeah," Zarek concurred. "What he said, times a hundred."

"All right, then," Wulf said, heading for his house. "Let me get my things and we'll be on our way."

As he walked off, he saw Talon move to stand beside Ash. "This is the part where you normally say if everyone does what they're supposed to, everything will work out as it's meant to. Right?"

Acheron's face was impassive. "Normally, yes."

"But?"

"We're dealing with something greater than the Fates tonight. All I can honestly say is it's going to be one hell of a fight."

Wulf laughed at that as he left hearing range. That was okay by him. Fighting was the one thing he and his people excelled at.

They arrived at the Inferno just before midnight. Oddly enough, the bar was completely empty of patrons.

Dante met them at the door, dressed in black leather. He didn't have his vampire teeth in, and he looked extremely angry.

"Ash," he said, greeting the Atlantean. "Been a long time since you've darkened my door."

"Dante." Ash shook his hand.

Dante looked down at the baby with a knitted brow. "Simi?"

The baby smiled.

Dante let out a low whistle and stepped back. "Damn, Ash, I wish you would warn me when you're planning on bringing your demon here. Do I need to warn the guys the feeding machine has come visiting?"

"No," Ash said, swinging the baby lightly. "She's only here to munch Daimons."

"Where is everyone?" Wulf asked.

Dante glanced to the wall to his right. "I caught wind of what was going down tonight so we closed the place."

Wulf followed his line of vision and saw the pelt of a panther mounted there. He recognized the hide by the streak of red in it. "Your brother?"

Fury darkening his eyes, Dante shrugged. "The bastard was working with the Daimons. Feeding them information about us and you."

"Man," Talon breathed. "That's cold to kill your own blood."

Dante turned on him with a feral sneer that more than betrayed the fact that Dante wasn't human. "My brother betrayed *me* and our people. If I were as cold as I'd like to be, his hide would be on the floor so everyone could walk on him. Unfortunately, my other brothers were a little disturbed by that so we compromised with the wall."

"Understood," Ash said. "Where's the rest of the pack?"

"In the back. We're staying out of it. We don't like to kill our own."

Zarek snorted at that. "Unless it's your brother."

Dante approached Zarek and the two of them had a mutual sneer-off. "Law of the jungle. The betrayee gets to eat the betrayer."

Zarek gave him a droll stare. "Law of my jungle. Kill them all and let Hades sort them out."

Dante actually laughed at that. "I like this one, Ash. He understands us."

"Gee, Z," Ash said jokingly. "I think you may have

found a new friend after all. That should make Astrid happy."

Zarek flipped him off.

Ash ignored it. "All right, game faces, guys."

Dante went to guard the front door while Ash removed his baby from the carrier and handed her to Wulf who was a bit hesitant to touch the little girl demon.

She eyed him speculatively, then smiled. "The Simi won't bite you if you don't drop her."

"I will try not to drop you then."

She flashed her fangs at him, then settled back in his arms, the perfect image of a relaxed infant.

"Should we hide?" Julian asked. "Take them by surprise?"

"We can't," Ash said. "Stryker isn't a normal Daimon."

"More like Desiderius?" Kyrian asked.

"Worse. In fact, my best advice to all of you"—Ash directed a warning glare at Zarek—"is to let me handle Stryker. I'm the only one of us he can't kill."

"And why is that, Acheron?" Zarek asked. "Oh, wait, I know this. Fairbanks will hit one hundred and ten Celsius in January before you answer that."

Ash folded his arms over his chest. "Then why ask it?"

"Just to piss you off." Zarek moved across the floor. "When are they supposed to get here, anyway?"

The air above the dance floor shimmered and hissed.

Zarek's face broke into a wide grin. "Oh, goodie. Let the bloodbath commence."

Kyrian pulled his sword out and extended the blade while Talon pulled his circular srad into his hand. Julian unsheathed his Greek sword.

Zarek and Ash didn't make a move for their weapons.

Neither did Wulf. His goal was to protect Simi, Erik, and Cassandra.

The bolt-hole flashed a second before Stryker came through it. A full legion of Daimons came out with him, including Urian.

Urian's face was completely stoic as he met Wulf's gaze. It was hard to believe this was the man who had married Wulf to Cassandra. There was nothing on his face or in his eyes that indicated Urian knew him. Kat was right, the man was one hell of an actor.

"How nice," Stryker said with an evil laugh. "You brought dinner for my men. If only everyone could be so considerate."

Several of the Daimons laughed.

So did Zarek. "You know, I almost like this guy, Acheron. Pity we have to kill him."

Stryker slid a sideways glare to Zarek before his gaze went to Acheron. The two of them stared at each other without a word or emotion.

But Wulf saw the momentary confusion on Urian's face as he noticed Acheron.

"Father?"

"It's all right, Urian. I know all about the Atlantean. Don't I, Acheron?"

"No. You just think you do, Strykerius. I, on the other hand, know your every flaw, right down to the one that enables you to believe in the Destroyer while she toys with you."

"You lie."

"Perhaps. But perhaps not."

Oh, yeah, no one could play the game of vagueness better than Acheron. He was a master at saying nothing and making people doubt the very air they breathed.

Finally, Stryker turned to Wulf. His gaze dropped to the baby Wulf held. He cocked his head and smiled.

"How sweet. You went to so much trouble, didn't you? All of you did. I should feel flattered."

A bad feeling went through Wulf. Something wasn't right about this.

Did the Daimon know Simi wasn't his?

Stryker moved to stand next to Urian. He draped an arm over his son's shoulders and kissed him on the cheek.

Urian scowled at the action and grew rigid.

"Children are the very thing we live for, aren't they?" Stryker asked. "They bring us joy. Sometimes they bring us pain."

Urian frowned even more as his father played with the leather laces holding Urian's blond braid.

"Of course, you'll never understand the pain I mean, Wulf. Your son won't live long enough to betray you."

Before anyone could move, Stryker slashed Urian's throat with his hand that wasn't human anymore. It was the shape of a dragon's claw.

He shoved Urian away from him. Urian fell to the floor gasping, holding his hands against his neck to stanch the blood flow while his father faced the Dark-Hunters.

"You didn't really think I was stupid enough to fall for this trick, did you?" His gaze bored into Wulf and when he spoke, it wasn't Stryker's voice he heard . . . it was the voice of Cassandra's father. "I knew you would never bring me the baby. I just needed to get the guardians away from Elysia for a while."

Wulf cursed at his words as he moved to attack.

Stryker vanished into a black cloud of smoke while the Daimons attacked.

"Ak'ritah tah!" Acheron shouted.

The portal opened.

One of the Daimons laughed. "We don't have to go through—" Before he could finish the sentence, the Daimon was violently sucked through the opening.

The others quickly followed.

Ash ran across the floor to where Urian lay in a pool of blood. "Sh," Ash breathed, covering Urian's hands with his own.

Urian's eyes were filled with tears as he stared up at Acheron.

"Breathe easy and shallow," Acheron said, his tone soothing and deep.

Wulf and the others watched in stunned silence as Ash healed the Daimon.

"Why?" Urian asked.

"I'll explain later." Acheron stood up and lifted the hem of his shirt until his lean, well-defined stomach was exposed. "Simi, return to me."

The baby shot out of Wulf's hands immediately. She turned from an infant into a tiny dragon, then laid herself over Acheron's skin until she became a tattoo over his left ribs.

"I always wondered how your tattoo moved," Kyrian said.

Ash didn't speak. Instead, he raised his hands.

One second they were in the Inferno, the next, they were in the middle of Elysia.

More than hell had broken loose since Wulf and Kat had left earlier. Unending screams rent the air. There were scattered bodies of Apollite men, women, and children everywhere. Apparently, they didn't disintegrate like Daimons did unless they died on their birthdays.

Dread and fear tore through Wulf.

"Phoebe!" Urian cried, running for his apartment.

Wulf didn't bother to call out. No one could hear above the screams. So he ran as fast as he could toward his wife and son.

Several Daimons tried to stop him. His gaze glazed by fury, Wulf cut through them.

No one would get between him and his family.

No one.

He got to the apartment to see the door had been kicked open. Shanus's dead body was lying just inside the living room.

Wulf choked on fear until he heard fighting from his bedroom. Best of all, he heard his son's angry squall.

Running through the room, he reached the bedroom and paused. Chris stood in the farthest corner, holding Erik against his chest. Chris's two Apollite friends, Kyra and Ariella, stood in front of him as if they were a barrier to protect him and Erik.

Stryker and three more Daimons were attacking Kat and Cassandra, who were fighting them off with admirable flair and skill.

"You can't hold your shield forever, Katra," Stryker growled.

Kat looked at Wulf and smiled. "I don't have to hold it forever. I only had to hold it long enough for the calvary to arrive."

Stryker hesitated, then looked over his shoulder at the same time Wulf attacked.

Wulf killed one Daimon, then went for Stryker. Stryker turned around and blasted Wulf with a god-bolt that knocked him back into the wall.

Hissing in pain, Wulf saw movement out of the corner of his eye.

It was Ash and Zarek.

Kat immediately vanished while Stryker cursed.

Wulf and Zarek went after the last two Daimons while Ash and Stryker faced each other.

"Go home, Stryker," Ash said. "The war is over."

"It'll never be over. Not so long as my father"—he spat the word out—"lives."

Ash shook his head. "And I thought my family was dysfunctional . . . Let it go. You've already lost. My God, you just killed your own son, and over what?"

Stryker roared with anger, then attacked Ash.

Wulf grabbed his son from Chris at the same time Zarek pulled Cassandra behind him. Wulf wanted to get them out and to safety, but they couldn't reach the door while Ash and Stryker fought in front of it.

Stryker shot a god-bolt at Ash who took it without flinching. Instead, he gave the Daimon a blow that knocked him up into the air and slammed him against the wall.

Wulf whistled low. They all knew Ash was powerful, but he'd never seen the Atlantean do something like that.

Stryker attacked again. But for some reason, Ash didn't kill him. The two men slugged it out as if they were humans and not . . .

Whatever the hell the two of them were.

His face bloody, Stryker shot another blast at Ash.

He deflected it. Ash raised his hand, and as he did so, Stryker was lifted from the floor.

Stryker shot a bolt at him that caused Ash to stagger back and release him.

The Daimon hit the ground running. He wrapped his arms around Ash and rammed him into the wall.

But before he could strike Acheron again, a yellow-fleshed demon appeared out of nowhere. Her eyes flashing, she wrapped her arms around Stryker and then vanished into nothingness.

Acheron snarled at that.

"While you're at it, Apollymi," Ash shouted. "You better keep him there."

"What the hell are you?" Wulf asked Ash as he turned to face them.

"Don't ask questions you don't want answered," Zarek said. "Believe me. You're so not ready to know the truth."

"Is Stryker gone?" Cassandra asked.

Ash nodded.

Cassandra hugged Wulf, then took Erik from his hands and held him against her shoulder to quiet him. "I know, baby," she cooed. "But the scary man is all gone."

"What grabbed the Daimon?" Kyra asked. "Where did they go?"

Ash didn't answer. "You're safe now, guys. At least for a little while."

"Will he be back?" Cassandra asked.

Ash gave an odd half-laugh. "I don't know. He's one of the few creatures beyond my powers. But like he said, it's not over. He might be back in a few months or a few centuries. Time passes differently where he lives."

Kyrian, Talon, and Julian came into the room.

"The Daimons have all vanished," Talon said. "We killed some, but the rest . . ."

"It's all right," Ash said. "Thanks for the help."

They nodded, then walked out of the bedroom, into the chaos of the living room.

"Man, it's going to take days to clean this up," Chris said, looking around in disbelief.

Then, before their eyes, the destruction was cleared. All that was left behind were the bodies.

Zarek snorted. "You better stop while you're ahead, Acheron."

"I'm not ahead, Z. I can't fix what was really damaged here tonight." Ash's gaze went to Shanus's body.

Wulf shook his head as he picked up Shanus to carry him to the town's center.

There were Apollites everywhere, crying and screaming over their dead.

"They didn't deserve this," Wulf said to Acheron.

"Who does?" Ash asked.

A woman came up to Wulf. She had the bearing of royalty and it didn't take much to ascertain who she was.

"Shanus?" she said, her eyes filling with tears.

Wulf laid the body down for her. "Are you his wife?"

She nodded as her tears glistened in her eyes. She cradled his head in her lap and wept quietly.

Cassandra moved forward. "I'm so sorry."

The woman looked up, her eyes filled with hatred. "Get out. All of you! You're no longer welcome here. We helped you and you destroyed us!"

Zarek cleared his throat. "That might not be a bad piece of advice," he said to Wulf, looking around at the others who were directing killing glares toward them.

"Yeah," Ash agreed. "You guys help Wulf and his family get out of here. I'm going to see about someone."

Wulf knew he meant Urian. "Do you want us to wait for you?"

"No. There'll be a couple of SUVs waiting for you topside. Head home and I'll catch up later."

"SUVs?" Kyrian asked.

"Again, I repeat, don't ask questions you don't want answered," Zarek said. "Just accept the fact that Acheron is a freak of nature and let it go."

Ash cast him a droll glare. "I may be a freak, but at least I don't throw lightning bolts at my brother."

Zarek laughed evilly at that. "At least I haven't struck him with one . . . yet."

Ash watched as Zarek led the group out of the city.

He stood in the center, surveying the damage around him. He started to clear it out just as he'd done with Wulf's house and the apartment, then stopped. The Apollites would need something to focus on other than their pain.

Rebuilding the city would take their minds off their grief. At least for a little while.

Deep in his heart, he wept along with them.

Just because you can, doesn't mean you should . . .

He forced himself to walk down the corridor without yielding to the need inside to fix everything.

By the time he'd reached Urian's apartment, Ash was disgusted by the bloodshed Stryker had wrought in the name of Apollymi.

There was no sense in this, but then she was the Goddess of Destruction. And it was why he had to make sure she was never released from her prison.

Ash found Urian on his knees in the center of the living room. The man held a small gold locket in his hands as he wept silently.

"Urian?" Ash said in a low, steady tone.

"Go away!" he snarled. "Just leave me alone."

"You can't stay here," Ash said. "The Apollites will turn on you."

"Like I care." He looked up and the empathetic pain Ash felt from Urian made him take a step back. It had been a long time since Ash had come into direct contact with so much hopeless grief. "Why didn't you let me die too? Why did you save me?"

Ash took a deep breath as he explained it to Urian. "Because if I hadn't, you would have sold your soul to Artemis over this and killed your father."

"You think I'm not going to kill him over this?" He turned on Ash with a growl. "There's nothing left of her. Nothing! I don't even have anything to bury. I . . ." His words broke off as he sobbed.

"I know," Ash said, placing his hand on Urian's shoulder.

"You don't know!"

Ash gripped his chin and lifted it until their gazes locked. "Yes, Urian, I do know."

Urian struggled to breathe as he saw images flickering through Ash's swirling silver eyes. There was so much pain in them, so much agony and wisdom.

It was hard to maintain eye contact with him.

"I don't want to live without my Phoebe," Urian said, his voice breaking on the words.

"I know. For that reason, I'm giving you a choice. I can't lock on to your father to monitor him. I need you to do that. Because sooner or later, he'll be back after Apollo's lineage."

"Why would I protect them? Phoebe died because of them!"

"Phoebe lived because of them, Urian. Remember? You and your father were responsible for killing her entire family. Did you ever tell Phoebe it was you? You? Who killed her grandmother? Or her cousins?"

Urian looked away shamefaced. "No. I would never have hurt her."

"Yet you did. Every time you, your father, or one of your Spathis killed one of her family, she felt the pain you feel now. Her mother's and sisters' deaths tore her apart. Isn't that why you saved Cassandra to begin with?"

"Yes."

Ash stepped away from him while Urian wiped his tears away.

"You said I had a choice?"

"The other is that I will erase your memories of everything. You'll be free of all of this. All your pain. The past, the present. You can live as if none of this had ever happened to you."

"Will you kill me if I ask it?"

"Do you really want me to?"

Urian stared at the floor. To most people, his thoughts would be unknown. But Ash knew them. He heard them as clearly as he heard his own.

"I'm no longer a Daimon, am I?" Urian asked after a brief pause.

"No. Nor are you an Apollite, exactly."

"Then what am I?"

Ash took a deep breath as he spoke the truth. "You are unique in this world."

Urian didn't like that any more than Ash liked being unique. But some things could never be changed.

"How much longer will I live?" Urian asked.

"You're immortal, barring death."

"That doesn't make sense."

"Most of life doesn't."

He felt Urian's frustration with him, but at least it was lessening some of the man's grief. "Can I walk in daylight?"

"If you want, I can make it so. If you choose amnesia, I will make you fully human."

"You can do that?"

Ash nodded.

Urian laughed bitterly as he raked a cold look over Ash's body. "You know, Acheron, I'm not stupid, nor am

I as blind as Stryker. Does he know of the demon you carry on your body?"

"No, and Simi isn't a demon, she's part of me."

Urian's gaze bored into his. "Poor Stryker, he's so screwed and he doesn't even know it." The intensity of Urian's gaze burned. "I know who and what you are, Acheron Parthenopaeus."

"Then you know if you ever pass your knowledge along I'll make sure you regret it. Eternally."

He nodded. "But I don't understand why you hide."

"I'm not hiding," Ash said simply. "The knowledge you carry can't help anyone. It can only destroy and harm."

Urian thought about that for a minute. "I'm through being a destroyer."

"Then what are you?"

Urian let his thoughts wander through the events of this night. He thought about the aching pain inside him that screamed over the loss of his wife. It was so tempting to let Acheron erase it all, but with that he would lose all the good memories he carried too.

Though he and Phoebe had only had a few years together, she had loved him in ways no one ever had. Touched a heart he had thought was long dead.

No, it hurt to live without her, but he didn't want to lose all connection with her.

He fastened her locket around his neck and rose slowly to his feet. "I'm your man. But I warn you now. If I'm ever given a chance to kill Stryker, I will take it. Consequences be damned."

Chapter 17

Stryker snarled in outrage as he found himself in the Destroyer's throne room. "I was so close to killing them. Why did you stop me!"

Still the demon Sabina held him.

For once Xedrix wasn't in the room with his mother, but Stryker didn't have time to ponder the demon's whereabouts. His thoughts were too consumed by hatred and vexation.

His mother sat on her chaise completely poised, as if she were holding court and hadn't just destroyed all their years of careful planning.

"Do not raise your voice to me, Strykerius. I will not take insubordination."

He forced himself to level his voice even while his blood simmered in fury. "Why did you interfere?"

She pulled her black pillow into her lap and toyed with a corner of it. "You cannot win against the Elekti. I told you that."

"I could have beaten him," Stryker insisted. No one could stop him. He was sure of that.

"No you couldn't," she said firmly. She dropped her gaze again and ran her hand elegantly over the black satin. "There is no pain worse than a son who betrays your cause, is there, Strykerius? You give them everything, and do they listen? No. Do they respect? No. Instead they shred your heart and spit on the kindness you would show to them."

Stryker clenched his eyes shut as she voiced the very thoughts inside him. He had given Urian everything and his son had repaid him with a betrayal so profound that it had taken him days to come to grips with it.

Part of him hated Apollymi for telling him the truth. The other part thanked her.

He had never been the kind of man to cradle a snake to his bosom.

Stryker would never do to his mother what had been done to him. "I will listen to you, Mother."

She cradled the pillow to her breast and sighed wearily. "Good."

"So what do we do now?"

She gazed at him with a small, beautiful smile. When she spoke, her words were simple, but her tone was purely evil. "We wait."

Wulf sat on the couch with Cassandra beside him. Erik slept peacefully in his mother's arms, oblivious to the violence and deaths that had occurred tonight.

Oblivious to the fact that the world the baby was just coming to know had almost ended.

Since they had returned home, Wulf had refused to let either one of them out of his sight.

Chris was helping Talon bandage his arm, which had gotten shredded by one of the Daimons. Julian sat with an ice pack on the back of his head while Kyrian poured peroxide over his bloodied knuckles, into a bowl.

Zarek stood like a statue against the wall by the hall-way that led to the kitchen. He, alone, appeared un-scathed by the fighting.

"You know," Kyrian said, pausing long enough to hiss as he poured alcohol over the peroxide. "The fighting was a lot easier when I was immortal."

Talon snorted. "I still am immortal and I'm pretty banged up. That was a hell of a fight."

The phone rang.

Chris got up to answer it.

"That better not be Stryker," Cassandra said breath-lessly.

It wasn't. It was her father.

Chris handed the phone off to her and her hand shook. "Daddy? Are you all right?"

Wulf held her against his chest as she wept and talked for a few minutes, then hung up.

"It was what you said," she breathed to Wulf. "They never had him. Stryker had used the same trick to get you to leave the city that he used on me to open the apartment door. Damn that bastard!"

The phone rang again.

"What is it?" Chris snapped. "A full moon?"

"Yes," all the men said at once.

"Oh." Chris answered it, then handed it over to Kyrian.

"Hello?" Kyrian said. "Oh, hi, hon. No, I'm okay." He cringed a bit. "No, hunting was good. We'll . . . uh . . . we'll be home tomorrow."

He paused, then glanced to Julian. "What head wound?" He cringed even more. "No, tell Grace, Julian is fine. Just a little bump. We're all fine."

Wulf laughed at the way the ex-Dark-Hunter was squirming.

"Yeah, okay, will do. Love you too. Bye." Kyrian hung up the phone and let his gaze go to everyone. "Jeez, never marry a psychic woman." He looked at Talon, then Julian. "Guys, we're so screwed. The women know we didn't go hunting."

Zarek made a rude noise at that. "You think? What idiot came up with that lie?"

"I'm not an idiot," Talon snapped. "And it's not like I lied. I just omitted what exactly we were hunting and where we were doing it."

Zarek made another noise of disagreement. "Like your wives wouldn't know better?" He glanced to Kyrian. "When was the last time Mr. Armani hunted something that didn't have a price tag on it?" His gaze then went to Julian. "Oh, and the loafers and trousers are perfect camouflage."

"Shut up, Zarek," Talon snapped.

As Zarek opened his mouth to retort, a knock sounded on the door.

Grumbling, Chris went to open it and let Acheron and Urian into the room. Wulf rose to his feet as they entered.

Urian looked bad. He was pale, his clothes still covered in blood. But the worst was the restrained fury and pain in his pale eyes.

Wulf didn't know what to say to the man. He'd lost everything and gained nothing.

"We were getting worried about you, Ash," Kyrian said.

"I wasn't," Zarek said. "But now that you're here, do you need me for anything else?"

"No, Z," Ash said quietly. "Thanks for coming."

Zarek inclined his head. "Any time you want me to help rip something apart, just give me call. But in the future, could you pick somewhere warmer to do it?" Zarek flashed out of the room before anyone could respond.

"You know," Talon said. "It really pisses me off that he's a god now."

"Just make sure you don't piss *him* off," Ash said in warning. "Or he might turn you into a toad."

"He wouldn't dare."

Kyrian snorted. "We are talking about Zarek, right?"

"Oh, yeah," Talon said. "Never mind."

Kyrian stood up with a groan. "Well, since I'm one of the few nonimmortals in the room, I think I'm going to head to bed and rest."

Talon flexed his bandaged arm. "Sleep sounds like a plan to me."

Chris threw the medical supplies back in the plastic box. "C'mon, guys, and I'll show you where you can crash."

Cassandra stood up with Erik. "I guess I should—"

"Wait," Urian said, stopping her.

Wulf tensed as the Daimon approached his wife and son. Ash put his hand on his arm to keep him from interfering.

"Can I hold him?" Urian asked.

Both Cassandra and Wulf frowned. Urian had barely looked at the baby before this.

Cassandra glanced to Ash who nodded.

Reluctantly, she handed Erik over to him. It was obvious Urian had never held a baby before. Cassandra put her hands on his and showed him how to support Erik's head and hold him so as not to hurt him.

"You're so fragile," Urian breathed at the baby who eyed him sweetly. "And yet you're still alive while my Phoebe isn't."

Wulf took a step forward. Ash tightened his grip.

"Will you stay and guard your family?" Acheron asked quietly.

"My family is dead," Urian snarled, casting a heated glare toward Ash.

"No, Urian, it's not. Phoebe's blood is in that baby. Erik carries her immortality with him."

Urian closed his eyes as if hearing those words was more than he could bear. "She loved this baby," he said after a brief time. "I could tell how much she wanted her own whenever she spoke of him. I only wish I could have given her one."

"You gave her everything else, Urian," Cassandra said, her own eyes filling with tears as she spoke of her sister. "She knew that and she loved you for it."

Urian wrapped an arm around Cassandra and pulled her close. He laid his head down on her shoulder and silently cried. Cassandra joined him as she finally let out the pain she, too, had been holding back.

Wulf felt uncomfortable with their grief. Cassandra was so incredibly strong. He felt Phoebe's loss too, but not nearly as much as the two of them did.

But he would know Urian's grief all too soon.

After a time, Urian let go and handed her Erik. "I won't let your baby die, Cassandra. I swear it. No one will ever hurt him. Not as long as I live."

Cassandra kissed him on the cheek. "Thank you."

Urian nodded and withdrew from her.

"What an alliance, huh?" Wulf said after Cassandra had left them. "A Dark-Hunter and a Spathi united to guard an Apollite. Who would have ever imagined?"

"Love makes strange bedfellows," Ash said.

"I thought that was politics."

"It's both."

Urian folded his arms over his chest. "Would you mind if I slept in the boathouse?"

"Sure," Wulf said, knowing Urian wanted to be someplace where he had memories of Phoebe. "Consider it yours for as long as you want it."

Urian drifted out of the house like a silent phantom.

"Is that what I have to look forward to?" Wulf asked Ash.

"Life is a tapestry woven by the decisions we make."

"Don't give me that pseudo quasi psychobabble bullshit, Ash. I'm tired, I had my ass kicked, I'm still worried about Cassandra, Erik, and Chris, and I really feel like shit. Just once in eternity, answer one fucking question."

Ash's eyes flashed to red so fast that for a moment, Wulf thought he might have imagined it. "I *will not* tamper with free will or fate, Wulf. Not for you, not for anything. There is no power on this earth or beyond that could make me do such a thing."

"What has that got to do with Cassandra?"

"Everything. Whether she lives or dies depends on what both of you do or don't do."

"Meaning?"

He was wholly unprepared for Ash's next statement. "If you want to save her life, you have to bond her life force to yours."

That didn't sound too hard. For the first time in months, he felt some hope. "Great. Any chance you're going to give me a clue on how to do that?"

"You feed from her and she feeds from you."

A feeling of dread shrank Wulf's stomach. "Feed how?"

Ash's swirling silver eyes met his and the look in them

chilled Wulf to his soul. "You already know that answer. It's the first thought that went through your mind just now."

How he hated it when Acheron did that.

"Have you any idea how disgusting the thought of drinking blood is to me?"

Acheron shrugged. "It's really not so bad."

The words stunned Wulf. "Excuse me?"

Acheron didn't elaborate. "It's all up to you, Viking. Will you at least try it?"

What the Atlantean suggested was impossible. "She doesn't have fangs."

"She will if she needs them."

"Are you sure?"

Ash nodded. "It's really simple and yet it's really not. You drink from her neck and she drinks from yours."

The ancient Dark-Hunter was right. It sounded so simple at first. But could he and Cassandra really do that when everything they both believed in forbade it?

"Won't my blood kill her? I thought Dark-Hunter blood—"

"You're not a Dark-Hunter, Wulf. Not really. *You* never died. You have always been different from the others."

Wulf snorted in derision. "Yet again you tell me something that should have been made known to me years ago. Thanks, Ash."

"Things are always given to us when we need them."

"That's so not true," Wulf said.

"Actually it is. You just have to decide if you're strong enough, brave enough, to seize it and make it yours."

Ordinarily, Wulf would have had no doubt whatsoever about his strength or courage.

But this . . .

This required both of them.

And it required a lot of faith that Wulf wasn't sure he had anymore.

Cassandra sat there in stunned silence after Wulf had told her of the possible out.

"Are you sure it'll work?"

Wulf took a deep breath. "I don't know what I believe anymore, but if there's a chance, shouldn't we try it?"

"And you're sure this Acheron isn't trying to kill me too?"

Wulf offered her a small smile and refrained from laughing at the idea. "That is probably the only thing that I am certain about. I trust Ash, at least most of the time."

"Okay, then, let's do it."

Wulf cocked his brow. "You sure?"

She nodded.

"Okay then." He moved to stand just in front of her. She tilted her head to the side and pulled her hair off her neck.

Wulf put his hands on her waist.

He hesitated.

"Well?" she prompted.

He opened his mouth and placed his lips on the warm skin of her neck. Wulf closed his eyes as he felt her heart-beat in the vein and he grazed her skin with his teeth.

Mmm, she tasted good. He loved the way her skin teased his lips.

Cassandra cupped the back of his head with her hands. "Hmmm," she breathed, "you're giving me chills."

His body erupted at her words and the image he had of her naked in his arms.

Bite her . . .

He added pressure with his teeth.

She tightened her grip in his hair.

Do it!

"I can't," he said, pulling back. "I'm not a Daimon or an Apollite."

She looked up at him from underneath her lashes. "Now you understand what I meant when I told you that I couldn't cross over."

Yes, he understood.

But so long as neither of them was willing to do this, Cassandra was destined to die.

Chapter 18

Wulf was in the nursery with Erik. He sat in the antique rocking chair with his son asleep on his shoulder while he stared idly at the wall in front of him. It was covered with pictures of babies who had been born to his family over the last two hundred years.

Memories poured through him.

He glanced down at the baby he held. The thatch of black hair and the serene, tiny face. Erik's mouth worked in his sleep and the baby smiled as if in the midst of a happy dream.

"Are you talking to him, D'Aria?" Wulf asked, wondering if the Dream-Huntress would watch over his son as well as him.

He touched the tip of Erik's nose. Even while asleep, the baby turned to suckle his finger.

Wulf smiled, until he caught the faint scent of roses and powder on the baby's skin.

Cassandra's scent.

He tried to imagine a world without her. A day when she wasn't there to brighten everything. To place her silken hand on his skin, to run her long graceful fingers through his hair.

352 SHERRILYN KENYON

Pain lacerated his chest. His sight dimmed.

You're a wandering soul, looking for a peace that doesn't exist. Lost you will be until you find the one inner truth. We can never hide from what we are. The only hope is to embrace it.

At last, he understood the seer's words.

"This is bullshit," he said in a low tone.

There was no way he would let go of the best thing that had ever happened to him.

Wulf Tryggvason was only one thing in life.

He was a barbarian.

Cassandra was in Wulf's bedroom, looking for her box, when she heard the door open behind her.

She was mostly lost in thought when she felt two strong, powerful arms wrap around her and turn her to face a man she had only glimpsed one time before.

The first night they had met.

This was the dangerous warrior capable of shredding Daimons apart with his bare hands.

Wulf cupped her face in his hands and kissed her desperately. That kiss reached deep inside her and set fire to her blood.

"You are mine, *villkat*," he breathed. His tone possessive. "Forever."

He pulled her close to him, tight. She expected him to take her. He didn't. Instead, he sank his fangs into her neck.

Cassandra couldn't breathe as she felt the momentary pain that was quickly followed by the most erotic sensation she had ever known.

Her mouth fell open as she breathed raggedly, her head spinning. She saw colors swirling before her eyes, felt her heartbeat synchronize to his as everything around her became hazy, dizzy. Pleasure erupted through her body with an orgasm so strong she cried out from it.

As she cried out, she felt her incisors growing. Felt her fangs returning . . .

Wulf growled deep in his throat as he tasted her. He'd never felt so close to anyone in his life. It was as if they were one person sharing one single heartbeat.

He felt everything she did. Every hope, every fear. Her entire mind was laid open before him and it overwhelmed him.

And then he felt her bite into his shoulder. Wulf gasped at the unexpected sensation. His cock swelled, making him wish he were inside her.

She reached down between their bodies as she drank from him, and unzipped his pants. Wulf moaned deep in his throat as she guided him straight into her.

With no control over himself, he took her wildly, fiercely, as they bonded their life forces together.

They came together in a furious orgasm that slammed through them both at the same exact moment.

Weak and spent, Wulf pulled away from her neck. She looked up at him, her eyes glazed as she licked her lips and her teeth receded.

Wulf kissed her deeply, holding her tight.

"Wow," she breathed. "I'm still seeing stars."

He laughed at that. He was too.

"Do you think it really worked?" she asked.

"If it doesn't, I vote we follow Zarek's advice of taking Acheron out and beating him."

Cassandra laughed nervously. "I guess in a few weeks, we'll know."

Only it didn't take that long. Cassandra's eyes widened as she started gasping for air.

"Cassandra?" Wulf asked.

She couldn't respond.

"Baby?" he asked again.

Her gaze was filled with pain as she reached up, laid her hand against his whiskered cheek, and shuddered.

In less than three seconds, she was dead.

"Acheron!"

Ash jerked awake at the shrill pitch that rattled through his head. He was lying naked in his bed with his black silk sheets wrapped around his lean body.

I'm tired, Artie, and I'm sleeping. He sent the mental note through the cosmos to her temple on Olympus in a much calmer tone.

"Then get up and come here. Now!"

Ash let out a long sigh. *No.*

"Don't you dare roll over and go back to sleep after what you've done."

And that is?

"You released another Dark-Hunter without consulting me!"

The corners of Ash's lips twitched as he understood her latest rant. *Wulf had bitten Cassandra.*

He smiled, relieved at the truth. Thank the gods, Wulf had chosen wisely.

"That was not the way this was supposed to turn out and you know it. How dare you interfere!"

Leave me alone, Artie. You've got more than your share of Dark-Hunters.

"Fine," she said, her voice brittle. "You bent the rules of our agreement, then so shall I."

Ash bolted upright. "Artie!"

She was gone.

Cursing, Ash willed his clothes back on his body and flashed himself from his home in Katoteros to Wulf's house.

It was too late.

Wulf was in his living room with Cassandra in his arms. Her face was pale with a bluish tint to it.

As soon as the Viking saw him, his teary eyes blazed with hatred. "You lied to me, Ash. My blood poisoned her."

Ash took Cassandra from Wulf's arms and laid her gently on the couch.

Erik started wailing as if he understood what had happened. As if he knew his mother was dead.

Ash's heart stopped beating.

He'd never been able to stand the sound of an infant crying. "Go to your son, Wulf."

"Cassandra—"

"Go to Erik!" Ash snapped. "Now, and get out of the room."

Luckily, the Viking obeyed.

Ash cradled Cassandra's head in his hands and closed his eyes.

"You can't resurrect the dead, Acheron," Artemis said as she flashed into the room. "The Fates won't let you."

Ash looked up at her and narrowed his eyes. "Don't mess with me right now, Artie. This doesn't concern you."

"Everything you do concerns me. You know our bargain. You gave me nothing in exchange for Wulf's soul."

Ash rose up to his feet slowly, his eyes flashing.

Artemis took a step back, recognizing the fact that he was in no mood to play with her.

"You never had his soul, Artemis, and you know it. You

used him to protect your brother's line. What better way than to release him to watch over his immortal wife and breed equally immortal children who are strong enough to survive those who want them dead?"

"Wulf belongs to me!"

"No he doesn't. He never did." Ash closed his eyes and touched Cassandra's forehead.

Her eyes fluttered open slowly.

"No!" Artemis snapped.

Ash looked up, his eyes glowing red. "Yes," he hissed. "And unless you wish to take her place with Hades, I suggest you back off."

Artemis flashed out of the room.

Cassandra sat up slowly. "Acheron?"

"Shh," he said, moving away from her. "It's okay."

"I feel so strange."

"I know. It'll fade soon."

Cassandra frowned as she looked around the room.

Wulf returned. He froze as soon as he saw Cassandra sitting up. Faster than Ash could blink, he was across the room so that he could scoop her up and hold her.

"Are you all right?"

Cassandra looked at Wulf as if he'd lost his mind. "Of course. Why wouldn't I be?"

Wulf kissed her, then looked at Ash in disbelief. "I don't know what you did, but thank you, Ash. Thank you."

Ash inclined his head. "Any time, Viking. All I ask is that the two of you enjoy your time together and have lots of children." He folded his arms across his chest. "By the way, as a wedding present, I'm revoking the daylight curse from you and your children. No one born to either of you will ever again have to live at night. Not unless they choose it on their own anyway."

"Am I missing something?" Cassandra asked again.

One corner of Ash's mouth twisted up. "I'll leave it to Wulf to explain. For the time being, I'll go back to bed." Ash flashed out of the room.

Wulf picked Cassandra up and carried her toward his bed.

Artemis was waiting in Ash's bedroom for him to reappear. The look on her face told him she was planning on making the rest of his day miserable.

"What, Artie?" he asked irritably.

She swung a medallion from her finger. "You know who this belongs to?"

"Morginne."

"Wulf."

Ash smiled evilly. "Morginne. Loki is the one who has Wulf's soul. Think about it, Artie. What is the one law of souls?"

"They must be freely given."

He nodded. "And you never agreed to give up hers. Using Daimon venom, Morginne drugged Wulf so that he unknowingly gave his to Loki. The spell Loki used to trade their souls wore off after a few months and Morginne's soul returned to you while Wulf's went back to the amulet Loki holds."

"But—"

"There aren't any buts, Artie. I'm the one who made Wulf immortal and gave him his powers. If you want to put that soul back inside someone, then you better call Loki and see if he's willing to release Morginne to you."

She shrieked in outrage. "You tricked me!"

"No. This was the way things were meant to be. You

needed someone to breed with Apollo's heiress. As much as I hate your brother, I understand why Cassandra must live and why Apollo can't die."

"You planned this from the beginning," she accused him.

"No," he corrected. "I only hoped."

She glared at him. "You still don't understand the source of your Atlantean powers, do you?"

Ash drew a ragged breath. "Yes, Artemis. I do. I understand them in a way you'll never comprehend."

And with that, he brushed past her and lay down on his bed so that he could finally get some well-deserved sleep.

Artemis crawled into his bed behind him and snuggled up to his back. She nuzzled his shoulder with her face. "Fine then," she said softly. "You won this round against me and Apollymi. I'll credit you with that. But tell me, Acheron . . . how long can you continue to defeat both of us?"

He glanced over his shoulder to see the evil glint in her iridescent green eyes. "As long as it takes, Artemis. As long as it takes."

Epilogue

Cassandra awoke on her birthday, half afraid all of this was a dream.

Even Wulf never ventured far from her side, as if he were afraid she would evaporate the moment he left her.

He'd come rushing back to her at odd times throughout the whole afternoon. "You still here?"

She'd laugh and nod. "So far nothing's going south."

By the time the sun set and she looked the same as she had that morning, Cassandra realized the truth.

It was over.

They both were free.

Her heart sang in relief. Wulf no longer had to hunt her people and she no longer had to live in terror of her birthdays.

Ever again.

It was perfect.

Three years later

It wasn't perfect.

Cassandra bit her lip as she stood in the middle of the backyard with her hands on her hips while Wulf, Chris, and Urian argued over the swing set she was trying to have installed for Erik.

The workers had withdrawn to the front of the house while the three men argued it out in the back.

"No, see the slide's too high," Wulf was saying. "He could fall and get a concussion."

"Forget that," Chris snapped. "He could rack himself on the teeter-totter."

"Teeter-totter nothing," Urian said. "The swings are a choking hazard. Whose idea was it for him to have this?"

Cassandra rolled her eyes while Erik held on to her hand and wailed because they were taking away his swing set.

Looking at her distended belly, she sighed. "Take my advice, little one. Stay in there as long as you can. These guys are going to make you crazy."

Cassandra picked Erik up and carried him to his father. She forced Wulf to take the crying toddler. "You explain it to the baby while I go inside and add more padding to his nursery walls."

"You know," Chris said, "she's right. We do need more padding . . ."

And the men were off on that subject.

Cassandra laughed. Poor Erik, but at least he knew he was loved.

She opened the sliding glass door and returned to the house.

Two seconds later, Wulf was there, scooping her up in his arms. "Are you completely mental yet?"

"No, but I think you are."

He laughed at that. "An ounce of prevention—"

"Is worth ten years of therapy, easy."

Wulf growled low in his throat as he carried her through the house. "Do you really want him to have a swing set?"

"Yes. I want Erik to have the one thing I never had."

"And that is?"

"A normal childhood."

"Okay," he said with a sigh. "I'll let him have one, if it's that important to you."

"It is. And don't worry. If he's anything like his father, and he is, it'll take a lot more than that to concuss his thick skull."

Wulf feigned indignation. "Oh, now you insult me?"

Cassandra wrapped her arms around his neck and laid her head against his shoulder. "No, my sweetie. I'm not insulting you. I'm admiring you."

He smiled. "Good, safe comeback. But if you're serious about admiring me, I can think of a better way to do that."

"Oh, yeah and how's that?"

"Naked and in my bed."

Still hungry for more?

Turn the page for a sneak peak
at another thrilling
Sherrilyn Kenyon novel

Night Play

Welcome to the dark side . . .

Lilac and Lace Boutique on Iberville
The French Quarter

Stunned, Bride McTierney stared at the letter in her hand and blinked. She blinked again.

It couldn't really say what she thought it said.

Could it?

Was it a joke?

But as she read it again for the fourth time, she knew it wasn't. The rotten, cowardly SOB had actually broken up with her via her own account.

> *Sorry, Bride, but I need a woman more in keeping with my celebrity image. I'm going places and I need the kind of woman at my side who will help me, not hinder me. I'll have your things delivered to your building. Here's some money for a hotel room tonight in case you don't have any vacant rooms.*
>
> *Best,*
> *Taylor*

"You sorry, sycophantic, scum-sucking dog," she snarled as she read it again and pain engulfed her so profoundly that it was all she could do not to burst into tears. Her boyfriend of five years was breaking up with her . . . through a letter that he'd charged to her business account?

"Damn you to hell, you filthy snake!" she snarled.

Normally Bride would sooner cut her own head off than cuss, but this . . . this warranted serious language.

And an ax to her ex-boyfriend's head.

She fought the urge to scream. Or better yet, the need she felt to get into her SUV, go over to his television station and pound him into itty-bitty bloody pieces.

Damn him!

A tear fled down her cheek. Bride wiped it away and sniffed. She wouldn't cry over this. He so wasn't worth it.

Really, he wasn't, and deep inside she really wasn't surprised. For the last six months, she'd known this was coming. Had felt it every time Taylor put her on another diet or signed her up for another exercise program.

Not to mention the important dinner party two weeks ago at the Aquarium where he had told her that he thought it best he go alone.

Still it hurt. Still she ached. How could he do such a thing?

Like this! she thought angrily as she waved the letter around like a lunatic in the middle of her store.

But then she knew. Taylor had never really been happy with her. The only reason he had ever gone out with her to begin with was because her cousin was a manager at the local television station Taylor worked for. He'd wanted a job there and like a fool she had helped him to get it.

Now that he was safely ensconced in his position and his ratings were at the top, he pulled this stunt.

Fine. She didn't need him anyway.

She was better off without him.

And all the arguments in the world didn't ease the bitter, awful pain in her chest that wanted her to curl up into a ball and cry until she was spent.

"I won't do it," she said, wiping away another tear. "I won't give him the satisfaction of crying."

Throwing the letter away, she seized her vacuum cleaner with a vengeance. Her little boutique needed cleaning.

You just vacuummed.

She could just vacuum again until the damned carpet was threadbare.

Vane Kattalakis felt like shit. He'd just left Grace Alexander's office where the good (and he used the word with full rancor) therapist had told him there was nothing in the world that could heal his brother until his brother was willing to heal.

It wasn't what he needed to hear. Psycho-babble was for humans, it wasn't for wolves who needed to get their stupid asses out of Dodge before they lost them.

No matter what the Peltier bears told him, he knew the truth. Both he and Fang were living under a death sentence and there was no place safe for them. They had to get mobile before their pack mates realized they were still alive.

The minute they did, a team of assassins would be sent for them. Vane could take them on, but not if he had to drag a ninety-five-pound comatose wolf behind him.

He needed Fang awake and alert. Most of all, he needed his brother willing to fight again.

But nothing seemed to reach Fang. Nothing.

"I miss you, Fang," he whispered under his breath as his throat tightened with grief. It was so hard to make it alone in the world. To have no one to talk to. No one to trust.

He wanted his brother and sister back so badly that he would gladly sell his soul for it.

Sighing, he tucked his hands in his pockets and turned onto Iberville as he walked through the French Quarter.

He wasn't even sure why he cared anymore anyway. He might as well let the others have him. What difference did it make?

But then, Vane had spent the whole of his life fighting. It was all he knew or understood.

He couldn't do as Fang did and just lie down and wait for death. There had to be something out there that could reach his brother.

Something out there that could make both of them want to live again.

Vane paused as he neared one of those women's shops that were every few feet in the Quarter. It was a large red-brick building trimmed in black and burgundy. The entire front of it was made of glass that showed inside where the store was littered with lacy women's things and delicate, feminine tchotchkes.

But it wasn't the merchandise that made him pause.

It was *her*.

Bride.

He'd seen her only once and then only briefly as he guarded Sunshine Runningwolf in Jackson Square while the artist had sold her artwork. Oblivious to him, Bride had come up to Sunshine and the two of them had chatted.

Bride had been the most beautiful woman Vane had ever seen.

She still was.

Her long auburn hair was pulled up into a messy bun on her head. She wore a long, black dress that flowed around her body as she jerked a vacuum cleaner around on the carpet.

Every animal instinct in his body roared to life as he saw her again. It was primal. Demanding.

Needful.

Against his will, he found himself headed toward her. It wasn't until he had opened the burgundy door that he realized she was crying.

Fierce anger tore through him. It was bad enough that his life sucked, the last thing he wanted was to see someone like her cry.

Bride paused her vacuuming and looked up as she heard someone entering her shop. Her breath caught in her throat. Never in her life had she seen a more handsome man.

Never.

His long wavy, dark-brown hair was worn back in a sexy ponytail. His white t-shirt was pulled tight over a body that most women only saw in the best magazine ads. It was a body that had been meant for sex. Tall and lean, that body begged a woman to caress it just to see if it was as hard and perfect as it appeared.

His handsome features were sharp, chiseled, and he had a day's growth of beard on his face. It was the face of a rebel who didn't cater to current fashions, but who lived his life solely on his own terms.

He . . . was . . . gorgeous.

Bride couldn't see his eyes for the dark sunglasses he wore, but she sensed his gaze. Felt it like a smoldering touch.

This man was tough. He was fierce and it sent a wave of panic through her.

Why would someone like this be in her shop that specialized in women's accessories?

The vacuum, which she hadn't moved a single millimeter since he'd entered her store, started to smoke. Drawing her breath in sharply, she quickly turned it off and fanned the motor with her hand.

"Can I help you?" she asked as she struggled to put it behind her counter.

Heat suffused her cheeks as the motor continued to smoke and added a not-so-pleasant odor of burning dust to the potpourri-scented candles she used.

She smiled lamely at the devastatingly hot god who stood so nonchalantly in her store. "Sorry about that."

Vane closed his eyes as he savored the melodic Southern lilt of her voice. It reached deep inside him, making his whole body burn.

But she was scared of him. His animal half sensed it. And that was the last thing he wanted.

Reaching up, he pulled the sunglasses off and offered her a small smile. "Hi."

It didn't help. If anything, the sight of his eyes made her even more nervous.

Damn.

Bride was stunned. She wouldn't have thought he could become better-looking, but with that devilish grin, he did.

Worse, the intense, feral look of that languid gaze made her shivery and hot. Never in her life had she seen a man even one-tenth as good-looking as this one.

"Hi," she said back, feeling like nine kinds of stupid.

His gaze finally left her and went around the store to her various displays.

"I'm looking for a present," he said in that deeply hypnotic voice. She could listen to him speak for hours, and for some reason she couldn't explain, she wanted to hear him say her name.

Bride cleared her throat and put those stupid thoughts away as she came out from behind her counter. If her cute ex couldn't stomach her looks, why would a god like this one give a rat's bottom about her?

So she decided to calm down before she embarrassed herself with him. "Who is it for?"

"Someone very special."

"Your girlfriend?"

His gaze came back to hers and made her tremble even more. He shook his head slightly. "I could never be so lucky," he said, his tone low, beguiling.

What an odd thing for him to say. She couldn't imagine this guy having trouble getting any woman he wanted. Who on earth would say no to *that*?

On second thought, she hoped she never met a woman that attractive. If she did, she would be morally obligated to run her over in her car.

"How much are you wanting to spend?"

He shrugged. "Money doesn't mean anything to me."

Bride blinked at that. Gorgeous and loaded. Man, some woman out there was lucky.

"Okay. We have some necklaces. Those are always a nice gift."

Vane followed her over to an alcove against the far wall where she had a mirror set up with a multitude of beaded chokers and earrings.

The scent of her made him hard and hot. It was all he could do not to dip his head down to her shoulder and just inhale until he was drunk from her. He focused his gaze on the bare, pale skin of her neck...

He licked his lips as he imagined what she would taste like. What it would feel like to have her lush curves pressed up against his body. To have her lips swollen from his kisses, her eyes dark and dreamy from passion as she looked up at him.

Even worse, he could sense her own desire and it whetted his appetite even more.

"Which is your favorite?" he asked, even though he knew the answer.

There was a black Victorian choker that had her scent all over it. It was obvious she had tried it on recently.

"This one," she said, reaching for it.

His cock hardened even more as her fingers brushed the black onyx stones. He wanted nothing more than to run his hand down her extended arm, to skim his palm over her soft, pale skin until he reached her hand. A hand he would love to nibble.

"Would you try it on for me?"

Bride trembled at the deep note of his voice. What was it about him that made her so nervous?

But then she knew. He was intensely masculine and being under his direct scrutiny was as excruciating as it was disconcerting.

She tried to put the necklace on, but her hands shook so badly that she couldn't fasten it.

"May I help?" he asked.

She swallowed and nodded.

His warm hands touched hers, making her even more jittery. She looked up in the mirror to catch sight of those gorgeous hazel-green eyes that stared at her with a heat that made her shiver.

He deftly fastened it. His fingers lingered at her neck for a minute before he met her gaze in the mirror and stepped back.

"Beautiful," he breathed huskily, only he wasn't looking at the necklace. He was staring into the reflection of her eyes. "I'll take it."

Torn between relief and sadness, Bride looked away quickly as she reached to take it off. In truth, she loved this necklace and hated to see it go. She'd bought it for the store, but had wanted to keep it.

But why bother? It was a six-hundred-dollar, hand-made work of art. She'd never have anyplace to wear it. It would be a waste and the pragmatic Irishwoman in her wouldn't allow her to be so foolish.

Pulling it off, she swallowed the new lump in her throat and headed for the register.

Vane watched her intently. She was even sadder than before. Gods, how he wanted nothing more than to have her smile at him. What did a human male say to a human female to make her happy?

She-wolves didn't really smile, not like humans did. Their smiles were more devious, seductive. Inviting. His people didn't smile when they were happy.

They had sex, which to him was the biggest benefit to being an animal over a human. Humans had rules about intimacy that he had never fully understood.

She placed the necklace in a large white box that had a cotton pad in the bottom. "Would you like it gift-wrapped?"

He nodded.

Carefully, she removed the price tag, set it next to the register, then pulled out a small piece of paper that had been precut to the size of the box. Without looking up at him, she quickly wrapped the box and rang his sale.

"Six hundred and twenty-three dollars and eighty-four cents, please."

Still she didn't look at him. Instead, her gaze was focused on the ground near his feet.

Vane felt a strange need to dip down until his face was in her line of sight. He refrained as he pulled his wallet out and handed her his American Express card.

It was laughable really that a wolf had a human credit card. But then, this was the twenty-first century and those who didn't blend quickly found themselves exterminated. Unlike many others of his kind, he had investments and property. Hell, he even had a personal banker.

She took the card and ran it through her computer terminal.

"You work here alone?" he asked and quickly learned that that was inappropriate since her fear returned with a scent so strong it almost made him curse out loud.

"No."

She was lying to him. He could smell it.

Good going, jackass. Humans. He'd never understand them. But then, they were weak, especially their females.

She handed him the receipt.

Aggravated at himself for making her even more uncomfortable, he signed his name and handed it back to her.

She compared his signature to his card and frowned. "Katta . . ."

"Kattalakis," he said for her. "It's Greek."

Her eyes lit up just a bit as she returned the card to him. "That's very different. You must have a hard time spelling it for people."

"Yeah."

She tucked the paper into her drawer, then placed the wrapped box in a small bag with corded handles. "Thanks," she said quietly, setting it on the counter in front of him. "Have a nice day."

He nodded and headed for the door, his heart even heavier than before that he had failed to make her happy.

"Wait!" she said as he touched the knob. "You left your necklace."

Vane looked back at her one last time, knowing he

would never see her again. She was so beautiful there with large, amber eyes set in a pale face. There was something about her that reminded him of a Rubens's angel. She was ethereal and lovely.

And far too fragile for an animal.

"No," he said quietly. "I left it with the woman I wanted to have it."

Bride felt her jaw go slack as his words hung in the air between them. "I can't take this."

He opened the door and headed out into the street.

Grabbing the bag from the counter, Bride ran after him. He was quickly making strides down toward the center of the Quarter and it took some serious rushing to catch up to him.

She grabbed his arm, amazed at the tautness of his biceps as she pulled him to a stop. Breathless, she looked up at him and those beguiling hazel-green eyes. "I can't take this," she said again, giving the bag to him. "It's way too much."

He refused to take it. "I want you to have it."

There was so much unfathomable sincerity in those words that she couldn't do anything more than gape at him. "Why?"

"Because beautiful women deserve beautiful things."

No one unrelated to her had ever said anything so kind. Today more than any other, she needed to hear it.

Overwrought with his kindness, she burst into tears.

Vane stood there feeling completely at a loss. What was this? Wolves didn't cry. A she-wolf might tear out a man's throat for pissing her off, but she never cried and especially not when someone had complimented her.

"I'm sorry," he said, completely confused by what he'd done wrong. "I thought it would make you happy. I didn't mean to hurt your feelings."

She cried even more.

What was he supposed to do? He looked around the street, but there was no one there to ask.

Screw the human in him. He didn't comprehend that part of himself either. Instead, he listened to the animal part that only knew instinctively how to take care of someone when they were hurt.

He scooped her up into his arms and carried her back toward her store.

Sherrilyn Kenyon's award-winning paranormal romances have topped the *New York Times* bestseller charts, offering readers a world full of dark and dangerous heroes, feisty heroines and a richly imagined mythology. Sexy, fun and utterly addictive, this series is best described as *Buffy the Vampire Slayer* meets *Sex and the City*.

From the world of the Dark-Hunters comes the most anticipated book to date . . .

ACHERON

Eleven thousand years ago a god was born. Cursed into the body of a human, Acheron endured a lifetime of hatred. His human death unleashed an unspeakable horror that almost destroyed the earth. Brought back against his will, he became the sole defender of mankind. Only it was never that simple . . .

For centuries, he has fought for our survival and hidden a past he never wants revealed. Now his survival, and ours, hinges on the very woman who threatens him. Old enemies reawaken and unite to kill them both. War has never been more deadly . . . or more fun.

978-0-7499-0927-7

The Dark-Hunter Companion is a must-have book for every Dark-Hunter and Sherrilyn Kenyon fan!

THE DARK-HUNTER COMPANION

'We are Darkness. We are Shadow. We are the Rulers of the Night. We, alone, stand between mankind and those who would see mankind destroyed. We are the guardians. The Souless Keepers. Our souls were cast out so that we would not forewarn the Daimons we pursue. By the time they see us coming, it's too late. The Daimons and Apollites know us. They fear us. We are death to all those who prey upon the humans. Neither Human, nor Apollite, we exist beyond the realm of the Living, beyond the realm of the Dead.
We are the Dark-Hunters.
And we are eternal.'

The *Dark-Hunter* Creed

Sherrilyn Kenyon's *Dark-Hunter Companion* is essential reading for anyone who has recently made that once-in-a-life-time deal with Artemis. Packed with insider knowledge and secrets mankind are rarely privy to, it's also a valuable guide to the Dark-Hunter series for lesser mortals. It includes a Dark-Hunter directory, a handy reference guide to Dark-Hunter and Greek mythology, useful tips on dealing with daimons and squires, lessons in conversational Greek and Atlantean; there's even a section on how to handle unexpected visits from ancient gods. The companion also includes a brand new short story from every Dark-Hunter's favourite writer Sherrilyn Kenyon.

9780-7499-4095-9